INHERIT THE WORD

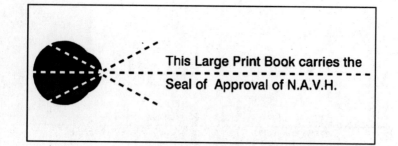

This Large Print Book carries the
Seal of Approval of N.A.V.H.

A COOKBOOK NOOK MYSTERY

INHERIT THE WORD

DARYL WOOD GERBER

WHEELER PUBLISHING
A part of Gale, Cengage Learning

GALE
CENGAGE Learning

Farmington Hills, Mich • San Francisco • New York • Waterville, Maine
Meriden, Conn • Mason, Ohio • Chicago

GALE
CENGAGE Learning®

LIBRARY OF CONGRESS CATALOGING-IN-PUBLICATION DATA

Gerber, Daryl Wood.
  Inherit the word / by Daryl Wood Gerber. — Large print edition.
    pages ; cm. — (A cookbook nook mystery ; #2) (Wheeler Publishing large print cozy mystery)
    ISBN 978-1-4104-6897-0 (softcover) — ISBN 1-4104-6897-6 (softcover)
  1. Cooks—Fiction. 2. Bookstores—Fiction. 3. Murder—Investigation—Fiction. 4. Large type books. I. Title.
PS3601.A215I54 2014
813'.6—dc23   2014016550

Published in 2014 by arrangement with The Berkley Publishing Group, a member of Penguin Group (USA) LLC, a Penguin Random House Company

Printed in the United States of America
1 2 3 4 5   18 17 16 15 14

To Nancy,
for your love and constant friendship

ACKNOWLEDGMENTS

Family is not an important thing. It's everything.

— Michael J. Fox

Thank you to my family for loving me and understanding the crazy schedule it takes for me to write a book. Thank you to my sweet lifelong friends for your love and friendship. Thanks to my talented author friends Krista Davis, Janet Bolin, Kate Carlisle, and Hannah Dennison for your words of encouragement and insight. Thanks to my brainstormers at Plothatchers. Thanks to my blog mates on Mystery Lovers Kitchen and Killer Characters. And thanks to SinC Guppies for your enthusiasm for the written word.

Thanks to those who have helped make the Cookbook Nook Mysteries a success: my fabulous editor, Kate Seaver; Katherine Pelz; Andy Ball; Kayleigh Clark; and my cover artist, Teresa Fasolino. I am so blessed.

Thank you to my business team. The amount of work it takes to launch a book is amazing to me. You are truly appreciated!

Thank you librarians, teachers, fans, and readers for sharing the world of The Cookbook Nook in Crystal Cove, California, with your friends. I am learning so much from all of you.

Thank you to Dr. Rivas for your invaluable technical information. And last but not least, thanks to my culinary bookstore consultant, Christine Myskowski. You have made exploring cookbooks such a joy for me!

CHAPTER 1

I clambered down the ladder in the storeroom of The Cookbook Nook carrying a stack of cookie cookbooks in my arms. My foot hit something soft. I shrieked. Tigger, a stray kitten that had scampered into my life and won my heart a month ago, yowled. His claws skittered beneath him as he dashed from my path.

"Shh, Tigger. Hush, baby." I had barely touched him with my toe. I knew he wasn't hurt. "C'mere, little guy." I arrived at the floor, knelt down, and spied him hunkering beneath the ladder, staring at me with his wide eyes. "It's okay," I cooed. As I scooped him up one-armed and nuzzled his neck, I felt a cool stream of the unknowable course its way up my spine. Tigger was a ginger-striped tabby, not a black cat. His passing beneath a ladder wasn't a bad omen, was it? Why did I suddenly feel like seven years of bad luck was lurking in the shadows?

"Miss Jenna, yoo-hoo," a girl squealed. "Miss Jenna, come quick!"

Fear ticked inside me. We had invited children to The Cookbook Nook for a cookie-decorating event — Aunt Vera's idea. She was a master cookie baker herself, with an extensive personal collection of cookie cookbooks. Had one of the children gotten hurt? Was that the dark cloud I'd sensed in the storeroom? I raced into the shop and skidded to a slippery halt in my flip-flops.

"Look at my killer shark." A girl with frothy orange hair was standing beside the tot-height table in the children's corner, brandishing a deep blue, shark-shaped cookie.

Nothing amiss. Kids being kids. No one hurt. *Thank the breezes,* as my mother used to say.

I steadied my racing heart and said, "Cool cookie." I set the cookbooks on the sales counter, then put Tigger on the floor and gave his bottom a push. Brave feline, he meandered beneath the children's table, probably hoping to score a crumb. "But please, kids, call me Jenna. Not Miss Jenna. I'm not a teacher."

The girl's father frowned. Guess he preferred decorum. I wasn't so hot on it. I liked to live fast and loose . . . sort of.

"But you're so tall," the girl said.

I grinned. I wasn't an Amazon, but at five eight, I was slightly taller than her doughy father. "Just because I'm tall doesn't make me a teacher."

"If you say so."

The first Friday of September was a perfect time in Crystal Cove to invite children to an afternoon cookie-decorating class. The weather hovered in the low seventies. The sun shone brightly. And school and homework hadn't taken over the kids' total concentration quite yet. For the class, in addition to ordering a fresh batch of cookie cookbooks like *The All-American Cookie Book,* Betty Crocker's *The Big Book of Cookies,* and *Simply Sensational Cookies,* we had stocked up on fun cookie-decorating sets complete with squeezable icing bottles and interchangeable design tips. Our theme for today's class was "Creatures of the Deep."

"Did you bake the cookies, Jenna?" one of the parents asked.

"Me? What a laugh." I was barely adept at making cookie batter — my limit of ingredients for recipes was a *daring* total of seven — but as an occasional artist, I embraced piping icing out of a squeeze bottle.

"Miss Jenna, look at my octopus." A boy with gigantic freckles wiggled his green,

11

gooey octopus cookie in the air, and then shoved his gruesome creation toward the face of the frothy-haired girl. She squeaked.

Aunt Vera, a flamboyant sixty-something and co-owner of The Cookbook Nook, moved to my side, the fabric of her exotic caftan billowing and falling. "Don't you love kids?"

Me? I adore them. Except for the time I did a photo shoot at Taylor & Squibb, my previous employer, for Dabble Doodles. A few prankster boys squeezed the contents of their glue and glitter pens onto the girls' clothing and — *gag me* — hair. Parents were livid.

"Yoo-hoo, Jenna. Kids?" my aunt repeated.

"Uh, sure. Love 'em." I didn't want any of my own. Not yet. I wasn't quite thirty. And a widow. Timing was everything. I said, "Absolutely. How about you?"

She chuckled while adjusting the silver bejeweled turban on her head — my aunt would prefer giving tarot card readings to figuring out how to market our joint enterprise. "I would have loved to have a dozen just like you."

"Aw. I love you, too." My aunt on my father's side had doted on me from the day I was born. When I moved back to Crystal

12

Cove to help her open the cookbook shop, she offered me the cottage beside her beach house. I felt blessed to have her in my life, especially with my mother gone.

"While the kiddies finish up," Aunt Vera said, "let's discuss the town's other ventures for this month."

"As far as I know, the mayor has planned a dozen new events for September, including a Frisbee contest, a paddle boarding race, and Movie Night on the Strand." Crystal Cove was a lovely seaside town on the coast of California, with beautiful rolling hills to the east and a glorious stretch of ocean running the length of the town to the west. The mayor of our fair city was always on the lookout for events that would lure tourists. "To pay tribute to the events the mayor has fashioned, I've ordered dozens of new cookbooks with beach and/ or movie themes."

"Ooh, lovely. You've included *The Beach House Cookbook,* I assume?"

"I have." *The Beach House Cookbook* had beautiful photographs of food and the seaside. In our business, cookbooks with enticing pictures were guaranteed sales. I still couldn't believe it, but some people bought cookbooks merely to peruse. Prior to my new enterprise, I was a function-and-use person. If it didn't have a function, I didn't use it. "I've also brought in *At Blanchard's Table: A Trip to the Beach Cookbook.*" This particular cookbook included recipes that were as delicious as they were simple. Prosciutto bundles? Balsamic goat cheese? They sounded easy enough that even I could make them. "Also, I ordered *Good Fish: Sustainable Seafood Recipes from the Pacific Coast.*" The Seattle-based author of *Good Fish* was a seafood advocate who really educated her readers. I especially loved that she had brought in another knowledgeable source to pair the fish with wine.

"That title's a mouthful."

"Between you, me, and the lamppost," I said, "some titles on cookbooks go on forever."

"They do, but competition is fierce and specificity matters. An unpretentious title like *Good Food* won't light a fire under the intended audience."

My aunt was right. She was always right. She knew cookbooks backward and forward. Me? I was just getting the hang of how popular they were. At my aunt's behest, last month I returned to Crystal Cove to run The Cookbook Nook and the café because, well, my life in San Francisco, as I'd

14

dreamed it, was over. I needed a new beginning. My aunt needed a marketing whiz.

"I love what you've done in the bay window," Aunt Vera said.

Our store was one of many in the Fisherman's Village complex. The bay window faced the parking lot and was our first calling card to passersby. In keeping with the town's monthly events, I had set out a seaside-themed display, complete with bright yellow oars, aqua blue Frisbees, and coral and white sand toys. Near the decorative kitchen items that we carried, I had set up our movie-themed display, which included the women's fiction books *Chocolat* and *Like Water for Chocolate,* both of which had been made into movies, and a mystery series about a cheese shop, which I heard might become a television show à la *Murder, She Wrote.*

"Jenna." My best friend and new assistant in the store, Bailey Bird — Minnie Mouse in size and Mighty Mouse in energy — hurried into the shop. "Whee! You'll never guess."

"What's with you?" I grinned.

"No caffeine. For twenty-four hours. I feel so-o-o good."

I liked a cup of coffee each morning, something with a little zip, but I didn't drink

15

it throughout the day. Bailey, on the other hand, nursed a coffee or cola about every two hours. She was off the stuff? When would she crash? My aunt gave me a worried look and began to rub the phoenix amulet she wore around her neck.

"Listen. Listen." Bailey spun in a circle. The skirt of her silky halter dress fluted around her well-formed calves. Sun streaming in the big plate-glass windows highlighted her short copper hair. "I just spoke with the mayor, and she wants us."

"For what?"

"To hold the Grill Fest."

"But Brick's always hosts the Grill Fest." Brick's was a barbecue restaurant about a half mile from Fisherman's Village.

"Brick's is going under. It just declared bankruptcy."

"How horrible."

"It is, isn't it? Tragic. However, the mayor doesn't want to delay the four-day fest. She's afraid that could hurt the town's economy," Bailey rushed on. "Tourism —"

"Can't afford any setbacks," I finished, quoting the mayor.

"It takes money to run this place, she says. The squeaky wheel gets the biggest piece of the pie."

"Excuse me?"

16

"The mayor messed up the wording, not I."

Our mayor, a frizzy bundle of raw energy, was nothing if not Crystal Cove proactive. Without tourists and the taxes they paid, how else could we finance our infrastructure? Only a few thousand people, including part-timers, lived here. Though many residents had incomes well above normal, the town couldn't manage to maintain the elaborate maze of windy roads, the parks, the aquarium, the junior college that offered a specialized degree in the study of grapes, and The Pier, which was a major go-to spot, complete with a boardwalk, restaurants, stores, and more.

"I suggested we have the Grill Fest at the shop," Bailey said, polishing her fingernails on her silky bodice. "I said, 'Jenna and Vera will think it's a fabulous idea.' You do, don't you? Think it's a good idea?" She slurped in an excited breath.

The contest consisted of four rounds, eight contestants. All contestants would participate in the opening round. After each round, judges would make their determinations, and two contestants would be eliminated, until only two contestants remained. They would vie for the grand prize — a medal and boasting rights.

"Well?" Bailey said.

My aunt and I nodded. How could we disappoint her?

"We can set up portable cooking stations, like we do for cooking classes," Bailey continued. "We'll ask the kitchen shop down the way to provide the tools and grills or sauté pans, depending on a contestant's preference. Think of the traffic. The cross-promotion. The conflict. The press."

Last year's Grill Fest had garnered all sorts of media coverage thanks to one contestant — the winner for eight straight years — who lambasted the runner-up for her grilled steak recipe. They ended up in a spatula fight. Someone had filmed the spectacle, which went viral on YouTube.

"And think of all the grilling cookbooks we can stock, like *Simply Grilling: 105 Recipes for Quick and Casual Grilling,*" Bailey said, the title tripping easily off her tongue.

See what I mean about long book titles?

"The author not only gives a clear account of the types of grilling and the utensils needed," Bailey went on, "but she also includes a recipe for one of my all-time favorite foods, Buffalo Sliders with Blue Cheese Slaw. And the pictures? Family-style adorable." Bailey had a mind like a steel trap. She could probably recite the contents

18

of every book in the shop.

"What's this year's challenge?" I asked.

"Grilled cheese."

Aunt Vera applauded. "Yum. We'll serve delectable sandwiches at the Nook Café." The café was an adjunct to The Cookbook Nook. During the opening month, we hadn't landed on a name for the café, and then we settled on the obvious. "Folks will flock to us for lunch and dinner. Ka-ching." My aunt was not interested in money. She had plenty because, years ago, she had invested wisely in the stock market. But she was all about bragging rights. She took great pride in our tasty enterprise.

"Ka-ching is right," Bailey echoed. She was all about dollar signs. Back at Taylor & Squibb, Bailey, who had been in charge of monitoring on-air, magazine, and Internet campaigns, would visit my office daily and give me a rundown of our earnings. Not our, as in Taylor & Squibb, but *our,* as in *ours.* Hers and mine. Every Christmas, she found out early, down to the penny, what we were earning for our holiday bonuses. She needed to, because she had to budget for her monthly clothes-buying sprees.

"Meow!" Tigger raced from beneath the cookie preparation table and leaped onto the counter by the register.

"I didn't do it." The freckle-faced boy threw his hands in the air, which of course meant he had done whatever *it* was.

I hurried to the counter and scooped up Tigger, a new wave of anxiety gushing through me. "Shh, fella. You're okay. Why are you so jumpy today?" I checked him out, making sure he didn't have icing in his eyes or ears — he didn't — and breathed a sigh of relief. I frowned at the boy, whose mother was giving him a quiet talking-to. I imagined pulling a cat's tail had been one of his crimes. He nodded obediently to her, but I could see he was holding back giggles.

As I set Tigger on the ground and encouraged him to be brave and mingle with the public again, I heard a jangle.

"Phone's ringing," Bailey said as she sidled behind me to set down her things.

I rummaged through my purse, which I had stowed on a shelf beneath the antique National cash register, and retrieved my cell phone. The readout said: *Whitney.* Wholesome, wondrous Whitney. My sister was brilliant at most things, but being a home-business entrepreneur, she was a tad dim when it came to knowing the hours other people kept at work. I asked Bailey to mind the shop, then sneaked to the storage room with my cell phone and pressed Send. "Hey,

Sis. I can't talk right now. We have a kids' soiree going on." Not to mention a café to run and more cookbooks to inventory.

"Jenna Starrett Hart, listen up."

I was single when I had established myself in my advertising career. After David and I got married, I decided not to change my surname to his, Harris. Hart . . . Harris. People would have gotten confused.

"Jenna," my sister barked.

"Don't have a tizzy." I laughed. I loved pushing my sister's buttons. "What's up?"

"You know I'm here in Crystal Cove."

"No." If she was checking up on me after my encounter with a murderer last month, I was going to clock her. I didn't need a reminder. I had put the past behind me. And I could clock her. I had six inches on her and a lot more hard-earned muscle, especially since I'd returned to a daily routine of running on the beach.

"Well, I am. I'm at The Seaside Bakery on The Pier getting the cake for Dad's surprise party tonight. You know it's tonight, right?"

I would have if she had clued me in. To anything. Ever. Well-meaning, warped Whitney. All my life I'd slung *W* adjectives together for my sister. She did the same to me: *jazzy, jittery Jenna.* Luckily I didn't have plans.

21

"Anyway," my sister continued, "I need you to pick up —" She halted, then screeched, "Omigosh!"

"What?"

"Get down here. Right. Now."

"No need to shout. Where are you?"

"The Seaside Bakery. Aren't you listening? I mean it. Come right now. And bring Bailey. Her mom, Lola. I think she's going to throw a punch."

CHAPTER 2

I grabbed my purse, snagged Bailey, and hurried out of The Cookbook Nook. She kept pace, which surprised me. Usually her short stride was no match for my long legs.

"What's going on?" she cried.

"Your mom."

Bailey blanched. "What about her? Is she okay?"

"Yes. She's . . . Whitney called . . . Punch." I couldn't form a coherent sentence.

"Your sister wants us to join her for a drink?"

"No."

"How does this involve my mom? I don't understand."

"Get in." I pointed to my VW bug.

Even though the car sputtered and hiccupped, I drove to The Pier in lickety-split time. The extensive parking lot to the south was nearly full, but I found a spot at the farthest end. By repeating our buddy dash, we were running on the boardwalk in less than three minutes.

"Do you see your mom?" I held a hand above my eyes to block the sun.

"There must be hundreds of people here. Why are you so worried?"

Hordes of tourists as well as locals were milling about. Many with shopping bags. Others with surfboards. Loads with corndogs on a stick. A line ran out of the barn-shaped Bait and Switch Fishing and Sport Supply Store. The place was probably having a sale. I darted around the throng and made a beeline for The Seaside Bakery. I couldn't make it past the crowd outside Mum's the Word Diner.

Bailey grinned. "What do you bet someone from the diner is tossing out tickets to win a free brunch again?"

A hoot of encouragement erupted from a guy in the swarm. A second onlooker let out with a whoop of football-fan-like glee.

A third man standing quietly at the back of the crowd made me stop in my tracks. For a second, I was struck by just how much he reminded me of my deceased husband, and the memories caught up with me.

Over two years ago, David had gone sailing. Two days later, another sailor discovered his empty boat. The investigators determined that David must have struck his head and fallen overboard. David wasn't a master sailor, but he was a strong swimmer; he refused to wear a life jacket. For the first two years after his death, I was distraught without him. Moving to Crystal Cove had been the right decision for me. I started over. I was making new memories. I was finding my smile.

Until right now. Where in the heck was Bailey's mother, Lola?

"Is that Whitney?" Bailey pointed. A woman, also near the back of the pack, had short blonde hair, but she was not my older sister.

"Forget Whitney. Do you see your mom?" I pushed my way through a couple of thickset men who looked like they regularly ate at Mum's the Word, or as the locals called it, the Word.

Bailey followed. As we reached the front of the pack, she yelled, "Mom, don't!"

Lola Bird, as tiny and curvy as her daughter, stood with her fists primed.

Bailey tried to press forward. I held her back. "Wait. I think she's okay. She looks like she's in control." I adored Lola; she was like my second mother. I had her to thank for my love of books.

Though Lola's foot drilled the boardwalk,

her face seemed composed. She was standing opposite Natalie Mumford, the owner of the Word. Natalie, who was in her fifties with perfect teeth, perfect gold-blonde hair, and a perfectly plastic demeanor, was the instigator of last year's Grill Fest fiasco.

"Admit it, Natalie," Lola demanded.

"What does my mother want Natalie Mumford to admit?" Bailey asked.

"I don't know," I said. "Whitney didn't tell me, and if you didn't notice, I just got here myself."

"This looks serious. Check out my mother's skin. She's pale. Is she going to faint?"

Lola did not appear remotely ashen. She had copper-toned skin and her cheeks were flushed pink. By the glisten in her eyes, she was having a good time. Before buying The Pelican Brief Diner down the road, Lola had worked as a lawyer defending the poor and downtrodden. During her lucrative career, she had challenged some of the state's staunchest attorneys. I adored her wit and saucy personality.

Someone in the gathering erupted with another hoot. I glanced around. Were people expecting a catfight? Were they betting on the outcome?

"Admit it," Lola repeated.

"I did not steal him," Natalie said. A harpy

couldn't have sounded shriller.

"He left my employ for yours," Lola said, her voice steady. "I'd like to know why."

Bailey dragged me over to Natalie's business manager, Sam Sykes, the husband to Natalie's Grill Fest nemesis. With his weathered skin, thick nose, and crinkly eyes, he reminded me of a mature cop in a TV drama. "Who are they talking about, Sam?"

"Your mother thinks Natalie stole her chef," he said.

"Did she?"

"He's working days at Mum's the Word now."

Natalie raised a fist. "I don't steal. I have never *stealed.*"

"Stolen," Lola said, correcting her.

Natalie seethed. She took an ominous step toward Lola.

"Mother. Don't." Natalie's rail-thin daughter, a woman about my age and a regular at The Cookbook Nook, scuttled from the pack of lookie-loos, cinched the belt of her oversized sweater, and grabbed her mother by the hand. "Please. Stop. Let's go back inside the diner."

Natalie shook free. "Let me go. You have no idea what's going on. You never do."

"But —"

"Ellen, I said back off."

Natalie's daughter plucked at her pixie-style haircut; her China-doll cheeks blazed red.

Her husband, a buff man in his early thirties with a fashion model's smoldering eyes, took hold of her by the shoulders. "Let me handle it, honey." Natalie's daughter didn't argue as her husband barged around his mother-in-law and blocked her. "Natalie . . . Mother . . . don't make a spectacle —"

"Out of my way, you fool." Possessing more strength than I would have given her credit for, Natalie shoved him aside. Maybe all those years working at the diner had built up her core muscles. "I am standing my ground. With this liar. On my boardwalk."

"This is the town's boardwalk, Natalie," Lola said. "And the town's pier. You do not have particular rights to it. You did not have the right to steal my chef, either. What did you do, threaten him?"

"*Threaten* him?"

"Tell him you were going to reveal some tawdry secret he was keeping?"

"Don't be absurd. I doubled his salary."

"There," Lola said, playing the crowd like a jury. "She admitted it. He quit last Sunday because she lured him away."

Natalie sucked in a breath. Her face started to turn purple. I scanned the crowd for Sam's wife, Mitzi. If she were here — which she wasn't — she would be reveling in this public shaming of Natalie Mumford.

"Uh-oh," Sam said. "I think I should intervene." He hurried to Natalie and tapped her shoulder.

She pivoted and nearly punched him in the nose. When she saw whom she'd almost assaulted, she pulled her arm back, and quickly said, "I'm sorry." In girlish fashion, and totally out of character, she swooped a loose curl back into her perfect coif. "I didn't know you were here, Sam." More twirling. Was she flirting with him? "Say, has something been bothering you lately?"

"No."

"You seem distracted."

"I'm focused."

"Is your health okay?"

"Everything's good. Ticker's ticking." Sam knuckled his chest; he was definitely flirting with her.

"Good to hear, because I sure don't want you balancing the books if you're a little off." She winked.

"Nope. I'm fit as a fiddle." He grinned.

"Well, then" — in a flash, Natalie's girlie behavior vanished, and she became as icy as a cold front — "what the blazes do you want?"

Sam flinched. For years, he had worked for Natalie. He assisted other business concerns around town, including a couple of the shop owners at Fisherman's Village. Every time I'd run into him in the past, I had felt like he'd wanted to offer his services, but I hadn't given him the opening. We didn't need him, as well respected as he might be. My aunt was an ace bookkeeper. Bailey ran a close second.

"Let's go inside and talk, Natalie," Sam said.

"Can't you see I'm in the middle of something?" She hitched a thumb at her adversary.

"Lola is goading you. Don't take the bait."

"I heard that, Sam Sykes," Lola said. "I'll have you know I am not goading her. I'm telling the truth. She did what she did to spite me. To hurt my business. She needed another chef like a hole in the head. And if you say anything to the contrary, I won't serve you your favorite cheeseburger smothered in bacon and guacamole anymore."

Natalie gasped. "Sam, say it isn't so. You go" — she clapped her hand dramatically to her chest — "to her restaurant?"

Sam petted her arm. "I go to lots of restaurants, Natalie. So do you."

"Traitor."

"C'mon, enough of this nonsense," Sam said. "Let's go inside the diner. Tend to the customers. Do what you love. And let's apologize to your daughter."

Natalie yanked away from him. "I knew it. I knew you'd turn on me."

"Natalie —"

"Sam, I adore you, but I hired you to advise me on numbers not on relationships."

Ouch. I eyed Sam, who did his best not to react.

"Hoo-hoo-hoo," Lola cried. "Natalie, if you keep spurning family and friends like that, you're going to burn every relationship you have."

"Stay out of my affairs, Lola. I'm warning you."

"Really? You're warning me? *I'm* warning *you.*" Lola gestured to the rapt crowd again. "In fact, if you're not nicer to everyone around here, someone's going to hit you upside the head with a fry pan to knock sense into you."

"Is that a threat?"

"Nope." Lola's bright blue eyes glimmered with humor. "Just an observation. One diner owner to another."

Natalie stabbed a finger at Lola. "Then let me advise you that you might be the one that needs some sense knocked into her."

"How so?"

"You don't pay your staff enough. You're cheap."

"I'm what?" Lola's voice skated up a scale of notes.

"And you entered the Grill Fest. What were you thinking?"

"I'm not following," Lola said.

Bailey whispered, "I'm not, either."

"You're not using your noggin, Lola." Natalie tapped her temple. "You know you'll lose. Why on earth did you enter?"

"Uh-oh," Bailey said. "Look at my mother's hands. She's balling them up again."

Energy rippled up Lola's arms. "You have some ego, lady."

"I should," Natalie countered. "I'm the winner eight years in a row. Eight. Count 'em."

I stiffened. Even the top salesman at Taylor & Squibb, a proud peacock if ever there was one, couldn't have looked as smug as Natalie.

"Not this time," Lola said. "You're going down. If not to me, then to one of the other contestants."

"No way will I lose to you, unless you bribe the judges."

"Bribe? Me? Why you . . ." Lola was gritting her teeth so tightly her jaw muscles were twitching.

"That's my cue," Bailey said and dashed to her mother. "Mom. Whoa. Breathe."

Natalie's family and friends corralled her.

At the same time, my cell phone buzzed. I whipped it out of my purse and glanced at the text from my sister: *Sorry, I had to run.* Another text quickly followed: *On my way to set up Dad's surprise party. See you there.*

Wretched, witless Whitney.

I went to my father's birthday party. Taking the high road, I didn't chide my sister for forgetting to invite me. When we said good night at the door, she bussed my cheek and promised to keep in touch. I lied and said that would be nice.

The moment I entered my cottage, which was a study in simplicity — one expansive room with a bachelorette kitchen, a bay window facing the ocean, a fireplace, a wall of books, a niche for my art supplies, and a beautiful wrought-iron bed — Tigger attacked me. Why was he so freaked out? I had only left him home for two hours. He leaped on my leg and slid down, digging his claws into my bare calf to slow his progress. Yeow.

"What's up, buddy?" Adrenaline pumped

through me. I switched on a few lights, fetched a huge flashlight and hammer from the kitchenette drawers, and dashed through the cottage, checking behind doors and in all the closets. Intruders and I weren't fast friends. Finding no one, I murmured, "We're safe. We're alone." So why wouldn't my pulse stop chugging?

Choosing to do ordinary things to calm myself, I filled the kitty's water bowl, fished a kitty treat from a jar, and picked him up.

He yowled.

"I understand," I said. "I need to be the leader in the calm department. I'll work on it."

When both of us settled down, I gave him the treat and put him on the floor. Taking my aunt's sage advice, I decided to cook. She guaranteed that the aroma of freshly baked cookies in the house not only soothed her but helped her sleep better. I gathered oatmeal, flour, sugar, eggs, and raisins for a simple dump-in-a-bowl cookie recipe, and then, instead of putting on Judy Garland music — many of Judy's heartfelt renditions brought me to tears, and I didn't want to cry — I set a positive-thinking tape into the CD player.

After a minute of recorded ocean waves lapping upon the shore, an instructor began to speak. She told me to relax my shoulders. To loosen my jaw. To breathe deeply. She said, "Repeat after me: I will keep my head up and my heart open. Good things will come into my life."

As I measured the dry ingredients, I repeated the mantra.

Next, the instructor said, "Good. Let's continue. Repeat after me: To go upward, I must go onward. C'mon, say it loudly."

I started to giggle. The gal was a yoga teacher in Hollywood, but I figured she must have been a cheerleader at one point in her life.

"C'mon," she reiterated, as if she knew her listeners were breaking into hysterics.

At the top of my lungs, I said, "To go upward, I must go onward."

Tigger, who had nestled into his comfy bed in the kitchen, leaped to his feet and dashed to my side.

"Chill, cat," I said. "I'm meditating. To go upward —"

He dove at my sandal-clad feet as if they were monsters.

"Cut it out." I nudged him with the side of my foot.

He tore away and pounced onto the red Ching cabinet. Before I could stop him, he careened into the ten-inch-tall, gold Lucky

Cat figurine that David and I had purchased on a rainy day in San Francisco. The sculpture, a bobtail cat holding its paw upright, was meant to bring good fortune. Ever since I had brought Tigger home that first night, he'd had it in for that fake cat.

"Oh no," I cried and rushed to stabilize the porcelain statue. I had saved the Lucky Cat numerous times before, but this time I was too late. It tumbled off the cabinet, hit the wood floor, and shattered into dozens of pieces.

I stared at the wreckage and gasped. Not because of the mess, and not because of the loss of a prized gift from my husband. But because scattered among the ruins were gold pieces. Lots of them.

As I bent to retrieve one, someone knocked on the door. I lurched to a stand. I wasn't expecting anyone. Had my aunt heard the crash? No way could she have made it to the cottage from her house in a few seconds; her place was a good thirty yards away.

"Who's there?"

"Me." *Bailey.* "I would've called, but I didn't want you to tell me not to come over. I need to talk. Let me in. Please."

I dashed to the door and opened it.

Bailey tramped inside hugging an over-

36

sized tote bag to her chest. "Thank you. I'm sorry to bother you this late, but I'm so exhausted. My mother has been bending my ear for hours. She's distraught over the loss of her chef and the damage it's going to do to her business. And —" She ogled the porcelain mess on the floor. "What happened?"

I rubbed my mother's heart-shaped locket, which hung around my neck — David's picture was inside — and I gawked at the shambles of the statue.

"Hey, are those gold pieces?" Bailey tossed her purse onto the loveseat and hurried to the heap. "Vintage American Eagles." She picked up a coin and examined it.

"How do you know what they are?"

"My uncle is a numismatic."

"A numis-*what*?"

"A coin collector. A geek, if you ask me. He focuses on the varieties within a series of coins, not simply the dates. Wow, there are some Philadelphia Type Ones and Twos here. Was this your piggy bank?"

"No." I wrapped my arms around my ribcage. "David . . . It was a gift from him." I remembered the day we bought it. David had been adamant about purchasing that specific Lucky Cat. I had preferred a white one. As we dined that night, he said, *You*

*deserve a gold cat. You are my golden trea-
sure.* Had he commissioned the cat? Had
he planted the gold inside? A month before
he died, David mentioned that he owed
someone money. He never said how much,
and no one ever dunned me for repayment.
What if the debt was huge? What if David
had decided not to pay? What if he had
invested all his cash in gold coins and hidden them? For me or for himself. Did it
matter? My thoughts flew back to the day
he died. Did someone follow him onto the
ocean that fateful day to rob him? Did
someone attack him on the sailboat and
throw him overboard? Not knowing what
happened, having no closure, ate at me. I
said, "I had no idea there were coins inside."

"At upward of two thousand dollars a
coin, you're looking at maybe a hundred
thousand dollars. Are there more?"

"More?"

"Did David keep other coins in the safety
deposit box?"

"We don't have a safety deposit box."

"Then what's that key for?" She pointed.

The key that used to hang around the
Lucky Cat's neck, the same key that David
said was *the key to his heart,* lay on the floor
near the fireplace. I picked it up and examined it. David often gave me trinkets that

were sentimental but worthless — as a joke. I figured the key belonged to a defunct luggage lock or something insignificant like that. "This is a safety deposit box key?"

"I think so."

Bailey helped me put the broken pieces of the porcelain cat into a Tupperware box, which I left on the kitchen table. I wanted to attempt to repair the statue. Then we gathered up the gold coins and stowed them in a second Tupperware container. I set that one beneath my bed for safekeeping.

"Thank you," I said. For Bailey's efforts, I poured her a glass of wine.

After taking a sip, she smiled. "Now, all you have to do is figure out where the safety deposit box is located."

CHAPTER 3

For days, right through Tuesday, which was the single day a week that we closed the shop, I called banks in San Francisco. My husband hadn't owned a safety deposit box at any of them. I spoke to some of David's friends, as well. A coworker of David's said he didn't know anything about David having acquired gold assets; he wouldn't even speculate. When I hung up from that call, I was frustrated and dry-mouthed with fear. What if David had done something criminal? No, I wouldn't even entertain the possibility. David had been an investor. He had capitalized on people's money. He was stalwart and true. There was a reasonable explanation, only I couldn't see it — yet. *Yet* was the operative word.

On Wednesday morning, though my heart was heavy with thoughts of David, I knew I had to focus on the Grill Fest, which began today.

After taking my VW to the repair shop —
that sputtery sound I'd been fretting about
for weeks turned out to be a bad carburetor
— I headed to work.

"Jenna, dear." Aunt Vera beckoned me to
the sales counter.

I set down the half dozen copies of a new
vegan cookbook that the local farmers'
market manager had raved about, *Sundays
at Moosewood Restaurant,* and I joined her.

"I'm worried about you," she said in a low
murmur, unwilling to disturb the many
customers browsing The Cookbook Nook.

"Why?" I heard the snag in my voice.
Dang.

She must have heard it, too. She tilted her
head. "The lights were on at the cottage late
last night. Why are you worrying the hard-
wood floor to distraction?"

"I'm not pacing. I'm baking."

"Minor detail."

"I'm getting good at biscuits." I'd made at
least five batches. My waistline was suffering.

"Good for you, but you can't sidetrack
me, young lady. Talk to me."

Other than Bailey, I hadn't told anyone
about the contents of the Lucky Cat, because I didn't know where David had gotten the money to buy the coins. Before he

41

died, he'd told me everything was *in order.*
What had he meant? Why hadn't I ever
noticed how heavy the statue was? Tigger,
the little imp, must have sensed something
was amiss from the moment he set foot in
the cottage.

"I'm fine," I assured my aunt, unwilling
to tell her more right now. I had a shop to
run and an event to publicize. *Buck up or
wither,* as my father would say. I planted a
fresh smile on my face and, forcing light-
ness into my tone, said, "Let me show you
the flyers I've created for the Grill Fest." I
brandished a ream of flyers announcing the
fest and the competitors involved. The
mayor had selected the entrants based on
the recipes submitted. "I'm going to visit all
the shop owners and bed-and-breakfasts.
Everyone in town, including tourists, should
know about our store and the competition.
I made up bookmarks, too. Simple give-
aways. Who doesn't like something for free?
Take a look at what I've added to the displays."

To honor the Frisbee contest — I had to
honor it; I'd played a lot of Frisbee with
David, as well as in college — I had ordered
a variety of pizza cookbooks: *Pizza on the
Grill: 100 Feisty Fire-Roasted Recipes for
Pizza & More; Pizza: How to Make and Bake*

More Than 50 Delicious Homemade Pizzas; the list went on. "How is this for a recipe title: Thai One On Pizza?"

My aunt chuckled.

Inspired by the paddle boarding contest — paddle boarding, or surf riding while standing, was depicted in Polynesian art as far back as the 1700s — I'd ordered a few cookbooks by Sam Choy, the chef and television personality who was known as the founder of Pacific Rim cuisine. Granted, Choy hadn't written any recent books, but some of our customers only care about the quality of the recipes within. Choy's were fabulous. Our supplier gave us a great discount.

"And specifically for the Grill Fest," I said, "I selected grilled cheese books. *Grilled Cheese: 50 Recipes to Make You Melt* and *Great Grilled Cheese: 50 Innovative Recipes for Stovetop, Grill, and Sandwich Maker.* My favorite is *Grilled Cheese, Please! 50 Scrumptiously Cheesy Recipes.*" The author, an expert when it came to grilled cheese, had instilled the book with photos that made my mouth water. She had also included helpful tips about the variety of cheeses that melted well. The recipe I wanted to try, when I was braver as well as more knowledgeable about how to handle a fry pan sizzling with hot butter, was a crab Swiss melt with asparagus. I remembered my mother making tasty appetizers with the same ingredients.

"Hello, hello." Katie Casey, our inspired chef, entered from the hallway connecting the shop to the café. She was carrying a tray of what looked like bite-sized sandwiches. Katie and I had known each other since kindergarten, and we had been best friends in high school, but we had grown apart during college. When she applied for the chef's position and wowed us with her first-rate culinary skills, we'd snapped her up. She stopped beside the vintage kitchen table. "Treats for the sweets. Hot from the grill." With a nod of her head, she gestured to the tray. I stifled a smile. No matter how hard Katie tried, she always appeared ready to lose her chef's toque. Her mass of curly hair bobbed with the hat. "And, hoo-boy, might I say that these are perhaps the best grilled cheese goodies I've ever made. Pears and blue cheese on the left. Brie, turkey, and green apple on the right. Take one. Or two."

I nabbed the Brie version. My aunt took the other. "Wow," we said in unison as we gobbled our goodies.

"I know, I know." Katie bubbled with enthusiasm. "I'm setting these lovelies on the tiered china plate." We had positioned a long table in the hallway so our guests could sample the café's wares. As Katie pivoted, she whispered, "By the way, when are they due?" *They,* meaning the eight competitors.

"At three P.M.," I said, after the lunch customers had thinned.

"Will we need a referee?" she joked, referring to the fact that Lola Bird and Natalie Mumford were among the contestants. Would they reenact the spat that had entertained the crowd on The Pier? "I'll volunteer," Katie added. At six feet plus, I didn't doubt Katie could out-bounce a professional bouncer.

"And how do you think Mitzi Sykes will act this year?" my aunt said. Mitzi was the eight-time runner-up. "Will she and Natalie have another spatula fight?"

I grinned. "Wait and see."

At noon, I made a tour of the town and handed out flyers. At 2:30 P.M., we started preparations for the contest. Katie helped. Though the contest would be held in the shop, we had closed the café because Katie and her staff wanted to watch the proceedings. Katie thought she might swipe some of the recipes, her prerogative, seeing as The Cookbook Nook was the host for the event.

With Aunt Vera and Bailey's help, we rearranged furniture, put out folding chairs, and relocated the roller-footed bookstands from the center of the shop to the sides. Afterward, we wheeled in four portable cooking stations, each set with two burners.

At 3:00 P.M., I wedged open the front door of the shop and let in the eight contestants. A horde of customers, eager to get inside, already stood in line.

Natalie Mumford, drenched in a floral perfume, crossed to the left-center cooking station, set her cell phone on the console, stowed her tote on the shelf beneath, and tugged on the hem of her blue suit jacket. Then she squared her shoulders and waved like a beauty queen at people peering in through the shop's windows. My aunt confided to me that Natalie was superstitious; she wore the same outfit at every competition. I understood. Back in college, I wouldn't take a test if I hadn't donned something white. Superstitions are silly, but I didn't fault anyone for having them.

Bailey's mom, Lola, clad in a hot pink sweater and snug jeans, wasn't to be put off by Natalie's choice of stations. She joined Natalie at the left-center console and gave her a broadbeamed *I'm-gonna-win-this-time* grin. Natalie responded with an equally

46

sassy smile. A moment of panic flitted through me as I imagined the two of them going at it like Helena and Hermia to win the heart of the handsome Demetrius in *A Midsummer Night's Dream.* Or worse, going at it like female mud wrestlers.

Please, please, I prayed. *Be civil, you two.*

Mitzi Sykes, the eight-time runner-up and costar of last year's YouTube spatula fiasco, strode to the end station closest to the sales counter. Though Mitzi was at least fifty years old, she didn't look a day over forty, with her savvy hairstyle, svelte shape, and ultra-smooth skin. She pulled a water bottle and a recipe card from her oversized purse. As she scanned the recipe card, her lips moved. I wondered if the mayor of our fine town had warned Mitzi and Natalie to behave. Maybe the mayor was secretly hoping for a reprise? Some claim that even bad publicity is good publicity.

Four more contestants entered, including Flora Simple who was a local shop owner wearing a hand-beaded outfit, a hunky fireman who was the poster model for the fire department, a baby-faced teacher, and a lanky librarian.

Tito Martinez, our local reporter, an irksome, full-of-himself man, entered last and was forced to take the position at the cooking station closest to the exit. He didn't seem to mind. While twirling a key ring around his index finger, he said, "It matters not where I stand. I will cook circles around all of you. I am the fittest and most prepared." Like I said, irksome to the max. He sniggered like a middleweight fighter egging on his opponent. The muscles of his chest pressed against his black silk shirt; his cocoa, canine-alert eyes blazed with serious intention. He pocketed his keys with overly dramatic flair, then set a leather-bound book on the countertop beside his burner. "I will be making a *muy especial* grilled cheese." Tito loved to throw occasional Spanish phrases into his speech. "From my personal recipe collection," he added.

His *personal* collection? Like *he'd* created them? I nearly laughed. Last month, he claimed that every recipe he owned came from his dearly departed *abuela* — *grandmother.*

"You'll go down first, Tito," Natalie said.

"Over my dead body," he replied, messing up the metaphor, which caused the corner of his mouth to turn up in a snarl and start to twitch. The poor guy would be lousy at poker.

"All right, all right." Our mayor, in a burgundy suit that underscored her squat shape, clapped her hands. "Let's stow it."

Ignoring the mayor, Natalie leaned forward and peered around the beader at Mitzi. "Where's my business manager aka your husband?"

"At a money management conference in San Jose," Mitzi said.

"Wow. Talk about not showing spousal support. Tsk-tsk." Natalie lasered her opponent with a smug look.

"Why, you . . ." Mitzi flushed pink. "I'll have you know that I have plenty of clients here." In addition to her home vegetable- and fruit-canning business, Mitzi was a personal chef who created in-home, gourmet meals for clients as far north as Los Gatos. I had never sampled her cooking, but I'd heard it was excellent, albeit a little froufrou. "Besides, my husband is dedicated to his work."

"Speaking of loyalty, Natalie," Lola said with a snarky bite, "where's your daughter and your son-in-law?"

Natalie raised her chin. "At the diner. Someone's got to run the place. It's a thriving business, unlike your own."

The mayor said, "Natalie, c'mon."

"C'mon, yourself, ZZ. You may be a dear friend, but you cannot make me curb my tongue."

Lola laughed. "I told you the other day on The Pier, Natalie, that you're going to lose friends if you keep this up."

Mayor Zoey Zeller, or ZZ to friends, said, "Yes, she did."

Natalie shot the mayor a scathing look. "You weren't there."

"Sure, I was. Watching two of my best friends duking it out. My, my, how the two of you" — she eyed Natalie then Lola — "went at it. Remind me never to cross either of you."

Lola smiled. "Natalie, in spite of you poaching my chef, The Pelican Brief is doing very well."

"I didn't poach," Natalie said.

"Liar, liar."

The fireman snorted. The baby-faced teacher and the librarian giggled between themselves.

Natalie said, "For your information, Lola, if it'll make you feel any better, your former chef is already gone."

"Gone?"

"Vamoose." Natalie waved a hand. "He got a great gig in Las Vegas, and he eighty-sixed this town as of last night."

"Good riddance."

"Contestants, please," Mayor Zeller tried again. "We're about to get under way. No more chatter. Please stow all water bottles, gadgets, and recipe cards. You should have your recipes fixed in your brains. And everyone, turn off or silence your cell phones."

As the contestants' sarcastic banter abated and they settled in for the long haul, I opened the front door and allowed the general public to enter. I recognized many of our regular customers and lots of fresh new faces. Bailey caught my eye and made a *ka-ching* gesture. I grinned, remembering a time at Taylor & Squibb when a client, the very wealthy owner of the Jiggy Jogging stores, barged in on a private board meeting. My boss was upset until Jiggy declared he wanted to quadruple his account, thanks to my brilliant idea of holding a running race with kids. Hopefully, thanks to Bailey winning us the Grill Fest, we would see a bump in sales. Ka-ching, indeed.

The mayor moved in front of the cooking stations to address the assembly. "Ladies and gentlemen, welcome." She gave a brief history of the Grill Fest and how much it meant to Crystal Cove to see so many people flock from far away places like San Francisco, Sacramento, and Los Angeles. "I want you all to know that I officially declare September, not April, Grilled Cheese

Month in Crystal Cove."

Applause erupted from the onlookers. I joined in. I wasn't quite sure who had established April as National Grilled Cheese Month — someone had set months for almost every food, including oatmeal and sweet potatoes — but celebrating one of the all-time best comfort foods in the world twice a year sounded like a good idea to me.

"And finally," the mayor continued, "I'd like you to meet the judges. I think you all know Pepper Pritchett."

The sixty-something, thickset woman who owned Beaders of Paradise, a beading shop on the first floor of Fisherman's Village, stepped forward. Dressed in a black-and-white frock and strands of marbled beads, she looked sharp and almost jaunty. Pepper hadn't been happy when I'd returned to Crystal Cove. In the past month, however, she and I had put our differences aside — all due to a misunderstanding with my father. His apology to her had helped us mend fences. On occasion, she even smiled a hello to me. She offered a thumbs-up sign to the beader contestant, who wiggled a pinky in response.

"And I'm sure many of you know Rhett

Jackson." The mayor nodded in his direction.

Rhett waved to the audience. I would never forget my first glimpse of the man. Tousled dark hair, a sly grin, and jeans that fit just right. Today he had dressed up a notch for the occasion. He wore a blue jacket over a white shirt tucked into chinos, as handsome as ever and hunkier than the fireman contestant.

"For those of you that might not know him, Rhett is the owner of Bait and Switch Fishing and Sport Supply Store. He's a fabulous chef, I might add."

Previously Rhett was the chef at The Grotto restaurant, which had been located on the second floor of Fisherman's Village until it burned down over a year ago. Rumor was that Rhett had started the fire, but Rhett swore he hadn't. My father, my aunt, and pretty much everyone else in town believed him. Rhett was certain that the owner had set the fire, run off with millions in artwork, and reaped the insurance benefits; however, he could never prove it. Disheartened, he'd left the restaurant business behind. He was taking a week off from his latest business venture to judge the contest because the mayor, who adored him, had begged and pleaded. It was hard to say no to Mayor Zeller.

I felt a tap on my shoulder and pivoted. Cinnamon Pritchett, daughter of the beading shop owner and Crystal Cove's chief of police, flashed a copy of *Grilled Cheese, Please*! "You should carry this in the shop," she said.

"We do. It's on the display table with the others."

"Guess I should become more familiar with the product in your store."

"Guess you should."

Cinnamon, in her mid-thirties, reminded me of a perky camp counselor with her bobbed hair, fresh face, and brown-on-brown uniform, but she had a crisp, no-nonsense attitude that a mother superior could appreciate. Now that the brouhaha of her suspecting me of murder was over, I was eager to foster a friendship with her. We had gone out for coffee and sweet rolls a couple of weeks ago and had talked about our love of good food. We agreed to set another outing, but we hadn't found the time. "Is there any place I can stand where I might be able to see better?" she asked.

"Kids' section is over there," I teased. Cinnamon was a few inches shorter than I.

"Very funny." She maneuvered through the throng and found a spot by the wall.

The first round got under way. While Katie fetched the contestants' preparations, which we had stored in the café's refrigerators, the contestants, starting with Tito, would explain what they were making.

"I will attempt a grilled cheese *al carbón,*" Tito said, "which includes jack cheese, marinated steak, crisp bacon, slices of avocado, and a smoky salsa."

For his first entry, the fireman was making a three-alarm chili grilled cheese. I told Katie that I wanted her to duplicate the guy's recipe. I would dedicate it to my mother, who made a chili that was so hot it nearly seared my stomach. Delish.

Natalie intended to make a classic croque-monsieur. She didn't elaborate for the sake of the audience, which annoyed me, but I kept my opinion to myself.

Lola, in contrast, was effusive. "I'm making a tilapia grilled cheese. I'll be using Port Salut. Do you all know that cheese?" She eyed the audience. "It's delectable. Made in the region of Brittany, France."

"Cheese doesn't go with fish," Natalie cut in. "Anybody knows that."

Lola ignored her. "I offer all sorts of fish-and-cheese dishes at The Pelican Brief."

"Maybe that's why your clientele is dwindling."

Lola forced a smile. "I'm adding an avocado aioli."

The audience *ooh*ed, which made Lola beam and hushed Natalie.

After each contestant described his or her concoction, Lola raised her hand and said, "Sorry, weak bladder. Can we take a break?"

The mayor declared a fifteen-minute recess. When everyone returned, she would tell the contestants, "Start your burners." She directed people to use the upscale portable bathrooms in the parking lot, brought in especially for the occasion.

Lola hurried to me. "Jenna, is it okay to use the shop's loo?"

I nodded. "For you, anything."

As she raced to the restroom in the hall between the shop and the café, Aunt Vera and I moved behind the sales counter to prepare for what we hoped would be an onslaught of sales. The buzz in the shop was electric. A racing event couldn't have been more exciting.

"I hope everyone in attendance will purchase at least one item from the shop," Aunt Vera said.

Sure enough, as if she had cast a spell over the crowd, customers started filing toward us.

While I was ringing up an order of checkered oven mitts, a set of red-striped measuring cups, and *The Absolute Beginner's Cookbook,* which was a book that taught novices like me how to boil an egg, a blare rang out.

"What the heck?" Bailey, who had been pitching grilled cheese cookbooks, darted toward me. "Fire? Where's the fire? None of the burners are on. The café's closed."

"You," Pepper said, and eyed Rhett, who was hovering by the vintage table chatting with Katie. He raised his hands — *innocent.* Pepper was one of the few who thought Rhett was guilty of arson.

"Out, everyone," the fireman contestant shouted. "Let's go." A number of his ever-at-the-ready buddies were in attendance. They scattered, some down the hallway toward the café and others out the exit along the boardwalk of Fisherman's Village.

Rhett, who was not a fan of fire — he had been trapped in The Grotto's blaze — hurried out with the rest.

"Shoot!" I said. The customer tried to pay for the items. "I can't, ma'am. Let's do what the firemen say. I'll leave your purchases right here. You'll be first in line when we're allowed back in. Promise." I inhaled. I didn't smell smoke.

Cinnamon rushed to the exit and motioned for people lingering inside to hustle.

"C'mon, everyone," she said with authority. "Go now. Hurry."

I grabbed Tigger and followed the pack to the parking lot. Poor little guy chuffed his concern. I whispered into his ear that this was a false alarm. At least, I hoped it was.

In minutes, the fireman contestant and a few of his pals returned. Holding his hands over his head, he addressed the panicked people. "No fire, folks. Nothing's going to go up in flames."

But then he sidled up to Cinnamon and spoke softly. Her eyes went wide. She said something to him sotto voce, and suddenly his pals bolted to the perimeter of the throng and stood, military-style, at attention.

"Listen up, people," Cinnamon said, addressing the crowd. "I want you to remain calm. We've had a casualty."

A collective gasp rose from the throng. Questions ensued.

Cinnamon said, "I'm sorry. I have no answers yet. Please stay put." Then she raced toward the café.

CHAPTER 4

Stay put? How could I stay put? This was my shop, my café. I sprinted after Cinnamon as she cut through the dining room and the kitchen. Cinnamon flung open the exit door to the alley and stopped. I came to a halt behind her. "What happened?"

Someone bumped into me. I turned. Pepper Pritchett, Cinnamon's mother, stood right behind me.

"Mother. Jenna. What are you —" Cinnamon blew out a quick burst of frustrated air. "Go back to the shop, both of you."

"This is my café," I argued.

"And my shop is in Fisherman's Village," Pepper said. "I want to know what's going on."

Cinnamon said, "The alley is public property."

"Okay, I'll grant you that, but —" I peeked over Cinnamon's shoulder and gulped.

Pepper gagged, made a U-turn, and

raced away.

I said, "Is she —"

"Dead?" Cinnamon said. "Yes."

Natalie Mumford lay slumped against the far wall, her hair mussed, her head bloody. I gulped, but I couldn't pull my gaze away. Natalie's blue dress hugged her thighs; her legs were splayed. Her clutch purse lay open, out of reach. A grooved panini sandwich grill about the size of an extra-large waffle iron rested beside Natalie's shoulder.

"Are you kidding me?" I said. "Someone hit her upside the —" I pressed my lips together. The other day at The Pier, when Lola and Natalie had verbally sparred, Lola warned that Natalie should be careful or someone would hit her upside the head with a frying pan. Everyone there had heard Lola say it.

Cinnamon cut me a look. "What?" I could tell the wheels of her super-sharp brain were trying to piece together a puzzle. "Jenna, answer me."

"Nothing."

Cinnamon waited for more. I didn't oblige her. I couldn't implicate Lola.

"You look pale," Cinnamon said. "You're in shock. Go back to the shop. Drink some water. And whatever you do, keep what you've seen under wraps. My team is on its

60

way. When they're on task, I'll question the group." Her command of a situation astounded me. Was she made of steel? She added, "I'm so sorry this had to happen today."

"Or ever."

"Right."

Natalie Mumford may have been an overly confident, semi-nasty woman, but she hadn't deserved to die.

Cinnamon ran a hand down the length of her neck. "Go on." She returned to the scene and knelt beside Natalie. I'm pretty sure she thought I was gone when she grasped Natalie's wrist and said, "You poor thing," under her breath.

I returned to the shop and found Aunt Vera sitting on the stool behind the sales counter petting Tigger with long, rhythmic strokes. My aunt appeared in shock; Tigger looked like he was in heaven. Oh, to be as oblivious as he was.

Mayor Zeller joined us. She unbuttoned the single button on her blazer and leaned forward, elbows on the counter. "Well?" she said. "What happened?"

Minding our police chief's caution not to reveal details, I said, "Natalie's dead. Someone hit her."

"Heavens." The mayor's eyes filled with

tears. "Hit her? Why?"

"I don't know."

After a lengthy silence, the mayor said, "Will you have to close the shop?"

"I'm not sure. Chief Pritchett said the alley was public property."

"The horror," Aunt Vera said. "What if this scares off customers? What if —"

"It won't." I rested my hand on my aunt's shoulder. "No one will blame us."

"She's right, Vera," the mayor said. "And I'm not ending the Grill Fest simply because of this. Natalie would be appalled if I did. She —" Her voice caught. "It's a tragedy, but Natalie would be the first to say, 'The show . . .' " She twirled a finger to gesture *must go on.*

"Two murders in such a short time span," Aunt Vera said. She was referring to the shocking murder of my friend, a celebrity chef, last month. "What is this world coming to?"

"We're no less vulnerable to crime than the rest of the world," Mayor Zeller said. "That's why I will continue to promote our fair town and keep our police force one of the most vital in the state."

In the hallway that linked the café to the shop, two women started shouting at each other. I recognized both voices. Pepper and Lola.

"You did it," Pepper yelled. "You killed Natalie Mumford."

"I did no such thing," Lola responded.

"During the break, right before the alarm sounded, I saw you heading into the café area."

Though we could hear every word, I urged my aunt and the mayor to hurry to the hall.

Pepper jabbed a finger at Lola. "Tell the truth."

Lola batted Pepper's finger away. "I didn't go anywhere near the café area. I went to the restroom." She pointed to the ladies' room. "I got trapped inside. The door wouldn't open."

"You appeared out of nowhere right after the fire alarm went off," Pepper said.

A crowd formed behind my aunt, the mayor, and me. Everyone, heads craning right and left, watched the combative women as if they were participants in a tennis match.

"I'm telling you, I was in the restroom," Lola said. "It's the truth. The door stuck. I was so frustrated that I tried to call my daughter on her cell phone."

I scanned the throng for Bailey but didn't see her. Where was she?

"I couldn't get a signal," Lola went on.

"A likely story," Pepper jeered.

"Look, if you don't believe me." Lola displayed her cell phone.

Honestly, signals were hard to drum up anywhere in Crystal Cove. We had a couple of nearby cell towers, but being on the coast, we often experienced dead zones, as telephone companies call them. At present, the phrase made my stomach turn.

Lola continued. "After a few minutes and a lot of tugging, the door opened."

"Why were you running from the café to here, then?" Pepper asked.

"I got turned around. The alarm . . ." Lola pointed to and fro.

Bailey wedged into place beside me while rasping, "Out of my way."

"Where were you?" I said.

She blanched. "In the stockroom ogling the two-hour-old coffee. I was about to succumb when I heard my mother and Pepper screaming. Do something." She nudged me. "My mother isn't lying. You know that bathroom door sticks."

I had asked my father, a master handyman, to fix it. He hadn't gotten around to tweaking all the items on the shop's to-do list.

"Look, Pepper." Lola spread her hands.

"I'm as sorry as the next guy that Natalie is dead, but I'm innocent."

"You threatened her on The Pier. Everyone heard you."

"Do something," Bailey repeated.

Seeing as our chief of police was otherwise occupied, I presumed I was in charge. I hurried toward the women. "Pepper. Lola. Let's calm down."

Pepper said, "I will not. You heard her the other day. She was teed off that Natalie nabbed her chef. She's got motive."

"Not enough to end someone's life," Lola cried.

"Pepper," I said. "Please. Don't jump to conclusions. This isn't ours to dispute. Your daughter, Chief Pritchett" — I thumbed toward the café — "is good at her job. She'll figure this out."

"But Lola did it," Pepper said.

Why was she so sure? I had convinced myself that I could like this woman, but suddenly I felt hotter than a broiler oven. She had accused me of murder not too long ago. I wouldn't let her continue to assail Lola, as well. "Pepper, please."

"Somebody arrest Lola Bird," Pepper said.

"That's it." Lola waved her arms overhead. "I'm out of here. I will not take this abuse. If you need me, I'll be at my restaurant." Like Moses parting the Red Sea, she forged through the crowd. Magically, the onlookers separated. When Lola reached the end of the pack, the group closed the gap.

Time seemed to stop. No one moved. Not even Pepper. For a few seconds, we existed in a vacuum. But then Pepper started her rant again, and chatter rose to a frenzied din.

Cinnamon appeared and clapped her hands. "Everyone, listen up."

She couldn't continue because her mother grabbed her by the elbow and said, "Go after Lola Bird, Cinn. She killed Natalie. She left."

"She what?" Cinnamon glowered at me, like I had something to do with Lola's departure.

I splayed my hands — *not guilty.*

With even greater emphasis, Cinnamon said, "People, stay put. Do. Not. Leave. My associate is going to question you." She hitched a finger at a massive male subordinate with prominent ears and mooselike jaw. "Get statements."

As the Moose ordered everyone to line up, Cinnamon marched out the door and headed north on Buena Vista Boulevard, the main drag.

Bailey gripped my upper arm. "We have

to follow them. We have to save my mother."

"You heard what Cinnamon said. Don't worry. Your mother will do fine on her own." She would. I was certain. Lola Bird was one of the spunkiest women I knew. She was well read. She used words on a regular basis that most people didn't know existed. If she could defend the neediest of the needy without any assistance, she could defend herself. On the other hand, Lola was like a mother to me. Because Bailey and I had spent so much time together as girls, I had called Lola *Mom* as a teen. She had helped me define my career path.

"Please," Bailey said. "I'm begging you. I would do the same for your mother."

When my mother died, Lola had let me cry in her arms for a long time. I owed her. Big time.

Bailey and I rushed into The Pelican Brief Diner. The place was bustling with customers. The luscious scent of fried foods filled the air. Soothing guitar music filtered through speakers. We were anything but calm.

The hostess, a perky California-born Latina who was dressed like a sailor, picked up on Bailey's concern. "Your mom's in the kitchen."

Without missing a beat, Bailey hurried across the sawdust-laden wood floor, past clusters of wooden tables. I followed. Bailey rounded a corner toward the kitchen and caught a wrist bangle in one of the nets filled with fake fish that adorned the walls. As I disentangled her, a foghorn bleated.

Bailey said, "Did you hear that?"

How could I not? A sense of foreboding shivered down my spine. *No, no, no,* I thought. *This cannot happen. Lola is innocent.*

I edged ahead of Bailey and entered the kitchen first. Lola stood at a stainless steel prep table dicing tomatoes with a vengeance. A plate filled with the makings of a seafood salad sat before her. Cinnamon Pritchett stood a few feet from Lola, one hand on her revolver. The toe of her hiking boot drilled the floor. Swell.

Despite the standoff, a female chef and numerous sous-chefs scurried around the kitchen while filling orders. The clatter of voices and dishes was deafening. Many of the staff glanced sideways at Lola.

A waitress with her hair cinched in a hairnet whisked by and said, "What's going on?" Lola cut her a scathing look. "None of my business," the waitress chimed. "Got it." She continued on her mission of fetching a pair of breadbaskets.

Bailey and I sidled between Cinnamon and Lola. "She didn't do it," we said as if we had rehearsed.

Perspiration coated Lola's face. With her ruby lips pressed together, she seemed to be as focused as an Iron Chef in the final moments of competition.

"Give me the facts, Mrs. Bird," Cinnamon said.

"Lola," Bailey interjected. "Call my mother Lola. No one calls her Mrs. Bird." Bailey hated her last name. She wished her mother had switched back to her maiden name after her divorce. Bailey would have latched onto the surname Hastings in a flash. Her father, a decent guy who practiced law in San Francisco, would have been upset, but he would have allowed it.

"I'm waiting, Lola," Cinnamon said, granting the informality.

Lola blew out a quick burst of air, then reiterated what she had told Pepper back at the shop. She had gone to the restroom. The door stuck. Yada yada.

Right as she finished her account, in strode my father, a Cary Grant look-alike, who was, as luck would have it, named Cary. He didn't have the actor's charming swagger; he was a former FBI analyst and moved like a military man. He greeted Cinnamon, who nodded respectfully back. The two of them had a unique relationship. A month ago, I was surprised to learn that my father was Cinnamon's mentor. Her father had bailed on her at birth. In her teens, when she was going off the rails, acting up and committing juvenile-style crimes, my father, who had a history with Cinnamon's mother, stepped in to offer support. When Cinnamon showed an interest in the law, my father steered her back to Crystal Cove. Long story short, he now cared for her like a daughter.

My father hurried to Lola and put his hand on her elbow. "Put the knife down, darling." Another big shock for me . . . Recently, I'd learned that my father and Lola were dating. My mother would've been happy that my father had found someone, especially Lola. She and Lola had been good friends. "You've got plenty of staff to do the cooking," Dad said. As always, he was as tranquil as a summer sea.

Lola turned to him, her blue eyes wide with dismay. "How did you hear? You weren't at the competition."

"I arrived at The Cookbook Nook late. I'm so sorry. Of all days to have a run on T-nuts." After retiring, my father, who didn't need money because his FBI analyst work had filled his coffers to overflowing, had purchased a quaint hardware store; he opened the shop when he cared to.

"I didn't do it," Lola said.

"I know." He stroked the nape of her neck. "Everyone in town knows you didn't."

"Not her." Lola eyed Cinnamon.

"Hush, Lola." The mayor emerged through the archway. "Don't say another word. I'm going to represent you." She, like Lola, was also a licensed lawyer; however, her clients were mainly real estate purchasers, not criminals. Not that Lola was a criminal. She wasn't.

"I don't need you, ZZ," Lola said. "Besides, you can't. That would be a conflict of interest. You're my friend."

The mayor wagged a finger. "Only a fool represents herself."

"What is this, a convention?" Cinnamon said. "Everyone out."

Lola gazed at the burgeoning crowd. Suddenly, as if doused with awareness dust, the lines in her forehead smoothed out and she stood taller. With a command befitting a judge, she said, "Chief Pritchett is right. Out, everyone, otherwise I'll have the health authorities on my case. Out. Chief Pritchett, my office. Please." She whipped off her

71

prep gloves, tossed them in the trash beside the sink, and marched from the kitchen.

Near the hostess desk, I caught up to Cinnamon. "Lola didn't do this."

Cinnamon paused and held up a hand. "I respect your passion, but I heard about the argument between Lola and Natalie in front of the Word the other day." One of her colleagues must have filled her in after I left the crime scene.

Bailey joined us. "Natalie Mumford was the one who was livid."

I concurred. "Lola was making light. She always does. She never holds a grudge."

Cinnamon muttered something under her breath. As she entered the office, the feeling of apprehension that hit me earlier returned. The office seemed as stark as a prison cell: one desk fitted with a blotter and an in-and-out box, a chair, a file cabinet, a couple of pictures of Lola with her staff or with Bailey, and one lonely wooden totem of fish going upstream that Bailey had carved at Girl Scout camp. Lola stood beside the metal desk, arms by her sides, chin raised defiantly.

I said, "Chief, I'm guessing you've got something more on Lola, something other than supposition and your mother's biased statement, or you wouldn't be here."

"We have a document."

"A document?" Bailey bleated. "What kind of document?"

At Taylor & Squibb, I was the lead for the Legal Easy campaign, a do-it-yourself approach to law. In each ad, a ghostly paper assaulted a Scrooge-like man. Each paper was scrawled with his signature. An image of a confession signed by Lola floated before my eyes.

Bailey said, "Mom, do you know what document the police found?"

Lola nodded. "That's what we were discussing when all of you barged into the kitchen."

"What is it?" Bailey looked as if she was trying to brace herself for the worst.

"A letter of resignation from my chef. It's nothing."

"I wouldn't call it nothing," Cinnamon said. "That's what the basis of the argument was between you and Natalie, correct?"

"Not the letter," Lola said. "The deed."

"The deed to the diner?" Bailey asked.

"No." Lola faced Bailey. "The deed. The *act*. Natalie stole my chef."

Cinnamon said, "I heard Natalie Mumford promised your chef a bigger salary."

Lola snickered. "I'll bet that's not all she promised."

"Lola, don't," Mayor Zeller warned.

"He made advances at me. What do you want to bet—"

"Lola, enough," the mayor cut in. "No more answers. No more innuendos. I happen to know Natalie had no romantic involvement with your chef."

"Right. You were her friend, too," Lola said, a distinctive nastiness to the final word.

Cinnamon pressed on. "Receiving the resignation letter could have made you mad enough to attack Natalie."

"Oh, please. I received the letter nearly ten days ago, the day he quit. I tore it up and tossed it into that." Lola pointed at the trash can beside her desk.

"Because you were mad," Cinnamon said.

"If I'd wanted to kill Natalie because of her dastardly plot, don't you think I had plenty of time before today?"

"Lola, hush," the mayor said.

"Maybe she taunted you while you were on break at the Grill Fest," Cinnamon suggested.

"I was in the restroom," Lola said. "Besides, Natalie wouldn't have dared to take me on in private. She was always about public displays of *dis*-affection."

"Lola." Mayor Zeller clapped her hands once.

My father said, "Darling, listen to your lawyer."

"She's not my lawyer."

"Cool your heels." The mayor flicked Lola's arm with a finger.

Lola sealed her lips and mimed locking them with an imaginary key. Bailey grabbed my hand and squeezed like her life depended upon it. Cinnamon, who seemed sufficiently stalemated, pivoted toward the door.

A new idea came to me. I stepped in front of her. "Lola doesn't bolt the door to this office. You saw for yourself. We walked right in. Anybody could have stolen the destroyed letter. Where did you find it?"

"In Natalie's purse," Cinnamon answered. "Taped back together."

"Why would I put the letter in Natalie's purse?" Lola asked. "Do I look dumb?"

"The murderer must have planted the letter," I said. "Did you check the fingerprints on the tape? Are they Lola's?"

"How could I have discerned that in this short —" Cinnamon mashed her lips together. "There were no fingerprints. The tape appeared to be wiped clean."

"What about the weapon?" I asked.

"Also free of prints. However, I happened to notice that Lola wears prep gloves at the restaurant."

She was right. Lola had tossed a pair of latex gloves before exiting the kitchen. I said, "Where's the chef who quit? Maybe he killed Natalie."

"No," Lola cut in. "Natalie said he moved to Vegas."

Cinnamon said, "I will be following up on that aspect."

I gazed at Lola and back at Cinnamon. How had the killer timed Natalie's murder to the bathroom break? Then it came to me. "The fire alarm," I blurted out. "It was flipped on as a diversion."

Cinnamon threw me a baleful look.

"Of course you've thought of that," I said. Dumb me. Open mouth, insert head. "Do you know if any of our neighboring store-owners saw anything?" The alley was situated between Fisherman's Village and the next row of stores.

"I haven't had time to question anyone yet."

Of course not. We'd all dashed after Lola.

Bailey shivered beside me. "Chief Pritchett, I've heard that Natalie's family wasn't all that happy with her. She ruled them with an iron fist."

I liked Natalie's daughter. She was a regular customer at The Cookbook Nook. I hated to think her capable of murder, but I didn't want Cinnamon to consider Lola the only suspect, either. Did Natalie's daughter or son-in-law have an alibi? Neither had been in attendance at the Grill Fest.

I said, "Who stands to inherit from Natalie's death? She was pretty well-off, right?"

Our illustrious chief of police peered at me with frustration. "We're done here."

"But all I asked —"

"Done."

She was wrong. The murder had happened outside my store. My best friend's mother was a suspect. I was anything *but* done.

CHAPTER 5

Bailey and I returned to The Cookbook Nook, both of us perplexed as to what we could do to help her mother. In the Fisherman's Village parking lot, customers clustered in groups while Chief Pritchett's dedicated staff questioned individuals. On the boardwalk, people gathered around a table adorned with plates of cookies and an urn of coffee. Katie must have set it up so the disenfranchised wouldn't go hungry.

I paused in the shop's doorway and said, "Oh my."

Bailey said, "What the heck?"

Although the bookshelves had been returned to their rightful spaces, the shop looked as unkempt and as out of sorts as I felt. Customers had abandoned cascades of books on tables. Aprons were flung on chairs. When the firemen said, *Get out,* the masses had dropped everything. Shoot.

My aunt sat at the vintage kitchen table

turning over tarot cards for no one but herself. She said, "You can feel the bad karma, can't you?"

I nodded. This time I could.

"How's your mother, Bailey?" Aunt Vera asked.

"Fine, sort of." She sucked back a sob. "I'm going to the stockroom if you want me."

"I've got coffee brewing," my aunt said.

"No, thanks."

"No?" Aunt Vera eyed me.

I whispered, "She's off caffeine, remember?"

Bailey slogged through the shop, shoulders slumped, the spring gone from her step.

"Poor dear," Aunt Vera said as she stroked the amulet around her neck.

"Say a special incantation for her."

"I'm not a witch."

"You know what I mean." I surveyed the shop again. A little moan escaped my lips. It would take hours to clean up the mess.

"Don't worry, dear," my aunt said. "We'll get to it in time. It's not like we're opening again today."

"We're not? Why not?"

"Ask Katie."

"Where is she?"

"In the kitchen. Where else?" Aunt Vera

held up a finger. "By the way, that woman who owns the knitting shop down the street said she saw a UPS delivery person in the vicinity right before the fire alarm went off, but that's not unusual."

I continued on toward the café and gasped when I reached the archway to the cooking area. Halfway across the room, someone had pinned up yellow crime-scene tape. My stomach wrenched at the sight. *Not again,* I thought. I'd had nightmares about yellow crime-scene tape — twisting, writhing, and suffocating nightmares — all because of the murder of my friend on opening day. And now Natalie Mumford had been killed at our first town-sponsored function. What was going on? Did some otherworldly spirit have it in for my aunt and me? I wasn't sure either of our artistic souls could take the hit.

Buck up, Jenna. You can get through this.

"Katie, why is this tape here?" I said. "Natalie was killed outside."

She rushed to me, trying to placate me with hand gestures. "Don't panic. The police merely determined this was the route Natalie took before she met her doom."

"Why do you think she came to the kitchen?"

"I don't have the foggiest. Maybe she stole

in to grab some special ingredient for her Monte Cristo grilled cheese. The tape won't stay up forever. No longer than a day, so I've been told."

I calculated the financial loss, not that it mattered. Aunt Vera wouldn't mind. She hadn't opened The Cookbook Nook and café to make a profit. Back in the seventies, she and the love of her life had planned to open the shop, but life had taken a sour turn. For no reason that she could fathom, he'd left her at the altar. Nearly thirty years passed before she was ready to try opening the shop again. With me.

"The weapon, Jenna."

"What about it?"

"It was my panini grill. An old one I brought from home. I planned to take it and other kitchen items to the Goodwill store. The items were sitting on the ground outside."

"Are you kidding?"

"I told the police. One of our staff corroborated my story. Are you okay?" Katie gripped my arm. "You look pale."

"I feel pooky. I've got to get some fresh air."

"Why don't you go around town and pass out flyers telling everyone the café will be open again tomorrow?" Katie suggested.

"Tell them I'm planning an extra special menu for the occasion. It'll be right out of Julia Child's *Mastering the Art of French Cooking.* Her famous Veal Prince Orloff will be one of the items." She kissed the tips of her fingertips. "Ooh la la. Drop a few hints."

"Will do."

Katie screwed up her mouth as if she were afraid to ask me a question.

"Spit it out," I said.

"What's going to happen to the Grill Fest?"

"The mayor decreed that it would continue. She assured me that Natalie would have wanted it to go on."

"Re-e-e-ally?"

"I know. Ick, right?" Natalie had reveled in slaying the competition for eight straight years. Now she was the one that had been slain.

When I returned to the shop, Bailey reappeared. She had touched up her makeup, so she looked better but not refreshed.

"What's up?" She latched onto me. "You look like a woman on a mission."

I told her my plan.

"Let me join you. Vera, you can hold down the fort, right?"

My aunt didn't answer. She seemed to be transfixed by the site of a Tower tarot card, which many considered an ill omen. Lightning and chaos spewed from the top of the image.

I slipped beside her and whispered, "Are you okay if we leave?"

"Too-ra-loo." Usually she said that phrase with a light heart. Not this time.

The late-afternoon sun beat down on Bailey and me. Thankfully I had remembered to apply sun block. I was blessed with the Hart family's olive skin, but even olive skin can burn.

While dropping off flyers at the glitzy shops in the all-brick Artiste Arcade, Bailey said, "If you ask me, one of Natalie's family killed her. She was making big bucks at that diner. Have you seen the traffic?"

"I'm sure Cinnamon is looking into who will inherit Natalie's estate."

"Not if her grump of a mother has any say. Pepper thinks my mom is guilty with a capital *G*. Dagnabbit, but that woman is as bitter as hemlock."

I couldn't remember ever hearing Bailey say anything stronger than *dagnabbit*. If she was furious, she would simply say the word louder. But saying it meant she was perking up. "Don't worry about Pepper," I said. "I'm pretty sure Cinnamon has her mother under control." They'd had a mother-daughter argument a few weeks ago. If rumors were true, Cinnamon had told her mother to stop trying to run her life and go fly a kite. I think she also ordered Pepper to make peace with me. A week later, Pepper ventured into the shop and bought a discounted Martha Stewart cookbook. It was a start.

"What else could be a motive?" Bailey said. "Sex? Politics? Rock and roll?"

"Your mother insinuated that the chef who resigned made a pass at her."

Bailey flicked her hand. "Nah, not him. He was as gentle as a lamb and about as gay as they come."

"He's gay? Then why would your mother say that?"

"That's my mom. An instigator. She leaked the notion so others would latch onto it."

"Any reason the chef might have wanted Natalie dead?"

"I doubt it. Natalie doubled his pay. And didn't you hear? Mom said, according to Natalie, that the guy took a better gig in Las Vegas. The guy was all about *things*. He loved having money in the bank. Speaking of banks, any news on that safety deposit box key David left you?"

I shook my head. "I don't want to talk

about it."

"But —"

"Later."

After we made the rounds at the eclectic shops at the Artiste Arcade, we headed for a string of stores that I liked to call our mini–San Francisco. The complex was composed of an octet of narrow, two-story bayside structures. Each had charming windows and portholes. All of the structures were painted aqua blue with white trim.

Negotiating my way past an exiting pair of Frisbee enthusiasts, I led the way into Home Sweet Home, a delicious store filled with homemade potpourri, scented candles, and collectibles. As always, customers gathered near the year-round Christmas tree to find Crystal Cove–themed ornaments. The neon-colored surfboard ornaments garnered the most attention.

Flora Simple, the owner, who was the Grill Fest contestant who beaded all of her clothing, happened to be a good friend of Pepper Pritchett's. After Pepper's conciliatory visit to our shop, Flora had become a regular. She was particularly fond of chocolate-themed cookbooks. She hurried to us, offering a wave. "Hi, Jenna. Hi, Bailey." Her apple cheeks, which were usually gleaming with health, looked wan. She tucked a loose strand of limp blonde hair over one ear and toyed with the thick braid that she always wore pulled forward over one shoulder. "It's horrible, isn't it? Just horrible. Truly. Ugh." Her words came out in a gush. "Natalie, dead. I still can't believe it."

I flashed on Natalie lying in the alley, but I pushed the memory aside. Dwelling on the scene wouldn't solve anything.

"I hope it won't hurt your business," Flora went on. "I know we were all looking forward to participating in the Grill Fest. Natalie, especially. She would have won again, of course, and, well . . ." She sagged as if she had run out of air.

"We'll be up and running tomorrow," I assured her. "And the Grill Fest will continue."

"Really? I mean, how can you?" She covered her mouth then between parted fingers said, "Not *you* you. It's the mayor's decision, I guess."

I agreed that perhaps Mayor Zeller was moving forward like a steam engine on full throttle, but what could I do?

"I bet you'll have all sorts of new clientele," Flora confided. "There's no bad publicity, or so I heard a few people saying at the bank. That reminds me." She scanned the shop to see if anyone was listening to us. No one seemed to be. Sotto voce, she said, "I was just there, at the bank, making my usual late-afternoon deposit, and I caught sight of Mitzi. You'll never guess what she was doing." She didn't wait for us to beg her to continue. "Mitzi was hiding behind her car."

"Hiding?" I gulped. "Like someone was after her?"

Bailey said. "On the break, Mitzi said she was heading to the beach for her daily dose of vitamin D. Is it possible she saw the killer?"

At the end of the passageway between Beaders of Paradise and the Nook Café was a set of stairs that led to the public beach below. If Mitzi had gone that direction, she would have had a view inside the café. Maybe she'd seen Natalie's killer. On the other hand, what if Mitzi was the killer? She could have easily run from the patio, through the café, to the alley. She'd fought with Natalie at last year's fest. What if Mitzi confronted Natalie, and Natalie, true to form, said something that made Mitzi fly into a rage?

"I don't think she was hiding out of fear," Flora said. "I think she was spying."

"Are you sure it was her?" I said.

"Blonde chignon, chic Chanel suit. She was crouched behind her Toyota and peering into the bank."

"Who was she spying on?" Bailey asked.

"Sam was inside."

I shook my head. "I thought her husband was at a conference in San Jose."

"It must have ended early," Flora said. "Anyway, he was chatting up this Asian teller. You know the one I mean, with the tattoos." She fluttered her fingers along an arm and up her neck. "She looks like she's straight out of an anime graphic novel."

"You mean manga," Bailey offered. "Manga are the comics. Anime is the Japanese style of animation."

"That's it. Manga. Oh, if I could draw like that," Flora said. "I mean, I can draw, but not . . . you know, like that. The money I'd make. I have such a fertile imagination. I'd write books upon books. All about teens. I adored my teen years."

I said, "Back to Mitzi."

"If you don't believe me —"

"I believe you."

"I think she suspects Sam is cheating on her."

Why would Mitzi suppose that? By all I had ever witnessed, Sam adored his wife. She was pretty and smart and had a thriving business. On the other hand, he had flirted with Natalie on the boardwalk, and I was pretty certain Natalie had been flirting with him . . . until she'd turned to ice. I said, "Go on."

Flora glanced another time at her customers. More had joined the growing crowd by the Christmas tree. Two women were tussling over the last surfboard ornament.

"I don't think Sam has heard about Natalie's murder yet," Flora said. "He was doing business things at the bank. You know, very normal. Showing his ID, signing forms. He didn't seem to be upset in any way."

"Mitzi didn't go inside and tell him?"

"Like I said, I think she was keeping tabs on him." Flora folded her arms. "He'll be devastated. He adored Natalie. He'd been her business manager for almost eight years."

Bailey said, "What did Mitzi do next?"

"She started to cry, and she hurried off. Poor dear. It's hard to compete with youth. Don't get me wrong. Mitzi is great looking for her age, but married men and young girls" — Flora cradled a cheek with her hand — "it's a given, right?"

I cut a look at Bailey, whose face had turned crimson. She had been one of those young girls. Luckily, she had discovered the snake was married, and she ended the relationship before he could break her heart.

Flora continued. "That led me to thinking in a whole new direction, you know, about the murder. What if Mitzi wanted to get rid of another kind of competition? Don't get me wrong. I like Mitzi. Everybody does. But with Natalie dead, Mitzi stands a good chance at winning the Grill Fest, right?"

"You stand as good a chance," Bailey said.

"Me?" Flora waggled a finger. "No, no, no. I'll come in last, make no mistake. I know the things I do well." She gestured to the store. "I sew, I make potpourri, and I can fashion wax into the most glorious shapes, but I'm a moderate cook. I entered the competition because ZZ is a steady client, and I knew the recipe she would like. Grilled cheese made with Brie, pears, balsamic vinegar, and onions. She's a Brie fanatic. Why, last week she bought this gorgeous handblown plate I made for the sole purpose of serving Brie on it. Personally, I like harder cheeses." Flora tapped her temple. "Where was I? Oh, right, Mitzi. She's the one who stands to win the Grill Fest, which means, if for no other reason, she had motive to kill Natalie."

Flora talked for another fluid two minutes about how great a job the mayor was doing at promoting tourism before I cut her off by saying we had to make the rounds of all the shops before nightfall.

Crystal Cove was about six miles long in total; the shopping area along Buena Vista Boulevard ran about two miles in each direction. In between conversations with shop owners — none of whom proved as gossipy as Flora — Bailey and I tried to come up with other motives for murdering Natalie Mumford. Bailey's mother deserved our utmost at drumming up other suspects. According to Aunt Vera, who had filled me in on the Grill Fest contestants' histories while we had set up The Cookbook Nook earlier, Natalie Mumford had moved to Crystal Cove right before the first Grill Fest. She'd purchased the diner within a month, changed the name to Mum's the Word, and it instantly became a go-to place. Its location on The Pier was a good part of the reason for its success, but the food was the other. The diner offered hearty baked goods, sizeable portions, and supposedly the best potpie anywhere, bar none.

"I've been thinking," Bailey said.

"About?"

"Natalie was divorced."

"Talk about coming out of left field."

"Sue me. There was a murder in town.

91

That shakes me to the core. Anyway, Natalie left her husband back east. Why? Maybe there was animosity between them."

"You're wondering whether her ex is in town."

"Exactly. Would her daughter know?"

"Probably." I wondered how Natalie's daughter was faring. I bet she was shattered, unless she was the one who had killed her mother. No, not possible. She was a sweet, unassuming woman.

"Do you think any of Natalie's employees might have held a grudge?" Bailey asked.

"Good question and one I'm sure Cinnamon Pritchett is considering."

Bailey stamped her foot. "Jenna."

"What? Need a cup of coffee?"

"No." She did. She knew it; I knew it. "We've got to help my mother. We can't simply leave this up to the police."

"I know. Cool your jets. I'm on your side."

As we neared Latte Luck Café, I stopped. "Want a decaf?"

"Why tempt myself?"

"At least inhale."

She did then she shook out the tension from her shoulders, and we moved on.

An hour later, as the sun was setting, we returned to Fisherman's Village. The parking lot was filled with lookie-loos interested in catching a glimpse of our police force in action.

"Hey, Jenna." Rhett Jackson caught up with me on the boardwalk right outside The Cookbook Nook's front door. "I was hoping I'd get a moment with you." He touched my elbow.

A tingle of desire coursed through me. "What's up?" I managed to say. "Are you hoping to score some of Katie's cookies?"

"Nope. I've had my share." He patted his firm abdomen. "Actually, I was visiting a pal upstairs at Surf and Sea." In addition to The Cookbook Nook and Beaders of Paradise, Fisherman's Village included Ye Olde Irish Linens, Vines Wine Bistro, an art house movie theater, and Surf and Sea, a surf and beach games shop. "He mentioned seeing Mitzi Sykes on the café patio during the break when the alarm went off."

Bailey pivoted short of the door and hurried back to us. "There's no sunshine there," she said.

"I'm not following," Rhett said.

I explained. "Mitzi mentioned that she was going to take a vitamin D break. That means getting a few rays. She swears it's the part of her daily regimen that keeps her looking so young. Just enough sun to give her skin a flush but no damage. Twenty minutes a day. Except there's no sun on the patio. I had assumed she was headed to the beach."

"So why was Mitzi there?" Bailey said. "Do you think she pursued Natalie? Did she kill her? Mitzi was wearing a red suit. Blood —" She looked at me. "Was there any blood?"

I nodded.

"Blood wouldn't show on a red suit."

I caught sight of Pepper outside Beaders of Paradise. Dressed as she was in black stripes, her fist on her hip, the other hand shading her eyes, she no longer looked sharp; she reminded me of Smee in *Peter Pan*. A mental picture of her kicking up a leg and singing, "Yo-ho-ho," made me giggle and gave me an idea.

"I'll be right back," I said and hurried down the boardwalk. "Hello, Pepper. You look nice."

She mumbled something unintelligible.

I said, "Have the police questioned you already?"

"Their presence is ruining business."

I offered a consoling smile. "We're closed, too, if that makes you feel any better." It did. The glee in her eyes was unmistakable. "Say," I continued, "you left The Cookbook Nook before the fire alarm blared, right?"

Pepper raised an eyebrow. "I saw Lola. I'm not lying."

"I'm not concerned about that," I said, though I was. Deeply concerned. "Did you return to your shop? From this vantage point, you might have had a bird's-eye view of anyone who entered the café." For a nanosecond, I pondered whether Pepper might have motive to kill Natalie, but I couldn't come up with a reason. Pepper wasn't a competitor; she was a judge. And she and Natalie wouldn't have vied for the same men. Only recently had I found out that Pepper carried a torch for my father. Long story, but it was part of the reason she hadn't embraced my return to town.

"Yes, I could see," Pepper conceded.

I happened to know that Pepper, whenever her shop was empty, stood vigil by the windows, peering out. I would prefer to sit in a chair and read a book. During lull times, I had been browsing culinary mysteries about a domestic diva, a coffee store owner, a Key West food critic, and more. The downside? The more I read, the hungrier I became.

I said, "Okay, you could see, but were you looking?"

"I was." Pepper hurried to add, "For a moment. After I used the facilities."

"And did you see anyone? Like Mitzi Sykes?"

"Now that you mention it."

My pulse kicked up a notch. "On the porch of the café?"

"I saw her heading for the steps to the ocean."

Rats. Mitzi hadn't headed to the alley. Pepper's account put an end to that theory.

"However," Pepper added, "I didn't see her descend the steps."

CHAPTER 6

Elated to have drummed up a suspect other than Lola, I rushed inside The Cookbook Nook to the sales counter, grabbed the telephone receiver, and dialed the precinct. At Taylor & Squibb, my boss had loved whenever I wore my creative hat and my juices were flowing. The most unique work, he said, was a result of inspiration and boldness. I asked for Chief Pritchett. When Cinnamon answered, I spewed out my discovery. Mitzi was a much better suspect, I told her. Her motive? To knock off the competition. I gave details of Mitzi sightings when the fire alarm had gone off.

"Jenna," Cinnamon said sharply. "Stop."

How I hated that tone. "No." I refused to buckle. "Mitzi lost to Natalie for eight years in a row, and let's not forget about last year's YouTube fiasco. That could make anybody snap. And if Mitzi was already suspicious of her husband having an affair . . ."

"What are you talking about?"

"She was seen acting suspiciously outside the bank." I filled her in about Mitzi's spying adventure.

"You've been a busy girl."

"Lola is innocent." I crossed my heart and hoped to die, not that Cinnamon could see the gesture, but the move was something I had done since I was little. "By the way, did you track down the chef?"

"Yes. He is in Las Vegas, and he has a solid alibi."

"Did you find out who will inherit Natalie's estate?"

"Family members. All aboveboard. A standard will."

"Members, as in plural?"

"Ellen Mumford has a sister."

"Where is she?"

"On her way to town."

"And Natalie's ex-husband?"

"Have a good night." Cinnamon hung up.

So much for our budding friendship. I would have to tread softly and remind her along the way that communication was becoming a lost art. I envisioned a tongue-in-cheek public service ad campaign that might convey the message. It involved a woman rapping her knuckles on her friend's forehead, maybe like the V8 commercial. *Yoo-hoo, anybody home?* The bottom of the screen would be emblazoned with: *Talking. It's good for the soul.*

Thankful that my sense of humor had returned, I decided to get to work on straightening up the store. Aunt Vera was gone, but I had enough energy to power a thousand klieg lights. So did Bailey. She chose the children's corner. I went straight to work on the displays. Tigger bounded between us.

A half hour later, Aunt Vera bustled in waving a piece of paper. "Yahoo," she sang. "We're set to reopen tomorrow. I decided to be proactive. I went to the precinct myself, and I begged and pleaded with Chief Pritchett. I told her that, seeing as the alarm could have been triggered from the alley and Katie had discarded the weapon the day before, our store should not be penalized. Cinnamon agreed. It probably helped that I offered her a single-card tarot reading."

Harrumph. Couldn't Cinnamon have told me when I called that she was allowing us to reopen? Granted, being cleared to open didn't free me of the guilt I felt. Natalie had died on our watch, right outside our kitchen.

"You'll never guess what card I turned

over." Aunt Vera winked. "The Lovers."

The Lovers is the sixth trump or Major Arcana card in a tarot deck. It represents the obvious: a relationship or temptation.

"Cinnamon flushed pink," Aunt Vera said.

"Do you think she's in love?" Bailey asked.

"Or hopeful."

I doubted that receiving a positive fortune had anything to do with Cinnamon's decision to let us reopen, but why spoil my aunt's lovely mood? She did a sultry cha-cha across the floor, her caftan swishing around her ankles. She once told me that in her younger years she had been quite a dancer. I'd taken a few ballroom dance lessons in college and had wanted to take more with David; we had never gotten around to it.

Aunt Vera said, "An officer is on the way over to remove the yellow crime-scene tape. I'll tell Katie."

"I'll go," Bailey said.

I bet she hoped to sneak a cup of coffee.

As Bailey headed down the hallway and my aunt retreated to the stockroom, Natalie's daughter Ellen entered the shop with her adorable two-and-a-half-year-old daughter tucked into a stroller. The girl, who was sound asleep, had masses of curls and the longest eyelashes.

"Are you open?" Ellen said. Though the temperature hovered in the sixties, she was bundled in a mid-calf-length black coat and wore a cashmere scarf around her neck. Her cheeks were blotched with tears, her lips devoid of color. I didn't have the courage to tell her to wait to enter until a policeman removed the tape in the café. She had to be curious about where her mother had died.

"Come on in." Rather than pounce on Ellen and drub her with questions, I nestled onto a stool beside the counter and watched. As she always did, Ellen set the stroller in the rear near the children's section, then she wandered through the store from display table to display table. "Sorry for the mess," I said.

"Did the customers do this?"

"The fire alarm went off. The place was evacuated."

"I heard," she said in a monotone as she picked up a culinary mystery and flipped through it. "Oh, they have recipes." She brought one to the checkout counter along with one of the featured cookbooks particular to this month's local events. As she set down the pair, I noticed she had nearly chewed her fingernails down to the nubs.

"How are you doing?" I said.

"Okay." She rubbed both arms above the elbows.

"Are you cold?"

"No. Sort of. A little off, I guess."

"I'm sorry about your mother."

Ellen pressed her lips together. Tears pooled in her eyes. "She died in the alley?"

I nodded. "I don't know why she was out there."

"Business, probably. A private phone call. Who knows?" Ellen sighed. "The police said they have suspects, but they wouldn't name names."

Neither would I.

"As I was passing out flyers earlier," I said, "I noticed that you didn't close the Word."

"We can't. Food will go bad. The loss would be too great. And the regulars. They all want to pay their respects. I . . . well . . ." She shook her head. "I'm the acting owner, so I can't let them down. I've got to do all the ordering and such."

I recalled Bailey's assertion that whoever inherited Natalie's estate might be the killer, but I couldn't believe Ellen had murdered her mother. She seemed so fragile. "You were at the diner when it happened, weren't you?"

"No. Today's my day off, so I took my

daughter to the park at the south end of town."

Huh. I could have sworn Natalie had said that her daughter and son-in-law couldn't come to the competition because they were working. Perhaps she had lied because she was embarrassed to say she didn't have her daughter's support.

"The police questioned me," Ellen said. "They asked for my alibi, like you did."

"I didn't mean —"

"It's all right. I don't mind. In time, everyone will want to know. This town, like all small towns, thrives on gossip. I'm not sure the police believe me." She moved to her daughter and tucked the blanket under the girl's neck, then returned to me. "No one saw me at the park. It was empty."

"Because it's a school day."

"Exactly. The park is loaded with kids and parents on the weekends."

"If you don't mind my asking, why didn't you come to the Grill Fest?"

"Mother's wishes." The words had bite to them. "She told me never to come to the first round of the competition. She thought I would bring her bad luck." Ellen's voice caught. "Bad luck," she repeated. "I'd say being murdered is bad luck, wouldn't you?" Tears trickled from her eyes. She brushed them away with a knuckle. "I always did what she said. Always. If only this time . . ." She surveyed the shop, letting the regret hang in the air.

"I'm so sorry. I heard she could be rigid."

"Rigid?" Ellen blinked. "No. Firm. There's a difference. I felt no animosity. Ever. None whatsoever."

I remembered a line from Shakespeare: *The lady doth protest too much, methinks.* Something in Ellen's words didn't ring true. "Would your sister agree?"

"My sister? Who told you about her?"

"Chief Pritchett. I didn't know you had a sister."

"She's older."

"She's on her way to town, right?"

Ellen bobbed her head once. "Why were you talking to the police?"

"I had a theory to share. About Mitzi Sykes."

"Mitzi." Ellen almost spit the name. "She hated Mother. She wanted her husband Sam to stop working for her. I think she envied my mother's relationship with Sam. They were such good friends. I wouldn't put it past Mitzi to have murdered Mother."

"Ellen. Hon. There you are." Ellen's husband, Willie, strode into the shop wearing surfer shorts. His Hawaiian-style shirt

104

flapped open, exposing his chiseled chest, slick with oil. A thatch of hair drooped across his forehead. I'd seen Willie at the beach on numerous occasions. Despite his slightly crooked nose, he had never appeared so rakishly handsome. "I've been looking for you everywhere."

He strode to her and draped an arm around her shoulders. How sweet that he cared so much, I mused, until Ellen whispered, "How worried could you have been? You went surfing."

"A quick one." He matched her hushed tone.

"Did you drop by Die Hard Fan, as well?" Ellen said, referring to a sports memorabilia shop in town. She attempted to fetch something from his back pocket. "Is that a receipt?"

Willie grabbed her wrist to prevent her. "Don't." He immediately released her.

"Who's watching the diner with you gone?"

"It's cool."

"No, it's not. We have obligations."

"Chill." Willie offered a quirked-up smile. "I put some servers in charge of the place. It does them good to have more responsibility. You know that." He eyed the books on the counter and glanced at Ellen. He slipped his arm around her waist. "Are you planning on buying books, hon?"

A silent moment passed between them. Ellen flinched.

Then she said, "Jenna, I hope you didn't expect me to buy books today. I don't know what I was thinking bringing them to the register. I'm in a fog. I'm not myself, you understand."

"Of course. I'll keep them on hold."

"No need to do that."

"Okay. I can always reorder if we're out of them the next time you stop in."

Ellen picked up the books and returned them to their messy but rightful places. When she rejoined her husband, he said something more. She fetched the stroller with her daughter and gave me a little wave. "Bye, Jenna. Thanks for listening."

As they exited, I heard Willie ask what we had talked about. Ellen gave a shrug with one shoulder.

Aunt Vera emerged from the stockroom. She gestured at the exiting couple. "That was interesting."

"You heard?"

"Heard and saw. I was peeking through the split in the drapes."

I said, "Granted, they lost their mother and mother-in-law, respectively, but the dynamic —" In frustration, I dinged the bell that sat on the counter. "I'm not imagining things, right? He pinched her to coerce her to put the books back."

"Perhaps."

"Do you think they're tight on cash? Ellen had been concerned about him visiting Die Hard Fan, as well."

"Funerals can be costly."

I couldn't help revisiting Bailey's theory that whoever stood to inherit Natalie Mumford's wealth was the killer. Death would be mighty convenient if, say, a couple with a young daughter needed money. "Aunt Vera, what can you tell me about the Mumford family?"

"What do you want to know?"

She nestled into a chair at the vintage table. I ambled to a chair opposite her and sat as well. Tigger raced to my feet and pounced on them, backed up, and pounced again. I had taught him to play this game whenever I wore my fuzzy slippers at home. Because I was only wearing flip-flops on my feet, his sharp claws stung my bare toes like you-know-what.

I scooped him into my lap and kneaded his belly with my fingertips. "You served on a couple of Crystal Cove committees with Natalie, didn't you?"

"I did."

"What was she like?" I fitted together pieces of a grilled cheese jigsaw puzzle that sat unfinished on the table.

"Customers at the diner loved her. Council members adored her, too. She got things done. No pulling punches with her. She told you what she felt. No filter."

"Like Martha Stewart."

"Like many thriving businesswomen."

I grinned. "Like you."

"Very much like me. However, there were whispers. She was a taskmaster with her staff and her daughter."

"I've heard the same." I finished all the edge pieces of the jigsaw puzzle, which formed the crust of the grilled cheese. Then I started in on the centermost area, which was going to become an image of gooey Brie. "Natalie moved here eight years ago, right?"

"Yes. Ellen was seventeen. The older sister, Norah, chose to stay in the east."

"Norah. Pretty name. I never knew about her. Were she and her family close?"

"Natalie never talked about Norah. I think the girl might have chosen sides."

"You mean she opted to stay with her father?"

"I assume so. According to Natalie, he was

passive-aggressive. He'd say one thing then do another just to irk her. She was always so direct."

I thumped the table with my palm. "That's it. That's what has been bothering me about Willie. He's passive-aggressive. He didn't outright tell Ellen what to do, and yet I'm certain she bows to his will. A pinch here, a command there. I knew a young woman at Taylor & Squibb who suffered in silence for years."

"Relationships are complex, as you well know."

Tigger mewled. I scruffed his head and set him back on the floor. He bounded to the sales counter and leaped from floor to stool to countertop so he could play hide and seek with the cash register. He hid behind the spindle of bookmarks and peeked out. The old National didn't budge. Tigger pawed the drawer and hid again. Still nothing.

Watching my cat come up dry, I said, "Bailey's right. Money could be the motive for Natalie's death. Cinnamon said that Ellen and her sister stand to inherit Natalie's wealth. What if Willie thought getting rid of his mother-in-law would put that wealth in his pocket a little earlier?"

"Why Willie?"

"I can't see Ellen committing murder. She said there was no animosity between her and her mother."

"Wouldn't you, in this instance?"

"I guess so. She doesn't have a strong alibi. She was at the park with her daughter."

"Hmm." Aunt Vera tapped the table. "Playing devil's advocate, what if there isn't any money, ergo, no inheritance? As you well know, it's not easy running a business. We're not making much profit here."

"Yet."

"I've got money and you've got a partnership, but we're not rolling in it. Perhaps the diner, though it's busy, isn't making as much as it needs to survive."

"Other than money, why kill Natalie Mumford?"

Katie waltzed down the hallway carrying a platter. "Hungry?" She displayed the platter, which was set with three kinds of cheeses, a pot of honey, and slices of fresh fruit.

"Where's Bailey?" I asked.

"Pigging out on ice cream."

Uh-oh. Perhaps caffeine would have been the better choice. I know how she liked looking slim and trim.

"This is all I could whip up until the

police take down the tape, but it's coming down as I speak. Hooray. Thank you, Vera." Katie's sizeable chest heaved as she pumped her fist. "Boy, am I raring to go. Think we can get the word out to locals that we're open? Is it too soon for propriety? The kitchen staff and waitstaff are on their way in, in case."

I glanced outside. Although the police were long gone, a number of people stood in the parking lot staring and pointing at our store. "I don't think that's going to be a problem. Propriety or no propriety, we have customers. However, our clientele might be made up of the morbidly curious hoping to get a glimpse of something."

"Nothing to see." Katie set the platter on the table beside the puzzles. "By the way, taste this cheese. Tuscan Tartufo. So delicious. I've been communicating online with a cheese shop owner in Ohio who suggested I serve it with this honey." She spread thimblefuls of honey on two wedges of pale yellow cheese and handed them to us.

I downed mine in one bite and moaned with pleasure.

"To die for, isn't it?" Katie nestled into another chair. "I'm thinking we should start serving trios of cheeses as appetizers and desserts." She eyed the jigsaw puzzle, which

I had abandoned. "May I?"

"Be my guest."

"So what are you two talking about?" She broke apart the puzzle and started putting corners and sides together as I had. "I don't see any tarot cards, which means Vera isn't telling you a quickie fortune."

I filled her in on Ellen and Willie's recent visit.

"That Willie. He was a few years ahead of us in school." Katie was up to date on all the residents in town. I remembered the day we hired her. Aunt Vera had said: *That girl is good for gossip. She knows everyone at bookstores, libraries, shops, you name it.* Having never left Crystal Cove, Katie had her finger on the pulse of insider information. "Willie was a bit of a Romeo. Romancing this and that girl. Got kicked out of college for cheating."

"Cheating on what?" I asked.

"His final exam in economics. I think he learned his lesson, though. He might not have finished college, but he cleaned up his act. He's worked steadily. A variety of jobs. Mostly restaurants. Within days of the Mumfords arriving in town, he swooped in and won Ellen's hand. They married less than a year later."

"She was so young."

"Her mother was against the marriage, but Ellen went full steam ahead."

"Do they only have the one daughter?" I asked.

"Yep. Willie dotes on that girl. I've seen them at the petting zoo and the aquarium."

The Aquarium by the Sea, a beautiful establishment endowed by a widow, offered all sorts of educational children's programming.

"I've see them around town, too. He runs with her in that stroller," Katie added. "Very attentive."

"Do you think being a good dad speaks to his character? I mean, do you think he's too nice to have killed his mother-in-law to get his hands on her estate?"

"Whoa. No. I never said that. I wouldn't trust Willie as far as I could throw him. There's something off about him. All muscle-bound and pompous."

I nodded. "That's what I'm thinking. Did you know he went surfing on the afternoon of his mother-in-law's death?"

"Exactly." Katie tapped her temple. "He's not entirely topnotch in the brain department, and I've seen him at the restaurant. He's sort of, you know, mean to the staff. Very subtle. Very hush-hush."

Very passive-aggressive, I thought. My skin crawled.

CHAPTER 7

When the police declared us open for business, although it was officially closing time, we allowed people inside and sold more than our daily average of cookbooks and doodads. An hour later, I headed home with Tigger. I made a sweet omelet using a simple recipe from Mark Bittman's latest, *How to Cook Everything Vegetarian: Simple Meatless Recipes for Great Food,* a cookbook my aunt had suggested. Afterward, I cleared the kitchen table and eyed the Tupperware box that held the pieces of the broken porcelain cat. With the flurry of activity surrounding Natalie's murder, I had neglected addressing my own drama.

I popped open the box and peeked inside. The broken cat looked like a muddled mess. I put on a mixed jazz CD and then I grabbed a cutting board and a tube of superglue and started to piece together the cat, its rear end first. Tigger circled my ankles as if asking: *What's up?* I cooed that I was taking care of business. Fortunately, when the Lucky Cat shattered, some of the pieces remained large. I felt confident I could reassemble the entire thing. However, as the statue's belly began to take shape, my hands started to shake and my insides quivered. Feeling vulnerable and lonely, I fetched the necklace with the key that David had given me and whispered, "Where is the secret box you belong to? What will I find inside?"

As I asked the questions, I flashed on an incident when I was a girl. I had sought out my father and found him in the master bedroom closet. He was stowing something in a safe hidden beneath the floor. I asked what he was doing. He said that he was hiding his passport. He said it was a secret, and I couldn't tell a soul. He added, quoting Ben Franklin, *Three can keep a secret, if two of them are dead.* Then he chuckled. Little did I know that he was revealing a part of his life to me. As an FBI analyst, there were times he had donned a different persona. My mother had known. None of us kids had. Thinking about that incident, I wondered whether David, with what I now considered his secret life, had installed a keyed safe somewhere in our apartment?

116

He had lived there by himself for two years before I moved in with him. I never noticed a safe. I'd never thought to ask.

I glanced at the clock on the kitchen stove — 9:30 P.M. I dialed the tenant who had sublet my apartment in the city. The woman, recently divorced, answered after the second ring.

"Hey, Jenna," she said. "I was just thinking about you."

"You were?" My aunt would advise me to never dismiss an ESP moment. "Why?"

"I was online hoping to buy my sister a cookbook. She likes spicy food."

I sighed. *Online.* Everyone was buying online nowadays. I said, "Try *Susan Feniger's Street Food: Irresistibly Crispy, Creamy, Crunchy, Spicy, Sticky, Sweet Recipes.*" I remembered the title — another long one — because it had made me laugh. Bailey had shown me the book a couple of weeks ago. I loved the cover picture of the author-chef. She was so open and playful that I'd wanted to meet her. "And don't forget we sell cookbooks online through our store, too. No shipping charges if you purchase more than fifty dollars' worth of items."

She chuckled. "Silly me. I knew that. Will do. Why are you calling?"

I explained.

"Hold on," she said and set the receiver down. I heard her plodding through the apartment. Cabinet doors opened and shut. Drawers, too. *Slide, click, slam.* After a few minutes, my tenant returned to the phone. "I can't find a thing. Not under a mat. Not in a closet. Not behind a painting. I even checked under the sink in the bathroom. Sorry."

I thanked her and hung up and rubbed the key like an amulet, urging it to give me answers. It didn't, of course. So I called Bailey.

She answered in a hyper-chipper voice. "Hey, girlfriend."

"Still off caffeine?"

"Yep, and I have more energy than that teensy train in *The Little Engine That Could.* Who knew?" She was talking faster than a car salesman. "What's up?"

"Got a second?"

"For you, a whole minute."

"Funny. Listen, are you sure the key hanging around my Lucky Cat's neck was a safety deposit box key?"

"I'm never sure of anything. It was a first guess. Long, narrow, five notches. You're still drawing a blank?"

I told her about my search. "I wish David had left me some clue." My voice caught.

"Something tangible."

"You'll figure it out. I promise. But you can't drive yourself crazy about it."

"I know." I choked back tears.

"Are you okay?"

"Sure. I will be. I'm tired. With Natalie's murder . . . and —" I stopped myself from saying more or tears definitely would gush out. *Life is not all about you, Jenna.* Lola was the person we ought to have been concerned about. "How's your mom?"

"Hanging in. She's a tough cookie."

"Like the ones I bake," I joked.

"That's my pal. Find that sense of humor. Are you going to be all right?"

"Yep. Good night. See you tomorrow." I hung up and scooped up Tigger. He licked my chin. I kissed his nose. I considered calling Rhett and asking his opinion about the key but knew that wouldn't be a good move. He might get the wrong signals. And why shouldn't he? He wasn't a key expert. I would've been calling because, well, heck, I was attracted to him.

Instead, I dialed my father.

The next morning, I met my dad at The Pier to pole fish. He had suggested it last night when I wakened him. We stood at the end of the long stretch of boardwalk, bracing ourselves with our elbows on the railing, each holding a pole, its line dangling in the ocean. We never caught much. An occasional rockfish. We always threw them back.

By 7:00 A.M., The Pier was already packed with people. Some waited in line to buy food. Others were fishing, like us, or power walking.

"Look at those paddle boarders." My father pointed at the ocean.

A stream of adventurers, balancing on colorful surfboards and using long oars, glided across the cove. There wasn't a finish line. They were merely practicing for the Paddle-a-thon coming up in a week. On the beach, multiple groups of adults and children tossed Frisbees. Dogs joined in the fun.

"Dad, how's Lola doing?"

"She's worried and giving ZZ guff."

"I thought the mayor couldn't be her lawyer."

"She's not, but ZZ's got plenty of free advice."

"Lola isn't capable of murder."

"Do we ever know if someone is capable? A crime of passion is simply that, someone acting before he or she can change course." My father often made blanket assessments. "Cinnamon has asked Lola to come to the station again for more questions."

"Why is she riding Lola so hard?" I asked. "Don't you, as Cinnamon's mentor, have any sway over her?"

"I *was* her mentor. No longer. Cinnamon is her own person. She makes decisions based on theories and fact."

"Bailey is worried."

"She needn't be. Lola is one of the strongest women I know." Dad nudged me with his shoulder. "How are you? Why did you call me so late? Not just to set a fishing date."

I hoisted my pole, wound the line and hook around it, and propped it against the railing. "I've been thinking a lot about David."

"Why?"

"A ton of reasons."

My father peered into my eyes. "I'm sorry."

"If only —" I began.

"If only the police had found his body. If only there had been closure."

"Yes." I sighed.

"Something else is eating at you."

I told him about the Lucky Cat statue and the coins that had spilled out. I was just about to tell him about the mysterious key when, out of the corner of my eye, I spied a

121

man in the crowd who looked like David. Sandy hair. The right height. Broad shoulders. A confidence to his walk.

"Jenna." Dad gripped my shoulders. "You're hyperventilating. What's wrong?"

I stared harder at the man. It wasn't David, of course. Not even close. He was shorter, he wore glasses, and he had buckteeth. And he was very much alive.

Dad said, "Jenna, sweetheart. Talk to me."

"I see David everywhere. On the beach. In crowds."

"I see your mother, too, if that's any consolation."

"You mean I'm not crazy?"

"You're a wishful thinker. But watch out, next thing you know, you'll be seeing ghosts. O-o-ooh." My father imitated a wiggly-fingered specter.

I punched him. "Don't make fun."

"There's a local therapist you might want to talk to."

"The one who organizes the October benefit luncheon? Maybe." I indicated the flyers for the Grill Fest in my tote bag. After pole fishing, I had planned to roam The Pier and distribute them. "I'm going to get to work and put all this hoo-ha behind me. Promise. Got my pole?"

"I've got your back."

I kissed him on the cheek, and then I raised my chin and strode confidently down the boardwalk. I didn't feel self-assured, but thanks to working with actors for so many years, I could pretend like the best of them. Well, maybe not like Meryl Streep or Anne Hathaway, but you get the idea.

As I neared Mum's the Word Diner, my stomach growled like a motorboat on steroids. I had ventured into the restaurant a few times in the past, the last occasion over three years ago. The line outside was long, which meant the food had to be good. When I made it inside, the only spot available was at the counter. The place had undergone a facelift since my last visit. Turquoise checkered tablecloths adorned the tables. Beside the arced counter, fifties diner-style stools with metal rims and bright yellow cushions were anchored to the floor. Cheery turquoise-and-yellow window treatments and silver-framed photographs of The Pier finished the look. Copies of Natalie Mumford's self-published cookbook with her winning Grill Fest recipes sat stacked beside the register.

One look at the breakfast menu made me salivate: French toast with Grand Marnier sauce, a variety of omelets with homegrown herbs and vegetables, and a lobster-and-steak scramble. In honor of the Grill Fest, if a customer requested, the new chef would make a grilled cheese and serve it with homemade tomato soup.

Ellen, who looked healthier than she had when she'd stopped in The Cookbook Nook yesterday, swung by and greeted me. For a second, I thought she might want to chat, but a customer hailed her and she moved away. I didn't see her husband, Willie, which sort of disappointed me. As much as I hated to admit it, I had been hoping to see them together to observe how he treated her.

A vibrant African-American waitress with an asymmetric, purple-tinged afro and enchanting purple eyes, sashayed to the counter. As she wiped it down, she said, "Long time no see. Jenna, right?" Her nameplate read: *Rosie.*

"Good memory."

Rosie tapped her head. "Got a thing for faces, sugar. I do that mnemonic thing. You know, memory. 'Run over your granny because it's violent.' R-O-Y-G-B-I-V. Colors of the rainbow. Red, orange, yellow, green, blue, indigo, and violet."

"Nice. Never heard that one. What did you use for my name?"

Rosie laughed. "Jenna jumps jumping jacks." My sister never would have come up with something so nice for her string of *J* words. "You look real healthy."

"Thanks. Speaking of jumping, it sure is hopping in here."

"Business has increased big-time since yesterday when Natalie . . . died, rest her soul." Rosie crossed herself. "Public interest is a double-edged sword. It's sad but profitable. The economy . . . well, don't get me started. Things have been taking a downturn all over Crystal Cove. Haven't you noticed it at that shop of yours?"

"Business is pretty good, so far."

Rosie rapped her knuckles on the bar. "From your lips" — she pointed upward — "to His ears. Natalie was trimming services to cut costs until . . ." She placed two fingers over her mouth. "Pardon me. No talking about the dead."

"It's all right. I understand."

"She is missed. She was a good woman. Tough but fair."

That was along the lines of what Ellen had said to me at the shop.

"And Ellen?" I asked. "How's she doing?"

"She's okay. She's thinking outside the box. You probably noticed a promotional sign outside."

I hadn't.

"Children under six eat free. That's encouraged all sorts of new business. Kids can be such picky eaters. Parents don't want to spend for a kid's meal, know what I mean?" She hitched a thumb at Ellen. "Like you, she wants to have all sorts of special events. Pier Day. Super Sunday. Silly names, but catchy. She was also thinking of having a contest. A customer has to put a name and e-mail address on a slip of paper to be eligible to win a meal for four. What do you think?"

"It's a good idea." I ordered the French toast with Grand Marnier sauce and a cup of coffee. When Rosie returned with my meal, I said, "Where's Willie?"

"Off with his little one. Ellen is spending entirely too much time at the diner. It's the heartache that drives her." Rosie clucked her tongue. "And seeing as Grandma Natalie isn't around to help, well, Willie is doing most of the childrearing. He dotes on that girl of his."

"What's her name?"

"Bebe. Ellen named her after that actress on that old TV show *Cheers,* but Willie calls her his Bonnie Blue, like out of *Gone with the Wind.* Willie wanted to buy her a big new house, but now I guess he won't need to, seeing as they'll have Natalie's place all to themselves."

What a boon, I mused.

"He's sort of a nervous Nellie, if you ask me," Rosie went on.

"How is he to the staff?"

"A boor, but all bosses are, aren't they? He considers himself a big-picture guy. Says he can't abide the minor details." She leaned forward on her elbows. "But don't believe him. How that man goes on about the teensiest things when it comes to his daughter. If Bebe gets a scratch, he's on it with a bandage. She gets a snarl in her hair; he's the one to brush it. Why, he was so worried when there was a ping in the engine of his car, he went to Rusty's Repair Shop that minute."

Her words reminded me that I needed to pick up my VW at the shop. To get around, I had been riding my mother's old bike.

"That's where Willie was at the time of Natalie's murder," Rosie went on.

"He wasn't here?"

"Nope. Out getting his car fixed. Lord forbid if his car were to break down with his precious Bebe in it." Rosie rolled her eyes. "Mind you, sugar, I don't own a car. What do I know? But really, must he address every insignificant thing that very moment?"

"You're saying he misses a lot of work."

"Piles it all on Ellen." Rosie peeked past me. "Oh, there they are."

She wiggled her fingers and blew a kiss. Not at Willie, who was entering the shop, but at Bebe, who was awake in her stroller. Willie looked a little ragged in holey jeans with his rumpled shirttail out; however, he greeted people with an easy smile.

When he caught sight of me, something in his affable demeanor changed. His eyes narrowed. He scanned the restaurant and made a beeline for Ellen, who was chatting up an elderly couple. Willie parked his daughter in the stroller beside a table and pulled Ellen toward the kitchen door. Without releasing her, he ushered her beyond the door that divided the kitchen from the dining room. Through the glass porthole in the door, I could see him talking heatedly. Ellen cut a quick look at me — I was certain I was her target — and back at her husband. She shook her head.

Was Willie asking whether she had encouraged me to come to the diner? Wasn't I welcome? Maybe they were discussing Rosie, the waitress, but I didn't think so. Ellen flinched. She said something and then pushed through the door to return to the dining room. Willie followed and, in full public view, pointed at his cheek. Ellen, like an obedient spouse, leaned forward and gave him a peck, but she didn't look happy about it.

CHAPTER 8

Business that morning at the shop was busier than usual. By 10:00 A.M., I was exhausted. Downing two of Katie's lemon meringue mini-cupcakes after eating the oversized portion of French toast at the Word had something to do with my lack of pep. *Sugar blahs,* my mother called them. When I told Bailey and my aunt that I was going to take a twenty-minute catnap in the office, neither argued. Bailey, who was still off caffeine, was zipping around the store at the speed of light, reorganizing everything, soup to nuts.

While dozing, I suffered a muddle of dreams: Natalie and the chef's resignation letter; the Lucky Cat crashing to the floor; Willie locking his precious daughter in his car as something in the car went *ping, ping, ping;* David running away from me. Last but not least, I dreamed of the display in the bay window at The Cookbook Nook.

Something about it was off. I woke up with a crick in my neck. Eager to dismiss every dream as anxious nonsense, I focused on the window display.

In the advertising business, we had to be prepared to revise and rewrite as well as recast a role if an actor wasn't working out. I felt the same about the window display. Over the course of the next hour, I removed the oars, Frisbees, and sand toys, but I left the partial white picket fence. I set out beach towels and umbrellas. On the towels, I fanned a selection of the culinary mysteries we had in stock. All the books had cute titles like: *A Brew to a Kill, Death in Four Courses,* and *The Diva Frosts a Cupcake.* In addition, I placed decorative boxes nearby to indicate that the books included recipes. I added pretty floral aprons, mixing cups, and kitchen utensils, and I titled the area *Beach Reading with Flavor.*

Near noon, Katie, bless her soul, brought in a batch of open-faced crab melt sandwiches, made just for the staff. She had decorated each with a teensy umbrella. To my surprise, my stomach growled. I craved protein.

By mid-afternoon, a new wave of customers flocked into the shop. They perused the culinary mysteries with an enthusiasm bordering on frenzy. Everybody needs a book to read while basking in the sun, right? One of the women in the gathering, a charming woman and the leader of an eight-member book club, suggested I invite her book club to tea on a monthly basis so we could discuss food fiction. Pumped from the gusto in the shop, I jumped at the opportunity and asked if I might be able to grow the club. The leader was all for the idea. The more the merrier, she said, and then hinted that her pals might like to meet one of the mystery authors along the way. I had no idea whether an author or group of authors might come to quaint Crystal Cove, but I promised to do my best to lure them.

Around 3:30 in the afternoon, as I stood at the top of a ladder restocking shelves — my calf muscles were getting a great workout from all the sales. *Yahoo!* — Mayor Zeller entered arm in arm with Lola. I was thrilled to see that the lines in Lola's face weren't nearly as deep as a few days ago; her eyes glistened with energy.

I descended the ladder and joined them by the sales counter, where my aunt and Bailey were ringing up a steady stream of orders.

"Good news," the mayor warbled. "The Grill Fest will continue Friday, right after

Ellen holds the memorial for her mother."

"She's having a memorial instead of a funeral?" I said.

Mayor Zeller shook her head with regret. "Poor thing. Our chief of police won't release the body quite yet."

What more could Cinnamon glean from the corpse? Maybe the pieced-together resignation letter wasn't the only evidence she had found.

"When is the memorial?" I asked.

"Tomorrow morning," the mayor replied.

"Even better news" — Lola shot an exultant finger into the air — "Chief Pritchett is allowing me to participate in the fest."

"Yippee!" Bailey hurried to her mother and gave her a hug so fierce I thought she might be trying to wring some caffeine from her. "Mom, I'm so happy for you. That means you're innocent."

"Not so fast," Lola said, wriggling free. "I'm not out of the woods yet."

Bailey eyed me. "Jenna, tell them what we learned about Mitzi."

"What about her?" Lola asked.

"Two different people claim Mitzi was in the vicinity of the café around the time of the murder," I said.

"That doesn't put her at the crime scene," Lola argued.

"Near enough," Bailey countered.

"Why wasn't she in the parking lot with everyone else?" the mayor asked.

I explained Mitzi's supposed need for vitamin D and her claim that she was headed for the beach.

"That means she lied," the mayor said.

Lola scoffed. "We don't know that. Don't presume."

"Mom," Bailey said. "Mitzi held a grudge against Natalie."

Mayor Zeller nodded. "And rightly so. Mitzi was never going to win the contest as long as Natalie was alive."

"That's not true, ZZ," Lola said. "Mitzi is a creative chef. Her private clients rave about the uniqueness of her gourmet meals." Lola eyed me. "What about Natalie's heirs, Jenna? I heard you mention that angle to Cinnamon."

"No, I mentioned it, Mother," Bailey said. "By the way, did you know Ellen has a sister? The two of them stand to inherit."

Everyone looked as surprised as I had been. Talk about keeping family secrets in a closet.

I said, "However, just between us, I think Ellen's husband may have had a hand in Natalie's murder." I told them about my breakfast at Mum's the Word. "He seems overly concerned about Ellen talking to anyone." I explained how Willie coerced Ellen to return the books to the shelves yesterday. "I think they might be having financial difficulty. Ellen mentioned something about obligations. On the other hand, Willie has a solid alibi. He was at the car repair shop."

Mayor Zeller said, "I'll keep an eye on him. We don't want him giving Ellen and that daughter of hers any trouble. Now, Lola, let's go. Ladies, if anyone needs us, Lola and I are going on a shopping expedition." She ushered Lola out saying, "Hope you have your credit cards handy. We're celebrating your freedom."

"Temporary freedom."

"Don't talk like that."

Around 5:00 P.M. Katie tracked me down. Not with food, which disappointed me. I don't know why I was starved yet again. I thought being around the aroma of delicious food was stirring my appetite. If I didn't watch out, my waistline would double in no time. Perhaps an extra cup of coffee instead of sweets as a treat was a good alternative.

"Whew," Katie said while she tied on a white apron. "It's been crazy today. We've had so many customers I can barely breathe.

Can you do me a favor? I need you to go to the store. We had a run on the lunch special."

"The crab melt?"

"No, the Brazilian spiced fish salad. I need to make another batch of the tempero baiano, a Bahian seasoning. I'm completely out of turmeric, and I could also use some rosemary and thyme for the evening's soup selection. Would you go, please? I can't sparc any staff."

Bailey, edgy since her mother's departure, begged to tag along. How could I refuse?

The Crystal Cove Grocery Store was an intimate place, with wooden shelves, wooden bins, and a rustic wood floor. The owner, a baker by trade, made all the breads. A farmers' market couldn't have offered more fresh fruits and veggies. The herbs that Katie wanted, all locally grown, were offered in rattan-tied bunches. Hanging above the herbs were bags of spices.

I grabbed three bundles of each herb on Katie's list and a bag of turmeric. "You are jumpier than a dolphin in an ocean full of sharks," I said to Bailey, who hadn't stopped pulling on her left earlobe since we'd entered the store, a clear indication that she was tense. "How about downing some cola?"

"No. I'm good. Sure, I miss my caffeine, but I want to conquer my craving. A healthy body means a healthy spirit."

"Okay, Miss Zen, then what's eating you?"

Her voice drifted to a hush. "Mom. Right before we left, I called her to check in. She was still shopping with the mayor. She has a tendency to binge shop."

"Like you," I teased.

Bailey screwed up her mouth.

"Are you worried that she's running into money trouble?"

"No. Not at all. But binge shopping encourages her to buy things that don't, um, look good on her. You know, things that don't fit, though she convinces herself they do."

I laughed. "Don't worry about it. As long as she doesn't remove the sales tags, you can talk her into taking anything back."

"You're right. I'm acting crazy."

"Concerned."

"Nuts. Speaking of which" — Bailey knuckled my arm — "what's this I heard about you on The Pier this morning? You thought you saw David?"

My cheeks warmed. "Who told you? Dad?"

"Your aunt."

Which meant my father told her. So much for him thinking it was perfectly fine seeing my dead husband occasionally.

"She's worried."

Aha. That explained why my aunt had hovered near me while rubbing her amulet a couple of times today. I'd have to inform her that insanity couldn't be frightened off by a few positive prayers. On the other hand, going crazy was not on my agenda. I made a mental note to call the therapist and set an appointment. What could it hurt?

"Well?" Bailey said. "I'm waiting for a response."

"I've got David on the brain. It's this thing with the Lucky Cat and the key and the coins." I inhaled and exhaled slowly. "I want to know the truth."

I headed for the checkout line and saw Mitzi Sykes ahead of us placing item after item on the conveyor belt. She was wearing ginormous rings and multiple strands of necklaces. As she chatted up the clerk, using grand hand gestures, her metal bangles clanked. I flashed on the conversation with Flora, the Grill Fest contestant who was the owner of Home Sweet Home. She had spotted Mitzi spying on her husband. Mitzi wouldn't have been able to do so in that getup, I thought. Way too noisy.

I moved toward her. "Hey, Mitzi, who's having a party?"

Mitzi smiled. Her red lipstick made her luscious lips look even bigger. "Me. Well, not me. My client. You know the fellow who designed the Nature's Retreat Hotel?"

I did. Local architect. Big ego.

"He's such a gourmet. Snails. Lobster. Seven different kinds of cheeses. Bananas Foster for dessert."

I felt a bump on my grocery cart from behind and pivoted. Mitzi's husband, Sam, was trying to inch by me. Slung over his arm was a mini-basket filled with fixings for spaghetti.

"Sorry," he said. "Do you mind?"

I didn't.

He placed a dividing rod between his and Mitzi's purchases, then rummaged through his pockets, mumbling as if he had misplaced something. Mitzi paid for her goods, and the clerk bagged them. Then Mitzi rolled her loaded cart toward the exit.

"Babe, wait," Sam called.

A man who called his wife *babe* wasn't a cheater, was he? Perhaps I was too naïve for words.

"I'm not going anywhere, my love. You've got the keys," Mitzi teased. She pulled her cart to a stop short of the exit.

"No, I, um . . ." Sam scratched his neck. He caught sight of me watching him and instantly dropped his arm to his side. His cheeks burnished the same color as his chafed neck. "I seem to have misplaced my wallet."

Mitzi's face morphed from flirty to flinty. She strode to Sam and in a hushed voice said, "What?"

Sam sputtered. "I'm not sure what could have happened."

"You can't have spent the food allowance already."

Food allowance? I mused. What was up with that?

"No, I . . ." He dug again into his pockets. "I think I was robbed."

Mitzi huffed as if she had heard that excuse way too many times to count.

"Fine. Forget it. What do you care?" Sam left his items on the conveyor belt and bolted from the store.

Mitzi hurried after him but stopped at the door. As Sam tore from the lot in his Mercedes, Mitzi sagged against the jamb and dropped her forehead into her hands.

I thrust the cash to pay for our goods at Bailey and dashed to Mitzi. "Are you okay?" Closer up, she smelled faintly of alcohol.

140

Had she been taste-testing the brandy that was to go into her client's Bananas Foster dessert?

"I'm so embarrassed." Mitzi whimpered. "I know better than to have an argument in public. My psychiatrist has warned me to keep personal matters private, but do I listen? It's just" — she chewed her lip, taking off a layer of lipstick in the process — "I feel so raw, and Sam" — she sighed — "is a little raw, too. He . . . Oh, the whole world knows. He had a thing for Natalie."

I hadn't known.

"I thought with her gone that I could keep him interested, and for the past twenty-four hours, we've been good."

I stifled a gasp. Was Mitzi admitting that she had killed Natalie in a jealous rage?

"And then I go and do something stupid like this," Mitzi went on. "I bite off his head. What was I thinking? What do you bet he's already looking for a new lover?"

If Flora was to be trusted, Mitzi believed Sam was already looking. Why else would she have followed him to the bank? How had she tracked him down? Had she put a GPS device on his car?

"I can't prove he's involved with anyone, except he's always low on cash. What does he spend his money on? Flowers or trinkets?

Not on me."

"Have you point-blank asked him?"

"Sure." Mitzi fluttered her hand. Her bangles clanged again. "He swears he's investing his money here and there, but on more than one occasion he's claimed that he was robbed. He's innocent, he insists, and I'm the one who feels bad for asking. Same old, same old."

"No, I meant have you asked him about the affairs?"

"Of course I've asked. He says I'm the only one for him. Except" — she glanced left and right — "Natalie insinuated other-wise."

"What did she say? When? At the Grill Fest?"

Mitzi nodded. "She said I should keep an open eye. Can you believe the gall?"

"An *open eye* about what?"

"Can't you guess? Lovers."

"Maybe she was trying to rattle you." I couldn't believe we were talking about Nat-alie as though she were alive, but Mitzi seemed so needy that I felt obligated to help her through her crisis. "Maybe Natalie was the one who had a thing for Sam, but he didn't reciprocate," I suggested.

"All men reciprocate, don't they?"

I didn't know. Did they? No, I wouldn't

believe it. *Jaded, jilted Jenna.* No, it didn't fit me. "Mitzi, stop it. Sam is in love with you. I've seen the way he looks at you."

"You have?"

"He adores you."

"If only that were so." She dug into her purse, pulled out a tissue, and blew her nose, then stuffed the tissue back, withdrew a lipstick, and swathed on a new layer. "I do everything I can to keep him interested. I exercise. I eat right. I do a nightly bath ritual, scrubbing my skin all over so it's baby soft. Then I apply lotion using facial gloves I get from France. My skin is silky smooth. Feel." She jutted out her arm.

I flinched. She didn't really want me to touch her, did she? Guess not. She tucked her arm against her side. Phew.

"I often caught him texting Natalie," Mitzi said. "*Ping, ping, ping.* How I hate the sound of that darned cell phone. Naturally, he claimed every text was about business, but c'mon, do I look dense?"

I gaped at her. After what Flora had said, I began to wonder about Mitzi. Not only did she suspect Sam of having an affair with Manga Girl, but she believed he had been involved with Natalie. Was her husband a serial rover, or was she just plain paranoid?

"Dang it," Mitzi said and stood to her full

height. She smoothed her chignon. "I'm a catch, aren't I? I'm hot, I'm talented, and I've got a thriving business."

Bailey joined us. "What's going on?"

Mitzi cut her a bitter look. "Nothing. Not a thing in the world. Except I don't have a ride."

"We'll give you one," Bailey offered.

"Would you really?" Mitzi seemed so awestruck by the offer, I wondered again if she had been drinking.

As we walked to Bailey's Toyota RAV4, Bailey gave me a wink and said, "Say, Jenna, did you ask Mitzi if she saw anything suspicious when she was on the café patio yesterday?"

Mitzi stopped pushing her cart. "What are you talking about? I . . ." She sputtered. "I was never on the patio."

"Sure, you were," Bailey said. "One of the fellows who works upstairs at Fisherman's Village saw you. Pepper Pritchett, too."

Mitzi stiffened. "Wait a sec. Hold it right there. Are you implying that I was anywhere in the vicinity of the crime scene? Do you think I killed Natalie Mumford? No way would I get close to that woman when she's smoking like a chimney."

"Natalie smoked?" I said.

"On the sly. Why else do you think she

was in the alley?"

That explained Natalie's extra-heavy dose of perfume at the contest. Thinking back, I remembered seeing something that looked like a cigarette case in her opened purse.

"Miss Holier than Holy didn't think anyone knew," Mitzi went on, "but, of course, everyone did. It drove Sam crazy. Coffin nails, he called them. His mother died of" — Mitzi leaned in and whispered — "the big C."

My gut wrenched. My mother had died of cancer, too, but not because she was a smoker. She hadn't smoked. Ever. She was simply a tragic statistic.

Mitzi tilted her head like a curious bird; her gaze turned harder than granite. "On second thought, I'm going to take a cab home." Hurriedly, she fished her cell phone from her purse and started dialing. "It's out of your way to drive me."

"It's no bother," Bailey said.

"Yes, it is." Without another word, Mitzi made a U-turn with her grocery cart and headed back to the store entrance, her cell phone tucked between her shoulder and chin.

"Well, well." Bailey stowed grocery bags in her car. "I guess she didn't dare hang out with us for fear she'd spill more information. Care to fill me in on what went down?"

I told her about Mitzi's concern that Sam was having an affair with Natalie, her worry based upon Sam and Natalie's many telephone text exchanges.

"Interesting," Bailey said. "You know, I did hear a ping right before we took the break that day."

"Didn't the mayor tell everyone to turn off their cell phones?"

Bailey smirked. "Does anyone ever obey that request? I remember Natalie looking at her cell phone right before the break. What if Sam texted Natalie? Maybe he intended to meet her clandestinely after the competition."

"Except Sam was attending the conference in San Jose."

"But Flora saw him at the bank."

"Late in the afternoon."

Bailey let that notion brew for a second. "What if Mitzi was the one who texted Natalie?"

"I'm not following."

"What if Mitzi planned all along to kill Natalie? What if she nabbed Sam's phone with the express intent of texting Natalie so Natalie would meet her alone in the alley?"

"But she said that she wouldn't have gone

near Natalie when she was smoking."

"Where there's smoke, there's fire."

CHAPTER 9

Although I was beat, Katie had been adamant about giving me an after-work cooking lesson. Who cared if it was 9:00 P.M.? Not her. Tigger pranced around the cottage, checking her out as she set food items on the counter. We rarely had guests this late. Katie had brought her mother's old *Betty Crocker Cookbook,* the checkerboard cover splattered with who-knew-what. Bailey, Katie's accomplice, sat at the kitchen table, her finger propping up the raised arm of the Lucky Cat. Two minutes ago, she had affixed it with superglue. The appendage was so heavy, she couldn't let go until the glue set. *Tough break,* I thought with more than a bit of spite as I yawned and stretched.

"Making tomato soup isn't hard," Katie assured me. She set a pound of tomatoes, an onion, and herbs on a cutting board. Next, she pulled out a blender that I had yet to utilize. "A chop of this, a dash of that.

I use homemade chicken stock at the café, but when I'm in a rush at home, I put in a natural, no-additives broth. You don't pour in the cream until the very last because you don't want it to curdle. In thirty minutes, snap, it's done. Serve it with a chunk of bread, and you have a full meal."

"I ate dinner," I said. "I'm not hungry." By the time Bailey and I had returned to The Cookbook Nook after our grocery run, the store and café were bustling with customers. When the buyers at the shop petered out around 8:00 P.M., we closed, and I downed one of Katie's specials. The Brazilian fish had been so spicy, I had needed three glasses of water. But, yum!

"One can never turn down tomato soup," Katie said.

"It's the perfect complement to a grilled cheese sandwich," I replied. As I said the words, I thought of my mother. She had loved cold days with warm lunches. Perfect *painting-and-wrapping-oneself-in-emotions days,* she had called them. How I missed her and her positive attitude, her sunny smile, and our moments discussing artists' styles and nuances.

"Ooh, grilled cheese," Katie crooned, her eyes twinkling with mischief. "Do you have cheddar?"

"No-o-o," I said, putting a damper on her fun. "I'll agree to a light meal and no more. Then bed. I'm beat."

"Spoilsport," Bailey said.

I mock glowered at her. "We have a full day tomorrow. So much to do before Natalie Mumford's memorial." Out of respect, we had agreed to close the shop for those two hours. It was the least we could do.

Bailey said, "By the way, did you note the run on grilled cheese cookbooks today? It's a mania. I ordered an overnight shipment. Hopefully, we'll get them before the Grill Fest resumes tomorrow afternoon."

I popped open a bottle of chardonnay. Tigger startled and nearly did a somersault. "Cool it, kitty," I said then poured three short glasses of wine and handed one to each of my friends.

Bailey frowned. "How exactly am I supposed to drink that?"

"You have a free hand. Put down the tube of glue."

She glanced at the tube and laughed. "I think it's stuck to my skin. I've never been good at arts and crafts."

I helped pry her loose.

After she took a sip of wine, she said, "Better than caffeine any day. Now, did you tell Katie about the scene at the grocery store?"

"What scene?" Katie asked.

"Between Mitzi and Sam." I recounted the event.

"No way." Katie wagged a finger. "I don't believe Sam had a thing for Natalie. I mean, honestly, he's an upstanding guy. He manages so many accounts in town. Two at Fisherman's Village. Why, he even managed my former boss's account." Katie used to be the personal chef for an affluent widower who'd died at the ripe age of ninety-seven. "Sure, there was some talk."

"About Sam having an affair?" I said.

"No, nothing that risqué." She wriggled her nose. "I'm not one to gossip."

Bailey nearly snorted wine out her nose.

Katie skewered her with a look. "Okay, maybe I am. I like to be in the *know.*"

"Me, too," Bailey said. "Share."

"Mr. Powers, my boss . . . One day he asked Sam about a section of his portfolio. Sam had terminated it without Mr. Powers's approval, but Sam assured him that he had simply moved money to a better-positioned account. Sort of a day trade. In the end, Mr. Powers was satisfied."

Bailey moaned. "I dated a day trader once. The guy was as hyper as a three-year-old on a sugar diet."

I said, "That doesn't address whether

151

there's any truth to Sam having an affair with Natalie."

"Right." Katie laid a hand to her chest. "But I'm talking about character. Sam visited old man Powers often. He chatted him up as if he were his doting son. Never once did they talk about Sam's interest in anyone but Mitzi. And I listened in. You know me."

"Miss No Gossip," Bailey teased.

Katie shot her a scathing look. "I mean, I don't trust many folks. I didn't want Sam or anyone for that matter taking advantage of the old guy, you know?" She sipped her wine. "Wouldn't we have heard something gossip-wise at the shop about Sam before this?"

"I doubt it," I said. "It's not like Mitzi and Sam are regular customers. Do you know, Mitzi actually bragged to me that she never uses recipes from cookbooks?"

"The gall," Katie said.

"I thought it was sort of funny, like she had no filter."

"You could mention the alleged affair to Cinnamon," Bailey said.

My turn to spew wine. "Are you kidding? And make her think that I'm snooping?"

"You are."

"No, thank you. Not interested."

"Jenna, cut up tomatoes." Katie pulled a knife from the block and brandished it at me.

In the past month, I had become pretty comfortable mixing things with a spoon. And I was good with a steak knife when eating meat. But slicing and dicing things that could go squirt in the night . . . all by my lonesome? Save me.

"It's easy." Katie demonstrated, chopping as fast as one of the chefs on television.

I blanched. "Not a chance."

But Katie wouldn't let up. Relenting, I took the knife and slowly, methodically cubed the tomatoes repeating a new mantra in my head: *No fear. No fear. No fear.*

"Not bad," she said. "Practice makes —"

"Music," I finished, remembering another of my mother's favorite sayings. In addition to being an artist, she had played guitar. Much to my chagrin, I couldn't pluck a string to save my soul. I wasn't bad with a harmonica; I could play a few pieces on the piano, too.

As I attempted to snip rosemary with a pair of kitchen shears, Bailey asked, "What's this?" She displayed the bottom of the cat statue to me. "There's writing. I think it's Chinese. What does it say?"

I started for the Lucky Cat, but Katie

stopped me.

"No, ma'am. Do not lose your focus. Cooking requires your full attention. Put all the ingredients in the blender and turn it on." When Katie was certain I was on task, she headed for Bailey. "It probably says: *Made in China.*"

"I don't think so," Bailey said. "It looks handwritten, not factory-printed."

Katie peered at the writing. "Hoo-boy, that's a lot more than three characters." She fluttered her fingers. "Wait. I'm getting a vibe. It means . . . It means . . ."

"Oh, no you don't," I warned. "Don't start talking like Aunt Vera."

"But I really do think it means something," Katie said. "You know, like a fortune cookie fortune: *Avoid taking unnecessary gambles.*" She laughed. "As if any gamble is necessary."

Bailey said, "What if David is sending you a message from the beyond?" I shivered.

"Maybe the words say: *Every departure is an entrance to new adventures.*" Bailey rubbed the Lucky Cat's belly. "Speak to me, precious cat statue. Speak." She screeched out a cat's yowl.

Spooked, Tigger leaped at my legs.

"For heaven's sake," I said. "Stop it. You're freaking out the kitten." I reached down to

154

calm him at the same time that I hit Pulse on the blender. Like a volcano, tomatoes and herbs spewed upward. "Oh no!" Thanks to Bailey's banter and Tigger's surprise attack, I had forgotten to put on the blender's lid. I stabbed the Off button. It didn't matter. The kitchen looked like a crime scene: red goo upward, sideways, and everywhere.

Bailey and Katie cackled.

I grumbled. "It's not funny. Help me clean it up."

"Don't get snarky." Bailey set the porcelain cat aside; its arm held. She scrambled to her feet. "Really, you should find out what these words mean."

"I will."

An hour later, after I used three entire rolls of paper towels dampened with a mixture of vinegar and water to clean up the sticky tomato mess, and after I diligently made a batch of tomato soup that Katie said was pretty darned decent, my pals left.

Late into the night I searched the Internet for an interpretation of the writing on the bottom of the Lucky Cat, but because I was unable to draw the characters into the search bar — I didn't own a scanner, so I couldn't copy them digitally, either — I wound up stymied. The Chinese alphabet had thousands upon thousands of characters as well as countless styles: Ancient, Kai Shu, Xing. If I'd been so inclined, I could have learned to paint the characters with a choice of paintbrushes made out of rabbit, squirrel, or badger hair. Bleary-eyed, I fell into a restless sleep wondering whether the message on the bottom of the statue related to the gold coins, while at the same time hating David for leaving me with such a puzzle.

Except, of course, I didn't hate him. I missed him.

The next morning, I woke with a start. A slim ray of sunshine peeked through the break in the curtains. Tigger pounced onto the bed and kneaded my chest through the comforter.

"No way, mister." I plucked him off the spread and tucked him beneath the sheet. Instantly contented, he curled into me while I, wired and wide-awake, stared at the ceiling. What had awakened me? Had I dreamed something horrible? Had I heard a noise?

Unwilling to feel paranoid or sorry for myself, I clambered out of bed, donned my running clothes, knotted my hair with a covered rubber band, and headed outside for my daily walk/run.

A thick, foggy drizzle made it hard to differentiate between the ground and the ocean, not to mention that the sand felt mushy beneath my feet. Worried about twisting an ankle, I headed to the main road. With few cars out, I jogged in the lane instead of along the shoulder. I breathed in three counts and out four counts. After a few minutes, my shoulders relaxed. After five minutes, those teensy muscles that bind the ribcage together loosened.

As I was nearing The Pier, which due to the fog looked like a thin haze of charcoal gray, I heard a car coming up behind me. I twisted my head to look but couldn't see anything. No headlights. No blur of color. I moved to the right and peeked over my shoulder again. A car was nearing. A dark sedan. Suddenly it was bearing down upon me. In the bicycle lane.

"Hey," I yelled, like that would have done any good.

It didn't. The driver seemed to be aiming straight for me. I flailed my arms. The car continued to head in my direction.

Fight-or-flight took hold. With my heart ramming my ribcage like a sledgehammer, I dodged to my right, skidded on the gravel, and stumbled. I hit a soft spot that gave way, and I tumbled down a small decline held together by scrub brush and weeds. The branches scraped me, but their assault was nothing compared to the beating I could have taken from a two-ton vehicle.

"Jerk." I got to my feet and scrambled up the embankment to see if I could glimpse the offending car's license plate. I couldn't even make out what kind of car it was. I pounded pavement after the vehicle, but seconds into the chase I realized my pursuit was a lost cause. The fog had consumed any memory of the encounter.

Deciding that running on the sand might be safer after all, I headed back down the embankment. As I reached the sand, I glanced occasionally at the road, hoping that the driver would come back to check on me. No such luck. So much for having concern for one's fellow man.

During one of my head turns, I lost track of what was in front of me on the sand, which wasn't smart, since the fog had thickened to pea soup consistency. I ran smack into a pack of dog owners with dogs in tow. "Oops," I yelped then, "Whoa," as I tripped over a leash and took a header. From an embarrassing angle on my back-side, I peered up and realized all the owners and dogs were wearing some form of reflector shield. How had I not seen them? How had I missed hearing them? Well, actually, I hadn't *missed* them, had I?

One of them reached out a hand to help me up. "Jenna?"

Looking closer, I recognized Rhett. He gripped me by the shoulders. A black Labrador romped in a loop around me then sat on his rump, his head tilted as if asking who this killjoy was. The other owners and pets continued on their journey.

"Sorry," I said. "Guess the fog's a little thick for my own good." Understatement of the century.

"Are you okay?" Rhett asked. "You're shaking."

I told him about the near miss on the road.

"Perhaps you should wear reflectors," he said.

"The fog had lifted a bit. I could see the car. Don't you think the driver should have seen me?"

"You don't believe the driver swerved at you intentionally, do you?"

A chill ran through me. Was that what I was inferring? The driver hadn't aimed for me, had he . . . or she? That was unlikely, and yet —

"I'm not sure. But —" I paused again when I realized my fingertips were tingling. Aunt Vera said that was the kind of sensation she experienced whenever she truly connected to the spiritual world. If I was psychic like her, what next? Would I hang out a shingle and tell fortunes? No. Never. I was a businesswoman, a reader, a dabbler in the arts. Not a seer. And yet I had this gut feeling about my near run-in with the car. "I jog every morning."

"On the sand, not the road."

"You're right, I'm wrong. It couldn't have been intentional." Yet something about the event sent a shimmy of doubt through me. Had someone watched me leave the house and tailed me? Why would anyone want to harm me?

"Perhaps you should rethink your morning exercise routine. Maybe on these thick-as-mush days you should consider doing weights at home." Rhett rubbed my arms as if to console me. At the same time, the Labrador nosed him in the back of the legs. Rhett lurched into me. He held me firmly for a split second then self-consciously pushed away.

I laughed. "Who's this?"

"Rook. I just got him. I was missing Rufus something awful." Rufus, Rhett's Great Dane, passed away last year. I hadn't met him, but Rhett sang his praises. "What can I say? I love big dogs."

Rook nudged Rhett's hand.

"All right, fella, we'll get back to our run.

In a sec." Rhett tightened the leash. "Jenna, I guess congratulations are in order. The Grill Fest is back on."

"It is." I still felt anxious about the prospect. Natalie had died. Was her death a result of having been a contestant? Would others be targeted? Somewhere in the middle of the night, I'd had another dream pairing Natalie with David and a pot of gold. Was there something to be divined from the dream? If only I were a dream interpreter. Maybe that could be my calling once the fortune-telling talent kicked into high gear.

"What a collection of characters competing," Rhett continued. "Between Tito and the fireman and that funky beading gal."

"Flora. And don't forget the librarian. Have you heard her laugh? She's so full of life."

He grinned. "I look forward to taste-testing the competitors' entries, even though I'll have to exercise harder next week. Speaking of which, I'm hungry. Want to grab a bite to eat?"

Was he asking me on a date? I delighted at the notion. One night a few weeks ago, Rhett had shown up on my doorstep with a picnic, but that hadn't been a real date. Like many chefs, he'd had a late-night craving.

He'd arrived with spareribs and all the trimmings. A day later we went for ice cream, but that hadn't been a formal date, either. I was pretty sure I wanted to go out with him, but thanks to the conundrum my husband had left me, I wasn't ready to do so yet.

"Can't," I said like a scaredy-cat. "I've got to open the shop." I jerked my thumb back toward town. "And I've got errands, too. There's so much to do before Natalie's memorial at noon." Was I running away from life? I didn't want to. Not forever. I had to make myself emotionally available. Soon. "Are you going?"

"I'll be there. I think the whole town will. Everyone loved Natalie."

Not everyone.

CHAPTER 10

At 9:15 A.M., I exited the stockroom and surveyed the shop. Dozens of customers were browsing the cookbook shelves, but none appeared ready to buy. Bailey was kneeling beside a pair of munchkins in the children's section, pointing out the finer points of cake-pop decorating sets. They gawked at her as if she were the wisest person on earth. She was. Thanks to a couple of recent baking lessons from Katie, Bailey had taken up cake-pop art. Her latest batch, in honor of the beginning of the school season, were Oreo pops made with kitty cat faces. Tigger the imp lay sound asleep, stretched out on the back of one of the reading chairs. My aunt stood by the gadgets display, chatting up a pair of buyers who were engrossed with the embroidery on some potholders.

"Bailey, do you mind if I leave the shop for a bit?" I said as I exited the stockroom.

"I have three errands to run before Natalie's memorial."

"Feel free. Your aunt and I can handle the crowd, but" — Bailey snapped her fingers and beckoned me closer — "do me a favor. Stop by The Pelican Brief and check on my mom, would you? She sounded low when I called her this morning."

"Sure," I said. The diner was on the way to my first errand, the bank. I needed to withdraw cash. Rusty's Repair Shop was one of the few businesses in town that demanded honest-to-goodness greenbacks. No plastic. No ifs, ands, or buts. I certainly preferred when customers used cash at The Cookbook Nook and the café, but I wouldn't demand that they did. However, I understood the practice. The steep fees charged by credit card companies for services rendered could put small independent businesses in dire straits.

A short while later, I rolled out my mother's retro bicycle, which I now stowed in the stockroom — errands around town were more easily handled using the bike — and I pedaled to The Pelican Brief. I parked the bike in a rack on the sidewalk and secured it with a lock. As I entered the restaurant, Lola exited her office. She didn't look glum; in fact, she looked buoyant. Her face glimmered with subtly glittered rouge. Her large eyes were outlined in silver to match her hair and snug outfit. She carried a fashionable leather briefcase. She saw me and hurried over.

"Sweet Jenna." She grasped one of my hands and bussed my cheek. "What a bright spot you are in my morning."

"You look great," I said, meaning it.

She winked. "Fake it and you own it, as some famous actress used to say. Bette Davis, I think. Or maybe it was Mae West. I'm not sure."

"Where are you off to?"

"To see ZZ. She wants to discuss the finer points of my case."

"I thought she wasn't your lawyer."

"She's not. But she likes to have her say. Friends: Can't live with 'em; can't fire 'em." Lola chuckled. "She wants to discuss what happens if I'm arrested."

I squeezed her hand. "You're not going to be arrested. Chief Pritchett has nothing on you."

"One mustn't rely on what *should* be. Just like in a restaurant, preparation is everything. Seeing the pitfalls before they happen is vital." She pulled free and let rip with a seal's bark of a laugh. Bailey laughed with the same gusto as her mother. "Ooh, that chef of mine. He started this whole thing. If he hadn't left me for Natalie . . . I don't miss him. Not a whit. Yes, he was gifted with fish dishes; however, I found a superb new chef. Did you meet her the other day when we convened in the kitchen? She's a sprite. Not good with fish but fresh out of cooking school and so daring with spices. She'll give that Katie of yours a run for her money." Lola glanced at her watch. "Must hurry off. Tell my daughter to lighten up." She shook a finger. "Don't roll your eyes."

Had I? Of course I had.

"And don't try to tell me otherwise. I know she sent you to do reconnaissance. Don't worry. I'm coping. I didn't binge shop." Lola leaned closer. "Between you and me, I think Bailey could use a cup of coffee. It might take the edge off. Or maybe she could use a little you-know-what."

"What?" I said, then understood. A rush of heat warmed my cheeks.

Lola laughed again, then blew a kiss and dashed from the restaurant.

I made an about-face and started to head out when Keller Carmichael, a rangy young man who supplied ice cream to many of the restaurants around town — ice cream that he actually kept cold on the back of his bicycle by pedaling fast enough to energize a freezer — trudged in with a vat of ice cream balanced on his shoulder.

Blind to my exit, he nearly sideswiped me.

"Whoa," I said. Two near collisions in one day, although Keller wasn't one-tenth the weight of the car that had tried to run me off the road, made my heart skip a beat.

Keller swung around and caught sight of me. One-handed, he whipped off his cap and swooped a thatch of brown hair off his face. "Hey hey, Jenna. Sorry. Making a delivery." Keller rarely used a formal *miss* or *mister* when addressing anyone. His mother, the owner of the Taste of Heaven Ice Cream Parlor, a sit-down dessert shop up the street, acted appalled, but I knew she wasn't. She adored her entrepreneurial-though-quirky son, and why shouldn't she? He was as cute as all get-out with his quick, toothy smile. "How's that chef of yours?" Keller asked.

"Fine," I said, wondering why so many people were mentioning Katie today.

"I hear she's my competition in the chilled food category."

Katie made delicious ice cream.

"Only at the café," I said. "She's not about to pedal around town, like you." I had to admit that I wasn't completely sure about that. Recently I had learned that Katie liked

167

to parasail and Jet Ski. She didn't look the type, but what did I know? I didn't look like I would rappel off steep mountains, and yet I had done exactly that during a wilderness survival trip I'd taken with my brother during high school.

"Katie's missing out," Keller said. "You get to see all sorts of things biking everywhere around town." He grinned. "Say, someone I know . . ." He scratched his head in an odd way, right hand to left ear. "Can't remember who. Anyway, whoever it was said you were investigating the murder of Mrs. Mumford."

And we wondered how rumors got started.

"I'm not." I wagged a finger. "No-o-o." I sure didn't want Cinnamon Pritchett to get wind of the allegation.

"Well, in case you are, I've got a tidbit. No bigger than a chocolate chip, of course, but it's something. See, I was riding past The Pelican Brief a week or so ago. Sunday, I think." Keller hefted the vat of ice cream to his other shoulder. "The Mumfords were here."

"As in *here* here?"

"Yup. The Sykeses, too."

That surprised me. I didn't think Natalie would have deigned to enter her competition's restaurant. She'd seemed appalled to

168

learn that Sam had gone there. Had her outrage been for show? Did it matter any longer?

"It was a brunch day. I remember because, like, the line was down the block." Keller brushed his bangs off his face again. I wondered why he didn't simply trim them. "It was a warm day. I decided to take advantage and sold ice cream to the folks standing in line. Even though I had to pedal double-time to keep the ice cream cool, I was doing amazing business."

"I'll bet you were."

"I was offering caramel macchiato ice cream. One of my best flavors. The caramel is really rich."

I twirled a finger for him to continue.

Keller grinned. "Right. I do that a lot. Get off track. Not on my bike. With my thoughts. That Mrs. Mumford. I couldn't believe she was wearing a coat. Sheesh."

I twirled my finger a second time.

He chuckled. "Message received. Anyway, here's what I saw." Like a spy in training, he stopped talking as a couple of patrons edged around us to exit the diner. When the door closed, he resumed. "Mrs. Mumford . . . the other one."

"There's only one." There *was,* I corrected in my head.

"Right. Ellen's last name is Bryant, same as Willie's, right? I'm such a doofus." He shook his head. "Natalie, the mother, got all hot and bothered with Lola. I thought it was important because, you know, a week ago, they had a fight on The Pier and then . . ." He let the rest of the sentence hang.

"What did they argue about?"

"I don't know. See, I saw it go down in pantomime, like a Charlie Chaplin movie."

The Latina hostess sidled up to us. "I heard something that day." While fixing the collar of her white midriff shirt, she added, "Hope you don't mind, but I've been listening in on you two."

Keller flushed the color of cotton candy.

The hostess duplicated the spy-in-training move then said, "That was the day Lola caught Natalie having a private tête-à-tête with the chef. Lola was steaming. An hour later, the chef resigned."

Had Natalie hung around and fished the torn letter from the garbage can in Lola's office? Why would she have cared about it?

"I remember," the hostess continued, "because yesterday the police came in asking questions. Guess there were other witnesses who talked to them about the set-to already."

I was glad to hear that Cinnamon and her crew were on the job.

"I feel so bad for Mrs. Bird," the hostess went on. "She was simply trying to protect her turf."

"Does Lola know that you spoke to the police?" I said.

"Sure."

I glanced at the exit. Perhaps that was why Lola had been in such a hurry to chat with the mayor. She knew she wasn't in the clear. Not by a long shot.

I left the diner, glum from the bad news, and headed to Crystal Cove Bank. Last night, when I realized I needed cash for my car repair, I decided to ask someone at the bank about the mysterious key in my possession. Although I didn't believe David would have leased a safety deposit box account in town, I didn't want to overlook the possibility. At David's memorial — I hadn't been allowed to have a true funeral without a body — his mother had confided that David had intended to retire with me to Crystal Cove someday. He'd told her how much I loved the area. After that conversation, I had raced to the restroom and sobbed for an hour.

The bank, which was situated near the main intersection of town, wasn't busy. Two tellers, three customers. I headed toward the line but paused when I spied Willie Bryant talking to the Asian teller — Manga Girl, as Bailey had dubbed her — the woman whom Sam Sykes had been chatting up the afternoon Natalie died. Willie had cornered the teller by the entrance to the safety deposit box room. He was stabbing his finger at what I assumed was a savings passbook. The teller, clearly frightened, shook her head. Willie repeated the gesture. Tears filled Manga Girl's eyes. She placed a hand over her mouth and scurried past him. Willie charged after her. Manga Girl raced through a barred door and shut it seconds before Willie caught up to her. Like me, the other customers watched the scenario with wide-eyed interest. Willie booted the door, but the teller didn't open it.

Grumbling beneath his breath, Willie trudged toward the exit. The cartoon character Pig-Pen, who is always accompanied by his cloud of dust — or as my mother called it, his cloud of *gloom* — couldn't have appeared more annoyed.

As Willie neared me, I said, "Is everything okay?"

"What do you care?" He heaved a sigh. As he left the building, letting the glass entry door bang closed behind him, the others in the bank released a collective sigh.

I picked up a withdrawal slip, then got in line to wait. When it became my turn, as luck would have it, Manga Girl, who had returned to her post at the counter, gestured for me to approach. I was fascinated by the tattooed, aqua-green lizards crawling up both of her arms. Matching colors adorned her eyelids. How could Mitzi possibly think her husband was interested in this woman? On the other hand, many men found an exotic young female intriguing.

"Three hundred dollars, please." I pushed the slip toward her along with my ID and ATM card.

"Enter your pin on the pad."

As I punched in my four-digit code, I said, "I'd like to find out if my husband leased a safety deposit box."

"He'll have to come in with you."

"He's —" My chest tightened; my voice snagged. Her request caught me totally off guard. "He can't. He . . . he passed away."

"I am sorry," she said in a cool, impassive tone, either due to the hint of an Asian accent she retained or because all her emotions had been spent on Willie. She pointed across the room. "You will have to take that up with our manager."

"I've called other banks. They were able

to tell me right away."

"The manager is the redhead at the service information desk."

"You can't even tell me whether his name is in the system?"

"No. That is private. Your name would have to be on the account."

"I don't know if it is."

"If you have a certificate of death and your marriage license, you will learn more."

I had both, back at the cottage. They were stowed in a metal box with other valuable documents: a police report, our passports, our social security cards. I hadn't peered at any of them since David's death. The idea of opening the box filled me with dread.

Move on, Jenna.

"It's none of my business," I said as the teller pushed my money beneath the glass divider, "but I was wondering why Mr. Bryant was giving you such a hard time."

Her gaze turned ice cold. "You are right. It is none of your business."

"I'm asking because, when he left, he seemed so upset. Was there a shortage or something? Does he need cash for the memorial to cover the pastor or site fee?"

"Ma'am."

"Privacy. Got it. All I'm saying is that I would be glad to lend his wife Ellen the

174

money if she needs it."

"Next."

CHAPTER 11

I stood at the counter inside Rusty's Repair Shop waiting to pay, while Rusty, a freckle-faced chatterbox, kept talking and talking. About the weather. About the upcoming Frisbee contest, which he intended to enter. About the paddle boarders.

"What's up with that? Standing and rowing like one of them guys in Venice, Italy? *O sole mio,*" Rusty crooned. "No, sir." He typed the command for print on the computer keyboard. The printer started to whirr, then sputtered. "Dang." He fiddled with a jammed piece of paper, tugging hard. The paper ripped. He muttered, then opened and closed the back door of the printer. The machine hummed. Satisfied, Rusty started over. "FYI, your VW is in prime shape. There's no one better in town than me at fixing those beauties." He buffed his raggedy nails on his denim work shirt.

"There's no one *but* you," I teased.

"Yup. I'm a mastermind with machines."

Some machines, I mused. I wouldn't allow him near the printer at The Cookbook Nook.

"With proper care," he went on, "this car will last you a long time. Remember, only use synthetic oil. You don't want any more rattles or pings."

"Got that right. I'm not a ping kind of girl." Saying the word *ping* drew me up short. I flashed on what the waitress at Mum's the Word had said about Willie's alibi on the day of the murder. "You know, from what I hear, Willie Bryant isn't a ping kind of *guy.*"

"Ah, Willie. Sort of obsessed, poor fella."

"One of his coworkers said he comes in here for any little noise."

"Those Hondas. They're pretty good cars."

"He drives a Honda?"

"Metallic dark blue. Sharpest one in town."

My breath caught in my chest. Could Willie have been the driver behind the wheel of the sedan that almost ran me off the road? Yesterday he saw me questioning Rosie when I ate breakfast at the Word. The day before, he caught me chatting with his wife. Did he think I knew something about

Natalie's murder? Something that would implicate him?

"Hondas are reliable for the most part," Rusty went on. "The most common flaw in the 2001 model is transmission failure due to a design flaw. And the 2002? It's got everything from erratic SRS lights to seat belt latches. Rear tires' wear and tear is the main complaint on the 2007 models, caused by a faulty rear arm." He shook his head. "But like I said, Hondas are good overall. Better than a Kia. Don't get me started on those suckers."

Eager to glean more from Rusty, I said, "I heard Willie brought his car in here the day his mother-in-law died. He had some funky sound going on. Did he wait while you repaired it?"

Rusty scratched the stubble on his chin. "Nah. Wasn't that day. He was in the day before. I remember 'cause we got talking about the Giants game. The team is pathetic this year. What's with the pitching staff? It always comes down to pitching. Willie and me? We must've talked for an hour at least. He's got all the statistics in his head. He's a bright one, Willie is."

So he failed economics but he could manage baseball statistics. What did that say about the guy?

"Guess I was misinformed," I said as another notion struck me. Had Rosie the waitress gotten her story wrong about the day, or had Willie told her he was at the repair shop to establish an alibi? Maybe Willie thought Rusty, who was somewhat dim except when it came to fixing cars, wouldn't remember calendar days with such clarity. I wasn't sure how I could find out, but for Lola's sake, I had to.

Rusty hummed then said, "I did see him that day, however."

"You did?"

"Yep. At the collectible shop. You know the one. Die Hard Fan. Right next to the tuxedo store. My daughter's getting hitched, and me and my boy were getting fitted. Pain in the butt, know what I mean?"

"What time was that?"

"Must have been around noon. Willie was having a heated chat with the guy behind the counter. Lots of finger pointing. Pretty sure I heard him say, 'You'll be the first to get paid.' "

My mind raced. I recalled how upset Ellen had been when Willie showed up at The Cookbook Nook later that afternoon. She had mentioned something about him visiting the collectibles store. She'd rummaged in his swimsuit pocket. Had she found an

179

IOU? Had Willie hoped Natalie's demise would help him settle his debts? Had he left the collectibles store and tracked down Natalie in the alley behind my shop?

I paid and took the keys from Rusty.

As I was leaving, Rusty's assistant entered the shop while wiping his hands on an oil-stained rag. Right behind him entered Cinnamon.

"Good morning, Chief Pritchett," I said. "What are you doing here?"

"I've come to question a witness." She eyed me suspiciously. "What are you doing here?"

"Picking up my car." I jangled my keys, thrilled that I had a legitimate reason to be where I was. I didn't want her thinking I was a snoop, and I wasn't, really. Not on purpose, anyway. I glanced at Rusty, worried that he might tell her that I had been asking about Willie, but he was lost in another world, intent on clearing a second jammed paper from the weary printer. Lucky me.

At ten minutes to noon, I closed The Cookbook Nook for two hours, and I attended Natalie Mumford's memorial with Bailey, Katie, and my family.

Aunt Vera, who refused to dress in black,

wore a paisley caftan that was a tad over-the-top. "Dressing in cheery colors," she said when my father mentioned her outland-ish choice, "is good for the soul, and, my sweet brother, these Mumford girls could use some cheering up."

Ellen and her older sister, Norah — who looked strikingly similar to Ellen, right down to her pixie-cut hairstyle and slim form — stood on the top step outside of Mum's the Word Diner. Willie, clutching his daughter in his arms, hovered to the left of the sisters. Sam and Mitzi Sykes stood beside him. The sight of Mitzi caught me off guard. Even in a black mourning suit, she was radiant. More than radiant. The other day she had appeared younger than her age, but now she seemed late thirties at the most. Had her meltdown at the grocery store and worry about losing her husband prompted her to have work done to her face? Botox or Restylane injections, per-haps? I recalled hiring an aging actress for a Smooth and Luscious skin cream campaign, and everyone on the set nearly shrieked when they saw her. Face pulled tight. Lips ramped up to the size of caterpillars. Ugh. A little work, fine. A total makeover, who needs it? Not that Mitzi looked like that. But at her age, with her looks, why did she keep tweaking?

Hordes of guests, including Grill Fest contestants, the mayor, Cinnamon and her mother, as well as many townsfolk that I recognized as regulars at The Cookbook Nook, occupied the chairs that had been set in arced rows facing the diner. Rhett spotted me and waved. I responded with a smile.

Bailey elbowed me. "Psst." She pointed at the standing-room-only portion of the crowd. "What's she doing here?"

I caught sight of Manga Girl and said, "Everyone has come. Natalie was obviously loved or, at the very least, appreciated."

"Or everyone wanted the afternoon off."

"Don't be snarky."

"Mitzi's sending daggers the teller's way." Bailey hitched her chin.

I eyed Mitzi. She certainly was looking angrily at someone. Was her target the teller, or was there another woman she suspected of having an affair with her husband?

A lean, tan man in his forties whom I had dubbed Nature Guy because of his passion for preserving the coastal waters and saving other habitats around Crystal Cove joined Ellen and Norah on the topmost step. As a minister of the Internet-based Collective Life Church, he was allowed to preside over a variety of events. He raised his hands; the assembly hushed.

"There's my mom," Bailey whispered. "I'll be right back." She hurried to Lola and threw her arms around her. For a woman who, up until a few years ago, couldn't spend ten minutes with her mother without carping, as most young women do in their early twenties, Bailey was certainly in full support mode now. Maybe reducing her intake of caffeine was putting her in touch with her feelings. The tableau they formed tugged at my heartstrings.

Standing by myself — a pair of Aunt Vera's tarot-reading clients had given up their seats to my aunt and father — I surveyed the attendants. I had read enough mystery novels to suspect that the killer was present. Was Willie the culprit, as my gut insisted? Had he killed his mother-in-law so he could get his hands on her money? He was toying with the lacy collar of his daughter's dress, clearly disinterested in the event. Conversely, Ellen appeared engrossed with what Nature Guy was saying. She clung to her sister's hand as if it were a lifeline. Norah looked stoic, but I did my best not to judge her; I didn't know her. Sam's skin was a wretched color of gray. Mitzi, who had returned her attention to the proceedings, seemed forlorn. Was she for real? Though her eyes were dewy with moisture, I wasn't convinced she was innocent of murder. Even the most callous person would have had a hard time not tearing up as Nature Guy quoted from one of my favorite songs, "Into Each Life Some Rain Must Fall."

When Nature Guy finished the sermon extolling Natalie's virtues, guests rose and migrated toward two long tables filled with provender from the diner: bite-size sandwiches, cheese and meat platters, and cookies.

I wasn't hungry, but I forged ahead with the others. Near the beverages, somebody jostled me into Sam. I said, "Excuse me."

"Horrible." His tone was flat; his gaze, flatter. "It's just . . . horrible. Iced tea?" He held up a pitcher with his right hand. The action made his watch slide. Its metal band caught the sun's rays, which reflected directly into my eyes.

I squinted and ducked to avoid the gleam, then accepted a glass from him and took a sip. "I'm sorry for your loss."

"The girls will suffer the most. They'll be heartsick without her."

"How long did you know Natalie?"

"Years." The single word conveyed a lifetime of regret. "We met the day she arrived in town. I had handled the previous diner owner's finances. Natalie liked what she saw on the books. I keep concise accounts."

"So I've heard from my chef. You worked for her former boss."

"Mr. Powers. Cagey old coot." Sam smiled weakly. "Natalie and I became fast friends."

"Friends," I echoed, thinking about Mitzi's worry that her husband's text life with Natalie suggested an affair.

"Absolutely. I'm not buddies with many of my clients, mind you. I keep my distance, for the obvious reasons, but Natalie was different. She enjoyed discussing world politics and events. We were of like minds."

I wasn't picking up any impropriety in what he said. I wondered if Sam knew of his wife's suspicions. Had she ever given him the chance to dissuade her?

He frowned. "Now, of course, with Natalie gone, my work is under attack."

"What do you mean?"

"Willie, Mr. Big Picture Guy. He's —" Sam grimaced. "I shouldn't talk out of school."

"You don't like Willie?"

"He doesn't have a head for business. Natalie —" Sam stopped himself; he seemed to be searching for the right thing to say. "She knew he was a slacker, but he was good with her granddaughter, so she tolerated him." His shoulders sagged. "I won't deny Natalie held tight reins on the family, but she knew what was best for all of them."

"Are you saying she was controlling?"

"Don't put words in my mouth."

"I didn't mean to." I took another sip of tea, trying to formulate a question that wouldn't make Sam go running to Chief Pritchett to blab that I was butting in where I didn't belong. I decided simple was best. "Do you trust Willie?"

"He loves Ellen."

Sam didn't really answer my question. Was he purposely being evasive? Did he realize, although it wasn't evident to the typical observer, that Willie and Ellen suffered from marital issues? Maybe Natalie became aware of Willie's abusive nature, as veiled as it was, and decided to put a stop to it. Perhaps Willie killed her, not to get his hands on her cash, but because he was fearful she would alert the authorities to his behavior.

I said, "On the day Natalie died, do you know where Willie was?"

"I heard he was at the repair shop, but I wouldn't know for certain. I was attending that stupid conference in San Jose. If only —" He pressed his lips together and gazed into my eyes. "Wait a sec. You're asking if I think Willie, not Lola, killed Natalie?"

"Lola didn't do it." I wasn't naïve enough to mention that Mitzi had aroused my suspicion, too. Sam was her husband, after all. He would defend her.

"Didn't the police find evidence implicating Lola?" Sam said. "I heard something about a letter from her former chef. His resignation was the reason she and Natalie went at it on The Pier. Supposedly the letter was ripped into tiny pieces and pasted back together. The police found it in Natalie's purse."

"I think the murderer planted it there."

Sam considered my answer. "So what you're asking is whether I think Willie was capable of killing his mother-in-law? I wouldn't put it past him to have done it, but he does have an alibi."

"He wasn't at the repair shop that day."

"Are you sure?"

I explained. "I stumbled onto the information. I'm sure Chief Pritchett knows by now."

Sam folded his hands in front of himself. "I've often wanted to kick Willie out of the Mumfords' lives, but Ellen won't let me."

"Ellen? Not Natalie?"

"Natalie believed time would educate her daughter. Ellen's eyes would open. She

187

would see Willie for what he was. But she hasn't. She won't. Love is blind, no?"

Or bullied, I thought. Then again, maybe I was wrong about Willie. Perhaps he wasn't an abuser if Ellen wanted him to stick around. What was the truth? Lola's innocence could depend upon knowing it.

Sam tapped my arm. "I'd better get back to my wife." He hitched his chin.

I pivoted and saw Mitzi glowering at the two of us.

Sam strode to her and whispered something in her ear. Mitzi's face softened. Well, almost. Her forehead didn't budge. She smiled, as if mesmerized, then looped her hand through the crook of his elbow and leaned into him.

"Jenna." Bailey approached with her mother. "We're going to give our condolences to Ellen and her sister. Want to join us?"

The reception line, which until recently had stood at least fifty people long, was down to ten, my aunt and father among them.

"Sure. Then back to the shop."

We eased along the boardwalk toward Ellen and her sister. The closer we got, the more dissimilarities I found between the women. Norah radiated calm and self-assurance; Ellen looked self-conscious. Norah's eyes were intense, like deep ocean water and almost as unreadable; Ellen's were a soft green and vulnerable. Norah greeted each guest while Ellen held back, her hands tucked beneath her armpits.

When we drew near, Ellen's gaze jerked from Lola to me and back to Lola. "No, no, no," she said and started to sob. "You shouldn't have come."

Lola reached toward Ellen. "I didn't kill your mother."

"Don't touch me." Ellen threw up her hands as if defending herself from an attack.

Lola recoiled. "I'm sorry, Ellen. Truly I am." She shook her head, then said to Bailey and me, "Your mother's and my feud was always meant in good fun. Friendly banter. I promise you. She would have said the same."

Norah cut in. "Mrs. Bird, I'm so sorry for my sister's outburst. She hasn't found her center yet."

Lola said, "I understand. It's hard to lose a parent at any time, but in this ghastly way, I can't imagine. Ellen, darling, my sympathy is with you. You and your family are in my prayers."

Speaking of family, I said, "Ellen, is your

father here?"

"What? No."

Norah threw me a hard look. She reminded me of a teacher I'd had in elementary school who never believed anything I used as an excuse for missing homework. "Our father is as far from California as possible," she said, her tone crisp. "He has a new wife and a new life."

"A new wife?" Ellen gaped.

"I'll tell you all about her later. She's a real Southern belle." Norah gave her sister a nudge. "Go inside the diner. You've spoken to everyone out here. You look beat."

Before Ellen could grasp the doorknob to the diner, Sam, sans his wife, broke through the gathering and hurried to Ellen. "Sweetheart, are these women bothering you?"

Sweetheart? I curbed my suspicion. I was reading more into Sam's words than I ought. He had befriended Natalie. He cared about her daughter. He wrapped an arm around Ellen's shoulder. She leaned against him.

"Psst," Bailey whispered to me. "Get a load of Mitzi." She stood about fifteen feet away, her gaze filled with venom. "She can't possibly think Sam is involved with Ellen, can she?"

Why couldn't she? The thought had flitted

across my mind.

"The age difference is remarkable," Bailey added.

"Ahem." I smirked. "One might say you are the proverbial pot calling a kettle black."

Bailey glowered at me. ' "Youth is easily deceived because it is quick to hope.' Aristotle."

" 'Youth is a wonderful thing. What a crime to waste it on children,' " I countered then added, "George Bernard Shaw. He's much more fun to read than Aristotle." Bailey had read more classics than I — I had a bucket list of books I wanted to read before I departed this life — but I could keep up with her in the quote department. I loved inspirational quotes and posted them on my computer.

"But c'mon," she pressed. "Sam and Ellen? Ick."

I agreed. "I can't see it any more than I can see Sam and Manga Girl."

Norah, the model of composure, walked up and peeled Sam's arm off her sister. "Thanks, Sam. I've got this under control."

Her words took me aback. I reflected on Sam intimating that Natalie had been a bit of a control freak. Was the elder daughter taking over where her mother had left off? Had she killed her mother so she could influence her younger sister and manage the estate?

Stop it, Jenna. Norah just arrived in town. Cut her some slack.

Mitzi took advantage of the moment and barged into the group. She clutched her husband's arm and, mouth moving, steered him clear of onlookers. Whether she was scolding or extolling him, I couldn't be sure.

Norah, with her arm wrapped protectively around Ellen's shoulders, said, "Thank you all for coming. We are so appreciative."

I wasn't sure I believed her, but feeling sufficiently dismissed, I moved on with my friends. As we neared the end of the board-walk, something niggled at me. I turned back. Ellen, who was tickling her daughter's chin, looked engaged again and tons more relaxed. I didn't see Willie anywhere, but he wasn't the object of my search. Norah was.

I spotted her, lit cigarette in hand, standing at the far end of the diner looking as if she were about to disappear around the corner. She was talking animatedly into a cell phone, using her cigarette to make a point. She pulled the cell phone away from her ear, glimpsed the readout, stabbed in three digits, and pressed the cell phone back to her ear.

Call me crazy, but she seemed ticked beyond reason. Why?

CHAPTER 12

When we returned from the memorial to
open The Cookbook Nook for the afternoon, a flock of customers were already
standing in line to enter.

"Are we having a sale I don't know
about?" I said as I fished keys from my
purse.

Bailey grinned. "I think folks are excited
about the Grill Fest. I heard many on The
Pier talking about it."

Of course. The competition would resume
in an hour.

"Lots of people came early to purchase
cookbooks that have good companion recipes for grilled cheese," Aunt Vera said.

"Like chips or French fries," Bailey said
then clicked her fingers. "Jenna, that reminds me, we've got a cookbook with a
name you'll love: *French Fries.* Two words.
That's it."

She was right. That was my kind of title.

Short and to the point. Don't get me wrong. I could memorize litanies, if necessary, but *French Fries* . . . didn't that say it all?

"On the other hand," my aunt said, "customers might have come because they found out that Katie has spent hours putting together new sampling platters."

I grinned. "Whatever works." As a former advertising executive, I understood the power of free *anything*.

I opened the door, and customers shuffled inside. Tigger, who had been sleeping on the chair in the children's corner, leaped to the floor, flicked his tail, and made a beeline for the stockroom. He was a people-liking cat, but a massive incoming crowd could be overwhelming.

As I slid behind the counter and prepared the register for sales, I dialed Katie on the intercom and let her know we had returned. She promised treats in less than five minutes.

True to her word, Katie showed up with a three-tiered platter of cheese panini, each mini-sandwich grilled to perfection. I hurried to her, the flavorful aromas stirring my appetite. One selection, made with a specialty cheese called No Woman, a zesty cheese laced with Jamaican jerk spices, had me craving more.

195

"I've put all of these on the menu," Katie said to customers who joined us in the hallway. "I added some grilled cheese go-with snacks, too, using recipes I pulled from *The Everything Kids' Cookbook.*"

"You must have been reading our minds," I said. Or we had been reading hers. I peeked at Aunt Vera and mouthed: *ESP?* She tittered. I faced Katie. "I've thumbed through *Everything Kids.* All the recipes look delish. I've got to try the nutty caramel corn. But what an extraordinarily long subtitle: *From mac 'n cheese to double chocolate chip cookies — 90 recipes to have some finger-lickin' fun.* Whew!" I recalled a few of my advertising clients, back when I was working at T&S, who would grow supremely frustrated when we pitched extra-long slogans. Like me, they had wanted easy-to-remember, two-word phrases.

"May I address the crowd?" Katie said.

"Sure."

"Hey, everyone." With her sizeable height, her toque in place, and her arms raised overhead, Katie looked huge and fearsome until she smiled, and then any observer knew there was no one sweeter and less terrifying. "Come into the café after the competition, and if any of you are interested, next Saturday we're going to offer a cheese class at the café in honor of the Grill Fest, so sign up now. We have a special guest as the teacher. There will be taste testing involved."

Customers murmured their appreciation.

Before I could return to my post by the register, Katie nabbed me by the elbow. "Uh-uh, not so fast. Our local cheese monger from Say Cheese Shoppe passed on teaching the cheese class. She has a sick grandmother."

"Then why did you offer —"

"Because I want to have the class. I think it's good promo for the shop and café to be known as an educational place. So . . ." She grinned. The Cat in the Hat couldn't have looked sneakier. "It's your job to ask Rhett Jackson if he will teach it."

"What? No way." I flashed on Rhett's and my encounter on the sand after my near miss with the sedan. I'd run away. What a dope. "Ask him yourself."

"But you have the inside track with him. He's hot, hot, hot for you, and you're hot, hot, hot for him."

Was I? *Yes, yes, yes.* Then why did the notion make me feel guiltier than all get-out? Because I hadn't solved the mystery that my husband had left me. I needed to do so before I could move on. I loved a good puzzle, just not in my personal life.

"Fine, I'll do it." I pivoted to return to the shop, but Katie gripped me again and held me back.

"I'm not done."

I scowled at her. "No, I will not ask Rhett on a date."

"Did I ask you to? I have much more crucial needs. I need gossip. What's the scoop from the memorial? Who did you talk to? Who seemed desolate and who didn't? I'm a hound. Feed me." She bayed softly.

I laughed and said, "Help me rearrange the furniture, and I'll tell you." As we moved bookcases and set up chairs, I filled her in on my thoughts.

"Do you really think Mitzi could have killed Natalie?" she asked. "In so short a time?"

"Anyone who was in attendance at the first round of the Grill Fest could have."

"I think whoever killed Natalie knew she had gone out for a quick smoke."

"Exactly." Numerous times, I had pieced together the time line for Wednesday in my head. The competition started. We went on break. Nearly ten minutes passed. The fire alarm sounded. Soon after, a fireman discovered Natalie's body.

"Anyone who wasn't in attendance could have killed her, too," Katie said. "Like that older daughter you mentioned."

"Norah just arrived in town," I said, though I did have doubts about her. She seemed to be fashioned out of galvanized steel.

"And Natalie's son-in-law," Katie said.

I agreed. Willie. Not my favorite person. "Do you remember that science experiment we had to do back in grade school?"

"Your disintegrating onion fiasco?"

I nodded. The teacher had asked us to pick an item and record its growing process for weeks. Dumb me, I had chosen to put an onion on a long toothpick, hover it over water, and observe. An avocado seed could sprout, right? The onion didn't. It decayed layer by layer until all that was left at the center was a rotten yellow core. That was the beginning of the end for me as a budding scientist. Maybe that was one reason why I was so tentative in the kitchen.

"What about the experiment?" Katie said.

"That's what Willie reminds me of."

"Shallow and no substance." She bobbed her head. "You should give your two cents to Chief Pritchett."

"I'm afraid she'll want a dollar." I laughed and said, "Chairs."

After setting out twenty chairs, I dusted off my hands and noticed Katie toying with the ties of her apron.

"What?" I asked.

"Um, was that ice-cream-pedaling guy at the memorial?"

Before leaving for the memorial, I had told Katie about my chat with Keller Carmichael at The Pelican Brief Diner. "I can't remember seeing him. Why?"

"No reason."

I bumped her with a hip. "Out with it. Are you sweet on him?"

"Maybe."

"You should let him know."

"He wouldn't be interested in someone like me. I'm gawky and —"

"You're not gawky."

"I'm awkward anywhere outside of the kitchen."

So is he, I wanted to say, but feared a rebuke from her. If she liked the guy, then, like most women, she would defend her man to her last breath.

Katie glanced at the heirloom pocket watch pinned to her chef's jacket. "Hooboy. Time flies. I've got to move those portable grills into the shop before the contestants arrive. See you." She dashed away.

A half hour later, contestants and more spectators arrived. The judges entered as a trio and stood to one side, chatting among themselves. Rhett nodded in my direction. I mimed that I needed to talk to him later. He acknowledged with a thumbs-up gesture.

The hunky fireman entered after the judges. Like a gentleman, he had opted out of the competition so there would be two eliminations even though the primary round was never completed — Natalie, by her untimely death, being the first elimination. Polite applause welcomed him. He smiled and took a seat in the audience. A handful of women swooned audibly.

Flora strolled in behind him. She was clad in a black beaded sweater over black trousers and looked ready to dominate. So much for declaring herself least likely to succeed. The baby-faced teacher and the lanky librarian followed her. Both appeared eager to win.

Tito, in a loud shirt and jeans, moved to the center cooking station. Yesterday, the *Crystal Cove Crier* had posted an article written by Tito as a tribute to Natalie. His flair for prose filled with humor and wit surprised the heck out of me. Tito flourished a recipe card at the crowd. "This is the one, *amigos*. The recipe to beat."

Mayor Zeller winked and said, "I'll be the judge of that." The spectators laughed. The mayor added, "We're waiting on a couple of other contestants. When they move inside, we'll begin."

I spied Mitzi signing autographs outside the store. For the event, she had changed out of her funereal black and donned yet another red suit, this one with sequined lapels. I didn't have a signature color. I liked to wear hues that reflected my mood. Mitzi pulled a lipstick from her clutch purse and swathed her lips in a color that matched her suit, then checked her image in the window and strutted inside. I surveyed the swelling crowd for her husband, Sam. He stood near the back of the shop talking into his cell phone. Friday was a workday for many, after all.

A minute later, Mitzi moved inside and joined Tito at the center cook station. She placed a bottle of water and a recipe card on the counter and then tucked her clutch into the cubby below. As she rose, she bumped her head on the cook station. She popped to a full stand and, giggling, waved to the audience like a pageant contestant. "I'm fine. Just clumsy. Welcome. I'm so glad you all —"

Lola rushed in appearing frazzled, her silver hair spikier than normal and her breathing staccato. Mitzi offered a nasty glare, but Lola missed the look. She seemed to want to be anywhere but the competition. She caught hold of her daughter by the sales counter. Bailey said something and patted her mother's shoulder, then ushered her to the station next to Mitzi's.

I hurried to them and gave Lola a hug. "Go get 'em."

The mayor strolled in front of the cooking stations while banging the bottom of a saucepan with a wooden spoon. *Gong.* The group hushed. "Welcome, everyone, to round two. I'm sure you all just attended the memorial for Natalie Mumford, and we're sorry she is no longer with us, but as we all know, life marches on. And so shall we." She closed her eyes briefly, as if in prayer, then opened them, faced the contestants, and held out a hand. "Recipe cards, please." Although each contestant had submitted a list of ingredients yesterday in order for our kitchen to have them on hand, Katie had asked to review each recipe today before the competition started, in case a contestant had omitted an item from his or her list and Katie had to scrounge at the last minute.

"This feels wrong," Lola murmured.

Bailey frowned. "Mom, don't weird out. I'm sure you included all your ingredients. You've made a Grilled Cheese Tuna Tornado hundreds of times."

"That's not what I mean."

I said, "No one else is going to die, if that's where you're headed." A deputy was stationed in the alley, another on the café patio.

Lola shook her head. "What I'm trying to say is, should I be doing this?"

Mitzi leaned in and muttered, "Feel free to leave. You won't be missed."

We ignored her.

"Don't be nervous, Lola," I said. "It's merely a contest. My mother often told me, 'Winning will never make you better than anyone else.' "

"No, I mean it." Lola stamped her foot. "Out of respect for Natalie, should I be doing this?"

"No, you shouldn't," Mitzi hissed. "In fact, why are you allowed to compete if you're a suspect in a murder?"

Bailey gasped. So did I. What was that expression: *Toads and diamonds?* I remembered it from an old French fairy tale by Charles Perrault. The good sister helped a fairy, so the fairy blessed her by making diamonds fall from her mouth whenever she spoke. The bad sister rebuked the fairy, so the fairy cursed her with toads. Mitzi may have looked her best, but she wasn't at her finest. Did I smell alcohol on her breath?

"Leave, Lola," Mitzi continued. "Go. Now."

Bailey growled. "Stop it, you . . . you —"

Lola put her hand on Bailey's arm. "Honey, don't."

"Mother, I'm not going to let her goad you."

"Don't worry, darling. Neither am I." Lola threw her shoulders back. "In fact, Mitzi's diatribe is having quite the opposite effect. I'm innocent, and I'm staying right here to prove it." She nudged Bailey. "Join the crowd. You, too, Jenna. And you" — she aimed a finger at Mitzi — "be forewarned. I'm going to win this competition."

The mayor rapped the saucepan again. *Gong.* "All right. I've delivered your recipe cards to the kitchen. Chef Katie will return with the preparations in a few minutes. This is going to be fun."

The noise in the shop swelled. Excitement was in the air. I had to admit that I was itching to know what each contestant was going to prepare. Katie hadn't divulged a word. My mouth was salivating in anticipation.

When Katie delivered the competitors' ingredients on individual trays, the mayor whistled as loudly as a New Yorker hailing a cab. "Okay, people, here we go. Show your appreciation."

The audience applauded.

And then, before anyone could stop her, Mitzi grabbed a fistful of shredded cheese, hurled it at Lola, and shrieked, "I will not lose. Do you hear me? Not to you. Not to Natalie. Not to anybody."

CHAPTER 13

Rhett and the mayor raced forward and corralled Mitzi. Sam bolted from the back of the shop and wedged into the mix. The hunky fireman, like a true hero, leaped from the audience to shield Lola from further harm. Tito, ever ready as a reporter, whipped a recorder from his pocket and started talking into it. No doubt the fracas would make headlines in tomorrow's paper. What would the title be: *A Holey Cheese War? Cheese Catfight? A Cheesy Display of Non-Affection?* Was someone in the audience taping the incident on camera? Would we see another YouTube video before midnight?

I rushed to Bailey and linked my arm through hers. Aunt Vera and Katie joined me. Despite the tension in the air, we worked hard to stifle giggles. I mean, really, Mitzi threw cheese in Lola's face? What could she have been thinking? Luckily, she hadn't hurled the bowl. We talked among ourselves. Would the mayor suspend the competition? Would she eliminate Mitzi on the spot? More importantly, would Mitzi's erratic behavior move her higher on the police suspect list in the murder? Lola could benefit.

As if my thoughts of Cinnamon had conjured her out of thin air — I hadn't seen her in the audience; I'd forgotten she was an ardent grilled cheese fan — she forged to the front of the room while reminding everyone to remain calm. She kept a cool distance from Rhett. They didn't have the warmest relationship. They used to date, but after the fire at The Grotto, when Cinnamon hadn't believed Rhett's account that the previous owner had switched out the valuable artwork, the possibility of friendship was nil.

"Let's give the contestants some breathing room," Cinnamon said. "Emotions are running high."

The audience heeded her advice and took to scanning the shelves for cookbooks and knickknacks.

Cinnamon approached me. "What're you three smirking about?"

"We were commenting on Mitzi's instability," I said.

Cinnamon regarded Mitzi and the other contestants and then lasered me with a glare. "Don't go jumping to conclusions."

"I wasn't. I —" For heaven's sake, was I stammering? I had a right to my opinion, didn't I? At least I hadn't said, "Arrest her," like Cinnamon's mother had said to Lola the other day. I tucked a hair behind my ear and said, "If you'll excuse me, I've got customers to attend to."

A quarter of an hour later, as more people entered the shop to watch what was turning out to be a must-see event, the mayor pronounced Mitzi apologetic and properly cautioned that she would be disqualified if she engaged in any further antics. The mayor then situated Mitzi and Lola at opposite ends of the cooking stations, and the competition resumed.

An hour later, to the surprise of all, Tito Martinez won the votes of the judges with his barbecued chicken grilled cheese. When asked about his recipe, Tito claimed he had been motivated by a recipe in Grady Spear's *The Texas Cowboy Kitchen: Recipes from the Chisholm Club*. Tito admitted that Grandma Spear's Dr Pepper cake recipe, which inspired his addition of Dr Pepper to his barbecue sauce, was to die for. The instant the words *to die for* exited his mouth, he blanched. He must have realized the inappropriateness of the praise, given the circumstances. Mitzi came in second in this round. Lola and Flora rounded out the roster. The librarian and the teacher, though close in points, were cut.

After the competition concluded, the remainder of the afternoon flew by. We sold out of every barbecue cooking book and nearly all of the grilled cheese books. The spatulas with hand-painted handles that we had acquired from a local artist were a hit, too. When we closed the shop, Aunt Vera headed off to a meeting of her tarot-reading buddies, and Bailey, Katie, and I headed to B-B-Q, a lively new restaurant that featured country-western music and specialized in smoked ribs. Katie was nervous leaving, because she had taken on a new assistant chef and was giving him the run of the kitchen.

"Are you comfortable with the hire?" I said.

"All chefs are control freaks," Katie said with a wink. "What do you think?"

We crossed our fingers, knowing she couldn't continue to do every shift at the Nook Café.

Around 7:00 P.M., we entered the rowdy restaurant. We weren't surprised to find it

210

packed to the gills. Music blared from speakers. Dozens of people were line dancing on the sawdust-strewn dance floor. All the tables and stools in the bar, which extended the length of the narrow establishment, were filled. A waitress in cowgirl attire ushered us to a table at the far end of the restaurant. While we waited for our beverages and barbecued potato skin appetizers, the latest version of "Footloose," one of the all-time great line dances, began to play.

Bailey was never one to pass up dancing. "Party hearty," she said and prodded us to the floor.

As we joined the group and mirrored their steps — walk, walk, walk, *clap* — Katie said, "By the way, what was up with Mitzi steaming out of the parking lot? So what if she had a setback today? She's not out of the competition. There are two more rounds."

I said, "I think she was upset because Sam left right after the fracas. He didn't stay until the end. He didn't stand by his woman."

"Maybe he had appointments," Katie offered.

We all did a kick-ball-change and walked forward. *Clap.*

"If you ask me," Bailey said, "Mitzi might

be too in love with him, if that's possible. Jealous with a capital *J.* She doesn't trust him."

"Why do you think that is?" I asked as we executed a grapevine step, weaving one foot behind and the other foot in front. *Clap.* "He seems to be in love with her."

"Are you sure?" Bailey said. "I was watching this Dr. What's-his-name the other day on TV." She flicked her hand, unable to come up with the surname. People to the right of her copied the move and whooped, obviously thinking she was making up a new step. "He was talking about how you can tell if a guy is into you. He touches you in little ways. Your elbow. Your shoulder. If there's no physical contact, there's nothing. Oh, and the smile. If the guy is looking at you and his smile is turned up, that matters. If there's no smile in his eyes, get rid of him." Bailey brushed her shoulders as if ridding herself of dandruff. Neighboring dancers mimicked her move again. When she realized what they were doing, she winked at us and said, "Watch this." She did a scissor step.

The others copied her and sang, "Whoop, whoop."

"I think Sam looks at Mitzi with a smile," I said as we walked forward. *Clap.*

Bailey said, "He looks at everyone with a smile. He's got crinkly eyes." She demonstrated. "What if he's snowing her? What if he married Mitzi for her money?"

"How much money are we talking about?" I asked.

"Didn't you know?" Katie said. "Mitzi comes from San Francisco high society. Have you heard of Pacific Heights?"

Indeed, I had. It was a stretch of real estate populated by billionaires and located in one of the most scenic settings in all of San Francisco. From Alta Plaza, there were breathtaking, panoramic views of the Golden Gate Bridge, the Presidio, Alcatraz, and the bay. Before I met David, I had dated the son of a resident of Pacific Heights. The guy had proven to be a royal jerk. Money doesn't always foster class.

"When Mitzi's parents passed away," Katie continued, "she inherited everything."

"I knew she was wealthy," I said, "but I thought her money had come from her personal chef and canning businesses."

Katie chortled. "Don't be naïve. Those kinds of businesses can make a person a decent living, but they can't generate a fortune. Not unless the chef were to become, say, the next Wolfgang Puck."

"I repeat," Bailey said. "Did Sam marry

213

Mitzi for her money?"

Katie snuffled. "Mitzi isn't stupid. She would know if he did."

"Are you sure?" I said. "Love is a funny thing. In fact, Sam even told me at the memorial that love is blind. He was referring to Ellen and her husband, but still . . ."

"Everyone needs to enter a relationship with eyes wide open," Katie said. "We all have flaws."

Bailey laughed. "Some of us more than others. For instance, *me.*"

Playfully I whacked her wrist. "Don't even go there."

"I'm a mess when it comes to choosing the right guy, and you know it." Bailey did another kick-ball-change and led the pack in a corner turn. *Clap.*

"You're no worse than Mitzi," Katie said. "Did you know she was nearly married to another man, pre-Sam? She was twenty or twenty-one. Her father stepped in and proved the man was a bigamist. He had a wife in Wyoming."

"Wow. No wonder Mitzi worries about Sam playing around," I said. Walk, walk, walk, *clap.* "I think she's masking her anxiety with a nip or two of something. Did you see her bump her head before the competition? And what about that incident at the grocery store?"

Bailey said, "Do you think she's carrying a flask in her purse?"

Katie clucked her tongue. "Old man Powers had a lady friend that would stop by. She was so in love with him, but he didn't feel the same. She started turning up snockered. I think she was nervous, hoping she could reveal her feelings. I never figured out how she was getting so stewed until, one time, I offered to toss out a water bottle she had brought with her, and the woman turned into a tigress. We struggled over that bottle until realization hit me."

Kick-ball-change, kick-ball-change. Walk, walk, walk.

"That's it," I said, in unison with the clap. I was having a *duh* moment, as my brother would have called it. "What do you bet Mitzi's water bottle is laced with something stiffer than water?"

"Maybe Sam knows," Bailey said. "Maybe he threatened to leave her if she didn't pull herself together, and after that display today, he gave her an ultimatum."

Katie bobbed her head. Her curls bounced. "What if he was stupid enough to say he'd leave her for Natalie?"

"Yes." Bailey spanked her hip.

The group of dancers beside her did the

215

same. "Whoop, whoop."

"That could have made Mitzi mad enough to lash out," Bailey said.

I nodded. "Mitzi knew Natalie would go outside for a cigarette. She told me so. What if she pulled the fire alarm? What if she was the one who planted the resignation letter in Natalie's purse to divert suspicion from herself?"

"How would she have gotten hold of it?" Bailey said.

I told them what Keller had said about the Sykeses and Mumfords going to brunch at The Pelican Brief Diner. "They heard your mother fighting with the chef."

Katie said, "But why would Mitzi kill Natalie in such a public place? With a panini grill? Why not poison Natalie or juice up the car and mow her down? If Mitzi was drunk or even tipsy, she could have claimed it was an accident."

I gaped at her. "Mitzi drives a Mercedes."

"What's that got to do with anything?" Bailey said.

"She's impulsive, agreed?" I said as we executed a scissor step and a spin. Walk, walk, walk, *clap.* "What if she was the person who tried to run me off the road?"

"Why would she have done that?" Katie said.

216

"Because I was the one who found out Pepper saw Mitzi near the murder scene. Maybe Mitzi blames me for having Cinnamon follow up on that lead."

"Except whoever drove at you did it at seven A.M.," Katie said.

"Maybe that nightly ritual Mitzi boasts about includes a couple of extra strong snorts," Bailey said, "and she woke up in a stupor. She took a drive, saw you, had a tizzy fit, and *bam!*"

When the music ended and the group thinned out, I spied Manga Girl and a handsome Asian man close to her age among those leaving the dance floor. Holding her hand, he guided her to an intimate table. The twosome proceeded to kiss like a couple in a seriously romantic film.

I pointed her out to my pals. "Mitzi seems to be mistaken about the bank teller having a thing for Sam."

"She's mistaken about a lot of stuff," Katie said.

"We're reaching for answers," I concluded. "We have nothing on Mitzi. Not yet. Thankfully, Cinnamon Pritchett is on the case."

"Is she?" Katie asked.

"Yes," I said, defending Cinnamon. We weren't full-fledged friends, but I did believe that she, like my father said, wouldn't rest until justice was served.

"Well, then" — Bailey returned to the table, picked up her wine, and clinked her glass to mine — "let's shelve any discussion about murder and focus on you."

"Uh-uh," I settled onto my chair. "Not now. Not after I got all sweaty on the dance floor."

"I'm talking about your personal problem, goofy," Bailey said. "The safety deposit box key. Have you discovered what it goes to?"

Oh, *that*. "Not yet."

"You've contacted all the banks in San Francisco?"

"Yes. I even went to our local bank. Manga Girl was less than cordial."

"What about the Chinese lettering on the porcelain cat?" Katie said. "Did you decipher it?"

"Nope."

As we dug into the potato skins, which were loaded with barbecue sauce, grilled onions, and queso fresco — *muy delicioso* — we bandied about other phrases David might have written: *I love you; I worship you.* After a while, the phrases became sillier: *I dig you, babe,* or *Rub my bottom for luck.* Giggles are always good for the soul.

We joined a few more line dances and

around 11:00 P.M. bade one another good night.

At midnight, unable to set aside my friends' questions, I sat in bed with the pieced-together Lucky Cat in my hands. Tigger lay on top of the comforter, snuggled into my hip. Together we stared at the Chinese writing. What did the words say? What if I, like Mitzi, had deceived myself when it came to my husband? What if the words said: *We're through. It's over.* Tears pressed at the corners of my eyes. I squeezed my eyes shut and didn't let the tears fall. I would not let frustration get the better of me. No way, no how.

Saturdays were always busy on The Pier. Singles, couples, families, and packs of teens flocked to the site. Throw in special events like paddle boarding and the upcoming Frisbee contest, all of which had established temporary headquarters on the beach south of The Pier, and the place was hopping with activity.

Because Bailey was scheduled to open the shop, I had an extra hour on my hands, so I went to Bait and Switch Fishing and Sport Supply Store to propose the cheese education class to Rhett. Except he wasn't at the store. His assistant reminded me that he

219

had taken vacation days so he could judge the grilled cheese competition. I felt about as sharp as a bowl of Jell-O until the assistant informed me that Rhett was nearby.

I found him halfway along The Pier, sitting on a bench not far from Mum's the Word and whittling a tree limb. His black Lab lay by his feet. Rhett spotted me coming and set his hobby aside.

"Hey," he said. "Have you stopped laughing after yesterday's brouhaha between Mitzi and Lola?"

I grinned. "Never a dull moment at The Cookbook Nook. What are you working on?"

"A cane for a neighbor. The guy has a hitch in his step of late, but he's too stubborn to move into the flats." Rhett lived in a cabin in the hills.

"Nice. What's the knob going to be?"

"A duck's head. The guy is big on ducks. Want to take a stab at whittling?" He offered me a foot-long stick and a second Swiss Army knife.

I liked to sculpt; I had never tried my hand at whittling. I accepted his gifts and, without a clue as to what I would whittle, started paring away at the wood. Within seconds, I had crafted something akin to a number two lead pencil. Not very unique.

Rhett grinned. "It takes time to get the hang of it."

"I can see that."

"Why are you here?"

I told him.

"That Katie," he said. "She's determined to get me back into food services."

"Will you do it?"

"Sure. I love cheese. There's so much to learn. I own a collection of cheese reference books you should consider having on hand at the shop. *The Cheese Chronicles* by Liz Thorpe, one of the most knowledgeable women in the world on the subject. She loves American cheeses. Also, *The Cheese Primer* by Steven Jenkins, a cheese impresario in his own right. He adores French cheeses."

I made a mental note. "What did you think of the competitors' sandwiches yesterday?" My whittling project started taking shape. It was going to be a honey spoon. I would have to sand it to perfection.

"There were some good recipes. Tito's wasn't bad, but I liked Bucky's sandwich better."

"Bucky's?" I raised an eyebrow. Bucky was the hunky fireman who had sweetly withdrawn from the competition. "He didn't compete."

"Just seeing if you were paying attention."
Rhett chuckled. "By the way, the scuttlebutt
is Bucky is dating a friend of yours."

"Bailey?" I said, excited that she might
have met someone she actually liked in
town. She could be so picky.

"Got me. I'm in the dark."

"He's your friend. You must know. Tell
me."

He shook his head.

"Not fair," I said.

"Love is never —"

"Sam!" a man bellowed.

Willie stormed down the stairs of Mum's
the Word Diner, carrying the stroller holding his daughter. He set the stroller on the
boardwalk. The daughter joggled in her seat
and almost lost her grip on a huge lollipop.
Willie yelled again, "Sam!" He jogged while
pushing the stroller toward Sam, who was
tramping toward the parking lot. "Stop,
now."

Sam pivoted. "Leave it alone, Willie."

Willie jammed the brake on the stroller
and took a swipe at Sam, who grabbed
Willie's forearm, spun him around, and
pinned him up against the wall of the
nearby candy store.

"Maybe I should intervene." Rhett folded
his Swiss Army knife and pushed it into his

jeans pocket.

Before Rhett could rise to his feet, Sam cupped his hand and said something into Willie's ear. Willie stiffened. He glanced at his daughter and back at Sam. He gave a slight nod of his head. Sam released him, and Willie hurried to his daughter and wheeled the stroller in the opposite direction.

"Do you think the crisis is truly averted?" I said.

Rhett nodded. "Looks like it."

"I'm not so optimistic." I scrambled to my feet and raced after Willie.

Rhett groaned and leaped to his feet, probably wondering how he could rein me in like his Labrador. "Willie, hold up," Rhett yelled. At least he was pretending to be supportive.

Willie slowed. He wheeled around. Rhett's dog bounded to Willie and planted his paws on Willie's chest, nearly knocking him over. The guy scrambled for balance. He pushed the dog off, then bent down and rubbed the dog's ears. The interchange surprised me. A dog lover couldn't be all bad, right? Perhaps I had misjudged Willie.

"Is everything okay?" Rhett said.

"Between you and Sam," I added. "He's

got to be tense after Mitzi's outburst yesterday."

"What outburst?" Willie said.

I had forgotten that neither Willie nor anyone else from the Word had attended the competition. "Mitzi —" I hesitated. Tongues would be wagging inside the Word soon enough. No sense fanning the fire. "What just happened between you and Sam?"

Willie peered beyond me at the retreating object of his anger, and something curious crossed his face. He refocused on me, slumped slightly, and jammed his hands into his pockets. "Sam." He sighed. "Man, he's always trying to tell me how to raise my child, like he has any say in the matter. Kids eat sugar." He nodded at his daughter, who was merrily licking the lollipop. Her eyes were wide, her cheeks flushed. "Kids survive. But Sam claims he knows what kind of parenting style Natalie wanted for her precious granddaughter. So what if they were friends, huh? He has no right to tell me. He's not family. Bah!" He waved a hand. "Sam's not worth the breath." Willie bent and tickled his daughter's nose. She giggled. He bid us good-bye.

As Willie retreated, I questioned his performance. It had been a performance. I was certain. What did he want us to take away from it? He had alluded to Sam and Natalie's relationship. I reflected on Mitzi and her fear that Sam had had an affair with Natalie. Was Willie inferring that it was true? Had Natalie, who had confided in her trusted advisor Sam, fallen in love with him and he with her? According to Willie, Natalie had told Sam her concerns about Willie as a father and provider. Had she mentioned anything about Willie's abusive nature? Maybe that was what the two men had been arguing about.

"Earth to Jenna," Rhett said.

I told him my theory. "What do you think? Should I tell Cinnamon my suspicions?"

"You know how I feel about her."

"I have to inform her."

Rhett gripped my shoulder and offered an encouraging smile. "Do whatever makes you comfortable."

If I told Cinnamon that I thought Willie or Mitzi were better suspects than Lola in Natalie's death, would she listen? As an ad exec, I had often needed to plot out a campaign to ensure its success. Now, as a business owner, I was planning months ahead, thinking about the next great cookbook to stock or the next decorations to display. How could I get Cinnamon to take me seriously? Perhaps I should invite her to dinner at my place and "fatten her up," as the saying went. Did she have a boyfriend or fiancé that I should include? She had drawn the Lovers card when my aunt had offered her a one-card tarot reading. How little I knew about her. She had a persnickety mom and no dad. She'd led a wild childhood, she could sing like an angel, and she rocked as a roller skater. I knew she was a foodie and adored grilled cheese sandwiches. Could she cook? Did she prefer meat, or was she a vegan? Did it matter? I continued to concoct our imaginary meal. During the conversation, *Bam!,* à la Emeril, I would unveil my theories. Sated, Cinnamon would be so thrilled to hear my side, she would agree to back off Lola. But the more I replayed the scenario in my head, the more I was convinced the plan would backfire in my face.

Me? Cook an entire meal? That was edible? Fat chance.

At the very least, I had to consider enlisting Katie's help to carry out my scheme.

CHAPTER 14

Needless to say, I chickened out. I didn't go to the precinct. I went straight to The Cookbook Nook. Sure, I could be courageous on occasion, but after envisioning the scenario ten more times in my head, I couldn't see the value of approaching Cinnamon and possibly alienating her. So what if I had theories? Big deal. Every Tom, Dick, and Harriet had theories. I couldn't run headlong to the police with nothing but assumptions. My father was quick to say that we all knew what happened when one assumed . . .

No, in order to exonerate Lola and appease her worried daughter, I needed more facts that could be substantiated, in the same way that I needed more specifics if I intended to learn about David's safe deposit box key and the gold coins I'd found hidden within my Lucky Cat.

Performing routine tasks had always been

a way for me to clear my mind. When I was five years old, my clever mother convinced me that dusting was the best way to unclutter a muddled mental state. By the age of seven, I was onto her. I realized she was getting me to do her dirty work, literally, but over the years, rearranging bookshelves had become one of my favorite pastimes. Often I would sort books by color; other times, by title or by author. During high school, I had even volunteered at the library so I could feed my obsession. Straight-A papers were the result of busy hands. B's and C's occurred whenever I sat idle.

"Can you believe that Halloween and Christmas are right around the corner?" I set aside the empty plate, once mounded with scrumptious tuna salad that Katie had made me, and I shuffled from shelf to shelf, realigning our few remaining grilled cheese cookbooks while Aunt Vera and Bailey organized the gift items. "It's hotter than a pistol outside, and we need to come up with decorations for cool temperatures."

"Don't rush holidays," Aunt Vera said. "If there's one thing I've always claimed, it's that each month should stand on its own. We don't dream up new decorative themes until the old ones are taken down and stowed."

I agreed. I recalled an ad campaign I'd headed up in my first year at Taylor & Squibb for a Santa turkey. Talk about confusing. The actress in the commercial kept cracking up whenever she had to utter, "Gobble, gobble, ho, ho, ho!" Though we had hired her for her sense of humor, we had no idea she wouldn't be able to keep a straight face.

The door to the shop opened, and a warm breeze swept in along with a handsome couple who headed straight for the grilled-cheese-cookbook display. Ellen Bryant trailed them. She made eye contact with me and smiled weakly. After her upset with Lola at the memorial, I had expected her to spend the weekend resting in bed. Why had she come to the shop on a Saturday? And why was she dressed in a bulky sweater on such a balmy day? I flashed on what Keller the ice cream guy had said about Ellen wearing a coat on the day her family went to brunch at The Pelican Brief Diner. That was why he had remembered seeing her there. Had she purposely worn the coat so she could slip into Lola's office, filch the resignation letter, and hide it beneath her bulky coat?

Don't be silly, Jenna. Natalie snagged the

letter and stuffed it in her purse. Mystery solved.

So why had Ellen come to the shop? Maybe she wanted to tell someone — me — that she suspected her husband of murder.

Keen to get her to confide in me, I joined her by the stack of new foodie puzzles. Five hundred pieces, brilliant colors. My favorite was the vivid one of a slice of chocolate cake. Our culinary mystery readers were puzzle fanatics, too. "Ellen, what a nice surprise to see you here again."

Ellen cinched the belt of her thigh-length sweater and adjusted the strap of her tote bag. "Nice to see you, too."

"I set aside the books you put together the other day. They're in the stockroom."

"No, thanks."

"Do you have time to look at a few new books that came in?" I steered her toward the center of the shop. "I couldn't help but notice the darling aprons your waitresses wear at the Word." At the Grill Fest the other day, one of the customers told me that aprons were in vogue. The cuter the better. Not only that, but women wanted to know the history of an apron, and they were collecting them, too. "Did you know there are lots of people into designing aprons?" I held up *The Apron Book: Making, Wearing, and Sharing a Bit of Cloth and Comfort,* with its colorful cover of vintage apples-and-pears cloth. "Sort of like handmade quilts, I guess. And get this." I held up another book with the title *Apronisms: Pocket Wisdom for Every Day.* "I know I can always use a thoughtful hint or two about how to live my life, can't you?"

"Actually, I don't have time to chat." Ellen checked her watch. As she did, I noticed her raw fingernails again. She caught me ogling her and snapped her hand down to her side. "I've got to go."

"Stay for a minute." I tapped her arm ever so slightly. Call me crazy, but I had caught a rerun of *The Mentalist* on TV and had been fascinated by the way the lead character, a former carny magician, persuaded individuals to trust him by touching them on the shoulder. Ellen drew in a deep breath; her face relaxed. Presto chango. I felt nearly as powerful as my Aunt Vera. "I'm concerned about you."

"Don't be."

"You look pale. You always seem to be chilly."

"Oh, that." She rolled her eyes. "That's because I have Hashimoto's disease."

"What's that?"

"Cold intolerance. Hypothyroidism. It's a result of being anemic."

I could've kicked myself, not for being ignorant about the condition — I wasn't; a friend at the advertising agency had the same condition: brittle nails, joint pain — but for assuming, because of Ellen's propensity for wearing warm clothing, that she could be a thief, or worse, a murderer. What had I been thinking? She was a sweet, sensitive woman who didn't deserve my suspicion.

"There aren't really any medications I can take yet," Ellen went on, unaware of the argument I was having with my inner self. "My disease is not that advanced." She paused. "What's wrong?"

"Nothing."

She regarded me without guile. I needed to be honest with her.

"It's silly really. For some weird reason I was thinking about the letter the police found in your mother's purse."

"I'm not following."

How could she? Hercule Poirot would have had a difficult time following my circuitous train of thought, but I pressed on. "I wondered if the killer planted it there. To frame Lola."

"I gave my mother that letter."

My mouth dropped open. "You stole it?"

Ellen blanched. "It was in the trash."

"In Lola's office."

"I . . . I went in to ask her a question. About her biscuit recipe. She wasn't there. I saw the letter. Trash is public property, isn't it? I thought . . ." She faltered. "I thought my mother might have wanted the letter to, you know, rub in Lola's face. Mother could be vindictive that way."

"You gave it to her to gain her approval."

"Sort of. Yes. We had a complicated relationship, but she meant well."

Whack to the head. Ellen was nice. I said, "I'm sure she did."

"The reason I came in today . . ." Ellen checked her watch again, then hurriedly rummaged through her tote bag. She pulled out a crimson book with indecipherable gold lettering and offered it to me. "I heard you needed to interpret some Chinese phrases. This might do the trick."

Double whack to the head. Ellen wasn't just nice; she was really nice.

"Who told you that?" I said.

"Your aunt was in the Word with her tarot friends yesterday. She said you were looking into something that related to your past, and then she told me my fortune. 'Be wary yet be willing,' she said. 'The future is bright with new adventures.' " Ellen beamed as if she had found deep meaning in those words.

I glanced at Aunt Vera, who was playing with Tigger. As if sensing my gaze, she swiveled and winked at me. The sly dog. Had she been doing some sleuthing on her own?

"I've been studying Chinese at the junior college," Ellen continued. "I have a number of employees who are native Chinese. Talking their language, even with my stilted accent, seems to put them at ease. Have you noticed that Crystal Cove has become the ideal destination for people trying to get a fresh start?" Another glance at her watch. "Maybe you can find what you're after in that book. It's pretty basic."

I thumbed through the pages. Inside were images of Chinese characters, each with an English interpretation and instructions about how to draw them using radical strokes. None, via a cursory glance, jumped out as the words written on the bottom of the Lucky Cat. "Thank you. I truly appreciate it."

Ellen started for the exit. At the same time, the door opened and Pepper Pritchett entered. Though she wore pink, a color that was good with her skin tone, she looked disgruntled and sour. Her mouth drew into a thin line of disapproval. Uh-oh. What was wrong now? How I wished she could be happy. What would it take? I knew her beading business had increased since the Grill Fest began.

Pepper marched to Ellen and blocked her departure. "Well, well, well. Mrs. Bryant. I would expect nothing less. No sooner than the memorial is over and you're gallivanting about buying cookbooks."

"I wasn't," Ellen said, standing a tad taller.

"You have shown no respect for your mother, young lady. The Word should be closed at least for a day or two."

My aunt, who was not given to scrambling, *scrambled* to her feet and stomped toward Pepper. "Mind your tongue, Pepper. You have no right to antagonize the girl."

Taking my lead from my aunt, I said, "Yeah. No right." Honest to Pete, Pepper still scared me. Though she was inches shorter, she had a scowl that would frighten hyenas. And the way she knitted her brow? There was definitely rhino DNA mixed in with hers. Her daughter Cinnamon was lucky to have missed that part of the gene pool, although, truth be told, she could have her moments of being prickly — like, for instance, with Rhett.

Ellen said, "Vera and Jenna, thank you, but I can handle this." She rolled her narrow shoulders back and showed pluck that I thought she lacked. "For your information, Mrs. Pritchett, my mother would commend me for my actions. Mum's the Word meant everything to her. If she'd had her way, she would have opened the Word twenty-four hours a day, every day of the week. She wanted her regulars fed and satisfied. Furthermore, despite wagging tongues and low funds, I intend to carry on my mother's tradition." Tears pooled in Ellen's eyes. "I have nothing more to say to you, except that you are welcome at the restaurant if you ever care to drop in. Good day." Ellen faced me. "Jenna, I've changed my mind. Please put one of the apron books on hold for me along with the other two books you set aside. I'll be back." Head held high, she strode from the store.

Pepper planted her hands on her hips. "Don't let her snow you."

"What do you mean?" I asked.

"I happen to know a thing about Natalie Mumford's last will and testament."

"How is that possible?" Aunt Vera said. "You and Natalie weren't close. In fact, I have heard you make scathing remarks about the food at Mum's the Word."

"Lest you forget, I am the mother of the chief of police."

"Cinnamon wouldn't have revealed any-thing to you," I said, then eyed my aunt. "I'll bet the will is public now. That's how Pepper knows something." A will starts as a private document, but once the testator dies, the executor — I had been David's — petitions to open probate. Once in probate, the document becomes public.

"What does the will say?" Aunt Vera stared down Pepper, who took a reluctant step backward.

"Both of Natalie's girls inherit equally."

"Big whoop," I said. "I had already as-sumed that."

Pepper folded her arms over her chest. "I wouldn't be surprised if the two of them plotted to do her in."

"What?" I nearly shrieked.

"I've mentioned my theory to Cinnamon. She's keeping an eye on them. In fact, she's keeping an eye on each of the Mumford clan. And that, missy" — she pointed at me — "I know for a fact."

Missy? I seethed. "I would bet that your daughter wouldn't want you sharing this information with us."

"Bother." Pepper stabbed the air. "The word will get around town one way or another. The gossip mill is churning."

After she left, I smiled. Though Cinnamon

wouldn't have wanted her mother talking so freely, I was glad Pepper had. If Cinnamon was looking at the Mumford clan as suspects, then Lola was home free. Almost.

CHAPTER 15

At 6:00 P.M., I scurried around The Cookbook Nook clapping my hands. "Let's go. Chop-chop. Time to close for Movie Night on the Strand."

Bailey set a stack of teen cookbooks on the checkout counter. My favorite, *Teens Cook Dessert,* was among them. The sisters who had written the book clearly stated, in teenage language, how to make teen-friendly desserts. They had included fabulously tasty photos, and who could resist their cute chapter titles? "Fancy Stuff," "Other Fun Stuff," and "Custards, Puddings, and Stuff."

"C'mon, Aunt Vera." I snapped my fingers for emphasis. "Time's a-wasting." My aunt was rehanging kitchen gadgetry so items would face outward. "Those will wait until morning. Let's go."

"Don't be bossy, missy," Aunt Vera said.

"Don't *missy* me," I teased. "Only Pepper gets to call me that."

My aunt chuckled. "That's my girl." She disappeared through the curtain to the stockroom.

I put the Chinese-character book that Ellen had brought me into my tote and scooped up Tigger. "C'mon, Bailey. We're going to be late."

"I'm not going," she said, still fussing with the teen section.

"No need to snap."

"I didn't snap."

Yes, she had. Earlier she had almost bitten my head off because I hadn't had enough sugar-free substitute for her *yucky* — her word — cup of decaf coffee.

"You're going," I said firmly. "Aunt Vera expects each of us to assist at the community outreach fund-raiser." We were selling hot dogs and cupcakes. The money raised would help one of the less fortunate communities on the north edge of town to build a new playground. "Katie made the most fabulous almond-flavored cupcakes with vanilla buttercream using a recipe she plucked from one of those culinary mysteries. They're called Blonde Bombshells. Don't you love it? Anyone who helps out gets to sample the wares for free."

"Gee, guess I'll miss out, then."

"You love cupcakes, and I know how you

240

feel about almonds." She could down a family-size bag full of nuts in one sitting. My teeth would ache for days with all that crunching.

"I already made my apology to your aunt."

I frowned. "What's going on?"

"Nothing." Bailey blew air at me. "Don't look at me like that."

"Like what?"

She mimicked my squinty eyebrow expression. "I'm fine. Promise."

I touched her forearm. "Is it the caffeine thing? Are you okay?"

"Look, no shaking." She held out her hands. "Steady as a seismograph."

"Then where are you off to? Got a hot date?"

"Maybe."

"With Bucky?"

"Who?" She tilted her head. Her mouth quirked up.

"Don't play coy. The hunky fireman."

"Not telling." Bailey chuckled. "You go ahead to movie night. I know you wouldn't miss this event for the world."

One thing I remembered fondly from my childhood days was movie night on the beach. Our whole family would go. The town owned a huge, drive-in-size screen. Only G-rated movies were shown, many age-old, but no one seemed to mind. Sometimes, if the screening was of a well-known musical like *The Sound of Music* or *Singin' in the Rain,* the audience would sing along with the characters. Everyone came with blankets and picnics. Vendors sold soft drinks, juice, and snacks. The night was simply fun.

"You're missing out," I said.

Bailey chuckled. "I'll suffer alone."

"Alone?" I quipped.

"Yes." She sighed. "Alone. I'm not going on a date. I'm taking a Spanish class at the junior college."

"But you speak Spanish."

"Two years in high school. Kerflooey. Not enough. I want to be fluent."

"Why?"

"Because. Of a guy. A very cute guy. Who doesn't speak English."

"Not the fireman?"

"Nope."

"Where did you meet this guy? Why is this the first I'm hearing about him?"

"That's all I'm saying. *Basta. No más.*" Bailey jammed a finger at my nose, then scuttled away. Darned if she couldn't be close-lipped, especially when I was hungry for gossip.

"I'll learn the truth," I said as she retreated

into the stockroom. "I always get the skinny."

Tigger purred. I scratched his ears. "Sorry, buddy, but you're heading home. Kitties can get trampled on the beach." He mewled his sorrow. "I know, I know. It's so unfair when you're not in charge."

By the time my family and I arrived at the beach, the area was packed. Banners on poles flapped in the breeze. A few people hurled, hucked, and bladed Frisbees, while others tossed around softballs. Visitors lugging coolers searched within the football-field-sized area to find a spot to nest. Huge klieg lights surrounded the perimeter. At the far end of the strand, a Road Runner cartoon played on the twenty-by-twenty-foot screen. *The Love Bug,* featuring Herbie the super car, was going to be the main attraction.

Aunt Vera and my father, who had lured Lola to help — I had the feeling my father didn't want to be apart from Lola in her time of need — stood by a long table already set up with oversize steamers filled with hot dogs. Beside the steamers were baskets of hot dog buns, accoutrements like ketchup and mustard, and rows of scrumptious looking cupcakes. The line of customers waiting to purchase food extended the length of the picnic area.

I took up my post near Lola, who offered her thanks for all the support I had given her. Though I wished I could tell her that the police were looking at the Mumford girls more closely, I didn't want to raise her hopes until I could confirm it was true from Chief Pritchett.

"Where's my daughter?" Lola asked.

"She's never been a movie buff. You know that." One of Bailey's favorite sayings after seeing a movie was: "If you liked the movie, read the book." "She's taking a Spanish class. There's some Spanish-speaking guy that she has her eye on."

Lola said, "I'll bet it's Jorge."

"Who?"

My father leaned over. "He's one of the paddle boarding experts."

Aunt Vera said, "Remember last month, when I said Bailey would meet a man in the village? It appears my prediction came true. Jorge is very tall and easy on the eyes."

Dang. How did everyone but me know about Bailey's infatuation? What good was I as a best friend if I didn't keep up to date with my pal's new crush? Why wouldn't she have told me? In a way I felt jealous. Silly, I know, but I did. Maybe she thought that, because I was her boss now, she couldn't confide in me anymore. Well, that was going to change.

As the line of customers dwindled and the familiar strains of Disney's theme song filled the air, I caught sight of Rusty the car mechanic spreading a blanket on the sand. Tonight's main attraction was right up his alley. I bet Rusty knew every line of the film.

Right beyond Rusty I spotted Cinnamon striding across the sand. I reflected on my reluctance earlier to share my suspicions about Mitzi and Willie and wondered if now would be a good time. While we chatted, I could corroborate her mother's claim that the Mumford sisters were suspects.

I asked my aunt if she minded if I ran an errand.

"Too-ra-loo," she sang. "You've done plenty here. In less than an hour, we've raised enough for the new playground, including the extra slide." She rubbed the special amulet hanging around her neck. "I told you I predicted record sales."

"You did, indeed."

"Oh, please," my father said. "Not again with the —"

Aunt Vera held up a warning finger. "Mind that tongue, Cary. I see the future, and that's all there is to it."

"Why can't you foresee something more important so we could be forewarned of death and devastation?"

"Cary," Lola nudged him with a hip.

Aunt Vera scoffed. "I told you, little brother, I don't see darkness. Only light."

"Pretty darned convenient."

"You're envious of my power."

"Power? Is that what you call it? More like vain obsession."

The two of them continued to lock horns as I slipped off my flip-flops and padded my way, barefoot, toward Cinnamon. Even at a distance, I could hear Lola acting as referee.

Before I reached Cinnamon, she stopped and struck up a conversation with Mitzi and Sam Sykes. My stomach did a teensy somersault in anticipation. Had she learned what I had? Had someone else clued her in? Did she think Mitzi's meltdown at the Grill Fest was in direct relation to her feeling guilty about killing Natalie Mumford? I continued on my path, ready and willing to offer my insight but paused when Sam, in response to whatever question Cinnamon had asked, pointed. She didn't linger. She marched off, her pace official, toward the ebullient waitress from the Word. As Cinnamon caught up with Rosie, it dawned on me that she might be interested to hear Rosie's take on Willie's whereabouts on the day Natalie died. Thrilled that our chief of police was doing her job — okay, sure, I'd doubted her before, but not now — I breathed easier. Lola would be exonerated, and all would be right with the world.

Feeling the urge to jump for joy, and not fully into watching *The Love Bug,* I ran to a pack of men and women playing glow-in-the-dark Frisbee outside the movie seating area. There is something wonderfully liberating about racing after a small, inanimate object that you can catch one-handed. I remembered David bounding like one of those lords a-leaping in "The Twelve Days of Christmas" and catching the Frisbee, mid-air, beneath his legs. He had been poetry in motion.

I approached a string bean of a woman, a Cookbook Nook customer who grew vegetables to sell in farmers' markets, and asked to be included in the game.

"Sure," she said. "Boys against girls."

"I didn't realize it was a competition." Though I had played sports when I was younger, my insides knotted, knowing I had plopped myself into the middle of an organized game. "I'll bow out."

"No, stay. We've got six Frisbees going at

once. Whichever side gets all of them, wins. But the Frisbees have to keep moving. Hands up. Eyes open. You don't want to catch one at the back of your skull."

"Duly noted."

"Shame about Mitzi," String Bean said.

Why couldn't I remember the woman's name? If only I had Bailey's steel-trap memory. Sarah? Sally? Sue? *Sue sells seashells down by the seashore.* It started with an *S*.

"I heard Mitzi lost it at the Grill Fest," the woman continued. Sometimes String Bean supplied vegetables for Mitzi's home canning business if Mitzi's personal garden ran short. "What is going on with her? Do you know? I mean, why is she so uptight?"

Maybe Mitzi was off caffeine like Bailey, I mused.

"She's always trying to be perfect," String Bean went on. "If only she'd relax. I would, if I were her and blessed with so many God-given talents. She cooks, she gardens, she's smart and beautiful, and she —" The woman yelped. "Lean left."

I obeyed. A split second later a Frisbee whizzed past my nose.

Nature Guy caught the disk. "You okay, Jenna?"

"Fine."

As quick as lightning, with his hand held overhead and clasping the disk with a backhanded grip, he hurled what ultimate Frisbee enthusiasts called a scoober. He rushed away while trying to intercept another pizza-shaped missile.

"Guess there's no chitchat during Frisbee," I said to String Bean. "Gotta stay alert."

"All I meant," she said, "was that I wish Mitzi would lighten up. She's got so much going for her. And yet —" She dove for a Frisbee and caught it. She scrambled to her feet and dashed away, leaving me to finish the sentence.

And yet Mitzi was insanely worried that her husband was stepping out on her. Was she justified in her concern? Moments ago, when Cinnamon had approached Mitzi and Sam, Mitzi had appeared to be the epitome of a contented spouse.

"Jenna," a woman called.

A gold disc was heading straight for me. I reached out. Nabbed it. At the same time, I saw a hulk of a shadow charging me, hands waving overhead. Rhett.

"Got you clogged," he said with an evil, yet fun grin spread across his face.

Clogged was the Frisbee term for standing in my way.

"No, you don't." I dodged beneath his arm and air-bounced the Frisbee toward String Bean.

"We did it!" String Bean yelled as she caught the sixth Frisbee. "Girls win. We have them all."

The ladies cheered; the men moaned.

Rhett buffed my arm with his knuckles. "Look at you, coming in at the last moment and saving the day. With an air bounce, no less. You're a pro. Don't deny it."

I didn't. I might not have been as graceful as David, and I didn't particularly enjoy competition, but I had good hand-eye coordination.

Rhett slung an arm around my shoulder. Warmth spread over me like a cozy blanket. "Want to grab a cupcake? I hear they're delicious."

"They're all gone."

"How about an ice-cream cone, then? I see Keller across the way." He pointed.

Close to the water, Keller sat on his stationary bicycle-style contraption, pedaling hard to keep the ice cream cold. A bevy of people stood enraptured by his wizardry. A pretty young woman was scooping ice-cream cones from the tub of ice cream strapped to the rear of the bike.

From among the onlookers I spotted

Norah with Ellen, who was wearing her heavy coat and holding her daughter in her arms. Norah's mouth was moving. She was talking to her niece. She drew a picture with her hands as she talked. The girl laughed. So did Ellen as she fiddled with her daughter's lacy white bonnet. Willie stood nearby, his Hawaiian shirt unbuttoned and hanging open. He rubbed his well-developed chest and abs with his fingertips and gazed at the multitude, totally disinterested in whatever Norah was saying. What a Neanderthal.

Suddenly, the sky blazed with fireworks. Red, white, green. Popping sounds echoed along the beach. Eight P.M. On the dot. Dark enough for a great visual, yet early enough for all the kids in the crowd to watch and get home in time for bed.

Instinctively, I curled into Rhett.

He chuckled. "Aha. You forgot about intermission fireworks, didn't you? Don't be frightened." He swiveled me toward him and lifted my chin with a fingertip. Without hesitation, he kissed me on the lips. Once. Soft. Giving.

Heat coursed through me. I relished the feeling for a moment, then broke away, lustful yet nervous.

"Did I do something wrong?" he said.

"Not at all. I liked it. I —"

Movement caught my eye. Willie was trying to wrestle his daughter from Ellen's arms while at the same time attempting to cover the girl's ears. When he gained control of her, he stared at his sister-in-law with unveiled hatred and said loudly enough for anyone to hear, "Butt out, Norah." Clutching his daughter to his chest, he marched away.

Ellen faced her sister, eyes pleading. Norah urged Ellen to run after Willie. Ellen obeyed.

An irrepressible urge to help swelled within me. I raced after Ellen. I could only imagine Rhett's reaction: *Oh no. Here we go again.* I reached Ellen seconds after she caught up to her husband.

"Give her to me, Willie," she shouted.

Willie whirled around. He caught sight of me and snarled. "What are you doing here?" He shook his hand at me.

Ellen said, "Willie. No. Don't."

"Stay away from me and my family. I don't want to warn you again." He gripped Ellen's arm, muscled her into the throng, and instantly disappeared.

What had Willie meant by *again*? Was he admitting that he had tried to run me off the road?

Worried for Ellen, I started to go after them, but Rhett grabbed my arm.

CHAPTER 16

Rhett spun me toward him and took hold of my shoulders. "Are you okay?"

Before I could answer, he kissed me hard on the mouth. When he released me, I felt as awkward as a schoolgirl in her first play. My mouth went dry. I needed a drink of water something awful. The toes of my right foot, kid you not, wormed their way into the sand. How foolish could an almost-thirtysomething woman act?

"Well, that was nice," I said. "The kiss, not the scene between the Bryants."

"I was worried about you. Willie . . ." Rhett ran a finger through a curl of my hair.

"He's so edgy," I said. "I was concerned that he might hurt Ellen."

"I'm sure the new responsibility is getting to him. He's got a lot to handle with a wife and a kid."

And extra cash and a new house, I thought cynically.

"Hey, look." Rhett pointed. "Over there. I see them. They seem fine now."

Ellen and Willie, clutching his daughter, stood apart from the rest. She was running her hand up and down his arm. Willie nodded passively.

"I've been into the Word a couple of times this past week," Rhett continued. "Willie seems in over his head. He's always got a ledger or a menu in his hands and a perplexed look on his face. Not everyone is meant to run a business." Rhett sighed. "Are you calmer now?"

"Yes." I glanced at Norah, who stood apart from her family. What had gone down between Willie and her? Had she, like Sam, butted in with parental advice, setting the stage for Willie's overreaction to my intrusion? Maybe she had called Willie controlling when he'd covered his daughter's ears to protect them from the loud noises.

"Care to try it again?" Rhett said.

"Try what? Oh, the kiss. Yes, but . . ." I balked. But *what*? Was I scared? Those gorgeous eyes. That delicious mouth. Why was I holding back with him, not only now but also on my run the other day? Six months ago, my therapist in San Francisco had told me I was "fit for duty" and ready to reenter the world. *Date. Have fun. Take a chance.*

When I'd called her to tell her I was moving back to Crystal Cove, she had cheered. I knew what she would advise me to do if she learned about the mystery involving the Lucky Cat statue that had sent me into a tailspin this past week, exactly what my father had advised: seek a local therapist.

"Jenna?" Rhett said.

I popped onto my toes, bussed Rhett on the cheek, and said, "Yes, I want to kiss you again, but we need to go on an official date first, okay?"

"Our picnic —"

"Not official. Happenstance. Call me old school."

"Okay, Old School, you're on. How's Monday night?"

"Why Monday?"

"You'll see."

Excited but also feeling like a skittish kitten, I squeezed his hand and ran off. Heaven forbid I stick around and continue the conversation like an adult.

When I arrived home, Tigger, speaking of skittish kittens, pounced on me. His kisses were sweet, but they were no substitute for Rhett's. The memory of the man's lips on mine made me, for some crazy reason, crave sugar. I set my tote on the kitchen table and then gathered the ingredients for Mexican wedding cookies. I had learned how to make the sweets a few weeks ago. The recipe only required five ingredients. The treats had quickly become my go-to dessert. After shaping the buttery, nutty dough into crescents, I set the baking pan in the oven.

While I waited for the cookies to bake — they cooked at a low temperature and wouldn't be ready to roll in powdered sugar for a long while — Tigger yowled, then leaped on the kitchen table and sniffed the book of Chinese characters in my purse.

"Good idea," I said to him. I pulled out the book and retrieved the repaired Lucky Cat from my bedside table. I leafed through the book, searching for each symbol on the bottom of the statue. The symbols proved to be pretty basic: one meant *sun,* another meant *rise.* When I realized the phrase translated to *The sun will rise,* tears filled my eyes. Whenever things were bad at the office, David would say, *The sun will rise; everything will work out.* He would make me repeat the phrase, and then as if he were a superhero because he had fixed the problem, he would flex his muscles and grin.

Not this time, I thought. He hadn't fixed things *this* time.

The timer on the stove *ping*ed. I hurried over, donned mitts, and removed the cookie pan from the oven. Per instructions, I waited a minute and then, using one of the polka-dotted spatulas I'd brought from the shop, lifted the cookies off and set them on a rack to cool. When I could touch them without scalding my fingertips, I poured a half cup of powdered sugar in a pie pan and rolled each cookie in the white fluff. My fingers grew sticky. As I licked off the sugar, I recalled an admonition my mother used to say: *Problems don't get solved in one quick lick.*

Thinking of my mother made me reflect on Bailey's mother. Was Lola's problem solved? Was she off the hook for murder? Every time I opened a book, I thought of how Lola, while I was growing up, had encouraged me to stimulate my brain cells. I didn't want her to go to jail. I loved her dearly. I hadn't confirmed anything with Cinnamon. Should I call her and bug her at this late hour?

Not on a bet.

"Chicken," I said as I poured myself a glass of milk. I nabbed a cookie, moved to the window, and pushed back the drapes. Looking out at the ocean, which was barely visible in the pitch-black of night, I stood transfixed as I ran through the events of the day: Mitzi's meltdown; Ellen's visit to the shop; Pepper's assertion that the Mumford sisters would inherit equally. Replaying the scene on the beach between Willie, his wife, and his sister-in-law sent a chill through me. Would Willie have hurt either of the women? Norah seemed to have a strong connection to Ellen. Had she ever been a part of the Bryants' lives before? The way she had commanded Ellen to hurry after Willie and the way Ellen had obeyed intrigued me. Was Ellen her sister's pawn? For some reason, I felt protective of Ellen. How could I learn more about Norah?

Frustrated because I had no answer to the questions cycling through my brain, I downed a second cookie, finished my milk, and headed to bed. In the morning, I would go to the Word and see if I could learn more about the Mumford clan.

Early Sunday morning at an hour when many were usually at church, Mum's the Word was hopping. A line of customers streamed down the steps and along The Pier. As I drew nearer, I understood the lure. A banner announcing *Fifties Day* hung above the diner's door. A black-and-red Ford Meteor sedan with sparkling fins was parked beside the diner. The Everly Brothers' "Bye Bye Love" played from a jukebox set up outside the front door. Looking closer, I realized all the customers were dressed in 1950s garb.

"Jenna," a woman called.

Mayor Zeller, dressed in snug jeans and a T-shirt that sported characters from the musical *Grease,* her frizzy hair looped in a rubber band and her face scrubbed clean, invited me to join her.

I popped into line beside her, doing my best to squelch a smile, because I couldn't ever remember seeing her wear anything other than business attire.

"We're all supposed to dress up," the mayor said, which told me I wasn't much good at hiding my amusement. "Didn't you get the notice?"

I shook my head.

"Norah Mumford handed out flyers yesterday. Don't worry. I'm sure the diner will let you in. I'm a nut for old movies and songs from the fifties," the mayor went on. "Elvis's 'Don't Be Cruel,' Bill Haley's 'Rock Around the Clock,' and Johnny Mathis's 'The Twelfth of Never.' I swoon." She patted her chest, then snapped to attention. "Heads up. We're moving." A kid hunting for the golden ticket in *Charlie and the Chocolate Factory* couldn't have acted more excited. "I'm going to order a big, juicy hamburger. How about you?"

"I'm hoping for breakfast."

"You're in luck. They're serving stacks of dollar-sized pancakes drenched in butter and syrup served with thick slabs of crispy bacon." The mayor used her hands to describe the meal. "I studied the menu."

I giggled. "I had no clue you were such a foodie."

"Always. Why else do you think I came up with the Grill Fest idea all those years ago? Natalie encouraged me to have it. She said she would win, of course. Her ego was intact."

"I don't recall her doing special events like this at the Word."

"Natalie wasn't interested. She ran a steady place. She'd have an occasional twofer-type promotion, but no galas. She liked consistency, and she liked to rule the roost." The mayor clicked her tongue between her teeth. "That came out wrong. Natalie was a good soul. But progress takes forward thinkers, like you and your aunt and, well, like all the wonderful business-men and women in our town. Natalie was a bit of a dinosaur. She believed she knew what was right and who should do what."

I tilted my head. Did I detect bitterness in the mayor's tone? Had Natalie told her what to do when it came to the Grill Fest? Had she ordered the mayor to declare her the winner each year — *or else?*

"I'm excited for the Mumford girls," the mayor continued, "especially the youngest." She pointed at Ellen, who stood outside acting as hostess. She was clad in a cute poodle skirt-and-sweater ensemble and looked about twelve years old. "I think she'll thrive with the changes, now that her sister is staying around."

"Are you saying that Norah is moving here for good?"

"Absolutely."

"She's willing to give up her life back east? What did she do for a living?"

"She was a hospital administrator."

"Really? That's a pretty big paycheck to turn down."

"The work was very depressing. She's fallen in love with Crystal Cove. What's not to adore?"

Ellen held up a finger. "One," she called. "We have a seat at the counter for one. Any takers?"

I peeked at the mayor, wishing I could break free from her gracefully. I was itching to know more about Norah. I would get more gossip from Rosie, the counter waitress, if I sat alone.

"Go ahead, Jenna." Mayor Zeller pressed me forward. "I can see you're eager to get going. I totally understand. You've got a business to run. Me? It's my day off. I'm going to di-i-ine." She dragged the word out with relish.

I waved at Ellen, who guided me inside to the counter while handing me a menu. As we walked, I told her about my success with the Chinese translation.

"I'm so happy to hear that," she said. "I'm thrilled to have helped. You've been such an inspiration to me."

"I have?"

"You picked yourself up after your husband died. You started a new business. And you won't take any guff from crusty people like Pepper Pritchett and her cohorts." She ruffled her pixie-cut hair. "It's because of you that we're having a theme day."

"I don't understand."

"You're always doing themes at The Cookbook Nook. I love the windows in your store. They're so creative. I tried to talk my mother into this fifties thing last month, but she wouldn't go for it. Thanks to Norah" — she eyed her sister, who was chatting up customers at the far end of the diner — "I found the courage."

"Hasn't Willie been supportive?"

Ellen hesitated. "Of course. Yes. Definitely. But ever since Norah drove in for the memorial, it's been different." I felt the urge to ask Ellen about the scene on the beach last night, but customers hailed her. She handed me a menu. "Enjoy your meal."

As she walked away, I considered what she had just revealed. In the advertising business, every word was chosen specifically to convey a meaning. Ellen said that Norah *drove* into town. Sure, a couple of days had passed between the murder and the memorial, so Norah had plenty of time to have flown from the East Coast, and, yes, she could have driven from the airport, but I would have said she'd *flown* in. Where had she been if she had driven in? Taking my reasoning one step further, could Norah have sneaked into Crystal Cove on Wednesday, the day of the murder, via automobile, without Ellen and the others knowing? With the advent of cell phones, identifying a person's exact location had become much more difficult.

Rosie, vibrant in a purple shirtwaist dress that matched the stripe in her hair, approached me with a water pitcher. "What'll it be, Jenna jumps jumping jacks?"

"I'm not sure, Rosie raises roosters."

"Ha! Funny girl. Mnemonics. Aren't they

264

a great tool?"

I scanned the colorful specials menu. "Seems like another busy day for you."

"Wish they were all like this." She poured a glass of water for me. The liquid sloshed over the sides. She mopped it up. "Say, you don't have need for another waitress at your café, do you?"

"Are you looking for a second job?"

Rosie glanced at Ellen and back at me. "Let's just say I wouldn't be averse to a lateral career move, if you catch my drift. Things have been a little lean around here lately. There's less help. Fewer specials — except for today, of course. Less security."

"Does a diner require security?"

"All businesses with cash registers do, sugar, even in gentle, peaceful Crystal Cove. Crime is everywhere nowadays."

I hadn't felt the need to install an alarm system at the shop. Should I? We had a lot of product, not to mention that there had been two murders in two months. In San Francisco, murder was a frequent occurrence, but I hadn't known any of the victims in the city personally. Had I somehow brought bad karma with me to Crystal Cove?

Stop it, Jenna. You are not the reason evil exists. And yet —

Rosie rapped her knuckles on the counter. "Willie thinks he can handle every aspect of the business himself, but if I might confide, the poor chump is failing. He's wound tighter than a spring and barking orders like a drill sergeant. He can't put in the hours required and take care of his daughter and home. Plus, I think he feels outnumbered, two to one, now that Norah's come to town."

"Tell me about Norah," I said, grateful for the opening in the conversation. "My aunt doesn't recall her having visited Crystal Cove before."

"Sure she has." Rosie placed the water pitcher on the counter and offered me a blue napkin and silverware setting. "Once a year on her sister's birthday. In and out. Never sightsees."

"I heard a rumor that she's moving here for good."

"It's true. She's worried about Ellen now that their mama is gone. She's very protective of her little chick."

"Ellen said Norah drove to town. Do you know from where?"

"She was down south in Los Angeles — that's where her corporate offices are. She was handing in her resignation letter the day her mama died."

So Norah had an alibi, and what the mayor said was true. Norah had quit her corporate job to be with her sister. Was that a sweet or calculating gesture?

I glanced at Norah and Ellen, who were standing shoulder-to-shoulder by the entrance of the kitchen. Norah was speaking out of one side of her mouth, looking for all intents and purposes like a conspirator. That made me flash on what Pepper had intimated. Was it possible that the sisters wanted a partnership so badly that they'd offed their mother in order to get their hands on their inheritance?

CHAPTER 17

On Sunday afternoon, I sat behind the sales counter at The Cookbook Nook, my focus on the computer screen. I was updating our website. When I'd worked at Taylor & Squibb, the pesky tech squad reminded me weekly, if not daily, how important it was to keep up the site. They asked for input, new designs, and announcements. They claimed that attracting those web bots — computer software that searches the Internet for new content and then ranks web pages accordingly — was vital to our company's growth. Most of The Cookbook Nook's business came from word of mouth, but we wanted to reach out to find new clients. Because there weren't that many specialty cookbook stores in the United States and none nearby — sure, a buyer could find recommendations for a cookbook online, or, based on cover art, a buyer could select from a huge assortment of cookbooks at a brick-and-mortar store — we prided ourselves on being the go-to place for cookbook knowledge; therefore, we needed to keep our website not simply current but stellar.

I had chosen to put the Grill Fest front and center on the home page. I was adding photographs that Bailey had taken. From what I'd heard, bots liked rotating photograph galleries better than almost anything else. However, I decided that we shouldn't post snapshots of Mitzi tossing cheese. Despite the fact that P. T. Barnum had claimed, "There is no such thing as bad publicity," I felt we might suffer a backlash from Mitzi or her husband if we reminded her of a weak moment. Why roil the waters?

"Hungry?" Katie entered the shop carrying a plate of gooey-looking chicken drumettes, the meaty sides of chicken wings. "I've roasted them in two different kinds of sauces. Both are savory."

Although I was full from the pancakes that I'd consumed at the Word, I made room. "Mm, tasty." I hummed my appreciation. "Love the pesto."

"Good, right? I plucked the recipe from this book." Katie tapped the top book on the stack of cookbooks she had set aside for me to peruse. *How to Grill: The Complete Illustrated Book of Barbecue Techniques* by the talented Steven Raichlen. "You know who this chef is, right? Cute, gray hair, beard, mustache, glasses." She mimed the look. The book offered concise and easy ways to grill for the beginner to the pro. "You had the drumette with the walnut-dill pesto sauce. I made an East-meets-West sauce, as well. Zesty-sweet. You could make these in a snap. Read through the —"

"Uh-uh." I held up my hand. "I don't have time. I can't be a slave to the kitchen. I've got to have a life, too, right?"

Katie gave me a mock-dissatisfied look. "A life? What's that?"

I noticed her pained expression. "How's the assistant chef working out?"

"Okay. Food's good. But the staff doesn't like him."

"Then let him go."

She sighed. "Yeah, I should." She set the tray on the counter. "Anything new on your Lucky Cat discoveries?"

I eyed the wings I hadn't tasted and debated whether I could handle another morsel. Deciding I couldn't, I abstained. "Only that the words on the bottom mean 'The sun will rise.'"

"Kelly Clarkson has a song with that title." Katie crooned out the first line.

"David used to say to me at the beginning

of every ad campaign I started: 'The sun will rise; everything will work out.' Except it hasn't worked out. *Life* hasn't worked out, and I haven't found out what that darned key belongs to."

Katie patted my hand. "You will. Be patient."

"Patience is not my middle name," I snarled.

"Don't I know it." She lifted the tray. As she bussed it to the hallway, I rued not taking the opportunity to sample the second drumette. Perhaps later.

Katie paused to chat with Pepper, who surprisingly appeared whenever Katie was setting out a new tray of goodies. I wondered whether the woman watched the shop through binoculars in anticipation. A month ago, I had talked to Aunt Vera about Pepper's sneaky visits to gobble up our wares. Aunt Vera agreed that Pepper was a bit of a scavenger, but she wouldn't deny her. She said Pepper fostered a huge beading community, and if even once a day Pepper talked about the food that the café was making, we would sell more food and cookbooks. Many of Pepper's clientele had become ours and ours had become hers. At that very moment, three beaders, including Flora, stood beside the far wall discussing

271

the pros and cons of the natural-food cookbook selections. One, written by Heidi Swanson, appeared to be their favorite: *Super Natural Every Day: Well-Loved Recipes from My Natural Foods Kitchen.*

"Every recipe is packed with veggies and protein," Flora said loudly enough for all to hear. "How about a tasty chickpea wrap in a whole wheat lavash?"

Her friends murmured their appreciation.

"Get this," Flora went on, proving to be quite the ringleader. "The author is a San Francisco farmers' market regular and a blogger."

"I wonder if we could meet her?" a pal said.

Knowing I had better things to do than to listen in on their conversation, I returned my attention to revamping our website.

Seconds later, the front door of the shop burst open, and Bailey, in the cheeriest outfit she had worn in days, raced inside. Her skin, however, looked pale. She skidded on her espadrilles. "You won't believe it. Willie —" She inhaled sharply.

"Willie, what?"

"Willie —" She drew in another breath, clearly out of any reserve air. She held up a finger. Another intake. "Willie —"

Horrible notions ran rampant through my

brain. *Willie had hit Ellen. Willie had hurt Norah.*

"C'mon already," I said. "Out with it."

"Willie is missing."

"Missing? As in, he left town?"

"He's gone."

"With his daughter?" Ellen would be heartbroken if Willie ran off with their little girl.

"I don't think so. I'm not sure." Bailey placed her hand on her chest to regain control of her breathing. "I was at the arcade buying these earrings." She batted a set of silver and beaded baubles.

I wound my hand in the air — *go on.*

"Right. I heard two women talking. One said she saw Willie at the bank yesterday. He was cleaning out his savings. Not one to believe a rumor without substantiated facts, I called the bank and spoke to a new friend of mine. We take Spanish together."

"A new *friend*?" I said, hoping she would elaborate about her secret boyfriend.

"Friend," she reiterated. "*She* is the assistant manager at the bank. She said that Willie had indeed cleaned out his savings. *His.* Under his name. He and Ellen had separate accounts."

"David and I had separate accounts. No big deal."

273

"Yeah, but I was intrigued, so I made my way down to The Pier and asked around. Not inside the diner, mind you. I'm not as daring as you. But the gossip is that no one has seen Willie since early this morning. He is gone with a capital *G*."

"Do you think he fled because he killed Natalie, and he found out Chief Pritchett is closing in on him?"

A woman gasped. I pivoted. Pepper tossed a drumette into the trash and dashed out the exit. Ten bucks said I knew where she was headed. To call her daughter and set Cinnamon on Willie's trail. Good.

On Sunday nights, we closed the shop early, and my aunt, my father, and I enjoyed a family dinner. This week, my aunt had offered to cook at her house. Little did my father and I know until we'd arrived that we would be put to work as sous-chefs. The windows were open; outside, the surf lapped the sand with calming regularity. I glimpsed my aunt's extensive collection of cookbooks. Only one was open and set into a book holder. Whew.

I rinsed my hands in the sink and said, "What do I do first?"

"Pare the pineapple."

I flashed on Willie and his Hawaiian shirts

and the egotistical way he wore them, flared open so people would admire his handsome physique. Where was the guy? There was one reason for him to have fled — he was guilty. He had killed Natalie because he wanted to get his hands on her money and have full control of Ellen, but Norah's arrival in town had blown his game plan. *Run away, Mr. Gingerbread Man.*

"Jenna, focus." My aunt pointed to the pork recipe in the cookbook. According to her, the menu she had chosen was simple fare. "Grilling is easy, but it requires your full attention."

The meal consisted of rice, beans, plantain bananas, and a pork roast. My father dealt with the beans, which weren't too difficult to make. We were using canned beans. The original recipe called for soaking fresh beans overnight.

After I removed the pineapple rind — ouch! — and cored the pineapple, I tackled the rice. I knew in my heart of hearts how iffy rice could turn out. Rice could wind up sticky or as dry as a bone. As I set the lid on top of the mixture to simmer, knowing I had followed the recipe directions to the letter, I was soaring with confidence, but then I skimmed the recipe for the pork marinade and nearly broke out in a cold sweat. The recipe required ten steps and at least twenty ingredients. Breathing like a Lamaze pro, I got the job done. Aunt Vera assisted twice. When it came to the actual grilling, my aunt was right. The dish was challenging. Working with a coal barbecue, which my father had to light — I couldn't figure out the cone thingy — I quickly learned that the temperature could vary. Not only did I have to baste the roast every twenty minutes, but at times I had to move it to another area on the grill so it wouldn't scorch. During the process, I was pretty sure I had sweated away five pounds from sheer worry.

We convened on the patio for the meal. Aunt Vera had set a beautiful table with cornflower blue mats, aqua glasses, and a mixture of blue silk flowers. The whoosh of the ocean's ebb and flow was all we needed as background music.

Midway through the meal — pieces of the meat wound up too crispy for my taste, though my aunt and father assured me that I was getting pretty good at this cooking stuff — my phone *ping*ed. Bailey had texted me that Willie was still missing.

My father frowned. "No texts at mealtime. You know that. Turn off your phone."

"But it's about Willie Bryant."

"What about him?"

Aunt Vera said, "Do you think Ellen knew he would flee?"

"Willie left town?" my father said, clueless.

"I can't imagine Ellen knew," I said. "Where did he go? Why did he leave his little girl?" I had called the diner to make sure he hadn't run off with his daughter; he hadn't.

"How is Ellen holding up?" my aunt said.

"I haven't talked to her."

"Did you ever question her about, you know, her finances?"

"What about them?" my father asked as he forked the remainder of his beans into his mouth.

"Jenna believes the Bryants were struggling financially."

I explained about the prickly encounter at the shop when Willie had prompted Ellen to return the books to the shelves. "I'm pretty sure he pinched her."

"Are you saying Willie is abusive?" My father's jaw tensed. In my lifetime, I had seen him take on a few tough guys. I recalled two specific incidents during my teen years: one to protect me at The Pier, the other to protect my sister on the beach. Karate moves had been involved.

"He's overbearing, that's for sure."

My aunt gazed at me. "Why does Ellen suffer his boorishness?"

"She lacks spine," I said. "According to a few folks, her mother treated her the same way. If Natalie commanded, Ellen obeyed."

My father frowned. "Have you been investigating, Jenna?"

"To clear Lola," my aunt said, defending me. "Text Bailey back and ask how Ellen's doing."

"Vera," my father said.

"I'm worried about Ellen," she countered. "And find out how her sister is faring as well."

"Norah," I said, an edge to my tone.

"You don't like Norah?" my father asked.

"I'm worried she's simply a replacement for the other dominant people in Ellen's life." I blotted my mouth with a napkin, then texted a message and hit Send. The message whooshed forward.

My father set his fork down. "Maybe I'm missing something, but Ellen seems to make a good team with Norah. The fifties event they did today was Ellen's idea, wasn't it? From everything I've heard, the event was a real hit. If Norah helped Ellen turn it into a reality, then perhaps Norah has empowered her sister."

I downed a scoop of rice flavored with deglazed white wine and onions, loving the combination, then glanced at my father. "Norah is moving here, Dad. Why would she quit a well-paying position at a hospital to run a diner?"

"She gave up her job?"

"According to a waitress at the Word, she turned in a resignation letter the day her mother died."

"This waitress," my father said. "She's a model of honesty?"

"I think so."

He raised an eyebrow. "Jenna, if there's one thing you are, it's too trusting. How long have you known the waitress? A day? Two? It takes years, as well as great insight, to know if someone is telling the truth or hornswoggling you."

"Hornswoggling?" I gawked at him.

"You know what I mean."

"Are you saying I'm not intuitive?"

"I'm saying at times you are gullible in a good way, Tootsie Pop."

Usually I didn't mind the nickname my father had given me. Tootsie Rolls were my favorite candy, followed by caramel and dark chocolate. But now, the term felt patronizing. I drummed the tabletop with my fingertips. "In what way can gullible be good?"

Aunt Vera scrutinized my father, stroking the amulet around her neck with dedication. "Cary . . ."

My father ignored her. "You're nice, Jenna, and you believe the best of people."

Not lately.

"And you tell the truth," he added.

"I can keep secrets that not even you, Mr. Super Secret Spy, could wrench out of me."

Although my father claimed his former line of work was as an analyst, there had been times when my siblings and I had questioned whether he had done more than that — possibly interrogation. Over the years, we had pressed him about his work. When he wasn't home, we dunned our mother. Where had Dad gone? With whom was he meeting? My brother had been the staunchest challenger.

Through gritted teeth, my father said, "Let's readdress the topic of Willie."

"Yes, do," Aunt Vera said. "Dessert?"

Both my father and I declined.

Aunt Vera rose and cleared dishes. Telling from her brisk gait, she was happy her magic had helped keep the peace. She was fooling herself. Neither my father nor I was calm.

I leaned forward and stared him down. "Let me pose a theory. What if Willie fled because he murdered Natalie?"

"Motive?"

I explained the inheritance. "He needed cash."

"You said he closed his *own* account not Ellen's. Why leave before the estate is meted out?" He had a point.

I said, "What if Ellen, with Norah for backup, denied him any of the inheritance?"

For five minutes, we went at each other, reviewing the rumors and/or facts, as I knew them. My father would not concede that Willie was the murderer.

"What if Willie was so stressed by Norah's influence over her sister that he gave up?" my father said. "Per your own account, he suffered Natalie's bullying for far too long. Maybe he'd had enough of all Mumford women."

"But he left his precious daughter behind."

My father rubbed his chin. "Maybe he's taking a respite. Hiding out for a few days to clear his head. Remember not to judge a man too harshly. Sometimes critical events in a person's life can alter a person's fate. You should understand that better than most." He pushed away from the table and stood. "No matter what, we're not solving this here and now. I would assume Cinnamon has been alerted."

"By her mother, if no one else," I said.

My father offered a wry look. "Let's call it a night, and I'll walk you home."

Minutes later, as I opened my door and bid my father good night, my cell phone rang. I hurried inside. Tigger dove at my ankles. I scooped him up while fishing in my purse. The moment I pulled the cell phone out, it stopped ringing. The readout said *Missed Call* and offered a number I didn't recognize. Who would be calling me at 10:00 P.M.?

Tigger yowled at the top of his lungs.

"Shush, cat." I stabbed the voice mail icon. Zero messages.

I hit *Recent* and saw the unidentifiable phone number. I pressed the number to automatically redial. I waited through two rings. On the third ring, a voice mail machine answered, and I heard Willie Bryant's voice instructing me to speak after the beep.

My insides snagged. Why had Willie called me? Why wasn't he picking up?

CHAPTER 18

All night long I tossed and turned, thinking about Willie and his odd phone call and David and the gold-filled Lucky Cat. *Everything will work out.* Had David written the Chinese words on the bottom of the statue? If he had, he had been wrong. Everything hadn't worked out. He'd died. I was alone. And I was left with a puzzle I could not solve.

At 6:00 A.M. Monday morning, dressed in my pajamas, I bounded into the kitchen and glowered at the mysterious key lying on the table. What kind of key was it? I had exhausted all banks and private mailbox locations in San Francisco as well as Crystal Cove. What else could the key fit? A bus locker? A train station locker? What secrets would I discover once I found the key's source?

"Darn it," I shouted and kicked a kitchen cabinet. It popped open. I jammed it shut.

Tigger bolted to the safety of the adjoining living room and skittered beneath the couch. He peered out, eyes wide with fright.

"Sorry, pal. I'm a goof. C'mere." I squatted and waited for him to trust me again. "Please. I'm sorry. I'm not just a goof. I'm an ogre. I'm mean and thoughtless and —" He crouch-crawled toward me. "That's it. Keep coming. I'm not going to hurt you." He nuzzled me with his head. I scooped him up. "Good boy. I'm getting dressed, and then we're going on an outing."

To soothe my soul, I needed a few answers to Willie Bryant's puzzle. Why had he called me, of all people, at 10:00 P.M. at night? Had he wanted to confess to murder? Why hadn't he picked up when I'd called back? Maybe he had lost his nerve. Perhaps he had called Chief Pritchett instead.

I headed to The Pier. As I neared Mum's the Word Diner, a pair of teen boys almost nailed me with a Frisbee. I cautiously ducked beneath their game and entered the restaurant. There were no themes today, no special deals, and there were fewer customers than the day before. Ellen perched on a stool by the counter. Sam sat beside her, his arm slung around her shoulders. I surveyed the place for Norah but didn't see her anywhere.

I approached Ellen and tapped her back.

"Hi, Ellen. Good morning, Sam."

Ellen broke free of Sam, spun her knees around, and leaped off the stool. She gripped me in a hug so intense I thought the breath might gush out of me. "Jenna, I'm so glad to see you."

I broke free. I needed air if I was going to make it past my thirtieth birthday. And Tigger. I wasn't sure how he had weathered the squeeze. I peeked into my purse. He peered up at me, as silent as a dormouse but none the worse for wear. I said to Ellen, "I heard that Willie might be missing. Have you heard from him?"

She shook her head, then tucked her hands beneath the armpits of her heavy sweater.

Sam stood up and edged toward Ellen. He didn't look miffed that my arrival had split Ellen and him apart. He seemed truly concerned for her. Fatherly. "I was on the horn all night calling around for him," he offered. "Mitzi, too, in between her nightly beauty treatments." He didn't say the latter with any malice, more as a statement of fact. "I talked to everyone. Hotels. Bars. The police." He grumbled. "They won't do anything until an adult has been gone at least forty-eight hours."

"Even though there's been a recent" — I

285

hesitated, unable to utter the word *murder*
— "death in the family?"

Sam frowned. "The deputy who took my call said they were 'on it,' as if that's any consolation."

"I checked the gym," Ellen said. "Sometimes Willie likes to work out late."

"It's hard keeping up those pecs of his." Sam clicked his tongue against his teeth, clearly not a Willie fan.

"I contacted the grocery store, too," Ellen continued, oblivious to Sam's judgment. "We were out of milk. I thought maybe he went there. He hates for our daughter to go wanting for anything. The owner hadn't seen him. Where could Willie have gone?"

"Surfing?"

Ellen's eyes widened, as if this was the first anybody had mentioned the notion. "Oh no. What if he got hurt? I hope . . ." She didn't finish the sentence. Doom seemed to grip her and drag her shoulders down.

"He hasn't contacted you in any way?" I asked.

She shook her head.

Out with it, Jenna. Speak. "He telephoned me, Ellen."

"You?" Her face tinged pink. "Why? When?"

"At ten last night. I don't know why. He didn't leave a message."

"Do you think it was a pocket call?" Sam said, referring to the thing that happens when a person forgets to lock his cell phone before inserting it in a pocket. If something bumps the cell phone, the phone might automatically trigger and contact the last name dialed.

"I don't know why he would have had my cell phone number in his phone. He's never called me." I petted Ellen's arm. She trembled beneath her sweater. "I was wondering whether Willie, knowing that I'm a friend of Chief Pritchett's, might have gotten in touch with me to —" I paused.

"To what?" The ceiling lights of the diner reflected in Ellen's eyes. She looked so vulnerable.

"To confess to your mother's murder." Although Willie topped my suspect list, it was probably wrong of me to implicate him without proof. Too late.

Ellen wagged her head back and forth. "No, no, no. He didn't kill my mother. He couldn't have."

"He might have ended our call and dialed Chief Pritchett instead."

"B-b-but" — Ellen stammered — "wouldn't Miss Pritchett, I mean Chief

Pritchett, have contacted me after that? And Sam called the police, and they —" Tears pooled in her eyes. "Poor Willie. He was angry at me. He —" She swallowed hard. "We had an argument. He stormed out of the house."

"You fought?" Sam said.

"We didn't *fight* fight. He didn't put a finger on me."

Not where anyone could see, I mused.

"Why didn't you confide in me?" Sam persisted.

"I didn't want to tell anyone."

"What did you argue about?" I asked.

At that moment, Norah exited the kitchen. She caught sight of the three of us. With stature as regal as a prima ballerina's, she strode to us and inserted herself between Ellen and Sam. "What's going on?"

"Willie," Ellen said. "I told you he's missing. He . . . he called Jenna." She explained as much as I had told her and faced me. "We argued about the diner. He wanted me to sell my half to my sister."

"Why?" I asked.

"He wanted out. He hates this place. He said it was too much work."

Norah raised her chin. "I told Ellen I have no interest in being a single owner. We're partners."

"Willie got mad when I said I wouldn't ask her," Ellen went on. "He said this place would be our ruin. It's sucking money like a Hoover."

"Are you having financial problems?" I said, thinking of what the waitress had said to me yesterday. They were cutting staff and trimming the menu. How badly off was the diner? Had the Mumford sisters inherited a money pit?

"No," Ellen said. "The diner is doing fine. Right, Sam?"

"It's been in the black for the last six years in a row," he said. "The first two years were investment years. Maybe Willie saw those figures and judged the diner's balances based on that."

Ellen sighed. "He's never had a head for numbers."

I recalled Katie saying that in college Willie had cheated in his economics course. I flashed on an image of him at the bank cornering Manga Girl. He had shaken what appeared to be a savings passbook. I'd assumed it was for his personal account. Had he, in reality, been questioning her about the diner's finances? Had he accused the teller of shorting the diner? Another scenario flitted through my mind, one that matched an occurrence at Taylor & Squibb.

What if Willie wasn't as stupid as everyone seemed to think when it came to economics? What if he had taken money from the diner's account? Maybe he was bleeding the diner dry. He transferred the cash into his own account and faked the scene at the bank to cover his actions. A third, darker possibility came to mind. What if Natalie found out what Willie was doing and approached him? He killed her, and a week later, he cashed out and split town.

I said, "My friend heard a rumor that Willie closed an account at the bank."

"Is this true, Ellen?" Norah said. Though she typically looked like her sister, she appeared nothing like her now. A hawk would appreciate her feral gaze.

"I've never paid attention to the money side of the business," Ellen said. "I've always been interested in the food and the customers. Mother" — she chewed her lower lip — "told me not to review the books."

I said, "I thought you had been doing the ordering since your mother died."

"True, but I've never written a check for anything. Willie took that over, didn't he, Sam? You know how the finances work. I mean, you did all the investing for Mother."

Sam drew in a deep breath. "Not all of it. I advised her, but she made every withdrawal and every deposit. She paid every bill. She was, as you know, very hands-on."

Ellen started to tremble. Her fingers clawed her sleeves. "I'm scared. What if Willie —" She grasped the counter.

I edged closer. "What if Willie . . . what?"

"What if Willie is dead?"

"Why would you jump to that conclusion?" Norah snapped.

Ellen's gaze swung between the three of us. "Maybe somebody at the bank saw him withdraw all that cash. Maybe he was robbed. Willie wouldn't leave home for good. Not without telling me. Not without Bebe. He didn't pack any bags. He didn't take his muscle T-shirts and his precious sports paraphernalia."

"What paraphernalia?" I said.

"Baseballs, bats, and gloves signed by famous players like Sosa, McGwire, and Bonds. He's a collector."

Rusty the car repair guy had seen Willie in Die Hard Fan, the sports collectibles store, arguing about a debt. Had Willie left town to avoid his creditor?

"Willie would never run off without his things," Ellen went on. "Or our daughter. He wouldn't leave her. What if he's" — her gaze flew between us — "been murdered, and the police think I killed him?"

"Ellen, hush," her sister said.

"I've got to find him." Ellen bolted toward the front door.

Norah ran after her and clutched her shoulders. "Ellen. Stop moving. Stop talking. Now."

Monday mornings at The Cookbook Nook were rarely busy. Weekend partiers slept in while tourists packed for home. I released Tigger from my purse. He scampered around as if he were the one on holiday. No kids. No adults. And no Bailey. I had given her the day off to browse Crystal Cove. She had been here two months and had never truly explored.

Tigger ran full bore toward the reading chair, ducked, and disappeared beneath. Seconds later, he reappeared and took off for the vintage kitchen table. *Mine, all mine,* I imagined the imp thinking.

I tossed my keys and purse on the sales counter. As I headed for the stockroom to stow my jacket — the morning air was a bit cool — thoughts about Ellen, Norah, and Willie raced through my mind. Who had done what and when? Was Willie alive? Why wouldn't he be? What if Ellen was right and he had been attacked after leaving the bank with all that cash? How much cash were we talking about? Were the Crystal Cove police searching for him by now? I dialed the precinct and got a busy signal. Swell.

I filled Tigger's water and snack bowls and switched on the remix that Katie had made of cheery food-related songs. "Sweet Potato Pie," a duet with James Taylor and Ray Charles, was first in the queue. Enlivened by the blare of horns and fabulous guitar, I danced a two-step to the café's kitchen — Dancing with the Stars, *watch out* — and fetched myself a cup of espresso from a machine in the café.

When I returned to the shop and settled onto the stool at the sales counter, I decided, given the lovely quiet, to spruce up the website even more than I had yesterday. As I woke up the computer, I paused when I caught sight of my key ring with the key David had left me added to it. Would pinning down the key's shape help me figure out what lock it fit?

The key was silver with a round head, its trunk long and narrow. There were five notches. I typed *Safety Deposit Box Key > Image* into the search line of an Internet browser page and hit Enter. Pictures of safety deposit box keys surfaced. Though many resembled my key, most had distinct ridges down the center of the key. Mine did not. I typed *Bus Station Locker Key* into the search line. Some of those looked like toothpicks; others reminded me of bottle openers. I typed *Key > Image,* and a slew of pictures came up, many of them stock photos or clip art.

Frustrated to the point of screaming but knowing yelling wouldn't accomplish any-thing — it rarely does — I gave up and returned my focus to The Cookbook Nook website.

In between customers' arrivals, purchases, and exits, I roamed the shop, taking photo-graphs of displays, then uploading them to the computer and adding them to the site. I inserted extra click-through buttons. I expanded the descriptions for gluten-free, vegetarian, and other specialty cookbooks. Both Bailey and my aunt had suggested those changes. They found customers didn't quite understand why there were specialty cookbooks. Some believed all cookbooks included vegetarian recipes. Hardly.

I worked straight through until 4:00 P.M., stopping briefly to put together a Swiss cheese, chopped olive, and mayo sandwich — one of my mother's favorites. It was easy to make, simple, and gooey. I also treated myself to one of Katie's afternoon sweets, a double-chocolate brownie. A girl needs her chocolate.

At 5:00 P.M., I stood to stretch my cramped limbs. At the same time, the front door opened.

Aunt Vera, dressed in a silver caftan and matching turban, sauntered in. She browsed the shop, then shook a reproachful finger. "What are you doing here by yourself, young lady?"

I flinched and felt my cheeks flush the way they had whenever the principal in high school had caught me doing something risky. Although I had been a good student, I had savored the challenge of racing into class right after the bell or slamming a locker door just because making loud noises was frowned upon. I didn't leap off any tall buildings, mind you. I wasn't that daring. Just full of myself.

"Well?" Aunt Vera tapped a foot.

"It's a work day. I work."

"Where's Bailey?"

"I gave her the day to play. From the moment she arrived in town, she's been working nonstop. Without her daily dose of caffeine, she's sort of on edge. I thought cool breezes and moderate sun would buoy her spirit."

"True. But you're all by yourself, Jenna. Why didn't you call me?"

"Because I figured you were busy doing private fortune-telling sessions. I didn't want to bother you. We've had a load of customers. Mostly moms. They bought that new grilled cheese cookbook we got in. *Grilled Cheese* by Spieler and Giblin."

"Yet another two-word title you can appreciate."

"I've got it memorized." Grinning, I tapped my head. "Many of the moms bought those new kiddie-food collections, too." Brightly colored cloth pizzas, fruits, and veggies. Adorable.

"Bless our young bakers."

"When the shop was empty, I devoted myself to the website. I feel like I accomplished a lot." Being so busy, my mind hadn't strayed to thoughts of Willie and Ellen and the tragedies surrounding our fair town.

"Dear girl, I'm getting vibes." Aunt Vera's eyes narrowed. She beckoned me to the vintage kitchen table, what we now called our meeting table. "Sit down."

"Aunt Vera."

"Sit."

I obeyed. Tigger leaped onto my lap and peered at my aunt as if he were the one in trouble.

Aunt Vera swept the skirt of her caftan out

of her way and took a seat opposite me. "Your hand, please."

Uh-oh. She intended to read my palm. She had read my right hand numerous times before. The lines hadn't changed. I possessed a strong heart line, good sexual desire, and a head for business. I would travel, but I didn't have wanderlust. Not bad, considering.

"You look lovely," I said. "The silver is perfect with your coloring."

"Don't flatter. Your hand."

I offered my hand, palm up. "Have you been telling fortunes all day? Your fingers are warm to the point of hot. Am I one more for the road?"

"Don't tease." She ran a fingertip along the surface of my skin. "You've got to relax."

"I am relaxed."

"No, I mean relax. Take the day off."

"Not on a Monday."

"Tomorrow the shop is closed. I expect you to take the entire day to have fun. Breathe."

As if I were under a spell, I inhaled.

"Walk on the beach," Aunt Vera went on.

I recalled the morning when I had almost been run off the road, and shuddered. "I will. Soon. But not tomorrow."

"Why not?"

"Because we have the continuation of the Grill Fest. Round three. Did you forget? The mayor asked us to remain open."

"Jenna, you need to have fun. Live your life."

"I am having fun. I went to The Pier this morning."

"To do what?"

Oops. Hoisted by my own petard. I could lie and say I had gone for a quick meal or to play Frisbee, but Aunt Vera, who was still holding my telltale palm, would sense the lie. A polygraph had nothing on her ability to pick up vibrations. "I wanted to check up on Ellen." I told her what had happened, from Willie's phone call to Norah's overprotection of Ellen. "I don't trust Norah, Aunt Vera. When did she really get to town? Could she have arrived before her mother died? Did she kill Natalie? She's so assertive."

"You're assertive. I'm assertive. We do not kill to get our way."

"What if Norah got rid of Willie so Ellen would be completely free of those who dominated her?"

"It's not unheard of, but why are you worrying about other peoples' lives so much?" My aunt clutched my hand. "You have enough on your plate."

"First, I got involved because of Lola. I wanted to make sure she didn't get railroaded into a conviction, not to mention that Natalie died on our watch, during the contest, right outside our property. I feel responsible. And now, there's Ellen. I like her. I'm concerned about her. She's fragile. A victim."

"Are you sure she's not capable of murder? Maybe she's manipulating everyone. She could be making all that up about Willie and his precious sports paraphernalia."

"No. I know for a fact that he buys stuff." I told her about the car repairman's account. "You've met Ellen. What is your sense of her?"

Aunt Vera released my hand. She pulled a tarot deck from the pocket of her caftan. "Draw a card."

"I don't need my fortune told."

"For Ellen."

"I'm allowed to do that?"

"Consider what you really want to understand about her situation, then ask."

I concentrated. "I want to know if she's guilty."

"Sorry, no. You can't do that. Ask what role you can play in her life."

"Aunt Vera."

"Do it."

Knowing my aunt wasn't going to give me a pass on this, I concentrated and then removed a card. Even without Aunt Vera's translation, I understood what I was looking at. I had pulled the High Priestess.

CHAPTER 19

My heart thrummed in my ribcage as I stared at the High Priestess tarot card. The priestess sat in front of the gate of Mystery, clad in a gorgeous blue dress. I knew from previous readings what she represents: knowledge, power, and truth. She mediates between light and dark, reality and illusion. The moon beneath her left foot represents her dominion over intuition.

"You see?" I said. "I'm bound by duty to continue to seek out the truth."

Aunt Vera let out a deep sigh.

"Oh, c'mon. You know I'm right." Although I didn't believe everything the cards revealed, I was more than willing to use them to my advantage, and I truly did want to help Ellen.

Aunt Vera took back the card and shoved it into the deck. "Have you told Chief Pritchett that you got a call from Willie?"

"Norah said she would do it."

"And has she?"

"How should I know?"

Aunt Vera ogled me.

I sighed. "Fine." I set Tigger on the floor, which didn't please him — he could have lounged in my lap until dawn — then headed for the telephone on the sales counter. Aunt Vera followed. I had the telephone receiver in my hand when the front door opened.

Rhett entered looking as rugged as the sailor I had once used in a sea-salt commercial: chiseled cheeks, bright eyes, a bit of a swagger. In a word, delicious. "Ready?"

"For what?" I said, then realized he had come to take me on a date. I set the receiver in the cradle. "It's Monday."

He aimed his index finger at me. "Give the girl two points."

"What's so unusual about Monday?" Aunt Vera asked.

Rhett unfastened the buttons of his pea coat. "We're hitting the town."

"Well, it's about time." Aunt Vera slotted the tarot deck into her pocket and whispered to me, "The High Priestess is patient." Then she moved to Rhett. "Where are you off to?"

"We're going lamp lighting."

"Oh my," Aunt Vera gasped. "I completely forgot. I've got to get cracking." She hustled behind the counter. "Jenna, where are the scissors? We have paper bags and candles, don't we? We keep them for emergencies, right?"

"Bags and candles for what?" I said, thoroughly stymied.

"You don't know?" Rhett grinned. "I thought you knew everything that went on in Crystal Cove."

"Not yet. What's going on? What's lamp lighting?"

"Stars," Aunt Vera said. "I'll punch stars in the bags." She glanced out the front windows. "Oh no. Pepper is way ahead of me. Go, you two. Have fun." My aunt shooed me toward the exit.

I dug in my heels. "What about Tigger?"

"Too-ra-loo. I'll take him home." My aunt scooped the kitten into her arms. "We'll have our own fun, won't we, fella?" She nuzzled his nose.

"I should contact Chief Pritchett," I said.

"I'm sure the Mumford girls did as promised." Aunt Vera gestured for me to leave and began to stroke the amulet around her neck.

"My car," I added, glancing toward the parking lot.

Rhett cocked his head. "If I didn't know better, Jenna, I'd say you were trying to get out of our date."

"No." I laid my hand on his forearm and something zinged inside me. A good something, filled with desire. I'd had a crush on the sea-salt guy, too. "I want to go with you. Absolutely. My purse."

I fetched my tote, slipped on my denim jacket, and returned in a matter of seconds. Grinning, I looped my hand around Rhett's elbow.

As he guided me toward the exit, I glanced over my shoulder. My aunt, the kook, smiled smugly. *Hocus pocus,* I mouthed. Chortling, she released her phoenix amulet and shuffled to the stockroom.

Lamp Lighting Night was like spending an evening in an enchanted fairy tale. As Rhett and I strolled along the sidewalk and the sun melted into the horizon, leaving a wash of orange and peach brushstrokes in the sky, little bags of light in front of the shops started to twinkle. Shop owners had cut intricate designs in paper bags and inserted either real or battery-operated candles into the bags. Disneyland at night had nothing on Crystal Cove.

We greeted couples and families. Most were bundled up; many hummed songs. I heard the strains of "Let It Be" and "Blowin' in the Wind," campfire-style songs that filled me with a warm glow.

A short while into our stroll, Rhett started humming U2's "All I Want Is You," which brought back memories of elementary school and a towheaded boy who wanted to kiss me. He had chased me around a tree while singing the song at the top of his lungs.

I started to laugh, and Rhett said, "What's so funny? Am I off-key?"

"No." I related the story.

"The kid had good taste."

"He had the worst breath."

"Should I chew a mint before we kiss?" He hesitated. "Perhaps that was presumptuous of me."

"I'm pretty sure we'll kiss before the night is over." I wasn't lying. I felt lighthearted for the first time in eons, and I was definitely attracted to my date. He had a quiet but strong presence. I felt adored by him. "If I recall correctly, my errant young suitor gave me a present that Christmas. I about freaked out when a frog leaped from the box. I think he was going for the frog-turns-into-a-prince metaphor, he being the hopeful frog."

"Did it work?"

"It failed miserably. I had no idea I could scream so loudly."

We laughed.

After a long, comfortable silence, Rhett said, "What was that, back at the store, about you needing to call Cinnamon?" So much for calm. Rhett's jaw worked back and forth waiting for my answer. I wished I could change Cinnamon's mind about him, but it wasn't my fight.

Not wanting to think about murder, or any crime for that matter, I said, "I don't want to talk about it, okay?" I switched the topic back to the present. "Who came up with the Lamp Lighting Night theme?"

"Mayor Zeller, the year after her husband died. She started the event as a night to focus on the future."

"You like her. I can tell."

"ZZ's a hoot. She never stops, that woman. She's always on the go, drumming up ideas to spark the economy. She's good for Crystal Cove. She makes it a destination place. Hey, look at that." He pointed at The Pelican Brief Diner. The entryway and front windows were outlined with blinking lights. A sandwich board sign stood in front with words written in chalk: *Warm Up Your Night with a Romantic Meal.* "Hungry?"

"Starved." I could go for my favorite fish sticks.

Beyond the diner, in front of Play Room

Toy Store, I spied Norah, Ellen, and her daughter. They were peering into the plate glass window, and no wonder. The toy store owner always created the most elaborate, good-humored displays. Norah held on to the handle of the stroller. Ellen's daughter was wiggling a pink baby doll animatedly at something in the window. Seeing the trio made me wonder if Ellen had heard from Willie. She looked pale and drawn. She was rubbing her arms briskly. Given her illness, why hadn't she worn her coat instead of a sweater? Norah said something; Ellen responded. As they chatted, the conversation with my aunt recycled in my mind. Was Ellen a victim or a manipulator? Did I need to be a high priestess on her behalf, or was she fully in charge of her own destiny?

As Rhett and I approached the diner's entrance, a blaze of flashing lights filled the street. Police cars. Three of them. Speeding toward us. No sirens. The first car came to a screeching halt beside the sidewalk, near Ellen. The other two lined up behind the lead car.

Cinnamon hurried from the passenger side of the lead car and approached Ellen and her family.

I broke free of Rhett's hold and raced forward.

He yelled, "Wait," but I didn't stop.

I pushed through the throng that had gathered around Ellen. She was tucked into herself and moaning. I asked one of the onlookers what was going on.

"Willie's dead."

A lump formed at the pit of my stomach. I snaked between a knot of onlookers until I reached the front of the group. The glow from the police car's interior light cast a greenish pall on Ellen's skin.

Cinnamon said, "He was found at the motel up the road."

Norah wrapped her arm around her sister and pulled her close. "How did you locate us?"

"My deputy is off tonight. She received an interoffice e-mail, spotted you, and sent me a message. Now, back away, everyone." Cinnamon raised her hands. "This is official police business."

The deputy who reminded me of a moose joined Cinnamon. He carried a handheld device and a digital-writing implement.

Ellen caught sight of me and called, "Jenna."

Cinnamon's gaze flew to Rhett and back to me. "What are you doing here?"

"We're taking in Lamp Lighting Night," I said.

Cinnamon's mouth turned down. If only I could change her mind about Rhett. Start fresh.

Focus, Jenna.

"What happened?" I asked.

"It's private," Cinnamon said.

"Please, Chief Pritchett." Ellen reached for me. "Let her stay. Willie . . . He called Jenna last night."

Cinnamon lasered me with another dismal look. Swell.

"He didn't leave a message," I said hastily. "I don't know why he called. It was odd, to say the least. What happened?" I moved closer to Ellen. She was shivering. "How did he die?"

Cinnamon ran her tongue across her teeth. "He was murdered."

Ellen gagged. Her hand flew to her mouth. "I knew it. I knew something horrible had happened."

Norah, who seemed as stunned as Ellen, eyed her niece. She crouched beside the girl and plucked the baby doll from her hands. Mean-spirited shrew, I thought, until Norah wiggled the doll in front of the girl's face to distract her. Norah played keep-away a tad longer, then handed the doll back. She sang the beginnings of "The Alphabet Song." Picking up where Norah left off, the girl crooned to the doll.

Norah rose and slung her arm around her sister again. "Willie has been missing since early Sunday."

Cinnamon arched an eyebrow. "Why didn't you report him gone?"

"Sam called the precinct," I said. "He was told that the police were 'on it,' but warned that missing adult cases are not taken seriously for forty-eight hours."

Ellen said, "Do you know who killed my husband? Or why?"

"No." Cinnamon assessed Ellen. "He was shot. Do you own a revolver, Mrs. Bryant?"

Ellen shook her head and clutched the collar of her sweater. She had been shivering before; now, she was downright quaking.

I felt awful for her. A friend at Taylor & Squibb, a freehand drawing genius, had lost her father to gun violence. Her art grew extremely aggressive. For two years, I begged her to seek help to guide her through the pain and the nightmares. Finally she agreed. She still went to support meetings as far as I knew.

"Your husband was shot at close range," Cinnamon went on. "We think it happened before midnight last night."

"You only just found his body?" I said.

"The motel manager called at three P.M. A maid discovered him. We've been working the case since then. The coroner thinks he died around nine P.M. last night."

"That isn't possible," I said. "He called me at ten."

"Why did he call?"

"As I said before, I don't know. He didn't leave a message. It had to have been a mistake. Perhaps a pocket call, though I can't understand why Willie would have entered my cell phone number into his directory. He's never telephoned me before."

Cinnamon addressed Ellen. "Where were you last night?"

Ellen hesitated. "I was out."

"The maid described a woman who looked like you at the motel," Cinnamon said. Her associate, the Moose, was taking furious notes. "She said the woman was wearing a knee-length black coat. You own a coat like that, don't you, Mrs. Bryant?"

"No," Ellen said. "I mean, yes. I do. I forgot it at the diner."

"No way could my sister have killed her husband last night," Norah blurted out.

"Why not?" Cinnamon said.

"She goes to meetings."

"What kinds of meetings?"

"FEW," Norah said spelling out an acronym. "Future Empowerment of Women."

I recalled my earlier estimation of Ellen, wondering why she hadn't dressed more warmly. She had been wearing the same sweater when I'd seen her at breakfast. Was her coat really in the diner, or was it at the dry cleaner's to remove blood? *Ick. Stop it, Jenna.* I didn't believe Ellen had killed her husband. I truly didn't.

Cinnamon regarded Ellen. "Your group meets on Sundays?"

Ellen nodded. "We convene twice a week, Sundays and Wednesdays, at a different member's house each time. Last night was at a woman named Yolanda's house. She's an ironworker. She sculpts out of her home. There were eight of us."

"Everyone at the meeting will vouch for my sister," Norah said. "She's been a member for the past year."

"How do you know so much about them?" Cinnamon asked.

"Because I was the one who encouraged her to go." Norah glanced at her niece and back at Cinnamon. "Let me start at the beginning. Ellen and I hadn't been in contact for a number of years, ever since our parents divorced. We found each other on a social networking site, and we became friends. She revealed, in some private messages, that her husband was . . ." Norah hesitated. "How should I put it? Cruel."

"Did he beat you, Mrs. Bryant?" Cinnamon said.

"No." Ellen shook her head. "He —"

"He bullied her in private," I cut in. "A pinch here, a poke there."

Ellen gawked at me. "You knew?"

"I had a hunch."

"I encouraged my sister to join FEW," Norah went on. "Willie was against it. I suggested she enroll in classes at the junior college, too. He told me to butt out, but how could I? Ellen doesn't want to be a waitress the rest of her life."

What money was Ellen using to pay for school? I wondered.

Norah drew her sister closer, and the thought occurred to me that Norah could have been the woman the witness had seen visiting Willie at the motel. Norah and Ellen looked so much alike, the narrow face, the pixie haircut. Had she donned her sister's coat and murdered her brother-in-law to free her sister from oppression?

Cinnamon must have noticed the similarity, too, because she said to Norah, "Where were you last night, Miss Mumford?"

"I was sitting Bebe." She nodded at Ellen's

313

daughter. "Around eight-thirty, she was feeling a little under the weather and started throwing up. We went to the emergency medical center. We were there until after ten."

A horrible notion made me queasy. Norah's previous job was in hospital administration. She probably had medical training. Had she deliberately made Bebe sick? Had Norah whisked her niece to the hospital and, afterward, when Bebe was groggy, had she swung by the motel where Willie was staying, left poor Bebe strapped in a car seat, and confronted Willie? Had she killed him and returned to the car in a matter of minutes? No, Willie was alive at 10:00 P.M. The timing of the whole thing made my head spin.

Timing.

"When did you arrive in Crystal Cove, Norah?" I said.

Cinnamon blazoned me with a look. I mirrored her. Questions had to be asked.

"Thursday, the day before the memorial," Norah answered. "Late."

"Did you take a red-eye from the East Coast?" I was testing her. Would she tell the truth?

"I wasn't on the East Coast. I was in Los Angeles."

"What were you doing in Los Angeles?"

"Jenna, cool it," Cinnamon said.

"It's all right," Norah replied. "I'll be glad to answer. I was at Hexagon Hospital headquarters." I knew of the company; it was a huge, nationwide organization. "I flew there to quit my job as administrator of the eastern division."

"You were in Los Angeles the day your mother died?" I said.

"Yes."

"Los Angeles isn't that long a drive from Crystal Cove, is it?"

Norah tilted her head. "What are you implying?"

"Did you plan to quit before hearing of your mother's death?"

Norah frowned, and then realization hit her. "Are you suggesting that I'm lying about resigning? That I cooked up the alibi so I could drive to Crystal Cove and kill my mother?" She blew out a stream of frustration. "Look, I've been planning to quit for months. You can ask my boss. In case you wish to check, she's been calling me ever since I quit, begging me to reconsider." Norah pulled her cell phone from her pocket, hit a button, and a list of messages from the same telephone number appeared on the face. Was that why she had stolen to the corner of the Word after the memorial, to return a call to her boss? She had seemed so sneaky, cigarette in hand, stabbing buttons on the phone. Norah turned to Cinnamon. "Are we through here?"

"No, we're not," Cinnamon said, now regarding Norah with suspicion. Perhaps she didn't appreciate Norah's testy tone. "Who saw you at the medical center last night?"

"At least three nurses, a doctor, and a number of patients."

"The maid said the woman had short hair," Cinnamon said.

"That could describe any number of individuals in town." Norah rubbed her fingers together as if she was desperate to get her hands on some calming nicotine.

I regarded her and her sister. Had they plotted together? Or had Willie, as Ellen theorized at the diner, simply been robbed because he'd had a wad of money on him? I wanted to believe Ellen was innocent.

"Willie was seen at the bank Saturday," I said. "Withdrawing a lot of cash."

Cinnamon eagle-eyed me. "Who says?"

"Bailey, who got it straight from her friend, the assistant bank manager. Someone might have seen Willie. Maybe that person followed him to the motel and mugged him."

"But why was he at the motel?" Ellen cried.

Cinnamon frowned. "Mrs. Bryant and Miss Mumford, I would like you to come to the station with me."

I knew that particular drill. Get finger-printed. Be questioned. Feel guilty. In Ellen's defense, I said, "Do they need a lawyer?"

Ellen, showing a hint of spine, stepped forward, her chin raised. "Do we?"

Cinnamon said, "Not yet, but it might be advisable."

CHAPTER 20

As Norah, Ellen, and Bebe were escorted to police cars, Cinnamon Pritchett sidled to me and whispered that I should go home and keep my distance. From whom? I wasn't sure. Was she referring to Ellen or Rhett? Sensing that she had meant the latter, I strode to Rhett, looped my arm through his and, rather than go to The Pelican Brief for dinner, invited him back to my place. Like a petulant teen, I made the offer loudly enough for Cinnamon to overhear. She didn't react. Perhaps I had been mistaken.

Rhett and I swung by The Cookbook Nook and retrieved my VW, and he followed me to the cottage. Before entering, we stopped at Aunt Vera's house to pick up Tigger. My aunt, who was decked out and wearing her favorite perfume, gave me a knowing wink. I blushed but winked back, which made her turn crimson. I didn't have the courage to ask if she was headed out on a date, but I guessed she was.

Minutes later, Rhett and I entered my cottage. The moment I closed the door and set Tigger on the floor, I felt a pinch of panic. Not because I was worried for my safety. Yes, another murder had occurred in our town, and a killer was most likely on the loose, but this feeling — this sensation — was personal. Something about going on a formal date with Rhett and inviting him into my home afterward made me feel as if I was betraying David. Call me crazy. *Dead husband, live man. You choose.* And yet my arms started to itch, and I couldn't stand still. Rhett, who picked up on my anxiety, ran a finger along my arm and suggested we take a stroll along the beach. The fresh air would do me good, he said.

We kicked off our shoes, slipped outside, and walked barefoot in the glow of a hazy moon. The crisp, cool breeze invigorated me. I pointed at a cluster of people playing with a glow-in-the-dark Frisbee by the shore.

"Let's join them," I said, eager to make new memories.

Rhett grabbed my hand. "You're on."

It never ceased to amaze me how hospitable people were in Crystal Cove. Without hesitation, the group welcomed us into their game. David and I had never encountered such friendly folks in Golden Gate Park. Rhett joined the guys; I teamed up with the women. A couple of times I had to race through the water to fetch a disk. We had a ton of fun. Near the end of the game, I found myself breathing heavily but freely.

When the game disbanded, Rhett and I ambled back to the cottage, arm in arm.

"I'm starved," he said as he opened the door and allowed me to enter first.

"I have the makings for a grilled cheese sandwich. Havarti melts well, doesn't it?"

"Like a dream. Do you have honey?"

"For tea."

"Bacon?"

"A fresh pack."

"Sit back and relax," Rhett said. "I'm going to make you a snack you won't forget."

Watching him move around my kitchen with such ease made me jealous. I wished my movements were as effortless. *Soon,* I thought. Maybe in a year or two. I was practicing new recipes daily. At times, Rhett had a way of tilting his head forward, as if his brain was locked in supreme concentration. The muscles in his back expanded and contracted as he sliced cheese or grilled bacon.

I set the table and poured each of us a glass of pinot noir. I preferred a light red wine with buttery cheeses.

"Voilà," he said as he set our plates on the table.

The first bite of my sandwich made me hum with satisfaction. The honey brought out the flavors of both the cheese and the charred-to-a-crisp bacon. "The Grill Fest competitors should be ecstatic that you're a judge and not one of them," I said. "The honey is inspired."

"Salt and sugar. Can't beat the combo. I've even added chocolate in one rendition." He dug in.

As we ate, we talked about little things. He had played soccer back in high school; I had dabbled in softball. He had skateboarded and snowboarded; I had roller-skated and skied. He liked long treks in the mountains; so did I. Bird-watching was a passion of his. Despite the many hikes I'd taken as a kid, I couldn't differentiate between a robin redbreast and a wren.

When we finished the meal, Rhett reached for me. He drew me toward him and ran the back of his hand down my cheek and along my jawline.

A quiver of desire spiraled through me until, out of nowhere, I flashed on David's face. Shoot, shoot, shoot. Now what? With great mental concentration, I hocus-pocused David's image away.

Rhett leaned in. So did I. We kissed, ever so gently. Then more firmly.

After a long, delicious kiss, I sat back with a grin on my face. "That was —"

Tigger, the imp, pounced into my lap and meowed. He rubbed his head against my chest.

Rhett laughed. "I guess you have a chaperone."

Tigger pushed off my thighs. He leaped onto the table, hopped across the placemat, and tiptoed toward the repaired Lucky Cat. If I'd been feeling guilty earlier about dating a new man, now I felt downright awkward.

"That figurine looks worse for wear," Rhett said.

I explained in brief detail how Tigger had decimated the statue. I even told him about the coins and the key. "I don't know why my husband did what he did, but I'm going to find out. It's the saying on the bottom that eats at me. *Everything will work out.* When? I'd like to move on, but —"

Rhett rubbed a thumb across the back of my hand. "Everything will work out, for you and your memories, as well as for us. Time is a great healer."

"What if it's too soon for us? What if we're not meant to be together?"

Rhett's eyes sparkled with intrigue. "Who knows the answers to those age-old questions? We'll take this one day at a time. You are something special, Jenna, and I want you in my life. I've never been so certain, in such a short time, about anything. I will be patient. Go solve this puzzle. Clear your head and your heart." He kissed my turned-up nose — a Hart family trait — and then helped me do the dishes. A total gentleman, he left without leaning in for another kiss. I closed the door and held on to the doorknob for an extra minute, my fingertips tingling with longing.

The next day, Tuesday, I awoke thinking of Rhett. Later, as I made coffee, I thought about Ellen. How had she endured the night at the police precinct? Had Cinnamon pried any more information from her or Norah? Had Cinnamon caught either of them in a lie?

I arrived at The Cookbook Nook with the same questions about the Mumford sisters rattling through my brain.

Bailey emerged from the stockroom. "Morning." Her eyes were bright; her skin had a healthy glow. She deposited a box of new books on the floor. "Whew. Just one more." She retreated to the stockroom and returned with the other. She set it beside the first.

"Why so chipper?" I said. "Did you cave and have a cup of coffee?"

"O ye of little faith. I'm still stimulant-free. This" — she drew an imaginary circle to indicate her face — "is the happy glow of contentment in my new city."

"You found an apartment?"

"A darling place. No more sounds of kitchen staff washing dishes in the diner at two A.M. I move in next week." She grew somber. "Hey, I heard about Willie's murder. I'm so sorry for Ellen, but his murder has to clear my mom, right?"

"Why?"

"Natalie's and his murders must be related. What's the possibility that two individuals from the same family would be killed within a week of each other? My mom has a solid alibi." Using an X-Acto knife, Bailey slit open one of the boxes. "What if Willie figured out who killed Natalie? What if he decided that, rather than turn in the killer, he could blackmail the fiend? You said Willie had an unpaid debt. He needed money." She pushed the opened box toward me with her foot and started in on the second.

I pulled open the flaps. "I'm worried for Ellen."

"Why?"

"She's got to be considered a suspect." I explained how Cinnamon had escorted Norah and Ellen to the precinct.

"If you want to find out what's going on, call the precinct or call Ellen."

"Or butt out."

"That's a third option."

"Let's not think about it for right now," I said. "We've got a lot to do before the third round of the Grill Fest starts." Inside my box was an assortment of dessert cookbooks. One caught my eye: *Sticky, Chewy, Messy, Gooey: Desserts for the Serious Sweet Tooth.* Yum. There was also a cluster of new culinary mysteries. The one about a caterer who cooked gourmet-lite food sounded like fun. "By the way, I'm sorry you had to come in today."

"*No problema.* You gave me the day off yesterday, which, in addition to finding my new apartment, turned out to be a glorious day."

"Why? Did you go paddle boarding?"

"Yes."

"With Jorge?"

She screwed up her mouth.

"*Verdad, amiga,*" I said. "Truth. Out with it."

"Aunt Vera!" Bailey shouted.

My aunt popped out from the stockroom. "What?" She gazed at Bailey, who planted her hands on her hips. Aunt Vera bit back a smile. "Busy. Sorry. Can't talk." She ducked back into the stockroom.

"Why wouldn't you tell me?" I rushed to Bailey and removed the X-Acto knife from her hand. "Because I'm your boss?"

"Because you'd tease me."

Okay, she was right. I would. She was dating a paddle boarder? Really? Did he say, *Hey, dude,* all the time?

"You'll ask me pointed questions," she added.

"I will not."

"Sure, you will. You're a snoop. You'll want to know his height, his weight, and the color of his eyes."

"Well?" I tapped my foot, waiting.

"Six foot two, brown eyes, one ninety. He's built." She patted her chest. "You know how I love a man's physique."

I did. She could wax poetic about the many Adonises she had met in her lifetime.

"You want to know about his family background?" she said. "Where he went to school?"

"Yes and yes."

"He didn't go to college in the States."

"No?" I did my best to rid my tone of judgment. I failed.

Bailey smirked. "Oh, he's educated. You know I need a man with a brain, but he's an émigré. His family lives in Mexico City. He went to university there. He's going through the United States' citizenship process."

"What did he study?"

"Engineering. He's working as a paddle board instructor to make ends meet. He earns good money. After he is granted citizenship, he's going to be hired by Lockheed. He's into physics, specifically aeronautics. Many companies are clamoring for scientists with dual citizenship. Did I tell you Jorge speaks five languages?"

I raised an eyebrow. When exactly did she think she had told me?

"All Latin-based languages," she went on.

"No English?"

"He's working on it. He's so clever."

Honestly, I was excited for my pal. I had never seen her gush over a man. The "one-night-stand queen," as she called herself, rarely got involved with anyone for more than a month, and I thought after her last fiasco, with the married man, she would cool her heels for at least a year.

"I want to meet him," I said.

"And you will. In time. We've only been dating a week. We can barely communicate."

I knuckled her upper arm. "I'm sure you've found other ways to connect" — hence the good color in her cheeks and the lilt in her step.

"Indeed. He's the best kisser."

I recalled my kiss with Rhett and was about to argue his merits, but I stopped as customers, eager for the Grill Fest to start, entered the shop. "I'm excited for you," I said. I truly was. "But we've got to set up. We'll talk more later, okay?"

While Bailey and I propped up folding chairs, Rhett, Mayor Zeller, and two of the contestants who had been eliminated last week entered. The baby-faced teacher appeared heartbroken. The long-limbed librarian prodded her pal to perk up. Mayor Zeller told them that next year's Grill Fest was going to focus on ribs. The teacher cooed with delight and reminded her buddy that both of them were barbecue goddesses.

The four remaining contestants entered the store as we wheeled out the portable cook stations. Lola seemed confident. Flora, equally self-assured, strode in behind her.

Pepper and Flora's beading chums accompanied her; all were chattering Flora's praise. Tito came in next and paused by the doorway as if expecting the audience to cheer his entrance. No one did.

Mitzi entered last, her hair tousled, her makeup slightly off. She teetered as she tossed her red coat and purse on the vintage table. Was she sick? I considered the theory that Katie, Bailey, and I had drummed up the other night, about Mitzi filling her water bottle with liquor. Maybe she was tipsy.

Before I could check on her, Mayor Zeller stood before the audience and invited the contestants to the kitchen to pick out their final items. Mitzi trailed the pack. Within seconds she returned, alone. She groped through her purse; I assumed she was looking for her recipe. Clearly frustrated, she hurled the purse away. She started toward the exit as if whatever she was seeking might be in her car. She stopped short of the door and pressed a hand to her chest. "He came," she said under her breath.

I followed her gaze. Her husband, Sam, who had arrived on a bicycle, was wedging his ten-speed into one of the slots of a bicycle rack. He secured it with a sturdy lock and hurried toward the shop.

When he entered, Mitzi threw her arms

around him and planted a solid kiss on his cheek, but then, as if she had been doused with ice water, she pulled something from his pocket and split apart from him. "What's this?" she said in a pitch meant for macaws. She brandished something that looked like a flyer. "Tell me."

Sam grabbed the paper. "A timetable." He reinserted it into his jacket pocket.

Mitzi snatched it back and opened it. "Liar. There's a ticket in here. To San Diego. Are you going to take a trip with *her*?"

Her *who*? I wondered. *Manga Girl? No way.*

"Babe, I'm going to San Diego for another money management conference. I have to stay current with the trends."

Battling tears, Mitzi said, "Why did you say it was a timetable?"

"You know how you get." He reached for her elbow. "Let's talk privately."

"I can't." Mitzi yanked free. "I'm late. Screw the makeup." She dashed toward the kitchen.

Sam's gaze flew from me to his wife and back to me. He shrugged. "She's nervous," he said as an apology. "She wants to win so badly. I —"

He halted, his attention snagged by Ellen entering the shop. She was clutching the

330

collar of her coat as if the temperature was close to freezing, which it wasn't. No daughter. No stroller. No handcuffs.

I moved to her. "How are you, Ellen? I'm assuming you're cleared since you're not at the precinct."

"I'm free, for now. The maid from the motel couldn't identify me from a lineup."

"And Norah?"

"She's watching Bebe."

That wasn't what I had meant. I'd wanted to know whether her sister was being held for more questioning. Norah had so much to gain from getting rid of not only her mother but also Willie.

"Find a seat," I said.

"Oh no. I can't stay for the contest. There's too much to do at the diner. I'm sorry to intrude. I had no idea that the contest would be going on today."

"You're not intruding," I assured her. "We haven't started."

"Good. I wanted to give you something as a thank-you for standing by me last night."

Sam joined us. "What happened last night?"

Ellen welled up. I couldn't imagine the anguish she was going through. Two loved ones lost in a week. "Willie didn't leave town, Sam. He was murdered."

Sam looked stunned. He reached for her hand. "What happened?"

Ellen spit out the main points. Sam hung on her every word. "Jenna was there when the police swooped in. She vouched for me. You were such a blessing, Jenna. I know Norah was there for me, too, but you offered a voice of reason to the chief. She listens to you."

I wasn't sure I agreed.

"To say thanks, I wanted to give you a few coupons to the diner, if that's okay." Ellen fished in her pocket and withdrew a clump of stuff: tissues, Post-its, coupons, and something else — a green cylinder. "What's this?" She held up a tube of lipstick. "Huh. Sassy Woman Red," she said, reading the label. "What a name. I guess somebody at work slipped it into my pocket."

"It's not yours?" I couldn't remember ever seeing Ellen wearing lipstick. ChapStick, maybe.

"Remember my coat was missing yesterday? I think one of the staff must have thought it was hers, put it on, and wore it home. Nobody confessed, but it was back on the hook when I went in this morning."

I glanced from the lipstick to Sam's face. Mitzi had kissed him, but she hadn't left a telltale lipstick mark. Mitzi never went anywhere without wearing bright red lipstick. I gazed at Mitzi's purse lying on the floor. Before rushing to the kitchen, she'd said, "Screw the makeup." Minutes ago, had she been searching for a tube of Sassy Woman Red lipstick? How had it wound up in Ellen's coat?

The reason exploded in my brain. "Mitzi," I said.

"What about her?" Sam asked.

Out loud, I scrambled to fill in the details. Mitzi had borrowed Ellen's coat. She was the woman the hotel maid had seen going into Willie's room.

"My wife does not have secret liaisons."

"No, Sam. I think she had another intention. Does she own a revolver?"

"You can't believe —" He inhaled sharply. "How dare you."

I realized Sam shouldn't be listening in on anything that I theorized about his wife, but I wasn't an officer of the law, and I couldn't slow down. I felt like I did whenever a great idea came to me at the advertising agency. Blabbermouth with Brains, Bailey had dubbed me. "What if Mitzi killed Natalie because she was jealous that you and Natalie were having an affair?"

"Natalie? What?" Sam sputtered. "We were talking about Willie."

I mentioned Bailey's theory that Willie must have figured out who had killed Natalie. "What if Willie was blackmailing Mitzi? He set an appointment at the motel to discuss terms."

"My wife couldn't have killed Natalie. She doesn't have a mean bone in her body."

I was pretty sure she did. She had thrown cheese at Lola. She had hurled curses at Natalie. Maybe she had a drinking problem and, therefore, had no recollection of what she had done.

"No, no, no." Sam's face turned three shades of purple. "She's innocent. Mitzi was home with me Sunday night. The entire night. She donned her mud mask at eight on the dot. It stays on for a full hour." He stabbed a finger to make his point. "Afterward, she removes it and devotes an hour to massage with a special cream. She's got this whole thing down to a routine."

"Sam —"

"I'm not lying to protect her. She was home. And while she was in the bathroom primping, I was calling around town searching for Willie. Everywhere. I called bars, restaurants. Ask anyone. Mitzi never left the house." He whirled on Ellen. "You're lying about the coat."

Ellen blanched. "No, Sam, I wouldn't."

"Maybe you're in league with your sister. I'll bet she's the mastermind. She blackmailed Willie. She told him to meet her at a motel where no one would recognize either of them. Willie agreed."

"No," Ellen said.

"Norah stole your coat," Sam continued, undaunted. "She put that lipstick in the pocket to frame my wife."

Ellen gasped.

"Or how about another scenario?" Sam said, his voice growing nasty and ominous. "Maybe the two of you killed your mother, and then you both conspired to do away with Willie."

"Why would they meet him at a motel?" I said. "Why not get rid of him at home?"

"I don't know. Because . . . because he was running scared. Because . . ." Sam splayed his arms. "None of this makes sense. Natalie dying. Willie dying. Any of it. All I know is that I will not have you accuse my wife of murder. This is not right. No matter how you spin it, I'm" — he sucked air through his nose — "ashamed of you, Ellen." Without another word, he pivoted and marched toward the kitchen.

Ellen sagged against me. Every ounce of her shook.

CHAPTER 21

I steadied Ellen and held her at arms' length. Her eyes grew misty. Customers in The Cookbook Nook started to stare.

"Let's get you some water." I ushered Ellen toward the hallway leading to the kitchen, popped a paper cup from the water cooler, and poured her a cupful.

Ellen slugged down the water. "Sam has never turned on me before, Jenna. He's always been supportive."

"Of course he's going to defend Mitzi, first and foremost. He's her husband."

"Whenever my mother criticized me" — Ellen hiccupped — "Sam took my side. He's been like a father." She began to weep. "I didn't kill my mother and husband."

"I know you didn't," I said as quarreling thoughts argued in my mind. Had she or hadn't she? Only her hairdresser knew for sure.

Ellen crumpled the water-cooler cup.

"You won't believe what Mitzi did this morning."

I said, "She came to the diner, am I right?"

Ellen's eyes widened.

"She needed to return your coat," I went on.

"No. That's not —"

"Mitzi was the one who borrowed it. She wore it to the motel."

"I didn't see her with the coat. You've got to be mistaken. What I was going to say is Mitzi cornered me in the kitchen and said she was interested in purchasing the diner."

"She wants to buy you out?" Granted, with Mitzi's wealth, she could afford to buy a lot of businesses, but why would she want to?

"Mitzi said she thought it would be good for Sam and her to own something together. She said that a couple that *cooks* together *sizzles* together."

From all indications, Mitzi and Sam's marriage was suffering. Mitzi had self-confidence issues. She worked hard on her looks. She worried that Sam was messing around with other women. She had blown a gasket when she found that ticket in Sam's pocket. Sam could deny, deny, deny and defend his wife as a knight should defend his ladylove, but why had he lied to Mitzi

337

about the ticket in his pocket?

"I can't believe this," Ellen said. "Mitzi
—"

"Hush." I put a finger over my mouth to caution her.

Mitzi and the other grill contestants were returning from the kitchen. Each carried a basket loaded with food items. They took their baskets to the portable cooking stations. Sam trailed the pack, giving Ellen a vile look as he passed.

When the mayor reintroduced the contestants to the audience, a notion came to me. What if it was true, and Mitzi did want to buy the diner? "Ellen, did Mitzi talk to your mother about purchasing the place?"

"I don't know. Mother never discussed business with me. She confided in Sam." Ellen sighed. "Willie would've been happy to sell. He said the diner would never help us build a nest egg."

"Didn't Sam mention yesterday that the diner's finances are in great shape?"

"Yes, but Willie . . ." Ellen fingered her hair. "You guessed right, Jenna. Willie and I were struggling financially. He didn't know how to cut back his spending habits. He is . . . was . . . a got-to-have-it-now kind of guy. He was always short on cash."

"I saw him arguing with a bank teller the

other day. Do you know what that was about?"

"He was probably asking for a loan. We have debt." Ellen gazed at her raggedy fingernails. "I was seriously considering Mitzi's offer —"

"Until Sam laid into you," I said.

"I don't think Mitzi has a clue what owning the diner could do to her marriage." Ellen's voice rasped with fatigue. "Ever since Mother died, Willie was angry and on edge. He . . ." The regret was clear. "If Mitzi wants it, I'll sell it. Good riddance," Ellen said with finality.

"Don't talk like that."

"I can't be a waitress forever."

"You're an owner now. That's much different. You have authority and prestige. What about your theme days? The scuttlebutt around town is how much fun everyone had at your Fifties Day event. You could do other decade themes. The Gay Nineties, the Roaring Twenties. Mitzi would never come up with these ideas."

"It's nice of you to try to cheer me up" — Ellen sniffed — "but it's not working. I'd better talk to Norah. We have to make plans. For a funeral. For —" She sank into herself. Her eyes filled with tears. "What am I going to tell our little girl? Willie wanted the world for her." She pulled her coat tightly about her and trudged out of the shop.

I returned to the Grill Fest and watched while Mitzi, her face flushed, dominated the event with her grilled cheese concoction as well as her foodie stories. The sandwich she had fashioned, made on cinnamon-swirl bread with Monterey Jack cheese oozing out the sides, won the votes of every judge based on visual appeal and flavor. By the end of the round, the judges ruled that Lola and Flora would be eliminated, and Tito, thanks to his zesty taco-style grilled cheese, would battle Mitzi for first prize.

Later that afternoon, The Cookbook Nook cleared of customers, and the contestants and judges — minus Rhett, who had urgent business to attend to at Bait and Switch — convened in the hallway to dine on cream cheese sugar cookies.

I spied Mitzi exiting the ladies' room. Though she had made it to the finals of the Grill Fest, she didn't look happy. Where had Sam gone? Had he slipped away before her name was announced? Mitzi teetered but steadied herself using the wall for balance, and then rummaged in her clutch purse. She pulled out a cell phone, dialed, and waited. When she didn't reach whomever she was calling, she hung up without leaving a message and jammed her cell phone back into her purse. Had she called her husband? Was she imagining him rolling around on a mattress with another woman? Had her suspicions and jealousy turned her into a murderer?

"Hey hey, everyone." Keller, carrying a sizeable brown ice cream vat on his shoulder, forged into the group. "Cold stuff coming through."

When Katie, who had been chatting up the mayor, caught sight of Keller, her cheeks flushed peppermint pink. She righted her toque and toyed with a few curls around her face. "Hi, Keller."

He grinned. "Where do you want this?"

"The usual place." She hitched a thumb.

"Got it." Keller strode into the café and made a hard left toward the kitchen.

I sidled up to my pal. "Aha. Your secret is out, and here I thought you made all your own ice cream."

"Whenever we have a run on a flavor, I call Keller. His ice cream is excellent. Today we ran out of fudge pecan swirl."

Quietly I sang, "Katie's got a boyfriend."

She swatted me.

"Go help him." I gave her a push.

She resisted. "No. Stop it. He'll be back."

And he was, in seconds. He walked with big loping strides. Without a vat of ice cream balanced on his shoulder, he reminded me of a gigantic puppy — big paws, floppy hair, sweet, soulful eyes. "Did I scare the folks away?" He laughed in his charming, yuk-yuk way.

"You didn't scare everyone away." Katie tittered.

During the time Keller had gone to the kitchen, Lola, Flora, and the mayor had departed. Pepper was doing her best to clandestinely snitch the last few cookies off the tiered tray. Mitzi was having a heated discussion with Tito, who was twirling his keys around his index finger and looking like he wished he could split without being rude. Watching the keys go round and round made me think briefly of the key David had given me. Tito was a reporter. Could my key fit a reporter's desk? No, David hadn't been a writer; he had hated writing anything, even a grocery list.

"Where's your amazing bicycle, Keller?" Katie said, stressing the word *amazing*.

I was tempted to roll my eyes at her but stopped. Who was I to judge her flirtation skills? I wasn't very good at the social sport myself. *Practice, practice, practice.*

"It's right out there," Keller said. "Don't

you see it on the sidewalk?" He yuk-yukked again.

Pepper whirled around and gave him the evil eye. "You." She must have recognized his distinctive laugh. She bounded toward him while jabbing a finger. "How many times have I told you, young man —"

"Not to park my bicycle near your shop," Keller finished.

"That's right. It's an eyesore."

"Sorry, ma'am."

"C'mon, Pepper," I said, using the tone my aunt employed whenever she needed to rein in Pepper. "He's a capitalist. You like businessmen."

"Door-to-door high jinks like his reflect badly on the community."

"They do not. They show the younger generation of Crystal Cove that not everyone needs a four-year degree to be successful."

"Bah," Pepper muttered.

Bah yourself, you sourpuss, I wanted to say, wishing I could inject her with a happy serum. Was there a five-ingredient recipe for something like that? Why didn't Pepper understand how entrepreneurs were good for our town? We had a slew of craftsmen in Crystal Cove: knitters, potters, bakers, and artists. Keller's mother, although she adored her son, hadn't been able to help him with college finances, so after high school, Keller had worked days and attended the junior college at night, taking basic economics classes. The day he graduated, he purchased his ice cream–making bicycle. The next week, he opened his alfresco business and became an instant hit. *Novelty,* as my first boss said, *cannot be purchased. Promoting novelty is a requirement of citizenship.*

"It's okay, Jenna," Keller said. "I don't need you to fight my battles." He removed his baseball cap and addressed Pepper. "I'm really sorry if I'm being a nuisance, ma'am. I wanted to stop in and say hi to Chef Katie."

Katie uttered a teensy peep. Her peppermint-tinted cheeks flushed strawberry red.

"I'll be moving the bike in three shakes of a lamb's tail," he went on. "Thanks so much for understanding. If I can make it up to you, I'd be glad to stop by Beaders of Paradise later this week and bring you your favorite ice cream. What is it, by the way?"

Pepper grew calm, as though someone had put her into a trance. "Dark chocolate," she said in a soft, girlie voice.

"Done. With an extra dose of chocolate."

Pepper nodded politely, then exited.

Shocked and thrilled, I glanced over my shoulder, fully expecting to see my aunt stroking her amulet. She wasn't there. Hmm. Had I somehow inherited her gift of persuasion? *Abracadabra.* A girl could get used to that kind of mental power.

"Who moves to the next round?" Keller said. "I assume Spa Lady will."

"Spa who?" I said.

Keller hitched his chin toward Mitzi, who was still lighting into Tito. "About a week ago, I saw her running out of the spa. You know the one." He did a hula-type move with his hips.

"The Permanent Wave Salon and Spa?" I said. A month ago, I'd had the luck to become personally familiar with the place.

Keller nodded. "That's it. Spa Lady — what's her name?"

"Mitzi," I offered.

"Yeah, she looked so ridiculous. She had on this terry cloth robe and turban." His fingers drew a coil above his head. "And a blue mask." He dragged his hand in front of his face.

I'd bet he was great at playing charades: *Two words. First syllable.*

"She was flagging me down as if her life depended on it. She caught up to me right in front of The Pelican Brief Diner. She

345

wanted ice cream. Rocky road. Tons of almonds. It's my best seller. I scooped her a cone, but it was a warm day. When chocolate started dripping all over her, she went nutty — forgive the pun — worried that the spa would be mad that she'd soiled their robe, so she rushed into The Pelican Brief Diner to clean herself off." He shook his head.

"She likes to keep up her appearance," I said.

"You're telling me. She's got a real thing for body stuff, because a couple of days later, I saw her heading into the tanning salon."

"The Golden D'or."

Keller tapped his nose as if I had guessed the right charades answer. "That was the day Willie caught up with her."

"Willie?"

Keller stroked his jaw. "Come to think of it, Willie was steaming. He accused Spa Lady of something. She yelled, 'How dare you.' Willie said something back. I could only hear Spa Lady because she was facing my direction. She said, 'You're loco!' Willie made a money gesture." Keller showed us by rubbing his thumb against his fingers. "Spa Lady hauled back. She almost slapped him, but she didn't. Like this, you know?" Keller demonstrated.

Katie, who was hanging on his every word, said, "What happened next?"

"Spa Lady huffed and went into The Golden D'or. Willie hesitated for a second, like he was making up his mind whether to go in after her."

"Did he?" Katie said.

"Yep. He entered. Seconds later, he exited looking pleased with himself."

I gazed at Mitzi, who had finished with Tito and was leaving the shop. Was Bailey's assumption correct? Had Willie accused Mitzi of killing Natalie? Had he blackmailed Mitzi and set a meeting at the motel? Was Keller's eyewitness account of Mitzi and Willie's confrontation enough for Cinnamon to bring Mitzi in for questioning?

I said, "You need to talk to Chief Pritchett, Keller."

"Why?"

"What you have to say might pertain to the murder of Willie Bryant."

"But my ice cream will melt."

"No *but*s. It's your civic duty." I ushered him to the sales counter and dialed the precinct. When I reached the clerk, she said Cinnamon was out on a call. There had been a crisis at the beach. A Frisbee player had accidentally on purpose hurled a Frisbee into another player's nose. The clerk

asked if I wanted to leave a message. I
didn't.

Instead, I ordered Keller to go to the
precinct. I offered to pay for any ice cream
sales he might lose. Good soul that he was,
he declined my offer.

CHAPTER 22

After the shop cleared, we removed the portable cooking stations and set the shop back to its normal layout. All the while, I kept hoping Cinnamon Pritchett would call to say, thanks to Keller's statement, she had finally solved the murders. The call never came.

Toward the end of the afternoon, we had a fresh influx of customers. Product was moving faster than ever: grilling books, gift items, and recipe holders. A few women detained me and asked for my expert advice on cooking a grilled cheese sandwich.

Me? Advice? I panicked. "Um, extra cheese," I said, riffing. "It's called a grilled *cheese.*"

One of the women thought I was the cleverest person in the world. Ha! Fooled her.

When the shop closed, I hurried to Katie and said, "Cooking lessons. Now." Although we had accommodated the mayor and kept The Cookbook Nook open for the competition, we hadn't opened the café. It was mine, all mine. "Make me bold, Katie. Confident. No fear. I want to be an expert chef by Thanksgiving. Got me?" When I set my mind to something, I could be relentless.

"You're on." Katie nabbed two cookbooks and went to the kitchen.

Bailey joined us. "I'm in, too. What are we making?"

Katie lodged the cookbooks into a pair of antique bronze book holders on the counter, then handed each of us hairnets, latex gloves, and aprons. "We're going to attempt eggplant-and-Parmesan soup and a Caesar BLT salad."

"That's bold? That's confident?" I said, donning my kitchen garb.

"It's delicious and challenging." Katie gathered eggplants, mushrooms, herbs, and shredded Parmesan from the refrigerator and set them beside one of the many wood butcher blocks. The recipe she was using came from an all-soup book called *New England Soup Factory Cookbook: More Than 100 Recipes from the Nation's Best Purveyor of Fine Soup*. From accounts online, there were two Soup Factory restaurants, both located in Massachusetts, both very popular.

Katie named Bailey soup sous-chef; I was put in charge of the salad.

"That will make me fearless?" I said.

Katie chuckled. "Never question the chef. First, you need to learn to wield a knife with flair. Fetch the ingredients for your salad, and then start chopping tomatoes. Use the serrated knife. Bailey, get the white wine, leeks, and homemade stock."

Bailey saluted. "Aye, aye, O, Captain, my Captain."

I threw Bailey a sardonic look. "You do know that's a line from a Whitman poem about Abraham Lincoln's death, don't you?"

"Yes, but . . . Oh, for Pete's sake. I was honoring Katie." Bailey sashayed to the refrigerator. "Don't tell my mother, but I like Katie's food better than my mom's chef's food."

I flashed on the chef whose resignation had ignited a firestorm of resentment between Natalie and Lola. Luckily for him, he had a good alibi for the day Natalie was murdered. I said, "Did you know your mother has threatened to steal Katie away?"

"She wants to steal me?" Katie said, apparently learning for the first time of Lola's interest. "I won't go."

"Of course you won't. I won't let you."

"Are you going to double my salary to keep me?"

"Not quite yet."

Katie chuckled. "It was worth a try. Don't worry. I'm sticking around for a long time. I love the café. It's my baby."

I set up my station with items for three Caesar BLT salads: lettuce wedges, avocados, tomatoes, hard-boiled eggs, already-cooked bacon, and blue cheese. While I was chopping tomatoes, Katie brought a bowl of ice water and placed it beside the lettuce wedges.

"What's my secret to great salads?" Katie said and didn't wait for a response. "Glad you asked. Prepping the greens properly. Now, Jenna, take the lettuce and dunk them in that ice bath I've prepared." She pointed to the bowl. "Don't over-handle them, or the lettuce will wilt. Simply agitate them a bit. Hoo-boy." She patted her abdomen. "Am I ever hungry. I couldn't cook like this at home. Papa would grumble and moan. Plain meat and potatoes for him." Katie's father was not the most sympathetic man in the world. Recently I'd learned that he had verbally abused Katie her entire life, calling her ugly and worthless. She was neither.

"Where will I find chicken breasts?" I said.

"In the refrigerator. Second shelf from the

bottom. Grab three eggs, as well."

I fetched the chicken breasts and, following Katie's lead, dipped the pieces in egg and then rolled each in seasoned flour. Next, tentatively — I had never fried anything before, and hot oil doesn't look all that friendly — I set the dredged chicken in a basket. *No fear, no fear.* I lowered the basket into a vat of bubbling canola oil and quickly moved back.

"Eight minutes," Katie said.

I was more than willing to be patient. There wasn't an oven mitt long enough to make my arm feel protected from hot oil. "Why does the oil have to be scalding?" I asked.

"Oil has to be hot enough to seal the outside of whatever you're cooking. If not, the food will absorb the oil." As Katie chopped up eggplant, she said, "Butter is different. We want the onion slices to absorb the butter."

Bailey sautéed the onions until they were brown, and then she slowly added the eggplant and herbs. "Jenna, any word on what your mysterious key fits?"

"No." I told them about my failed Internet search yesterday for a matching key shape. Since then, I hadn't had a moment to breathe, let alone do another search. I pictured Tito twirling his ring of keys, and although I had ruled out the key fitting the lock on a desk, I wondered if it might open an office door or a file cabinet. "I'll think about it tomorrow."

"Okay, Miss O'Hara," Bailey teased, referring to the literary Scarlett O'Hara's infuriating procrastination.

"I will. Promise. I just have bigger things on my mind."

"Bigger than the puzzle your husband left you?"

"Bigger, as in another person in town is dead and Ellen Bryant might be the police's main suspect."

"Don't you think Mitzi killed both victims?" Katie asked.

"Honestly, I don't know."

Katie hitched her chin at Bailey. "Toss in the leeks and mushrooms. Stir with a wooden spoon."

"I hope my mother is off the hook," Bailey said.

I hoped so, too. Why wasn't Cinnamon Pritchett being more forthcoming? I filled Bailey in about the fight Keller had witnessed between Mitzi and Willie. She laughed at the idea of Mitzi out in public, wearing only a salon robe and blue cream on her face. Next, I recapped Mitzi's flare-up with Sam at the shop, my suspicion that Mitzi had borrowed Ellen's coat, and Sam's verbal assault on Ellen.

"What about Ellen's sister, Norah?" Bailey said. "You don't trust her. What if she's framing Mitzi? What if" — she held up a hand — "and I know this is a reach, but what if Norah is the one lacing Mitzi's drinking water to make her appear tipsy and off balance?"

I said, "Don't you think Mitzi, if she's not a drinker, would have noticed something was different about her water?"

"Vodka doesn't smell."

"But it has a taste," I countered. "And how would Norah have gained access to the water? She wasn't here for the first round of the contest."

"Are you sure?"

I wasn't. Again I wondered whether Norah could have driven up from Los Angeles, sneaked into the alley, and killed her mother with no one the wiser.

Bailey continued. "Are you sure she re-signed her job as a hospital administrator?"

"Why would she lie?"

"To make herself seem vulnerable. Maybe she never intended to run the diner with her sister. Perhaps she put the bug in Mitzi's ear to buy the Word. Once the court settles her mother's estate and Norah gets the cash from the sale of the diner, she'll hotfoot it out of town."

I considered that possibility. "Norah said her boss was begging her to come back. She showed me her call list. There were tons of calls."

"Red or black numbers?"

"Red."

"What kind of phone does she have?"

"An iPhone."

"Same as me. Those are outgoing calls, not incoming. A technicality, I know, but it might matter." Bailey left her post and plucked a piece of blue cheese off one of the salads.

"Bailey Bird," Katie snapped. "Never, never —"

Bailey held up a hand. "Don't worry. I wouldn't touch food headed for customers, but that plate isn't going anywhere, and we're friends, right?"

Katie chuckled. "Yes. Forgive me. I'm in chef mode. I'm telling you, you do not want to hear restaurant horror stories. Chefs worry all the time about contamination and the like. If something happens to a customer, whether they get sick or hurt, the insurance claims can be ginormous."

"She's right," I said. "I don't want to think

356

about the financial consequences if we didn't have insurance coverage."

"Money, money, money." Bailey resumed stirring. "It's always about money. Back to Norah. What is the value of the Word? Would she make out like a bandit if it were sold?"

I said, "Ellen told me the diner wouldn't make them rich."

"That's if they held on to it," Bailey said, "but I keep thinking about what Flora said when we talked to her at Home Sweet Home. She saw Sam chatting up Manga Girl at the bank, right? What if he wasn't having an affair with her?"

"He wasn't. You saw her canoodling with that guy at B-B-Q the other night when we went line dancing. They looked hotter than hot."

"Exactly. So what if Sam was at the bank trying to secure a loan so he could purchase the Word? What if he, not his wife, asked Natalie to sell? Sam did the books. He would know if the diner is a cash cow."

"Ellen said Willie told her that the diner was sucking money like a Hoover."

Katie cleared her throat. "Ahem. Willie got kicked out of college for cheating on an economics test. I'm not sure if he could add two plus four."

"Willie met with the teller, as well," Bailey said. "He might have been asking the same questions we're posing."

I thought about the fight Keller had witnessed between Willie and Mitzi on the street. What if Willie had figured out that Sam wanted to purchase the diner? Then Willie told Mitzi, and she yelled, "You're loco!" Had Mitzi approached Ellen simply to find out if Sam had made an offer?

Katie said, "Jenna, you mentioned Manga Girl to Chief Pritchett, right?"

I honestly couldn't remember if I had. I had told Cinnamon that Willie had cleaned out his bank account the day he died. I wondered if she was following up on that lead.

Bailey tapped her temple. "If you ask me, that bank teller is the key to all of this, and yet —"

Crash! Glass shattered. Then more glass.

CHAPTER 23

Heart battering my ribcage, I whipped off my oven mitts, grabbed a carving knife, and raced out of the kitchen toward the café. The waitress at the Word had warned me to pay more attention to security. Had looters broken in? I paused at the end of the passageway, where the busboy trays hid from the diners' view. Katie and Bailey joined me, each armed. I signaled for them to become still, and I peeked around the edge of the partition. The overhead lights in the café were dim. The lights on the patio gleamed a warm, tawny yellow. I didn't see movement. I glanced in the other direction, toward the breezeway. The flower vase and preset glasses on a table for two were tipped over. The window beyond the table was intact. Store interior lights were on at Beaders of Paradise. I eyed the second floor of Fisherman's Village. Lights were on in Surf and Sea, as well. There were a few cars in the parking lot, and a nicely dressed couple was exiting a Mercedes.

Feeling braver because of the normalcy of the activity outside, I said, "Stay here," then I stepped from my hiding place. "Who's out there?"

A blur of orange raced at me. Tigger. He yowled at the top of his lungs, then dashed under a table.

"Kitty?"

Another meow.

"It's okay," I said to Katie and Bailey. "It's Tigger." No wayward teens. No burglar with a firearm.

I set the knife in the busboy tray and hurried to capture the cat. He eluded me numerous times, darting beneath tables and circling the legs of chairs. I almost had him when my head snagged on a tablecloth. As I backed out on hands and knees, the cloth and the entire setting came with me. More glass hit the floor. "Dagnabbit," I said loudly.

Bailey and Katie laughed.

"Don't," I warned.

After two more attempts, I nailed Tigger as he scurried down the hall, heading for the bookshop. "Gotcha, you little scamp." I held him high, his face meeting mine, my thumbs wedged beneath his forearms. "Did you think I'd forgotten you?" His plaintive eyes widened. *Yes.* He was right. I had. I was a terrible mother. Angst coursed through me. I tucked him close to my chest and nuzzled my chin into his fur. "I'm sorry. I've been so preoccupied. Forgive me." I took him into the stockroom and checked his food. Empty. More guilt. More apologies. When he was settled and I felt sure he knew I hadn't abandoned him, I cleaned up the mess our game of chase had made, and I returned to the kitchen.

"Back to Manga Girl," Bailey said as if we hadn't been so rudely interrupted.

I washed my hands. "Hey, guys. Maybe we shouldn't be obsessing like this." I meant what I said. My stomach was in knots. My heart, though calmer, hadn't returned to a moderate beat. I almost felt as if talking about murder was drumming up bad karma. Had Tigger picked up on it? "We aren't professionals. Crystal Cove has a solid police force with a savvy chief."

"You're wrong," Bailey argued. "We should be talking and theorizing." Using a Belgian accent à la Hercule Poirot, she added, "It keeps our little grey cells working. And lest you forget, this is our town. We want it to be a safe haven. And we need to exonerate my mother. Right?" She thumped the counter.

Her fervor reignited mine. "Right." So what if my insides were roiling? I had an obligation. "Back to Manga Girl."

Bailey rapped the counter a second time. "Good. Now, what if she is serving a dual purpose? What if she is arranging Sam's loan as well as having an affair with him?"

I thought of the ticket Mitzi had snatched from Sam's pocket earlier. She'd demanded to know if he was going away with *her.* Had she meant Manga Girl? I couldn't picture the bank teller throwing over her cute Asian boyfriend for a weathered man like Sam, but love, as Sam had reminded me at the memorial, could be blind.

Katie cleared her throat and fussed with her apron. "Um, Jenna, based on something you said while we were line dancing, I've been doing some digging on Sam." She held up her latex-covered hands as if under arrest. "Okay, I admit it. I'm a glutton for gossip. I wanted to know more about him, especially after Mitzi's meltdown at the grocery store last Thursday. You said that she adored Sam too much. I wanted to know why. I mean, he's not that special to look at. His nose is too thick, his forehead too high."

"He's got nice eyes," Bailey said.

"They're narrow and beady."

"Crinkly," Bailey countered.

I said, "I think he's sort of handsome in an aging-television-detective kind of way, and he seems engaged in the lives of those he loves."

"However, he hasn't been very supportive of Mitzi at the Grill Fests," Bailey countered.

"Today he was."

"Not really," Bailey said. "He left early again."

"Why did Mitzi marry him?" Katie asked. "She has oodles of money. She doesn't need him for financial reasons."

"Maybe he's good in the sack," Bailey said.

I laughed. "Maybe he's hypersexual, and that's why he's having affairs."

"Pfft." Katie waved us off. "If I were going to have an affair with a married man, I'd want him to be super hot."

"Super hot doesn't always mean good in bed," Bailey said.

"Keller isn't super hot," I noted. "He's charming, don't get me wrong —"

"I wouldn't have an affair with him," Katie said.

"You wouldn't?" Bailey and I chimed together.

"To be specific, you have an *affair* if one of the partners is married. Otherwise, it's called a relationship. *That*" — Katie held up a finger — "I would have with Keller. He's so . . ." She wriggled with enthusiasm. "But I'm straying." Using a teaspoon, she tested the soup, then tossed the teaspoon into a discard cup. "Mm, good. Anyway, I was chatting up one of Mitzi's best friends, the gal who runs The Enchanted Garden, and I got the inside scoop."

I knew the garden center, with its decorative arbors, eclectic garden art, and rows of perennial plants. It was a mini-wonderland. I had my eye on a wrought-iron, dragonfly-shaped wind chime.

Katie continued. "This gal knows Mitzi real well. The two are in a garden club together. Mitzi buys all her potted herbs from her. She was a fount of information. She revealed that, prior to moving to Crystal Cove, Sam managed a few businesses in San Francisco. They all failed. Sam lost a job at a big firm because of those mistakes, but money guys land on their feet, she said, and Sam was no exception. Another company hired him in a matter of months, the kind of firm that dismantles other companies."

"Like that guy in *Pretty Woman.*" Bailey snapped her fingers. "Richard Gere. I saw the movie multiple times."

"Didn't that come out when we were, like, seven?" I said.

"So? I belonged to a Richard Gere fan club. I saw all his movies."

"He did some edgy films," I said.

"My mother didn't know. Talk about Mr. Gorgeous. I would definitely have an affair with him. I don't care how old he is."

Katie clicked her fingers. "Yoo-hoo. Back to Sam. That's how he met Mitzi. One of her father's businesses, a lumber company, did well from the dismantling. Mitzi was running the place at the time."

I gaped. "Mitzi was a corporate woman? But she's got a thriving home business."

"Like the three of us, she had a previous career," Katie said. "When her father passed away, she inherited a gazillion bucks, so she gave up the corporate lifestyle to marry Sam, who, my garden lady friend confided, Mitzi claims is her soul mate."

"Why did they move to Crystal Cove?" I asked.

"I'll bet Sam instigated it," Bailey said. "He probably had to escape a bad reputation in the city."

"Nope." Katie wagged her head. "Mitzi made the determination. She wanted fresh air and no more corporate offices. She thought Sam would thrive as a financial consultant in a smaller community. As resourceful as she is, she knew she could build a business here."

Bailey sniggered. "I'll bet she wanted to wrangle him out of the city so he wouldn't have a bevy of gorgeous women from which to choose."

"We have lots of beautiful women in Crystal Cove," I said.

"Of course," Bailey conceded. "Just not as many."

As we continued preparing dinner, a string of what-if questions cued up like line dancers in my mind. Walk, walk, walk, *clap*. What if Sam resented Mitzi's bossy ways? *Clap.* What if he had hoped to revive his career in San Francisco, but because of her immense wealth, she held sway? *Clap.* What if he were having affairs to retaliate? *Clap.* Sam had gone to the bank and signed some kind of official papers. Why? Something wasn't adding up. What was I missing?

Katie said, "Bailey, ladle up three bowls of soup. Jenna, open the bottle of chardonnay, and pour us each a glass."

As Bailey and I obeyed, Bailey said, "What's going on in that brain of yours?"

I shared my muddled thoughts.

Bailey said, "Maybe Sam wanted to purchase Mum's the Word to prove to his wife he could run a business all by himself. Maybe he was under-stimulated in itty-bitty Crystal Cove. That could be why he is having affairs, too."

"If, indeed, he's having affairs," I argued. "Which brings us back to motive. We know what Mitzi would have gained from Natalie's death: the demise of a rival not only in the Grill Fest competition but also in the bedroom. What would Sam have gained?"

"Easier access to Natalie's daughters, so he could purchase the Word," Bailey said.

"What if he and Natalie weren't having an affair?" I cut off the protective seal from the wine bottle, set the automatic corkscrew over the top, and levered out the cork. "What if Natalie had evidence of Sam having other affairs and threatened to tell Mitzi? *Loose Lips Might Sink Ships,* as the old war posters claimed. Her death assured her silence."

"Jenna, it's time to remove the basket of chicken from the hot oil," Katie ordered. "Put on an oven mitt and carefully lift it out. Drain it over the vat to the right. Then arrange the lettuce on plates and top with all the other fixings."

As I followed orders — without fear, I might add — I recalled that day on The Pier

367

when Natalie had argued with Lola. Natalie had flirted with Sam. She had toyed with her hair and talked to him sweetly. And he had flirted in return. But then Natalie had turned icy cold. She had been a study in fluctuating emotions. "Here's another option: What if Natalie was in love with Sam, but he didn't reciprocate that love? What if she was pressing him to end his marriage?"

Bailey bobbed her head. "He worried that, if Mitzi found out, he would lose his meal ticket."

"Except she's not his meal ticket." I transferred the drained basket of chicken to the cutting board. "He has his own income."

"The question is, how much? You heard Mitzi and Sam at the grocery store. Mitzi gives him a food allowance."

"You don't know that. They could simply have a budget for each month. He does the home shopping; she does the purchasing for her business."

Bailey set bowls of soup on serving dishes. "They live in that fabulous house near your dad's. Sam drives a Mercedes. He wears expensive suits. Do you think he can afford all that on a business manager's salary? He makes, what, five percent per client? It's not like he's business manager to the stars."

"He has a couple of very wealthy clients,

and Mitzi said he invests."

"Didn't she also confide that he is invariably out of cash?"

"Jenna, I'll handle the chicken," Katie said. "You arrange the salads." With bare fingers, Katie removed the chicken from the basket. She set it on a cutting board and, using a super-huge blade, sliced the meat into long narrow strips.

I winced. If I'd touched the hot chicken they way she was, I would have been shrieking. Could I ever become as comfortable as she was in a kitchen?

"What kind of financial manager loses all his cash?" Bailey asked.

"The kind that messes up." I assembled three salads with avocado, crumbled blue cheese, diced hardboiled egg, and bacon on top of the lettuce, and proudly presented them to Katie.

Acting unimpressed — a chef rarely compliments, Katie said — she topped the salads with sliced chicken and then drizzled each with homemade Caesar dressing. She handed me finished plates. "Take the salads to the dining room. I'll be right there."

I did as instructed.

Bailey followed me, carrying the soup. "Those conferences Sam attends aren't cheap."

"Perhaps Mitzi covers all of those expenses and expects something in return," I said.

"Fealty or sex?"

"Both."

"Face it," Bailey said. "Mitzi already suspects Sam of having an affair, but she hasn't kicked him out. She loves him no matter what. For an attractive woman with tons of money, she's very insecure."

I set the salads at three place settings. "Women can be needy, even when looks, brains, and cash are in place." I'd seen it happen before. A woman I knew in the city, who was a ten in every way, discovered her husband was having an affair and became insanely jealous; her self-confidence floundered. She sought professional help. She even tried hypnotherapy, but nothing worked. In the end, she believed she would never be worthy of love again.

"The trail keeps leading back to jealous Mitzi," Bailey said. "I think she killed Natalie."

But we had no proof. Zip. Nil.

CHAPTER 24

At 10:00 P.M. I drove home, feeling fuller than a stuffed pigeon. Katie had insisted we make double chocolate soufflés with warm fudge sauce using a recipe she'd found in a magazine; a week ago, Bailey had suggested we stock a few foodie magazines like *Taste of Home* and *Simple & Delicious*. Our customers were reliably adding those to their purchases. Brilliant.

As I maneuvered the roads, theories skittered through my brain like pinballs, each one hitting a target and plunging toward the game's drain, only to be batted back into the field by mental flippers. I used to love playing pinball. My father was a pinball-machine collector; he had packed his den with game units. I remembered when he purchased Indiana Jones: The Pinball Adventure. Though I was primarily a reader, a girl needed silly downtime, too, and the gold and black colors and the *slam-*

bang-ping sounds of the pinball machine hooked me. It didn't hurt that, throughout the game, hunky Indiana Jones was staring straight at *me,* a gawky, boy-crazed preteen.

Ping. Who had killed Natalie? In my mind, Mitzi was the prime suspect. She had motive, opportunity, and she was loony enough to have killed on impulse. *Ping. Ping.*

Had Mitzi killed Willie? She could have donned Ellen's coat. The lipstick in the pocket was a clue. *Ping. Ping.* Score.

It dawned on me that maybe the Mumford family ought to fear other attacks. Did Mitzi intend to do away with the whole clan? *Ping. Ping.* Drain. Start over.

A mile from home, Tigger mewed in his travel cage. I said, "Almost there, buddy. Be patient."

Seconds later, my telephone chimed. I had received a text. At the first stoplight I reached, I glimpsed the phone, which was lying faceup on the passenger seat. Bailey had arrived home safely. I would never text while driving, so a response would have to wait, but I was relieved. My pal, a lightweight when it came to drinking, had imbibed an extra glass of wine while we cleaned and put away the dishes at the café.

A half mile later, something niggled at the edge of my mind. I eyed the cell phone again, and a new thought struck me. Bailey remembered hearing a *ping* sound right before the break at the first Grill Fest. She said Natalie glanced at her cell phone, even though Natalie was in cooking-combat mode, ready to defend her title and defeat the other contestants. What had she received: text, e-mail, or voice mail? Who would have dared interrupt her? On more than one occasion, Mitzi had caught Sam texting Natalie. She'd worried that Sam was having an affair with Natalie. He swore that his texts were about business, but what if they weren't?

I conjured up a possible scenario for the day of the murder. Sam texted Natalie to say he would hook up with her in the alley outside the café's kitchen. Natalie, who I was certain had interest in Sam, given the girlish albeit snappish behavior she had exhibited that day on The Pier, would have gotten a thrill out of duping Mitzi. Except Sam had not been in town at the time of the murder. He had attended a money-management conference. Or had he? What if he hadn't gone? I recalled the conversation with Flora at Home Sweet Home. She claimed to have seen Mitzi spying on Sam at the bank late on the afternoon of the murder. What if Sam had returned to town during the Grill Fest? Maybe he never left Crystal Cove in the first place.

I fashioned a new scenario with Sam, not Mitzi, as the murderer. He was a detail-oriented guy. He purchased a spot at the money management conference to establish an alibi, but he didn't go. Then he texted —

No, he wouldn't have needed to text Natalie. He knew her well. He would have known she would sneak away to have a cigarette. He could have laid in wait.

But what if he *had* texted her? What might he have written? That he was ready to throw aside Mitzi for Natalie, and he was coming back to town to see her. If Mitzi caught sight of the text, she would have gone berserk and —

On the other hand, what if Sam texted something entirely different? What if he wrote that he didn't want anything to do with Natalie? He begged her to steer clear of him, saying he didn't want to jeopardize his marriage. Natalie was the one who lost control. She saw the discarded panini grill and was ready when Sam showed up, but Sam surprised her and gained control. Sam struck Natalie. The fire alarm would have muted any screams. He disappeared down the alley and reemerged at the bank later that day.

Ping. Ping. The motive was weak. No score. Drain. Start over.

Sam's appearance at the bank on the afternoon after the murder still niggled at me. Needing to know more about his exact whereabouts, I sped home and raced with Tigger into the cottage. After I released him from his traveling crate and refreshed his water, I revved up my laptop computer, which sat on the kitchen table.

Online I found a site about the money-management conference in San Jose. The acronym was MONEY. Very subtle. The conference, a one-day event starting at 7:00 A.M. and running until 7:00 P.M., breakfast and lunch included, involved multiple tracks of seminars. Though the conference had concluded, I sent an e-mail to the coordinator. I knew from having conducted similar events for my former company that the coordinator wouldn't wrap up her work for months. Refunds, complaints, and tips regarding next year's event were expected. I asked whether Sam Sykes had attended the conference.

To my surprise, despite the late hour, I received a response almost instantaneously. Ten days ago, Sam had begged for a spot. Thanks to last-minute cancellations, the coordinator had been able to grant Sam's late request. That information supported my theory that Sam might have used the conference as an alibi.

I sent a follow-up e-mail asking whether the coordinator had any way of knowing whether Sam had really attended. Again, the coordinator responded quickly. She knew Sam personally and had seen him check in.

Rats. I sent off another e-mail: *Was he there for the whole day?*

The speed of the Internet never failed to astonish me. Seconds later, a reply arrived. The coordinator wrote that over one thousand people had attended the conference. Who didn't want to learn how to make a buck? she joked. She remembered seeing Sam around 10:00 A.M. and then again around 1:00 P.M.; however, there were at least three hundred individuals at each session. Sam wouldn't have been missed if he had left and returned.

Would Sam have driven to Crystal Cove and back a couple of times? San Jose was a good hour's drive from town. Even if I could check Sam's car for mileage, I wouldn't learn a thing. I wouldn't have a clue what the odometer had read before Sam left town. Would Mitzi know? She had tracked him down at the bank. When Flora told me that, I had wondered whether Mitzi had put a GPS device on Sam's car. How else would she have discovered his early return?

I refocused on jealous-beyond-all-get-out Mitzi. Though Mitzi acted impulsively now, pre-Sam, she had reigned in the business world. She had managed a corporation. Who knew what kind of manipulator she had been in her previous life? What if she had texted Natalie, claiming she was Sam using Mitzi's cell phone? Screwy, but possible. As Sam, she wrote that he had stolen into town. He needed to see her. Would Natalie have been naïve enough to buy that?

I paced the cottage, thinking of my comment earlier to Bailey and Katie about not obsessing over the murders. Why was I so focused on them? We had a strong police force. Cinnamon was a vital leader. I ogled the Lucky Cat and realized that the puzzle David had left me was the reason I was fixated. The more I concentrated on someone else's problem, the easier it was for me to avoid mine.

Back to Natalie. Who had wanted her dead?

What about Norah? What was her story? Maybe she was avoiding problems of her own. Maybe she had escaped an abusive relationship. Was that why she was so dead set on helping her sister exit hers? Perhaps Norah considered herself her sister's savior. Both Willie and Natalie had been overbearing. Ellen had been at risk.

I spun on my heel. "Why?"

Tigger, who apparently thought I was targeting him, darted beneath a chair.

"Cool it, buster. I'm not yelling. Boy, are you jumpy."

Like mother, like cat.

I scooped him up and scruffed his head. "Sorry, fella." He rumbled his thanks and burrowed into me.

As we paced the length of the cottage, my phone chimed again, and I realized I hadn't responded to Bailey. I set Tigger on the floor, punched in a quick text telling Bailey to sleep tight, and hit Send. As the message whooshed through the stratosphere, I thought again about the message to Natalie. Would the text, e-mail, or voice mail still exist on Natalie's cell phone? Was the killer clever enough to have erased it? Even if he or she had, I would bet a skilled technician could find it. I couldn't count how many times I had asked Taylor & Squibb's geek department to recover a deleted e-mail. As my father would say: *Fast fingers make for regrettable computer errors.* I had superfast fingers. Good for playing the Minute Waltz on the piano, not so good for business correspondence.

I spied the Lucky Cat that was once filled with gold coins and wondered whether there could be something hidden inside Natalie's cell phone, like a SIM card or backup recovery data solution. Could our police department tech geeks — if we had tech geeks; maybe we relied on the county for technical support — recover the information?

My cell phone dinged again. Bailey had written a response: *Don't let the bedbugs bite,* our standard phrase after that fateful week we had spent at summer camp when, indeed, bedbugs had plagued us. Gag.

As I considered a response, a game of mental pinball started up again inside my head. *Ping. Ping.* I flashed on the call I had received from Willie the night he died. Sam had suggested it was a pocket call. What if Willie hadn't called me? What if the murderer dialed my number to make it seem like Willie was alive at 10:00 P.M.? The coroner guessed that Willie died around 9:00 P.M. What if he'd died even earlier than that? Ellen's alibi covered her from 7:30 P.M. to midnight, but Norah's alibi wouldn't hold up. What if my original theory about

Norah's actions that night was correct? She'd left her ailing niece in the car, slipped into the motel, killed Willie, called me using Willie's cell phone, and fled.

Sam and Mitzi claimed to have been home for the night, but could I trust their accounts? According to Sam, Mitzi was involved with her nightly ritual. If she was primping, would she have noticed if Sam left the house?

No, I was wrong. The motel maid saw a woman visitor, not a man, in a black coat. Ellen found a tube of bright red lipstick in her coat pocket. I reworked the theory to fit Mitzi. What if Sam, who was making phone calls to locate Willie, hadn't noticed when Mitzi stole out the back of the house? The Sykes lived in an elegant one-level home. A path along the side of the house led to the rear patio. Mitzi could have sneaked away, done the deed, and tiptoed back in without Sam spotting her.

Were there other suspects I was neglecting to consider? The former chef who had fled to Las Vegas or Rosie the mnemonic waitress? What about Flora? She wasn't in the competition any longer, but she had been my first source of intel on Mitzi and Sam. Why would she have killed Willie? The two murders had to be related.

I plopped onto a chair in the kitchen and ran my finger along the Lucky Cat statue as if that would help me focus.

Bailey suspected that Willie had learned something and blackmailed the killer. What evidence could Willie have drummed up? Had he overheard something? Seen something? He'd cleaned out his account. He'd planned to run away.

I thought back to Willie's meeting with the bank teller. He had yelled at her. He had stabbed something that appeared to be a passbook. If only I knew the details of that conversation. Would Manga Girl talk to me now that Willie was dead?

CHAPTER 25

Through the night, I couldn't seem to get the Mumfords and Sykeses out of my head. In one dream, Natalie and Mitzi were going at it, hurling insults and tubes of lipstick. In another, Ellen and Norah laughed and danced around town while igniting candles in paper bags. In a third, Willie and Sam yelled in unison at Manga Girl. The poor woman cowered in a cage no bigger than Tigger's travel case. I awoke from each dream bathed in perspiration.

By 6:00 A.M. I was drenched. No more double chocolate soufflés with warm fudge sauce at night for me.

I rolled out of bed, peeked in the mirror, and gasped. My hair stuck out in all directions. The top looked like a hamster had nested in it. I threw on running clothes, donned a baseball cap, and headed out for a quick jog to clear my brain.

Still leery of running on the road, I walked

and ran on the sand. To the east, the sun cast a shimmering band of gold over the hills. To the west, seagulls circled above the placid ocean, each squawking eagerly for its morning meal. To keep my brain occupied so I wouldn't dwell on thoughts about murder, I counted my strides to and from my destination. I drew in deep breaths of air through my nose and exhaled through my mouth. By the time I returned to the cottage, I was rejuvenated and ready to face the day.

For the heck of it, seeing as I was feeling plucky, I dialed the precinct and left a message for Cinnamon. Supposition or not, she needed to know what was going on in my head. Maybe one of my theories would trigger one of her own.

After I hung up, I made myself a grilled cheese and tomato sandwich. Why? Because halfway into my exercise, I'd had such a craving for comfort food that I could barely stand it. As I sat at the kitchen table to eat — the sandwich was delicious — Tigger leaped onto the table and rubbed his cheek against the Lucky Cat's. I shooed him away and eyed the statue. If only I could resolve the issue about the key and the gold coins. I wouldn't be fully released from my past until I did. I thought of my father. I had started to mention the key to him that day when we met on The Pier to pole fish, but then I'd caught sight of a man who I had fleetingly believed was David. Why hadn't I remembered to consult my father again? He had a duplicating key machine at his hardware store. He might know what kind of key I had.

I dialed his home number, but he didn't pick up. When the call went to voice mail, it dawned on me that perhaps he was otherwise occupied. With Lola. A rush of embarrassment coursed through me. My cheeks flushed. Like a little kid, I wanted to put fingers in my ears and sing, "La-la-la." Too much information. I stabbed End without leaving a voice mail, grabbed Tigger, and flew to work. I would deal with the key later.

The moment I arrived, my aunt handed me a wad of twenties.

"Bank. Now. We need singles and fives," she said. Many of our customers paid in cash. "It's your turn to go."

"Where's Bailey?"

"She had a hankering for a double espresso."

"So much for being off caffeine."

"Some people don't have that natural get-up-and-go like you."

I didn't tell her that, until I had downed a

decent breakfast, my get-up-and-go had gotten up and went.

I settled Tigger in the stockroom and hurried away on my bicycle. I passed a number of serious cyclists on the road, heads down, dripping with sweat. Other riders looked as happy as I was to be enjoying the breeze and drinking in the morning sunshine. As I parked the bike in a bicycle stand outside the bank, removed my helmet, and secured both with a lock, the last dream I'd had replayed in my mind: Willie and Sam with Manga Girl trapped in a cage. Bailey had said the bank teller was key to the investigation. The word *key* made me flash again on the mysterious key. I assured myself that I would get personal answers *soon.*

I marched into the bank to make my transaction. Near the end of the line, I caught sight of Norah. She was unfolding the creases from a piece of paper. "Making a deposit?" I said.

"My last paycheck. My boss finally found the will to fork it over." Norah shook the check. "All it took was seventeen phone messages and a bit of screaming." She grimaced. "I'm so tired of automatic voice-answering thingies. You know the kind. Press one to hear a menu. Press two to go back. Press three to reach a real person, but then

a real person never materializes, only another prompt." She altered her voice to
sound like a machine: *If you feel you've
reached this recording in error . . ."* She
laughed.

So did I. A companionable silence fell
between us. I broke it. "I heard that Willie
died earlier than first believed. Probably
around nine o'clock."

"Really? I thought he called you at ten."

"The police have determined that the
killer might have made that call." Okay, my
vow never to lie just flew out the window. It
was a white lie and, therefore, acceptable,
right? "Your alibi covered from eight-thirty
on." I went silent, hoping she would elaborate.

"Yes, it did."

I remained quiet.

Norah frowned. She regarded the tellers
and returned her attention to me. "You
don't trust me. I get that. You want to know
every detail? Fine. Bebe was hungry."

"You said she felt ill."

"That was after we went to a drive-
through coffee place. You know, the one that
specializes in strawberry frappes. Bebe loves
them. I got her a kid's-size drink and, right
after, she felt icky. We went to the hospital
straight from there."

"Next customer," a teller said.

"That's me," Norah said and strode away. Guilty or not? I couldn't tell.

I scanned the other teller windows. I didn't see Manga Girl. Rats. When I approached a teller, I asked about her and was informed that she and her boyfriend had fled to Reno to elope. Her parents were distraught, but what could they do when it came to true love?

So much for that lead. I handed over the twenties and requested change.

As I was leaving the bank, I heard someone say, "Jenna." I surveyed the line of customers and saw Tito, chest puffed, twirling his keys around his index finger. What was it with those keys? Had he seen some macho guy in a movie doing it? He wasn't the one who had called my name; he was chatting up the frothy blonde next to him while lapping her up with his eyes.

Good luck with that, I thought.

So who had called out to me? I glanced toward the far end of the bank and spotted Rhett sitting in a chair beside the new-accounts desk. He waved.

I joined him. "What are you doing here?"

"I'm bringing in a partner for Bait and Switch, which means I have to make my personal accounts separate. Corporate transparency and all that."

"Why do you need a partner?" I asked, concerned.

"I don't. I simply don't want to work so hard. One of my regulars, a trust-fund baby, wants in. He's a good guy. Taking on a partner means I'll have time to go on a vacation now and then. How about you?"

"Vacations? Not for a year, I'm afraid."

"No, I meant what are you doing here?"

I waggled the money bag. "Small denominations."

"I know the drill."

"Hey, *chica,*" Tito said, interrupting us. He paused at the far end of the new-accounts table. He nodded to Rhett. "Hey, bro."

"Congratulations on making it to the final round in the Grill Fest," Rhett said.

"That's something, huh?" Tito jammed his keys into his jeans pocket. "Let's hear it for cuisine à la *mexicana.*" If he weren't always flexing his muscles and acting like a braggadocio, I would probably like Tito. His journalist pieces were funny — in writing, he had a Comedy Central–style of humor — and, like me, he enjoyed food, cookbooks, reading, and exercise. How did I know? Bailey had stumbled across Tito's computer-

dating personal page. Too funny. "Hey, *chica*
—"

And then there was that.

"Tito, call me Jenna, please. Not girl."

"*Sí, sí. Lo siento . . .* Sorry. Jenna," he said, the *J* soft. "I was wondering, what do you think about a triple-layer grilled cheese with jalapeños and bacon?"

"Sounds good. What if you added pico de gallo and avocado?" Those were two items I had wanted to add to my comfort food breakfast, but I hadn't had them on hand.

"Good idea." He scratched the stubble on his chin. "I think I'll head to the gym. A workout always helps me rev up my creative juices. *Adios.*" He paused and faced Rhett. "Hey, bro, it's okay if I speak of my creations in front of you even though you are a judge, isn't it?"

Rhett nodded. "I can't stop you."

As Tito sauntered out of the bank, ogling women to see if they were checking him out, I thought about what he'd just said. He was going to the gym. To work out. I flashed on the clue on the bottom of the Lucky Cat: *Everything will work out.* Was it possible that the key David had given me — the key to his heart — belonged to a gym locker? He had been an exercise fiend — mornings before work and evenings after work. He liked the adrenaline boost, and he wanted to be heart healthy. Following his death, I hadn't cleaned out his gym locker. His mother had begged for the chance. She'd said doing some of the final chores would give her closure. Though I'd assigned her a number of duties, she hadn't reported back on any of them. I had no idea what she had or hadn't accomplished. I'd let so much slide back then.

Quickly I bid Rhett good-bye and raced outside. In private I dialed David's mother on my cell phone. It was early for her — the woman could sleep more than an invalid — but I didn't care.

"Jenna," she said, apparently seeing my name or number on her phone. "How are you, dear heart?" She called everyone *dear heart,* her pet phrase.

I greeted her, my voice tight. How could I simply blurt out my question? I couldn't. I had to make small talk. I asked about her cat and her garden and her daughter. David's sister was an eminent endocrinologist. His mother loved to go on about her accomplishments. Five minutes into the conversation, she said, "Why have you really called, Jenna?" She wasn't naïve, just sluggish.

"David's locker at the gym," I began. I

didn't want to tell her about the gold I'd found within the Lucky Cat because, well, I wasn't sure about its source. "Did you ever clean it out?"

Silence. I heard her hum and lick her lips. "No, I don't think I did. I didn't even cancel the membership. I'm so sorry. Have you been receiving bills? I'll be glad to compensate —"

"No," I cut in. "That's fine. I simply wondered if you would mind if I emptied the locker myself."

"Of course." She coughed, but I knew she was covering a whimper. "I miss seeing you, dear heart. Will you stop by when you're up in the city?"

"I'll visit soon. Promise." I wasn't sure I would. I didn't think I could bear seeing pictures of David everywhere. Lying to his mother to protect her feelings, I reasoned, was an acceptable custom.

I bicycled back to the shop and told Aunt Vera my plan. She was more than supportive.

CHAPTER 26

In my VW bug, I sped to the city in record time. I entered the upscale gym, well known for its state-of-the-art weight machines, basketball court, cycle spinning rooms, personal trainers, and spa. The acrid scent of chlorine mixed with the pungent odor of sweat made my nose flinch. I approached the front desk, one hand clenching the strap of my purse, the other holding my key chain in a death grip.

"Good morning," I said. It was close to noon but still legitimately morning.

"Hey there." A perky blonde assistant with pigtails pushed aside her *People* magazine. "Sign in and show me your ID card."

"I'm not a member."

"Want to join? Would you like a tour?"

"No. My husband . . ." Words wouldn't come. My mouth felt as dry as a sauna.

". . . is a member and you want a family membership."

"No. He . . ."

Miss Perky peeked at her magazine. I didn't blame her. She couldn't wait to get back to the article about Justin Bieber. I would lay odds she had designs on him becoming her lover.

Speak, Jenna. "My husband died," I blurted out.

"I'm so sorry."

"Two years ago."

The assistant didn't look half as sorry as before. Two years was an eon to her. She pursed her lips. I heard her tennis shoe tap-tapping the floor. How dare I keep her from learning Justin's innermost secrets?

"My husband was a member here. We never closed his account. He had a locker. I'd like to empty it, if you wouldn't mind."

"I'll need to see your license."

I showed her.

"And, like, wow, this is going to sound weird, but do you have a death certificate?"

I gagged. "Not on me."

"Well, shoot."

Shoot, indeed. "Is your supervisor here?" I asked. Maybe he or she would be more merciful.

Miss Perky looked relieved that I would think of such a brilliant suggestion. "I'll be right back."

As she disappeared down a corridor of windowed cubicles, each space filled with a salesperson, I waited. How was I going to get around the death-certificate requirement? I needed answers. Now.

I glanced at the men's locker room door. I could slip in, pretend I had mistaken it for the ladies', but which locker was David's? The key didn't have a number on it. I couldn't insert it into every keyhole. And was it even a gym-locker key? For all I knew, my visit to the fitness center was a wild-goose chase.

Miss Perky reappeared. A man followed her. I recognized him. Shane something. He had worked at Taylor & Squibb in the sales department. Always tall, at one time Shane had been, um, hefty. He must have lost forty to fifty pounds. He looked as fit as an Olympic athlete. A striking streak of gray ran along the right side of his hair. A roguish dimple cut up his right cheek.

"Hello, Jenna."

"What are you doing here, Shane?"

"T&S downsized. I had to find something in this economy. Lo and behold, I was able to purchase a partnership in this venture."

"You're an owner?"

"We have eight clubs. Fewer hours. Easier on the heart." Shane wasn't much older than I was. His eyes twinkled with humor. "How are you?"

"Fine. I moved back to Crystal Cove."

"We have a club in Santa Cruz. You should check it out. Not that you need a gym. You look great."

I recalled a number of mixers thrown by our former boss. Shane, third-generation Irish-American and one of our premier salesmen, had the gift of gab. He could tell stories that made people hang on his every word.

"Do you like living on the shore?" he said.

"Love it."

"But you're here about . . . What was your husband's name?"

"David." I inhaled then exhaled slowly. "He had a locker here. Would this key fit it?" I opened my palm. The key had nearly made an imprint in my flesh.

"Yep, that's one of ours. Let's check out David's file."

Miss Perky said, "Doesn't she need —"

"I'll vouch for her," Shane said. "She's one of the most honorable ladies I've ever met." He hit the space bar on the gym's computer keyboard; the dormant screen came to life. "Last name Hart?"

"No. Harris. David Harris. Hart's my maiden name. I —"

"Got it," Shane said, sparing me from an explanation. He typed in a stream of letters and nodded. "Unit one eighty-eight. Let me clear the men's locker room, and I'll usher you in."

A minute passed before Shane returned and beckoned me. I followed him into the space, which was larger than I would have believed. Many lockers were day lockers with keys already hanging from the keyholes. An entire bank of lockers was reserved for members who paid a fee. David had never liked the idea of putting his gear into a locker where someone else's dirty clothes might have been. He wasn't fussy, just cautious.

I approached locker 188 tentatively. What would I find inside? I slotted the key into the keyhole and twisted. My hands shook as I opened the door. A navy blue gym bag sat inside. Nothing else. No towels. No shoes. No sign saying *X Marks the Spot.* Not wanting to open David's bag in front of Shane, I pulled it out — it was heavy — and hoisted the carry strap over my shoulder.

Shane said, "You'll want to close the account, I presume."

We completed that transaction in a matter of minutes, then Shane wished me well, and I returned to my VW.

In the dim light of the parking garage, sitting in the driver's seat, my lungs feeling like they were bound with Rocktape, I set the gym bag on the passenger seat and unzipped it. The zipper rasped from disuse. I pried open the bag and inhaled sharply. Inside were gold coins, similar to the ones that had spilled out of the Lucky Cat. Hordes of them. I ran my fingers through them. They were so cold. Beneath, I saw paper. I dug in and withdrew a slug of laser-printed financial sheets, each with a client's name in the header to the right and David's name, as investor, to the left. I didn't know what I was looking at except each account appeared to have lost money. What had happened?

I dug into the bag again and found an envelope with my name written on it in David's handwriting. My insides snagged. The envelope wasn't sealed. I removed the sheet of yellow lined paper, torn from a legal pad. It was dated the day he died.

Dear Jenna,
There are no words I can write to explain how I feel. I love you so much, and I am ashamed to admit my wrongdoing, but I borrowed money from my clients.

My hands shook. He had bilked his clients. How many? For how long? I continued to read:

I gambled on risky investments. The investments went south. I meant to pay back every dime, but I couldn't seem to get ahead of the trend. I am so sorry. I never thought something like this could happen to me. I tried to tell you so many times. On the vacation to Las Vegas. Over dinner at the Top of the Mark. The words wouldn't come. I love you, Jenna. I'm sorry that life didn't work out for us as I'd planned. I purchased the Lucky Cat and sealed the last of my wealth inside. For you, Jenna. The coins were purchased with the first money I ever made as an adult, so it's clean.

The imaginary Rocktape around my lungs grew tighter. What could David have been thinking? The money wasn't clean. The moment he borrowed his clients' funds, his earnings, all of them, were soiled.

If my crime is discovered, I will have to go to jail for a very long time. I can't let you live that life. What I am choosing to do is the right choice. For everyone. I love you so much, but you are better off without me. I hope you understand and will forgive me.

Love always,
David

"No," I said. I tossed the letter aside and pushed open the car door. I lunged out of the car. Emotions caught in my throat. I couldn't swallow. I remembered David calling me from the gym saying he was *ready.* I thought he meant he was fit to sail. What he meant was that he was ready to take his life. He committed suicide. He expected me to find this directly after the accident. I was in charge of his estate and effects. The letter went unfound because I had given his mother the task.

I wrapped my arms around me and keened like a wounded animal.

A woman exiting the elevator hurried to me. "Are you all right?"

"Yes. I'm —" I paused. What was I? Hurt that David wouldn't trust me with his secret. Sad that he hadn't found the strength to reform. Mad at myself for being blind to my husband's troubles. "I'm fine," I lied. "I received some bad news."

"I know an excellent grief counselor," she said.

I gazed at the woman, her concern touching me. Who was she? She had never met me and owed me nothing. My throat grew thick.

"If you want her number, e-mail me." The woman pulled a business card from her purse and pressed it into my hands.

Tears streaked my cheeks. "Thank you."

As I climbed back into the VW, I felt calmer. I would rise above this . . . betrayal. That was what it was. I believed I had known David, but I hadn't. Not fully. How could he have done what he had done? I recalled a line from *As You Like It:* "The fool doth think he is wise, but the wise man knows himself to be a fool."

Somewhere along the 280 freeway, I realized I would not be fiscally responsible to David's clients because our assets weren't community property. We had earned separately and had always kept our accounts distinct — David's rules. But I couldn't endorse that legal right. People had been hurt. Even if the courts didn't press me to pay David's debt, I intended to cash out the gold coins and allocate the money to David's clients. Would the gold cover the entire debt? I didn't know; I didn't care. I needed an exorcism. I wondered whether I should tell David's mother what had happened. I didn't want to cause her pain. It would crush her to learn her son had lied, cheated, and committed suicide. But perhaps she would find comfort in making things right. She had endless cash.

And then there was the matter of my broken heart. After my mother died, my father was prone to quote Rollo May, an existentialist who was popular in the sixties: "Courage is not the absence of despair; it is, rather, the capacity to move ahead in spite of despair."

No matter what my plan of action was in regard to David's misdeeds, I would move ahead with my life. From this moment on, my eyes would remain wide open. Always.

The first person I called was my father.

CHAPTER 27

After promising to meet Dad for dinner, I returned to The Cookbook Nook and waded through the day. Despite my sorrow, I was able to sell quite a few books. Naturally, my tastes leaned toward anything with a happy ending. No kitchen fiasco tales. No women's fiction that might make me cry. Customers seemed pleased with my choices. I was also able to move a lot of foodie jigsaw puzzles, mainly because I sat down at the vintage table and put together one after another to occupy my beleaguered brain.

Every so often my aunt, Bailey, or Katie, all of whom I had rounded up immediately to tell the news, would approach me. Aunt Vera would give me a quick hug. Bailey would pat my back without saying a word. Katie brought me homemade Oreo-style cookies and milk.

At closing, the trio corralled me. I felt nervous, as if they were going to pick me over like a pack of female gorillas. They didn't. My aunt instigated a group hug. As we stood in a cluster, she intoned, "Oh great Creator or Creatress, whichever you might be, may you provide Jenna with comfort during this time of need and give her hope for the future." She paused, then added, "That's it."

I giggled. "That's it? No *amen?*"

"You know that's not my style."

"No spells? No incantations?"

"Don't make fun, young lady."

I broke free and bussed her cheek. "Thank you all for your concern and your love." Bailey and Katie regarded me dolefully. "Stop it. I'm going to be fine. David is gone. At least now I know why. Solving that mystery will help me move on with my life. I promise. As Jane Austen said, 'Friendship is certainly the finest balm for the pangs of disappointed love.' "

We hugged again, and I left for dinner.

I stood next to the railing at The Pelican Brief Diner, staring out at the view. The sun, which was sinking into the horizon, gleamed a brilliant orange. Wisps of white clouds hovered high in the dusky blue sky. On the water, paddle boarders poled in a straight line toward The Pier. The picturesque moment should have made me feel calm and peaceful, but it didn't.

My father sat at the table. Lola nestled beside him. I could feel their gazes drilling holes into my back. After we'd ordered the evening's special, my father, who was never one to dwell on the negative, asked me how I was doing. That was when I stood and moved to the railing. How much time had passed since he had asked me the question? Two minutes? Five?

"Jenna, please sit," my father said. He didn't add, "Eat some fresh-baked bread." But I knew that was what he wanted. Two years ago, when I'd learned of David's death, I hadn't consumed much, and before I knew it, I'd lost fifteen pounds I could ill afford to have lost. Of course, all those pounds came back. My father needn't worry.

I swiveled and leaned against the railing. "I was surprised by David's duplicity," I said as if continuing a conversation. "Not just surprised. Shocked. Horrified. I thought we had this fabulous relationship. We told each other everything. I mean, he knew me to the last detail. I even admitted my greatest fear to him."

"Which is?" Lola said.

"A silly thing, but I feel so vulnerable

whenever I share it. Getting swallowed into the wall like that child in 'Little Girl Lost.' "

I wasn't much of a television viewer, but every New Year's Day, my father talked me into watching the *Twilight Zone* marathon. That particular episode gave me the heebie-jeebies beyond belief. "Why do you think David did what he did?"

Lola said, "I had a client once who did much the same thing. He bilked his investors, which shocked the heck out of all of us because he was a church-going, God-fearing individual, but it turned out he'd been hooked on gambling from a young age. He had hidden the signs and worked his rear end off to make all his payments until he couldn't keep up any longer. He was about David's age."

"I meant why did my husband commit suicide?"

"He went out in a boat," Dad said. "Maybe he hoped, given time, he could talk himself out of killing himself." He joined me at the railing and slung an arm around my shoulders.

Lola rose and stood on the other side of me. She tucked an arm around my waist. We made an odd Three Musketeers.

"It's over now, Tootsie Pop."

"Is it, Dad? I have the coins."

"Which I'll help you distribute. We'll get right on it next week. It'll take some time, but we'll make restitution. Okay?"

Our waiter arrived with our specials, which were beautiful in presentation: salmon seared with crosshatched grill marks topped with a salsa made with large chunks of avocado and mango, all set on a pile of luscious mashed potatoes.

My father guided me back to the table. I ate half my meal and pushed the plate away.

"Is something wrong with your dinner, Jenna?" Lola said.

"No."

"The recipe came from one of the cookbooks I bought at your store."

"You stole the recipe?" my father said, playfulness in his tone.

"That's the whole purpose of cookbooks, isn't it? To share."

"There's a subtle difference."

Their banter triggered something in my mind. A string of *S* words slewed together: *subtle, share, steal, scheming, sad.* Something jolted inside me. I couldn't stay seated any longer. I bolted to my feet.

"What's wrong?" Lola said.

"I need to walk. I need —" Emotions clogged my throat. I headed for the front door.

Lola rose. My father did, as well. They escorted me to the street. A cool breeze hit us as we exited the diner. I wrapped my arms around myself. Dad offered his jacket, but I declined. I walked north. They followed. I could feel their concern. I didn't make eye contact.

After a long silence, I said, "I saw Rhett at the bank this morning, Dad. Did you know he's taking on a partner?"

"No." My father was a regular at Bait and Switch. He loved everything about the store, from the fishing lures to the exotic knives.

"Rhett said he had to separate his accounts for the sake of transparency. If only David had been as transparent."

"He couldn't be, sweetheart. He was sick. Luckily he kept your accounts separate to protect you from future litigation."

"But don't you see?" I swallowed hard. "That means he knew ahead of time what he was doing." Additional *S* words joined the ones forming a kick line in my mind: *sly, slick.* "What if there's more to discover?"

"You mean like an offshore account?" Lola said.

"Lola, please," my father said.

"Eyes wide open, Cary. Lots of individuals create these accounts to protect themselves from malpractice suits. The bank routes funds through several corporate entities. An offshore account provides layers of protection. They're not illegal. All you need in order to get one is your passport, a reference from the bank, samples of your signature, and proof of residence." Lola nudged me. "Well, Jenna?"

"I honestly don't know, but I'm going to find out." One way or another. No more surprises. My cell phone buzzed; I fished it from my purse.

"I didn't hear your phone ring," my father said.

"It vibrated. Cinnamon sent me a text. Aunt Vera contacted her and told her about David. She's sending her condolences." I pondered what Cinnamon had to be going through, trying to solve two murders while keeping the rest of Crystal Cove safe. Tough job. "It was nice of her to take the time."

Although I would bet the last thing she wanted to hear were theories from the grieving wife of a suicide victim, perhaps I owed her a visit. We hadn't spoken since I'd left her a message the other day. Setting a goal made me feel instantly better and more in control of *me*.

There were a few empty spaces in the precinct parking lot. I pulled next to an

SUV, my VW bug looking like a pipsqueak beside it, and hurried into the building. The clerk informed me that Cinnamon wasn't in. She was — *wink, wink* — on a date, as if that were a big deal. Maybe it was. I wished I knew more about her. I vowed, starting tomorrow, to make an extra effort to develop our friendship.

As I exited the building, the moose-looking deputy with the huge jaw followed me. "Hey, Jenna, what's new?"

"Nothing."

He kept pace while pulling a lighter and a pack of cigarettes from his pocket. He was about to light up when he must have seen my frown. He tucked his paraphernalia away and hitched his jaw at the precinct. "Got word that something was up. Want to share?"

Share, steal, sly, scheme. I countered the onslaught of words with a childish invocation: *Rain, rain, go away. Don't come back another day.*

"No, thanks," I said politely. I wasn't about to theorize with a guy I didn't know. Let me rephrase. I did *know* the Moose. I'd met him when I first met Cinnamon weeks ago, but we hadn't really chatted. I didn't know his full name. I didn't know whether he had a family, a wife or kids. Was he from around here? Could he be trusted? In the long run, these questions mattered. If only I had been so wise years ago. Before David.

Doing my best to get a grip, I said, "Cinnamon and I had discussed grabbing a cup of coffee."

"Uh-huh. At ten at night?" The Moose was no dummy.

"I had a craving for a white chocolate mocha or a vanilla spice latte."

"I like them both." He displayed his left hand. No ring. He was baiting me.

"Yeah, well." I inched away. "Tell Cinnamon I dropped by."

"Will do. And if you ever want to talk to me . . ." He let the sentence hang.

I blushed. What was it about bereaved widows that turned guys on? Easy pickings? Not this one. I hurried to my car and sped away.

Home alone in the cottage, with only Tigger for company, the events of the day hit me hard. I felt lost. My stomach was raw, my throat hot. I wanted to cry but tears wouldn't come. I tried to force them out. Nothing. I growled, and Tigger echoed me.

"I'm not playing, kitty cat."

He nudged my foot with his nose. I nudged him with my shoe. He rolled onto his back, eager to tussle.

"Sorry, fella. Not now." I felt the urge to shout, but words escaped me. *David, David, David.* I slumped into the chair by the kitchen table and eyed the Lucky Cat and David's gym bag. If only my husband had confided in me. If only he had trusted me. Maybe we could have gotten him help. Maybe we could have worked through the problem and faced the future together. I loved him; there was no doubt. Yes, he had disappointed me, and yes, his decision to end his life would forever haunt me, but I would never stop loving him. I thought of his final letter, and an idea came to me. I fetched a piece of stationery and wrote a note to the detective in charge of David's case. He probably needed closure as much as I did. One cold case solved.

Unable to sleep, I decided to paint. Though I had made my career as an ad executive, I had always dreamed of being an artist. As was true for many artists, I was good but not great. Even so, painting relaxed me. I set up a blank canvas, chose a bristle brush, pulled my moisture-retaining palette from its drawer, and after removing the lid, dabbed a brush with black paint. Where to begin? I stared at the canvas. I had nothing. Nada. I paced the cottage waiting for inspiration to hit.

Two hours later, I still had nothing. Frustrated and in desperate need of an emotional release, I drew a game of tic-tac-toe. I played knowing I couldn't win. When I stopped painting and stared at all those *X*s and *O*s, they reminded me of unrequited hugs and kisses, and I lost it. I daubed my brush into red paint and smeared the color over the game. The result was a mess of grungy brown. It wasn't beautiful, but it was a start. *Angry Art,* I titled it.

Around 3:00 A.M., I put away my supplies and, crying, collapsed onto the couch.

At 7:00 A.M., I woke, puffy-eyed and ready to punch whoever was pounding on my door.

Chapter 28

As if propelled from a cannon, I bolted off the couch. The instant my feet hit the floor, I moaned. My head ached. I was wobbly. I hadn't had any liquor, and yet I felt as if I had imbibed a bottle of wine all by myself. Grief sucks.

More pounding. My aunt called my name. What was so urgent?

I grabbed my robe and hurried to the door. I peered through the peephole. Aunt Vera stood on the porch looking radiant in a sky blue caftan. She held up a steaming cup of something and a plate of poached eggs on hash. At least she wasn't demanding I run for safety. No fire. No UFO sightings.

I opened the door. "What?" I said, not too politely.

"Food for the soul."

"That usually includes sugar."

"Protein is better for you right now."

Without asking, Aunt Vera entered and set my breakfast on the kitchen table while noting that she had found the recipe for poached eggs on bacon hash from a beautiful cookbook called *The Art of Breakfast: How to Bring B&B Entertaining Home*, written by a woman who runs the Maine Innkeeping Academy. Who knew there was such a thing? Next, Aunt Vera pulled a necklace with an ice white quartz pendant from her pocket. "I also brought this. Good vibrations for healing and protection."

Even though my brain felt foggier than the San Francisco Bay, I could recite what my aunt had taught me through the years. Quartz was the universal crystal, and Crystal Cove, like much of the California coast, was rife with crystals and gemstones; hence, the name. Crystal, my aunt had told me on more than one occasion, could dispel negative energy and purify one's mental and physical planes.

"Put it on," she ordered.

"But I'm wearing my mother's locket."

"Not right now. I know what's inside."

David's picture.

"When you are ready to replace the photograph with a new love," she continued, "you can put the locket back on, but for now, do as I say."

I didn't know what chants my aunt had recited before coming to the cottage but, as if transfixed, I obeyed. Instantly — I knew it was nuts — I felt better. Lighter. Almost tingly.

Aunt Vera leaned in and kissed both of my cheeks. "A delightful future awaits you. Now, let's put on our thinking caps and come up with new ideas for the shop. Today is the last day of the Grill Fest. We need inspiration."

Over breakfast, I told her about my *no fear* motto in the kitchen. "I don't want to run the café, mind you. I could never replace Katie, but I want to learn. Everything." I told her that our clientele should have the same opportunity as I. We needed more cooking classes scheduled on the calendar. At once. In addition to Katie, we would book chefs from the local restaurants and diners, including Rhett.

Once I arrived at The Cookbook Nook, I collected all the how-to books we had in stock. Rachael Ray, known for throwing together quick meals, had penned a cookbook titled *My Year in Meals.* I browsed it and found easy-to-read, unpretentious recipes, each created because she had decided to write a food diary about her dining habits, similar in style to *Julie and Julia.*

Granted, given the list of ingredients Rachael used, I would have to add food and spices to my cupboards, but I was ready.

To enhance my increasingly upbeat mood, I switched on a mixtape of music. Bobby McFerrin's charming song "Don't Worry, Be Happy" was first in the queue. McFerrin didn't mention food in the lyrics — one of the requirements for the mixtape — but the song came from the movie *Cocktail*. Close enough, right?

As I set up for the afternoon's Grill Fest finale, Tigger, who had picked up on my jovial mood, followed me everywhere, prancing and attacking. The tickle of his claws on my exposed toes made me smile. I was alive and I had feelings. Yay for me.

Around 1:30 P.M., Katie showed up with a cookie bar made with peanut butter, crispy rice cereal, and chocolate that rocked my world. My aunt claimed she had predicted Katie's sugary treats; that was why she had fed me eggs for breakfast. I didn't believe her for a nanosecond.

Not too soon after the appearance of the goodies, Pepper Pritchett arrived. While munching, she paused in the archway leading to the hall and said, "The music is loud."

"Yes, I know," I said.

None of the customers, many of them

prospective audience members for the final round of the Grill Fest, seemed to mind. A few were swaying to the beat. Refusing to let Pepper get to me today, maybe not ever again — in addition to learning to be an expert cook, I was intent on creating a happy serum, or at the very least a happy spell, for Pepper — I did my best to grin like the Cheshire cat from *Alice's Adventures in Wonderland.* Tigger murmured his approval.

As Pepper moved to her spot at the judges' table, I wondered about her daughter, Cinnamon, and why she hadn't returned my call. I went to the sales counter and dialed the precinct. Cinnamon wasn't in. I was transferred to the Moose, who sounded miffed that I had called, as if I hadn't trusted him to relay last night's message. Perhaps he was ticked that I hadn't swooped in and accepted his offer of coffee. *Men.*

"I promise, Miss Hart," he said with an edge, "she will call. When she has time. We have lots of activities going on in town, which means set-tos and accidents."

Call me crazy, but a smidgen of worry pinched the edges of my mind when he mentioned accidents. "Is Cinnamon okay? I mean, nothing's happened to her, right?"

The Moose hung up on me. Steamed, I

slammed down the receiver. If he'd hoped to make a friend of me, he had ended that chance.

At the same time, Mayor Zeller, wearing a burgundy pantsuit, bustled into the store. "It's the finals. Are we ready? What a delight this whole event has been." She faltered. "Minus the sad tragedy of Natalie's demise, of course." She waved a hand in front of her face, as if to cool the flush of embarrassment. "Ah, here are the contestants."

Mitzi walked in looking like a gun-shy deer. Her eyes were pinpoints of angst; her smile thin. Sam was holding on to her arm. Making it to the finals must have really been doing a number on her. Sam released her, and she took up her post by her cooking station. Tito followed, appearing as relaxed as I had ever seen him. No dogged attitude, no swagger. In fact, he was grinning from ear to ear. His visit to the gym must have gone a lot better than mine.

My aunt leaned in to me. "Tito asked me for a reading yesterday. It was all very positive."

Rhett trailed the contestants. From his spot at the judges' table, he gave me a discreet wave. I considered telling him about David, but I didn't want to spoil my mood. The good news was, however, that I

418

was ready to move on. Two years was long enough to mourn. I stroked the quartz pendant, silently thanking my aunt for her gift.

The event got under way. Mitzi made a classic croque-monsieur, the same sandwich Natalie had planned for the first day of competition, with ham and cheese and a béchamel sauce. Tito, who couldn't hide his delight that Mitzi was playing it safe, came up with a food truck–style grilled cheese that involved macaroni, cheese, bacon, and peppers. The judges interviewed the contestants and sampled the sandwiches. A half hour later, they made their determination.

The mayor rose to address the audience. "And this year's Grill Fest winner is" — she paused for effect — "Tito Martinez."

Wow. I had seen it coming, but *wow*.

"Are you kidding me?" Mitzi spun to her right. She looked ready to deconstruct. "Sam?"

I perused the crowd and didn't spot him.

"Sam!" Mitzi yelled, clearly panicked.

"Has anyone seen Sam Sykes?" Mayor Zeller asked.

A woman waved her hand. "He left about twenty minutes ago."

Another woman added, "I saw him entering the Word right before I came here."

Mitzi moaned. "No, no, no. This is all *her* fault." She groped beneath her cooking station for her purse. "I've got to go."

"Wait, Mitzi," the mayor said. "Show a little decorum. Shake Tito's hand."

"I . . . I . . ." Mitzi drank in huge gulps of air. "No, I don't have time." She dashed to the door.

I raced after her and caught up with her beside her Mercedes. "Mitzi, slow down. I don't think Sam is having an affair with the bank teller."

"Of course he's not."

"But you said *her.*"

"Not *her,*" she said. "He's planning to run off with *her.*"

"Her, who?"

"Natalie's daughter." Mitzi whipped open the door.

"Ellen?" I said. "No, you're wrong. Ellen thinks of Sam like a father."

"As always, you don't know what you're talking about."

Mitzi scrambled into her car and started to pull the door closed. I grabbed the handle. She tugged. Man, she was strong. I released my hold. She ground the car into reverse, then tore out of the parking lot.

Mayor Zeller hurried to me. "What's going on?"

420

"Mitzi is jealous. At first, she believed Sam was having an affair with Natalie as well as another woman in town." I hesitated. Actually, the latter wasn't confirmed. Flora had provided that tidbit of gossip. What did it matter? "Now, Mitzi thinks that . . ." I paused again. Mitzi hadn't said Ellen's name. She'd said I was misguided. Had she meant Norah? What if Norah had come to Crystal Cove to be with Sam? I couldn't fathom how they could have met. On the Internet, perhaps. Norah said that was how she had reconnected with her sister. Had Natalie found out about Norah and Sam's relationship? Maybe she'd demanded that Sam end the affair. Maybe Norah didn't want her mother butting into her business; she rebelled and killed her mother. Willie found out. He threatened Norah and promised to reveal all to Mitzi. In retaliation, Norah killed Willie. No, that wasn't possible. She had an alibi. She was at the drive-through coffee shop with Bebe. Could she prove it? Would the drive-through person remember her? Did Norah have a receipt for that purchase with a time stamp on it?

I ran into the shop and told my aunt that I was going to the Word. I asked her to get hold of Cinnamon and send her to the diner. A hint of the apprehension that I'd

421

felt earlier resurfaced. Was Cinnamon okay? "And if you can't find her, call Dad."

As I sprinted to my VW, the mayor trailed me. "I'm going with you."

CHAPTER 29

Parking on the Pier on a Thursday wasn't too difficult. On a weekend, forget about it. As I pulled into a spot, I saw Mitzi racing across the pavement toward the boardwalk. A woman in her fifties wearing high heels was no competition for a long-legged, almost-thirtysomething in sandals. I caught up with her. Mayor Zeller lagged behind.

"Mitzi," I said, darting in front of her and blocking her progress. "Don't go off half-cocked. You can't be sure Sam is having an affair with Norah."

"It's all Natalie's fault," she said, not denying my claim.

"Natalie?" Did Mitzi, in her deranged state, believe Natalie had sicced her daughter on Sam to woo him away from Mitzi? Get real.

"Let me go," she said.

I wasn't holding on to her.

When she realized that, she dodged me

and barreled past the customers waiting in line at the diner. "Out of my way," she yelled.

I thought of the oft-misquoted line: "Hell hath no fury like a woman scorned," attributed to Shakespeare but really a line from *The Mourning Bride* by William Congreve. Had Mitzi, driven by misguided insanity, killed Natalie?

I charged up the stairs after her while bandying about a second notion. Was Mitzi really nuts, or was she faking it so she could publicly humiliate or possibly slay her husband? I remembered asking Sam whether Mitzi owned a gun. He hadn't said no. Was she packing now?

Mitzi barked at Rosie the waitress, "Where is he? Where is my Sam?"

Ellen and Norah, who were talking between themselves, stopped and stared. So did customers.

Rosie hitched a thumb toward the kitchen. Mitzi rushed in that direction. I hurried after her. By this time, the mayor, huffing and puffing, caught up.

"Heavens," she muttered.

Ellen and Norah bustled into the kitchen behind us, each asking, "What's going on?"

We found Sam sitting at a table at the rear of the kitchen. A ledger lay open in front of him. His laptop computer, its screen filled with a spreadsheet, sat to one side. Beyond the book and computer stood a glass of soda and a plate filled with a burger and fries.

"Sam," Mitzi said.

Sam raised his chin. His eyes went wide. He slapped the ledger and computer closed and leaped to his feet, knocking over an overnight suitcase that sat on the floor.

Mitzi yanked a pearl-handled gun from her purse and aimed. Even though I'd anticipated her possessing a weapon, I gasped. Everyone did. Ellen shooed her sister and the kitchen staff out of the area. Norah didn't budge. The others fled.

In my previous job, I had been a problem solver. I think-tanked ideas on a regular basis. I scoped out our competition and figured out how to wage a better campaign. What could I do, right here, right now? I couldn't wrestle Mitzi for the gun. It might fire; a bullet could hit someone. I couldn't sneak up on her. She seemed as alert as a fox and as crazy as a loon. I fiddled in my pocket for my cell phone and surreptitiously pressed Resend on the last number I'd dialed — the precinct. Would someone be able to listen in on the confrontation? Would my father or Cinnamon or even the Moose get here before this turned deadly?

In a decisive tone, Ellen said, "Mitzi, put away the gun. Please. I know you don't want to hurt anyone." I was impressed. Maybe Ellen's involvement with FEW was helping her grow a backbone. Her sister, usually the dominant one, was ashen.

Mitzi wavered, but she didn't stow her weapon. She waggled it.

"Tell me what's wrong," Ellen said.

"Him." Mitzi pointed the gun at Sam. "The two-timing jerk."

Sam held up his hands. "Mitzi, babe, what're you saying?"

"Don't speak, you . . . you . . . You're planning to run away" — Mitzi pivoted and pointed the gun at Ellen — "with *her.*"

So I hadn't guessed right about Norah; Ellen was Mitzi's target, after all. Shoot.

No. Don't.

"You abandoned me at the Grill Fest because she lured you here," Mitzi went on.

"I needed help with the books," Ellen said. "Honest. With Willie gone . . ." Her eyes misted up. "I asked Sam to stop by. He's being attentive."

"Liar."

C'mon, Jenna. Ideas. Pronto.

"Mitzi," I blurted out, "the real reason you're upset is because you're not sure who Sam is involved with."

426

"I'm not involved with anyone," Sam said.

"It's got to be someone. Why else are you out of money all the time?" Mitzi said, reiterating the same complaint she had made at the grocery store.

"You give Sam an allowance, don't you, Mitzi?" I said, vamping.

"Yes."

"It's for both of us," Sam protested. "For our household expenses."

"But you never seem to make it stretch," Mitzi said.

"In this economy —"

"When we got married," Mitzi continued, cutting off her husband, "my business manager warned me to keep our accounts separate."

"You have your own business manager?" I asked. Sam had to feel pretty emasculated in that scenario. "Do you have a prenuptial agreement, too?" My boss at Taylor & Squibb had drawn up a prenup when he'd married a child bride of twenty-two. Good thing he had. Their marriage had lasted two years.

"Yes, but Sam didn't mind," Mitzi said. "Why are you always out of money, Sam? Who are you spending it on? Tell me, who?"

Sam scanned the room. His gaze fell on Mayor Zeller.

Mitzi pivoted. Her face flushed a hotter shade of red; her nose twitched. I flashed on a routine I had seen in a Three Stooges movie. I wasn't a fan of the comedians, but David had begged me to watch one of their flicks. Slowly I turned . . . step by step . . . inch by inch. Was Mitzi faking this act of lunacy? She said, "Why did you come to my house the other night after the competition, ZZ?" Mayor Zeller took a step backward, obviously threatened.

"I asked you a question!" Mitzi shouted. "Why did you come over?"

"I . . . I was worried about you," the mayor stammered. "You had lost control of your senses. You threw cheese at the other contestants, for heaven's sake."

"You and Sam." Mitzi aimed a finger at her husband and then the mayor. "I see the truth now. You two are an item, aren't you? How did I miss the signs? You killed Natalie to keep him for yourself. Admit it."

CHAPTER 30

"No, Mitzi, that's simply not true." Mayor
Zeller turned winter white. She gazed at the
crowd in the diner's kitchen and zeroed in
on me. "Jenna, help me. Sam and I have
never been involved. Ever."

"You can't fool me, ZZ," Mitzi went on.
"I wasn't planning on being home that
night." She edged closer. "I had a dinner to
cook for the owner of the Aquarium by the
Sea, but my hairdo wasn't working and my
skin was dry. I was home, reapplying lotion,
but I wasn't supposed to be. Did you come
over to meet Sam on the sly?"

Mayor Zeller sucked in air. "No."

Sam said, "Mitzi, babe —"

"Hush up, Sam." Mitzi ogled the mayor.
"Your dear friend Natalie found out you
were having an affair with my Sam. Isn't
that so, ZZ? You killed her so she'd keep
quiet."

Mayor Zeller flapped a frantic hand. "Stop

this insanity, Mitzi. Do you hear what you're saying? I was with everyone outside The Cookbook Nook the day Natalie was murdered. Remember, the alarm went off?" She pumped her hand as if pulling the alarm's handle.

"I don't recall seeing you," Mitzi said.

How could she have? Two witnesses had spotted her near the rear of the café. I revisited my theory that Mitzi had killed Natalie. She'd had enough time to throw the alarm. She knew Natalie was a smoker. Was she casting all this suspicion on the mayor as a diversion?

"Natalie had a moment of conscience, didn't she, ZZ?" Mitzi continued to stalk her prey. "She threatened to tell me about the affair."

"No." The mayor worried her hands together. "Somebody do something. Stop her. Please. Your husband and I did not have an affair. Sam, tell her."

"I've tried," he said. "She always thinks I'm having an affair. You're not the first she's accused."

Mitzi ignored him. "Why did you want Sam, ZZ?"

"I didn't. I don't."

"You did. You do." Mitzi's hand started to shake. I was convinced more than ever that she had a drinking problem. Any second she could fire the gun accidentally.

Think, Jenna. What would Cinnamon or Dad do? I scanned the kitchen for a weapon to take down Mitzi. The place was filled with them: knives, sauté pans, trays. All out of my reach. I checked out the prep table: a salad bowl, tongs. Where was a weighty object when I needed one?

Mitzi continued her taunt. "You've always had eyes for Sam, ZZ. I can see. I'm not blind. You're sexy and scheming."

The mayor sputtered. She knew, as did everyone present, that an Ewok was sexier than she could ever hope to be.

"I will not share him with you," Mitzi said. "Not my sensitive Sam." She glowered at her husband. "How could you continue to screw around on me after all I've done for you?"

"Mitzi, babe. I am not having an affair with Mayor Zeller. I'm innocent. So is she. Let's go home. We'll talk."

"I know you didn't stay at the MONEY conference, Sam. I put a tracker on your car."

Aha! I knew it. Mitzi had used GPS.

"I did stay," he argued. "I was there all day."

"Why do you continue to hurt me so?

431

When I found out you borrowed my gloves, did I call you on it? No. I even moved the coat back to the right hook in the diner. And don't get me started about the car trash. All for you. I do it all for you. But what do you do? You fool around with ZZ and Ellen and Norah. Who else?"

Mitzi continued to rant, but I couldn't hear her as the words she had let slip replayed in my mind. She had *moved the coat*? To the *right* hook? That meant she presumed Sam had left a coat on the *wrong* hook. *Of course.* Mitzi was talking about Ellen's coat. The maid at the motel had seen the murderer wearing a knee-length black coat. The coat was long on Ellen; it hit her at mid-calf. Mitzi and Norah were about the same height as Ellen. But Sam was taller; the coat would have been shorter on him. He'd dressed like a woman to kill Willie. Had he murdered Natalie, too?

I thought of what Mitzi said about the gloves and the car trash, her words forming a picture the same way the edges of a jigsaw puzzle defined the center.

"The gloves." I whirled to face Sam. "Mitzi said you borrowed a pair of her gloves. Were they her prep gloves?" Mitzi, being a home chef, probably had tons of gloves. "No, she wouldn't have minded losing a pair of cheap prep gloves. You borrowed her facial gloves, didn't you, Sam?" The ones she uses for her nightly ritual. "I'll bet they're expensive. That would tick her off."

"Mitzi is missing a pair of her facial gloves," Mayor Zeller cut in. "She was counting them the night I showed up at her place. She was one pair short."

Mitzi was obsessive about her beauty treatments. Sam had said so himself.

Sam shook his head. "Babe, I never took your gloves. I know how precious they are."

"You wore them when you killed Natalie," I said. "Mitzi realized what you'd done when she found the gloves in the car trash."

"Me?" Sam sputtered. "Kill Natalie? You're off your rocker."

Was I? I flashed on Sam and Manga Girl and what Lola, my father, and I had discussed last night at dinner in relation to David. Suddenly a string of mnemonic words came to me. I glanced at the ledger in front of Sam. Rhett told me that Willie had looked perplexed while reviewing the ledgers. What if Mitzi's *sensitive Sam,* like David, was a *schemer*? What if he was *skimming* money from his clients? Not just from Mum's the Word but from all of his clients? What if he was *stowing* all that money in a special account at the bank? What if Natalie found out? On the day Natalie and Lola argued at The Pier, Natalie had asked Sam if everything was all right. She had wanted to know if something had been bothering him lately. She'd said he seemed distracted. When she teased him about not balancing the books if he was feeling a little *off,* she winked. What if she was discretely warning him that she knew he was skimming? A few days passed before she wound up dead. She could have confronted Sam. He would have denied any wrong-doing, or maybe he admitted his guilt and said he would fix it. Maybe Natalie even forgave him. But Sam didn't believe her. He started planning how he would kill her. He established an alibi by signing up for the conference. Midday, he returned to town. When the Grill Fest took a break, he struck.

I shared my theory out loud. "You did what my husband did, Sam. You moved funds from various accounts. You siphoned money into an account of your own. Natalie figured out what you were up to. Tell me if I'm warm."

Sam kept mum.

The day Natalie died, the woman at the knitting shop had seen a person in a UPS uniform. If Sam had dressed up as a woman, maybe he had dressed up as a deliveryman, too. I said, "I bet you look good in brown, Sam."

"What are you talking about?" he hissed.

"You donned a uniform to sneak anonymously into town. You stole down the alley. You knew Natalie would be there for a smoke."

"No way." Sam rubbed the nape of his neck with frustration. The action made me remember the moment when I'd run into Sam and Mitzi at the grocery store. Sam scratched his neck, supposedly because he couldn't remember where his money had disappeared to. When he caught me looking, he quickly dropped his arm. I'd noticed a rash on his neck. What if it wasn't a rash? What if it was a cigarette burn?

"You hate cigarettes, Sam," I said, trying out a theory. "You call them coffin nails because your mother died of cancer."

"Yeah, so?"

"I'll bet you told Natalie she shouldn't smoke, but she didn't attack you for nagging her. She lashed out when you pulled a gun on her. Natalie was a fighter, wasn't she? She scorched you on your neck with the tip of her cigarette. There's a mark, right beneath your shirt collar."

Sam jerked his chin reflexively.

"Her assault startled you. You dropped the gun or whatever weapon you showed up with. Maybe Natalie retrieved it, maybe not. You didn't waste time going after it. You saw another weapon, a discarded panini grill, and you remembered what Lola had said on The Pier. You grabbed it and hit Natalie upside the head. Then you ran."

"This is insane," Sam said. "You're cuckoo."

"Mitzi, you track Sam's comings and goings via GPS, right?"

Mitzi blinked a yes.

I said, "Sam went to and from the MONEY conference the day Natalie died, didn't he?"

"I was there the whole day," Sam countered. "You can check."

"I did check," I said. "On a whim. And yes, the conference coordinator remembers seeing you there, but she can't confirm you stayed the whole time. I think you went back and forth. It's an hour's drive, maybe less if you speed. You ran up the mileage on your car that day, which is why you've been riding your bicycle this past week, to keep the mileage down in case anyone got curious."

Sam huffed.

"Here's the rest of my theory. You purchased a ticket to San Diego. There's a suitcase by your feet. But you're not planning to run away with another woman. You're heading south alone so you can exit the country through Tijuana. You were seen signing all sorts of documents at the bank. Did you create an offshore account, Sam? Is that where you stashed all your skimmed earnings?"

Mitzi whispered, "Sam?"

"Willie was onto you, wasn't he, Sam?" I went on. "He wasn't as dumb as he made out. He figured the books weren't adding up. But Willie wasn't altruistic. He wanted in on your moneymaking scheme. That's what you two were arguing about that day outside the Word, not his child-rearing skills. You knew you had to get rid of him. You arranged to meet him at the motel, then you borrowed Ellen's coat. It's short on you. You put on makeup, including Mitzi's red lipstick, the lipstick Ellen found in her coat pocket." I eyed Mitzi. "You're missing a lipstick, right? Sassy Woman Red."

Mitzi bit her lip and nodded.

"Do you own any wigs?"

"Three," she muttered. "I wear them when my roots are showing."

"Is one short and spiky, like Ellen's hair?"

"No." She faltered. Her eyes fluttered.

"Sam cut one of them, didn't he?" I held out my hand hoping Mitzi would relinquish the gun. She didn't.

"Mitzi, don't listen to her," Sam said.

But Mitzi was listening. She wasn't as wild-eyed as before.

"Willie killed Natalie," Sam said.

"Willie figured out the discrepancies," I countered. "That's why he went to the bank teller and asked her about the diner's finances. Soon after, Willie was seen arguing with Mitzi." Without losing sight of Sam, I said, "Mitzi, Willie must have believed you were in on the scam. A witness said you called him 'loco,' but he confirmed what you already suspected."

"You're the one who's crazy," Sam said. He glanced at the exit door leading to the alley behind the diner. "None of this is true. And, for your information, I have an alibi for the night Willie died. I was home with my wife. I was making calls all around town looking for Willie. I spoke to lots of people. Tell them, Mitzi."

She said, "I . . . I . . . ."

"You didn't see or hear him, did you, Mitzi?" I said. "You were busy doing your beauty routine. He slipped out without you noticing. Using a cell phone, he could have made those calls from anywhere in town.

After you killed Willie, Sam, you dialed me to set the time of murder after ten P.M. Maybe you thought if I told the police about the call, it would be taken more seriously." I eyed Mitzi. "Sam is ready to let you take the fall, Mitzi. Why else would he have put your lipstick in Ellen's coat pocket?"

"No," Sam said.

Mitzi whimpered.

"What I can't figure out, Mitzi, is why you didn't turn in Sam the moment you suspected he was a murderer, but then it dawned on me. You didn't because love is blind."

"Not anymore." Bitterness flooded Mitzi's words. "The blinders are off. I tried to help you better yourself, Sam, but you're not worthy of me. I'm through with you." She aimed the barrel of the gun at him. "Through."

Sam retreated a step. "Babe, I didn't do any of what she's saying. I love you. Willie killed Natalie. She knew he was an abuser. She was going to turn him in. Willie admitted it to me that day on The Pier."

I thought of Tito, with his pec-flexing moves, and my old coworker, who was now the muscle-bound co-owner of a gym, and said, "Good try, Sam, but Willie wasn't physically strong enough to kill Natalie."

439

"Are you kidding? He was built."

I grinned. "Willie may have appeared fit, but he pushed like a girl. I remember you strong-arming him on The Pier, Sam, and the other day, Rhett's dog nearly knocked Willie off balance when the dog jumped up for a pat on the head." I addressed Ellen. "Willie had chest implants, didn't he?"

Ellen whispered, "Yes."

"Did he also have his abs etched?"

She nodded grimly.

"It's nothing to be ashamed of. One of the models we used at Taylor & Squibb did the same. He looked like he could bench press three hundred pounds, when in reality, he could merely press sixty."

Ellen said, "Willie wanted to be a surfer in the worst way, but he hated how weak his body looked."

"The surgery prevented him from being able to wield a punch," I said. "He was a quiet bully. He pinched, he ridiculed, but he didn't hit. And he couldn't have fought off you, Sam. You cornered him. You shot him at the motel at close range. With your wife's gun."

Mitzi ogled the weapon in her hand. A cry of despair escaped her lips.

In that moment of distraction, Sam charged Mitzi. He wrenched the gun from her hand and slung an arm around her neck. "Stand back" — he dragged her toward the exit — "or I'll kill her." He aimed the gun at her head.

"Sam, don't." Mitzi gurgled. "Stop. I'll get you help."

"You're the one who needs help, babe," he snarled. "You drink too much. You concoct all these ridiculous fantasies of me having affairs. I loved you, but after a while, it all became too much of a hassle."

"Turn yourself in, Sam," I said.

"Shut up." He pointed the gun at me.

My insides turned to mush. Where in the heck were the police? I glimpsed the knives and pots, still out of reach, and the salad bowl, still too lightweight. I peeked to my right. Two paces away I spied a row of empty plates sitting on a counter beneath warming lights.

Wait for it. Wait for it.

As Sam reached backward with his hand to open the exit door, I darted to the counter. I grabbed the top plate and hurled it like a Frisbee at Sam. It nailed him in the ribs. Sam stumbled. Mitzi twisted in his arms and elbowed him in the ear while letting rip with a slew of curse words. At the same time, Mayor Zeller and the Mumford sisters, each armed with frying pans, charged him and tackled him. All of the women and Sam fell into a pile.

Seconds later, the door leading to the diner opened and Cinnamon hobbled in on crutches. Her ankle was bound with aqua blue tape. The fireman — Bucky — hurried in after her. So did the Moose, gun aimed at the melee.

"Okay, break it up," Cinnamon yelled.

"Sam's the killer," I shouted.

She arched an eyebrow then gestured to her deputy to aim his weapon at Sam, who was trying, without success, to fight off the enraged women. "Want to tell me what went down here?"

"I called you," I said. "Didn't you hear anything?"

"No."

I pulled my cell phone from my pocket. The face was dark; the call hadn't gone through. How I hated dead zones. "Then why did you come to the diner?"

"Your aunt contacted me."

Right. I'd forgotten that I'd asked her to do so. I provided a quick recap. "I believe the black box for the GPS tracking will give you what you need to prove that Sam drove to and from Crystal Cove on the day of the murder." I told her about the trash, the gloves, and the possibility that Sam had money stowed in an offshore account. I said, "Did you happen to find a cigarette butt at the scene of the crime?"

"We did."

"You might want to test it for Sam's DNA. I believe he has a burn on his neck."

Cinnamon looked semi-impressed. I didn't expect more.

"What happened to you?" I said.

"Bucky and I were on a date. We went roller skating."

"But you're an ace skater."

"He isn't." Cinnamon grinned. "He lost control, grabbed me for support, and before you know it, we crash-landed."

"I'm such a klutz," Bucky said.

But cute. I thought of the Lovers tarot card Cinnamon had drawn from my aunt's tarot deck and grinned.

"Luckily, nothing is broken," Cinnamon said, "but the doctor wants to keep my ankle bound so it doesn't swell up."

Wasn't this an interesting turn of events? Bucky was one of Rhett's good friends. Perhaps if Bucky and Cinnamon continued to date, he could convince her of Rhett's innocence in the arson, and the four of us could double-date and . . .

A girl could dream.

CHAPTER 31

I returned to the Cookbook Nook. Fans of
the Grill Fest were still hovering about. No
one seemed aware of what had occurred at
Mum's the Word, but my father and my
aunt weren't born yesterday. They sidled up
to me. My aunt nudged me with a hip. I
gave the two of them the same quick recap
I had provided at the diner.

Aunt Vera tapped the crystal hanging
around my neck. "Good thing you were
wearing this."

"Indeed."

"C'mon," my father said, ever the cynic.
"You don't believe a crystal had anything to
do with the outcome, do you, Tootsie Pop?"

"Actually, I do, Dad."

"Swell." He glowered at my aunt. "Vera, is
your intention to turn our entire family into
a bunch of hippie-dippy New Age thinkers?"

"Watch it, Cary."

"Hey," I said, eager to end their feud. "What's going on over there?" I aimed a finger at Katie, who was chatting up Keller in the hall by the tier of snacks. Keller was yuk-yukking at something Katie said.

"He asked her for a date," Aunt Vera replied. "Aren't they adorable?"

I surveyed the rest of the shop. Customers were swarming Tito, who was signing autographs. "And over there?"

"That Tito." My aunt *tsk*ed. "He brought preprinted recipe cards with him, in case he won. I think he dreams of adding a food column in the newspaper."

"And over there?" I hitched my chin toward the stockroom. Bailey stood with a tall man, shaved head, stunning cheekbones, and a thin mustache. "Jorge, I assume." I remembered my aunt saying he was "easy on the eyes." He sure didn't look like an aeronautics engineer. Bad me for stereotyping. Back at Taylor & Squibb, I could have lost an account that way.

Dad grunted. "I'm not so sure about him now that I've had a few more minutes with him."

"Minutes? That's all it takes?" I teased.

"That's all it took with —" He halted.

I knew what he'd wanted to say: *with Da-vid.* My mother wasn't the only one who hadn't been won over by David's charms. I had battled them right up until the wedding. Why do twentysomething kids put up such a fight with parents? I wondered. Would I have kids who would do the same to me? I gulped. Did I want children? I had a cat.

"It's okay, Dad." I patted his arm.

"This Jorge guy is edgy, that's all," my father added. "Bailey deserves a guy who's nice and kind, like . . ." He scanned the room until his gaze landed on someone.

I followed the direction. "Like Rhett."

Rhett stood at the counter scratching Tigger's neck. The kitty rubbed his cheek against Rhett's palm.

"He's a good man, Jenna."

"I agree wholeheartedly, but I need to know all about him before I jump into a relationship."

A week later, by the time the town had settled back into a rhythm, Rhett and I had set a date for a hike, and Cinnamon and I had gone for coffee. Also, with my father's help and David's mother's cooperation, I was able to contact and reimburse all of the clients David had deceived. The relief I felt was infinite.

I was thrilled to hear that Norah was staying in Crystal Cove to help her sister with the restaurant. They intended to keep it open and build the clientele, if possible. Sam was booked on two charges of murder. Mitzi was facing charges of obstruction, but she had hired the best defense attorney in the state and, according to gossip, was bound to get off with community service, because a jury often ruled in favor of a duped woman in love.

Pepper, true to form, didn't like that Cinnamon was dating a fireman and came into our shop often to voice her concern. I doubted that she had ever liked anyone her daughter had dated, and I vowed to put more thought into creating a happy potion for her.

Was there a cookbook with that kind of recipe?

RECIPES

From Aunt Vera:
I gave this idea to Katie. Can you see me preening? It's one of my favorite sandwiches. Perfect for lunch or brunch. The cinnamon adds just a hint of flavor. It's like apple pie with a pack of protein, thanks to the turkey. Also, just so you know, cream cheese is a nifty little trick for any grilled cheese. When spread on the inside of a sandwich, it heats up fast and helps the other ingredients melt evenly. Enjoy.

BRIE, APPLE, AND TURKEY GRILLED CHEESE

(makes 2 sandwiches)

4 slices bread
4 tablespoons butter
4 tablespoons cream cheese

1 teaspoon cinnamon

1 green apple, sliced thin

6 ounces Brie cheese, sliced, rind trimmed off

6 ounces cooked turkey, sliced thinly

Butter each slice of bread on one side. Spread the cream cheese on the other side of the bread. Sprinkle with cinnamon. (Note: This is the inside of the sandwich; the butter side is the outside.)

To assemble: Top two slices of bread, cream cheese side up, with turkey. Place Brie cheese slices on top of turkey. Place apples on top of the cheese. Set the other slice of bread on top of the sandwich and press slightly.

If cooking on a stovetop: Heat a large skillet over medium heat for about 2 minutes. Set the sandwiches on the skillet and cook for 4 minutes, until golden brown. Flip the sandwiches with a spatula and cook another 2 to 4 minutes. You can compress the sandwich with the spatula. Turn the sandwich one more time. Press down with the spatula and remove from the pan. Let cool about 2 to 3 minutes and serve.

If cooking on a panini grill or sandwich maker: Set the sandwich on the grill surface and slowly lower the top. Cook for a total of

4 minutes. Remove from the griddle and let cool 2 to 3 minutes, then serve. Beware — the cheese filling might ooze out the sides. If the lid is too heavy, you might want to consider resorting to the stovetop method.

From Jenna:

Knowing how much I love ice cream, my aunt bought me a countertop ice-cream maker. And then Katie, who remembered how much I'd raved about Keller's caramel macchiato ice cream, wheedled this recipe out of him. She said it was a cinch. Yeah, right. Anyway, she walked me through the first batch, and it wasn't that hard. Katie says the trick to making homemade ice cream — which I guess Keller knew, too — is making sure there isn't too much "moisture" in the mixture. Moisture, aka water, turns to ice in the freezer. I guess there's a lot of water in milk. Who knew? Hence, you'll see evaporated milk in these ingredients. I've got to say, yum! If you're really daring, try making your own caramel sauce. Katie included that recipe below.

CARAMEL MACCHIATO ICE CREAM

(serves 6–8)

1 cup whipping cream
2 tablespoons espresso coffee (brewed, liquid)
3/4 cup sugar

1/8 teaspoon salt

1 12-ounce can low-fat evaporated milk

3 large egg yolks

3/4 cup caramel dessert sauce (I used Smucker's)

In a saucepan, over medium heat, cook cream, espresso, 1/4 cup of the sugar, salt, and evaporated milk. Cook for 3 to 5 minutes, until tiny bubbles form around the edges. Do not boil.

Remove from heat and let stand 10 minutes.

In a medium bowl, combine the remaining 1/2 cup sugar and egg yolks. Stir well. Gradually add the hot milk mixture to the egg mixture, stirring constantly.

Return the mixture to the saucepan. Cook over medium heat for 3 to 5 minutes, until tiny bubbles form again. Do not boil.

Remove the pan from the heat. Cool at room temperature and then set in the refrigerator for 2 hours.

Pour chilled mixture into ice-cream maker and freeze according to manufacturer's instructions.

Transfer half of the ice cream to a freezer-safe container, then spread half of the caramel sauce on top. Top with remaining ice cream, then remaining caramel sauce.

Using a knife, swirl the caramel through the ice cream.

Cover and freeze for at least 2 hours.

From Katie:
Making your own caramel sauce isn't that hard. And it takes no time at all! Enjoy.

CARAMEL SAUCE À LA KATIE

(yield: 1 cup)

2 tablespoons water
1 cup sugar
6 tablespoons butter
1/2 cup whipping cream

Note: Making caramel is a fast process, so have everything ready . . . right next to the pan. You don't want the sugar to burn. Promise! Also, the sugar gets really hot, so wear oven mitts. Okay? Ready . . . go.

In a 2- to 3-quart saucepan, heat the water and sugar over medium heat. Stir constantly. As soon as all the sugar has melted — the color will be a warm amber — add the butter. Whisk until the butter has melted. You will see bubbles around the edge of the pan.

Remove the pan from the heat and add the cream in a steady stream, whisking the whole time. *Note: This mixture will foam. It's so pretty.*

Whisk until the mixture is smooth, then cool a few minutes and pour into a glass heat-proof container and let cool completely. Remember the glass container will be hot until the mixture is completely cool. Store in the refrigerator for up to 2 weeks.

From Katie:
I love a good grilled cheese. I'm always trying different combinations, usually using items I'd consider putting in a salad, like pears and blue cheese. They are a perfect, um, pair. (Are you laughing? Sometimes I crack myself up.) For this sandwich, I decided to add grilled onions. I was inspired by the sandwich that Flora — you know, the gal from Home Sweet Home — made during the Grill Fest competition. Brilliant addition. The sandwich makes a delicious brunch or lunch meal. It's gooey, so you might consider having a fork and knife on hand. Say cheese!

PEAR AND BLUE CHEESE GRILLED CHEESE

(makes 2 sandwiches)

4 slices bread (Gluten-free bread works, too.)
4 tablespoons butter
4 tablespoons cream cheese
1–2 teaspoons balsamic vinegar
1 Bartlett or Bosc pear, cored and sliced thin
1/4 cup sautéed onions

4 ounces blue cheese, sliced

Butter each slice of bread on one side. In a small bowl, mix the cream cheese and balsamic vinegar. Spread the cream cheese–vinegar mixture on the other side of the bread. (Note: This is the inside of the sandwich; the butter side is the outside.)

In a small sauté pan, melt a tablespoon of butter over medium heat. Slice the onions thinly. Set the onions in the hot butter and stir for at least five minutes, until tender. (Note: The onions can be made a day ahead. If refrigerating overnight, bring to room temperature.)

To assemble: Top two slices of bread, cream cheese side up, with grilled onion. Place blue cheese (it will crumble) on top of the onions. Place pears on top of the cheese. Set the other slice of bread on top of the sandwich and press slightly.

If cooking on a stovetop: Heat a large skillet over medium heat for about 2 minutes. Set the sandwiches on the skillet and cook for 4 minutes, until golden brown. Flip the sandwiches with a spatula and cook another 2 to 4 minutes. You can compress the sandwich with the spatula. Turn the sandwich one more time. Press down with the spatula and remove from the pan. Let cool about 2 to 3 minutes and serve.

If cooking on a panini grill or sandwich maker: Set the sandwich on the grill surface and slowly lower the top. Cook for a total of 4 minutes. Remove from the grill surface and let cool 2 to 3 minutes, then serve. Beware — the cheese filling might ooze out the sides. If the lid is too heavy, you might want to consider resorting to the stovetop method.

From Katie:

I absolutely adore these cookies. They're so easy to make, even Jenna can make them. Shh. Don't tell her I was joking about her. But, really, they're easy. And they're gluten-free. I have a friend who can't eat wheat, so I make these for her all the time. They almost work like protein bars, though they're really cookies. Don't be fooled.

By the way, for all of you who *can* eat wheat, just substitute the gluten-free flour with regular flour and omit the xanthan gum. That's the ingredient that helps bind the gluten-free flour. Sweet dreams!

PEANUT BUTTER CHOCOLATE CRUNCH COOKIE À LA KATIE

Gluten-free

(yield: 12–16 cookies)

1/2 cup (4 ounces) unsalted butter, at room temperature
1/4 cup granulated sugar
1/2 cup light brown sugar, firmly packed
2 large eggs
3/4 cup smooth peanut butter

1 teaspoon vanillin
2 tablespoons water
1 cup gluten-free flour
1/2 teaspoon xanthan gum
1/2 teaspoon baking soda
1/2 teaspoon salt
2 cups crispy gluten-free rice cereal
1/2 cup semi-sweet or dark chocolate chips

Heat oven to 375°F.

Mix the butter and sugars in a large bowl. Add the eggs, peanut butter, vanillin, and water and beat with an electric mixer on medium for one minute.

In a separate bowl, mix the gluten-free flour, xanthan gum, baking soda, and salt. Add the flour mixture to the butter mixture and mix on low speed.

Fold in the gluten-free rice cereal and chocolate chips. Note: If you use Chex-style cereal, crush the pieces slightly in a plastic bag.

Line a 13″ × 9″ pan with parchment paper. Press the dough onto the parchment paper.

Bake until golden brown, about 12 to 15 minutes. Let cool for 15 minutes and then cut into bars or squares.

Note: These can also be made as individual cookies. Using a spoon, set scoops of dough about an inch or two apart on a cookie sheet. Press with a fork to flatten. Cook for 12 minutes, until golden brown. Let stand for 5 minutes before removing with a spatula.

From Jenna:
This is one of my all-time favorite sandwiches. I remember my mother making
appetizers of shrimp, mayonnaise, and
asparagus. She would put the salad on
melba toasts and top them with cheese
and then toast them in the oven. She
served them whenever a group of her
girlfriends came over to play cards or
simply shoot the breeze. My sister and I
would sneak in and steal a few for
ourselves. My brother wasn't a shrimp
eater. Boy, did he lose out! Here's to
you, Mom.

SHRIMP SWISS CHEESE MELT

(makes 2 sandwiches)

4 large asparagus spears, cooked to tender
4 large shrimp, diced
2 tablespoons mayonnaise
2 tablespoons cream cheese
2 tablespoons chives, chopped
1 teaspoon bouquet garni (or tarragon or
  parsley)
1/2 teaspoon lemon zest
Salt to taste
4 slices bread
2 more tablespoons mayonnaise

4 slices Swiss cheese

For the asparagus: Bring an inch of water to boil in a saucepan. Snap off the ends of the asparagus and cook, covered, in boiling water for 2 minutes. Pour off the water. Keep asparagus covered for 2 more minutes. Rinse in cold water. Slice in half and then cut into thin strips. Set aside.

For the shrimp salad: Remove tails from the shrimp and discard. Dice the shrimp. In a medium bowl, mix the shrimp together with 2 tablespoons of the mayonnaise, cream cheese, chives, herbs, and lemon zest. Taste and add salt if desired.

To assemble: For these sandwiches, no butter is required on the bread. Use the remaining 2 tablespoons of mayonnaise and spread on each slice of bread. Place all 4 slices of the bread, mayonnaise side down, on a cutting board. Spread the shrimp-cheese-mixture on 2 of the slices. Lay out the asparagus on the other 2 slices. Top each with Swiss cheese. Place the two sides together.

If cooking on a stovetop: Heat a large skillet over medium heat for about 2 minutes. Set the sandwiches on the skillet and cook for 4 minutes, until golden brown. Flip the sandwiches with a spatula and cook another

2 to 4 minutes. You can compress the sandwich with the spatula. Turn the sandwich one more time. Press down with the spatula and remove from the pan. Let cool about 2 to 3 minutes and serve.

If cooking on a panini grill or sandwich maker: Set the sandwich on the grill surface and slowly lower the top. Cook for a total of 4 minutes. Remove from the grill surface and let cool 2 to 3 minutes, then serve. Beware — the cheese filling might ooze out the sides because of the mayonnaise. If the lid is too heavy, you might want to consider resorting to the stovetop method.

By the way, the shrimp salad tastes fabulous all by itself, and can easily be used in a regular sandwich or on top of a crisp green salad!

From Jenna:
When I saw one of the Grill Fest contestants making this, I watched with fascination. When I tasted it — wow! I loved the combination of meats and cheese, mustard, and jam. Salty, sweet, and savory. I noticed that the cheese was sliced and not grated. I guess that's because dipping the sandwich into the egg mixture is messy, and if the cheese falls out, well, even messier.

But I have to admit that, after watching it all come together, I thought, I could do that.

Monte Cristo Sandwich

(makes 2 sandwiches)

2 eggs
2 tablespoons milk
1/4 teaspoon cinnamon
4 slices bread (White or a brioche-style bread works great; gluten-free bread works, too.)
1 tablespoon spicy mustard
2 slices cooked turkey
4 slices Swiss cheese
2 slices ham

2 tablespoons butter or vegetable oil (canola preferred)
Confectioners' sugar for decoration
2 tablespoons jam

In a pie plate, whisk together the eggs, milk, and cinnamon.

To assemble the sandwiches: Place the bread on a cutting board. Spread mustard on each piece of bread. Place turkey on 2 slices of bread. Top the turkey with 2 slices of cheese. Then add the ham. Put the remaining pieces of bread on top.

To cook: On medium-low, heat the butter or vegetable oil in a large nonstick skillet. Dip each sandwich into the egg mixture. Turn the sandwich to coat both sides. Set the sandwiches in the skillet. Cover with a lid and cook 3 to 4 minutes, just until the underside begins to brown. *Make sure you don't burn the bread.* Flip the sandwich with a spatula and press down with the spatula to compress the sandwich. Cook for another 3 to 4 minutes or until the underside begins to brown. If necessary, turn once more and cook until the cheese has melted completely, about 1 to 2 minutes.

Transfer to a plate, sprinkle with confectioners' sugar. Cut diagonally and serve with a spoonful of jam alongside.

CPSIA information can be obtained
at www.ICGtesting.com
Printed in the USA
FFOW04n1003120914